The Gateway to Imagia

The Gathering

To the Shark Lady!
Thanks for all your
excitement and support.
I hope you like this one!

2017

The Gateway to Imagia
The Gathering

Written by
Jessica Williams

Written by Jessica Williams

First Printing: 2017

ISBN-13: 978-1540725196

ISBN: 1540725197

Author and Illustrator: Jessica Williams
Kansas, United States of America
www.facebook.com/TheGatewaytoImagia

Dedication

To Silas.
Thanks for sticking with me, kid. Your patience is awesome. Thanks for being my biggest fan.
You rock.

Contents

Acknowledgements

As before, I'd like to take a moment to give a special thanks to my wonderfully supportive beta-readers:
Mike Wolff, Mom (Brenda Shaw), Aunt Rita (Crawford), Mandy Olson, and Jason Boyer.
Your support and help is greatly appreciated.
I'm one lucky writer.
Thank you.

Prologue

Sam could feel his heart beating in his ears. If ever there were a time for things to have gone wrong, this would definitely not have been the moment he'd have chosen. But that didn't stop things from spiraling out of control. He ducked as low as possible behind the bushes in his backyard, just below the window of his bedroom. He was nearly out of breath, but tried his hardest to not breathe for fear of being heard.

Next to him, growling low, Titus did his best to stay out of view. He whispered to Sam, "What are you going to do?"

Sam, eyes wide, shrugged as he searched his brain for a plan. He blurt out in a hiss, "I have no idea! What the heck am I *supposed* to do?" It was quiet outside.

Too quiet.

Sam risked a peek. He turned slowly, careful not to rustle the leaves.

"What are you doing?" Titus asked, fear touching his harried voice.

"Shhh. I've…got an idea." There was too much hesitation when he spoke, but he slowly parted the leaves and peered out into the backyard towards the dense forest. There, sniffing the air at the edge of the trees, was a beast of menacing proportions. It was sniffing for something in particular.

It was hunting for Sam.

"Can you see it?" Titus asked.

Sam turned to look at Titus and said, “Yeah. I don’t think it can smell us over here.”

“I can’t believe you created that monstrosity.”

“At least I imagined it was blind. Otherwise, we’d be in real trouble.”

Titus scoffed silently at Sam’s concept of real trouble. “What are you going to do now?”

“I’m gonna try to morph it, but I need to see it better. Do you think that we can get it closer somehow?”

Titus was in disbelief. “*Closer*? Are you kidding?”

Sam shook his head. “I can’t morph it properly if I can’t see it better. I’m kinda freaking out here, okay!”

Titus sighed. He muttered something under his breath then said, “Fine. I’ll take care of that. What’s it doing right now?” He braced himself for his next move.

Sam turned around to look out and see the beast again. But when he did, it was gone. He gasped and began to look around frantically.

Titus noticed Sam’s sudden wariness. “What’s happening?”

Sam kept looking around and said, “It’s gone.”

“*Gone*?” What do you mean gone?” Titus was panicking.

“I don’t know! It’s just…” Sam stopped mid-sentence when he felt the ground vibrating beneath his feet. He stopped breathing altogether when he heard the sound of something large sniffing. It was close. Titus didn’t move either. They both looked at each other, fear sweeping their faces.

Titus jerked his head in the opposite direction of the sniffing sound and Sam nodded. He began to crawl, not making a sound. Titus moved behind him, stealthily as he could.

Suddenly, they realized it had gotten much quieter. The sniffing had stopped. They both froze.

With no warning whatsoever, the bushes that were hiding them, along with several lawn chairs, were uprooted and thrown across the backyard. The creature threw his head back and roared, fangs glistening in the mid-day sun.

Sam screamed while Titus jumped in front of him, protecting his friend from what he feared would come next. He turned around while the creature was howling and yelled, “Run!” They both got up to run, but as they did, they immediately jumped forward when they saw the creature's immense fists come down – right into the corner of the house. Sam covered his head as debris flew around him. Titus was crouched low. The beast dug its claws into the house, ripping sections of the siding off.

Titus yelled sarcastically through the ruckus, "Is *that* close enough?"

Sam rolled his eyes as he flipped onto this back and looked up at the creature. It was sniffing the air once more, confused. It picked up the scent and bellowed. It had found them again. An angry fist hit the ground just inches from where Sam's legs were. Titus jumped back just before becoming a dog-shaped pancake.

Both comrades backed away. Sam had no choice but to scoot back using his elbows and feet. More debris flew through the air and the beast snarled when it finally pinpointed its target.

Titus saw what was about to happen and yelled, "SAM! NOW!"

Sam focused just enough on the beast. As the clawed fist came down, there was an unnatural gust of wind from behind them that picked the creature up and threw him back twenty feet. As it landed on the ground, there was no deafening thud of massive weight hitting earth. Rather, a beach ball sized pile of fuzz landed in the grass.

The tiny creature, which actually now looked like a large, creepy rodent, was disorientated and whimpering. Sam and Titus, both winded, walked up to the creature, brushing the dirt and rubble off of themselves as they went.

Titus looked at it and growled. "Now what?"

Sam looked at the terrified creature and then back at his destroyed house. He sighed and threw his hands on his head in disbelief. "I'm not worried about that," he said, pointing at the creature. "I'm worried about *that*."

Titus turned around to see Sam gaping at the shredded side of the house. "Yes. That could pose as a slight problem."

Just as Titus finished his thought, Sam heard his mom's car pull into the driveway and the garage door open.

Sam started to panic. "Oh no! Mom's home from the store. It's the first time she's left me alone and it looks like a tornado hit the house. I'm dead. Dead!" Sam paused and then had a thought. "Tornado," he whispered.

Titus cocked his head questioningly. "What?"

"Take cover. I know what I'm gonna do. This could get messy."

Titus almost barked when he said, "What are you…" but before he could finish his thought, the sky started to darken. "Oh no. You can't be serious."

Before Sam could answer, the wind picked up and the sky grew ominous for at least a half mile in each direction. Lightning struck and thunder filled the air. Sam looked around nervously, waiting for perfect timing. His mom would be coming in the house right now, so the moment was upon him. "Titus," he yelled, "let's get inside!" They ran to the back door, soaked in rain that had started to pour from the sky. He and Titus burst through the door. Sam spun and looked outside. He pinched his face in concentration and imagined a small tornado touching down just far enough away for him to be safe but close enough to look like it had just hit his house.

Sam's mom came running into the room and looked outside. She gasped and yelled to her son. "Sam! Get away from there!"

Sam glanced back at his mom who was about to grab him. But she stopped and stared out the door, unbelieving as to what she was seeing. The tornado was dissipating quickly and was gone before she had time to react further.

Sam stayed focused on the storm and it quickly began to calm down to just a light rain under dull gray clouds. Within another minute, all was calm, leaving only a slight overcast sky in its wake.

His mom knelt down and checked Sam over. She was in a mild state of shock. "Are you okay? Did you get hurt?"

"I'm fine, mom." He bit his lip and tried not to let her see. He didn't like what he was about to do. "It just happened so fast. We were outside and then the storm came out of nowhere. I barely had time to get inside." He hated lying. But he didn't know what else to do.

She hugged Sam tight and brushed his wet hair from his eyes. She went out the backdoor and Sam followed hesitantly, hoping his plan worked. When she rounded the patio and saw the back of the house she slapped her hand over her mouth and gasped loudly. "Look at the house! I don't understand. There was no rain in the forecast today. It must have been some kind of freak storm." She surveyed the damage and then said, "Sam, don't go in your room until we can get this taken care of. I need to go call your dad. Be careful. There's glass everywhere." She marched past Sam and Titus, muttering several concerns for neighbors and her annoyance with overpaid weathermen.

Now standing alone, wet, and exhausted, Sam and Titus exchanged very meaningful looks. Titus looked over his shoulder to make sure Sarah was out of earshot before quietly speaking. "Well…" he began, "that was interesting."

Sam snorted and tried not to laugh loudly. "I told you it was going to get messy."

"Yes. That you did. Where did the creature go?"

Sam pointed at something wedged up against what was left of the back fence. It was an old, ratty teddy bear. "I morphed it into that right before the storm."

There was no denying Titus' amazement. "Wow."

"Yeah."

They both stood there in silence for some time, reflecting on what all had just transpired. Several long moments went by before either spoke again. Titus spoke first, concern thick in his hushed voice. "Did you even know you were capable of something like that?"

Sam just shook his head slowly at first. He thought for a moment. His brow furrowed. "I don't think I should use my imagination anymore. I've never felt so…"

Titus looked up at his friend, waiting for him to finish.

Sam chewed on his bottom lip. "I've never felt so…dangerous."

Titus saw a sliver of fear escape his friend's face as he spoke those words. "You're not him, you know."

Nodding, he replied, "I know. Nadaroth was evil. But I don't think my power is meant for this world. I shouldn't even *have* my powers anymore. All of this," he gestured around his and his neighbors' yards, "is because I was being stupid while telling you about my nightmare. I've only been back a couple of months now and look at what I've done." He sighed. "I'm going to have to be really careful from now on."

Titus nodded and sighed pointedly. "Well one thing's for certain."

Sam looked down at him. "What's that?"

He grinned, "No more afternoon naps for you."

They both broke out into silent chuckles again.

As he was laughing, Sam couldn't help but to think that, all in all, it hadn't been that bad of a day. But life, so it seemed, was about to get much more complicated.

Almost three years later…

Chapter One: Secrets

The dusky forest was twinkling with the lights of early fireflies. There was just enough wind to lightly rustle the leaves of the trees, making the forest seem almost alive. It was nearly the end of another unseasonably warm spring day on Treetop Lane. And a boy and his dog were quietly gazing into the mysterious depths of the forest sitting just outside its borders.

Sam Little was mindlessly scratching behind his dog's ears as he stared into the forest longingly. It seemed to get more difficult to not go closer after knowing where it took him the last time he dared to venture inside. But he knew that it really had nothing to do with the forest itself. Rather, it was about the power of a wish he'd made on his tenth birthday.

Another day had passed without anything spectacular happening, and he dropped his hand from behind his dog's ears and sighed heavily. He turned his focus to his feet, like he so often did when he wanted to hide his true emotions.

His faithful dog looked to him. If a dog could show concern, then that would be the look that was on his face. His soft, caramel eyes looked over at his boy and watched as his face fell once again. The dog focused his gaze back into the forest. He sighed and then, with regret thick in his voice, he said, "It's been nearly three years, Sam. No matter how hard you try, you can never go back."

Sam continued to stare at his dingy, grayed tennis shoes and shrugged. “I know, Titus.” He couldn’t manage to say anything more that he hadn’t already said a hundred times.

Titus looked over his shoulder, past the yard, and into the house that they had left behind the night of Sam’s tenth birthday. He gazed into the glowing windows for any sign that Sam’s parents might be watching them. It had been difficult to refrain from talking since returning from Imagia, but it was necessary.

When he saw that they were in the clear, he growled in frustration then continued to speak. “I loathe this constant charade. I wish I could speak freely again. It really is degrading to have to bark every time someone asks me to speak.” He looked over to Sam who was smiling now.

“I know. It’s even harder for me though. You’re the only one I can really talk to and I can’t even do that without being told I’m crazy. At least all you have to do is roll over from time to time to be normal. Everyone expects me to be normal and I can barely do that. Every time I dream, I worry that I might use my imagination and then the house might be ripped apart from some random creature. Mom can’t even stand it when my room’s a mess. I wonder how long she’d ground me for if I destroyed the whole house? I’m not sure we’d be so lucky as the last time that happened.”

They were both laughing now. It was nice to have these moments away from reality. Since Sam’s return from Imagia, it’d been nearly impossible to fit in and return to life as he’d left it. The truth was, life could never go back to the way it had been. He’d never be a normal boy again.

No one knew exactly what would happen when Sam returned through his gateway over two and a half years ago. They weren’t sure if he’d age the same or if time passed differently at all. But the least of their worries was that he might actually retain his ability to imagine and that Titus would still carry the gift of speech. Unfortunately, those seemingly unpredictable scenarios had become the hardest to deal with.

No. Things were definitely not what anyone had expected. In fact, it was borderline impossible. It was so much harder than Sam thought it would be.

This evening was just one of the many nights he spent looking longingly into the dark forest hoping for some miracle to occur. But he wasn't alone in his yearning desire to return to Imagia. Titus' ability to speak and ever increasing intelligence made it torture for him to lead a life of deception. But being the realist that he'd become, he was always there to remind Sam that the hope he had of returning to a locked world was all for not.

As Sam sighed one last time, he heard the warning squeak of the backdoor hinges. He closed his eyes before throwing an annoyed glance at Titus who began to ritualistically thump his tail on the ground at he sound of his name. He really had become quite the convincing dog for what it was worth. "Time to come in Sam!" his mom hollered. "Come here, Titus! I have your dinner, boy!"

Both of them simultaneously rolled their eyes. Sam whispered, "It's time for your performance."

Titus whispered back as he trotted next to Sam, "You'd think she could manage to change it up a bit. The same dreadful kibble every single night for nearly three years. Are you sure you can't imagine me up something edible?"

"You know that I can't imagine food. I've tried. It has no flavor and it never fills your stomach. You're always hungry five seconds later." As they reached the halfway point and the back porch light cast its glow upon them, he knew his allotted time of mild freedom was up. He put one finger to his lips to quiet Titus and said, "It's show time."

Sam's mom gave him the same worried look that she gave him nearly every single night. She never seemed to stop fretting about how much Sam had changed since his disappearance. Nevertheless, she squeezed his shoulder lovingly as he walked in the door.

"Did you study for your history test?" she asked him.

"Yup." He waved vaguely over his shoulder to acknowledge her sign of affection.

One of the things that concerned Sam's mom was her son's lack of interest or passion in anything he did. He knew this, but he just couldn't muster the emotion that she needed to have from him. Sam was more than aware of this, but because his entire life had become lies built on secrets, he had no reasonable explanations.

It wasn't as if he had never tried to talk to his parents about the truth of his disappearance. He'd tried to tell his mom and dad, just once, that he'd gone to another world and met amazing creatures, fought a dangerous battle, and that Titus could talk. But his mom stopped him before he could say another word. He remembered how badly she freaked out and went on a rant about how he couldn't use his imagination as a crutch for such a serious situation. She then went on to say that if Titus *could* talk, she'd sell him to a science lab so they could pay for his college tuition and put an end to this ridiculousness. She'd stormed off so angry that day. And his father looked at him, shook his head slowly, sighed and followed his mom into the kitchen while she was hysterically prattling on about how Sam would end up in a crazy house at this rate. That was a bad day for Sam and he would never forget the way his parents looked at him.

So he and Titus both agreed that they'd never bring up the truth again. In order to protect himself from being labeled 'crazy', Sam never again spoke a single word about his other life in Imagia. When anyone asked him what happened, he'd always feign memory loss. People would naturally come up with their own theories after that. It seemed like such an easy decision at the time.

As Sam walked down the hall to the bathroom, leaving Titus to his mundane meal, he could hear her sighing. She hollered, as he was closing the bathroom door, "Don't forget to brush your teeth!"

Sam shut the door and instantly felt the pang of guilt for hiding things from his parents. With both hands placed on either side of the porcelain sink, he stared back at his reflection in the mirror. He pulled something out of his pocket. He carefully unfolded a tattered, well-loved photo.

The familiar image of his hairy best friend stared back at him. Aside of Titus, this picture was his only proof of the world he'd left behind; the world that he missed so dearly and yearned to return to. He couldn't help but smile at the goofy grin on Yetews' face and remember the moment that he'd morphed the photo from its original image of his family.

He looked at the image of himself in the picture and glanced into the mirror to compare the two faces. He felt like he'd changed so much in the last few years. His hair was a little longer, messier somehow. He was definitely taller now, no longer the smallest for his age. But the most noticeable change was in his eyes. The eyes in the mirror, though still blue, no longer held the same spark of adventure and joy they once had. There was too much sadness in them. They were not the eyes of a thirteen-year old.

Sam sat down heavily on the edge of the bathtub and ran his fingers through his untidy brown hair. He stared at the photo for a moment longer before reluctantly returning it back to his pocket. He had been very careful not to let his mom or dad find that picture. It would only create more problems that he wasn't prepared to deal with.

After his shower, Sam walked past the living room to tell his parents good night. They were watching the nightly news as usual. The news anchor was going on about another missing hiker in the forests of the Colorado Rockies. It hadn't been the first time he'd heard about missing people in that state. He couldn't help but think about how this world could be just as scary as Imagia at times.

The newsman was interviewing one of the locals about recent bear attacks in the mountains. Sam rolled his eyes as the man tried to explain that it had to be something more than just a bear. Even the news anchor had a skeptical look on his face. Sam's dad smiled from his run-down recliner. He snorted then said, "I can't believe the things people will say just to get fifteen minutes of fame on TV. One nut they talked to swore up and down it was bigfoot. Next, they'll blame it on aliens." He looked back at Sam, smiled and waved goodnight. "G'night, Sam." He started to wave his hands in front of him like he was trying to pretend to be frightening and said in his best Dracula voice, "Sleep tight. Don't let the big, bad, bear of Colorado bite!" he said mockingly.

Sam genuinely smiled and laughed. "Nice one, dad."

"George!" his mom hissed. "Are you *trying* to give him nightmares?" She shot a venomous look across the room at him and then looked back towards Sam. His dad winked at him when she had her back turned. Sam smiled again. His mom, worry still deep in the lines of her face, walked across the room to hug him. "Night sweetie. Sweet dreams."

"Thanks mom. G'night." As he turned to leave, he caught a glimpse of his mom biting her bottom lip and he felt the twinge of guilt resurface. He thought to himself that if she'd known half of the nightmares he'd had, she'd welcome man-eating bears into his dreams.

As he walked down the hall, he heard his dad saying quietly, "Honestly, Sarah. You've got to stop treating him like a china doll. You're pushing him away." Sam tuned them out past that point. He didn't need to hear another quiet argument about his fragile mind. He heard the clicking of Titus' claws on the hardwood floor as they fell into place at his side.

Another day was done.

Titus gazed out the window while Sam fought to find a comfortable position in bed. They had to be very cautious about speaking to each other, but now was the least risky time. The television was on and it was too early for his mom to peek in the room.

"I don't think my mom will ever stop looking at me like I'm crazy."

Titus didn't look away from the open window when he quietly replied. "She's just worried about you." He paused. He looked down and closed his eyes, deciding on something.

Sam noticed. "What's wrong? What is it?"

Titus let out an extra long breath and then turned to look across the room at Sam. He shook his head regretfully. "I heard your parents today when you left for school. They were talking about you."

"So? They do that all the time." Sam shrugged indifferently.

"Yes. Yes they do. But this time it was different."

Sam's brow furrowed and he sat up in his bed. "Different? What do you mean?"

Titus looked at his friend thoughtfully and then returned his gaze to the dusky night. "I think it's more your mom than your dad, but they don't think you're doing well since coming home. They think things are getting worse. They keep having discussions about how to break through to you and they've decided that it might be time to get help."

Unsure what he was getting at, but now concerned, he slightly shuddered at the grim tone in Titus' voice. "Tell me, Titus. I need to know what's happening."

His head hung low now as he spoke. "Sam…they want to send you somewhere. They think you need help that they can't give.

They're worried about what happened to you. And when your summer vacation comes…"

Sam swallowed hard. He and Titus had talked about different scenarios if his parents ever got too worried or suspected him of anything strange. Until now, he'd never really been concerned that it would get too serious.

"What are they gonna do?" he nearly stuttered.

"They are going to send you to a doctor. To a place called Hopeful Horizons Therapy for Children."

Sam felt his face grow pale and then suddenly flush with anger. "They can't send me to a doctor," he hissed as quietly as he could. "If they send me away to some weirdo doctor then who knows what will happen? And what about you? You'll go mad without me here. What do I do? How can I fix this?"

"I don't know. They want to know why you came back so different. They still don't understand why you stopped using your imagination. That's what makes your mom think something is very wrong." Titus paused before continuing. Then, carefully, he said, "Your mom said that sometimes she feels like it wasn't really you who came home. Imagination was such a big part of who you were. And now…"

Sam interrupted, "And now if I use it a wild hairy creature could end up diving into the neighbors' pool again."

The memory of Sam's first time using his imagination after returning from Imagia flooded his memory. It was enough to make them both laugh.

Sam had imagined a six-legged hairy beast of burden that appeared, as large as life, in front of them. It promptly ran amok through the neighbor's wooden fence and landed unexpectedly in their pool. Suddenly aware he retained his ability to imagine, he ran to the pool with Titus on his heels in a state of panic. He was lucky that it took Mr. and Mrs. Irving so long to hear the ruckus in their pool. By the time they managed to get outside, they had only caught a glimpse of the creature thrashing in the water. Sam had managed to morph it into a rather large deer at the last moment.

Titus was still chuckling, "Yes. Mrs. Irving might not be so easily convinced a second time. She was absolutely certain that deer had 'twice as much hair and too many legs'. It's a good thing you were still able to morph things as well."

Sam laughed low at the memory of the look on his elderly neighbors' faces. He sighed and became lost in his thoughts.

Fretting silently, he tried to think of ways that he could convince his parents that he was perfectly fine. Short of trying to tell them the truth again, he had no ideas come to mind. But if he tried to tell them the truth then they'd certainly be convinced he was crazy. And if he actually used his powers in front of them to prove his point, then he was sure they'd be terrified of him and send him away. He flopped backwards onto this bed and threw an arm over his eyes.

Titus turned around and sat down. "We still have a couple of months before you're done with school. We'll figure something out." The doubt was poorly masked in his voice.

Sam moved his arm so he could look at Titus. He gave a disbelieving look and snorted loudly. "Yeah. Great. Just a couple months left before they ship me off to the loony bin to see a bunch of doctors." Once his sarcasm was acknowledged, he finally rolled his eyes and covered them back up with his arm. He could feel the knots forming in his stomach. "What are we gonna do?" he asked hopelessly.

"I don't know. We'll think of something. But we probably need to be even more careful when it comes to our conversations as well."

Sam propped himself up on his elbows and cocked an eyebrow. "What do you mean? I thought we've handled that really well."

"Apparently not as well as we've thought. Your mom mentioned something else. It's another reason they're concerned."

"What now?" Sam asked, disheartened.

"She has never forgotten that conversation with you all those years back. She thinks that you really believe that I can talk to you, because she's overhead you speaking to me as if I'd respond."

"Great. Another thing to worry about."

"Well, look on the bright side."

Sam asked, "There's a bright side?"

"At least she…" Titus cut short and went rigid as the door suddenly opened.

Sam, still sitting up in bed, looked at his mother as if he'd been caught with his hand in the cookie jar. Quickly trying to cover up his shock, he asked, "What's wrong, mom?"

She looked down at him then over to Titus. "I thought I heard you talking to someone in here. Is everything okay?"

Sam shrugged innocently. "Yeah. Titus was whining at the window. I was asking him if he needed to go outside and potty before I got too comfortable."

She looked at him skeptically then looked back to Titus. "Titus, do you need to go outside and go potty?"

Titus knew what he had to do to erase her concern and started to thud his tail on the floor while cocking one ear and turning his head to the side inquisitively.

She opened the door wider and said, "Come on, boy! Outside!"

He jumped up and trotted to the door excitedly. But as Sarah turned to walk out, he made sure to let Sam see his annoyance for the ad-lib with his best canine scowl.

Sam heard his mom say she'd bring Titus back in shortly. He fell back to his pillow, eyes wide, and let out the breath that he must have been holding since his sudden panic.

Titus was back quickly. Sarah, obviously frustrated, said, "He just wanted to go chase bugs at the porch light. Crazy dog." She smiled again. "Night, sweetie."

"Night."

She looked at Titus again and he did his best dog-impression and spun around looking for an itch then pretended to find one on his hindquarter and chew at it fiercely. He finished his performance with a good scratch with his hind leg to his ear and then yawned before plopping himself down on the floor.

His mom shook her head and closed the door.

Sam sat back up and glanced at the door before turning to face Titus, fighting hard not to smile. "Sorry. I didn't know what else to do."

Titus didn't speak for a moment then said, "*That* was humiliating."

There was a brief awkward silence until he said, "I actually *ate* a bug!"

They both succumbed to quiet laughter. Even though it was a bit scary, it was actually one of those good moments that Sam really enjoyed.

They finally stopped chuckling. "What were you going to say before we were interrupted?" Sam asked.

Titus smiled his doggy-grin. "Well," he said, "Ironically enough, I *was* going to say that at least your mom hasn't heard me speak. If she had, I'd be a lab rat right about now."

Sam smiled too. They both laughed quietly again. "That was way too close. She isn't even knocking now?"

Titus shook his head. "Apparently not. Time to double our efforts, it seems."

Sam rolled onto his side so that he could look out the window into the edges of the shadowy, moonlit forest. He sighed. "Great."

Thoughts of being separated from the ones he loved, especially Titus, swirled through his mind. Images of the past, friends from another world, flitted into his thoughts as he drifted into his subconscious. The last image that he had in his mind as he slipped further into dreams was the dark mysterious trees of the forest. Two eyes gleamed out, watching him.

Sam could feel his heart skip a beat before he finally succumbed to a very restless sleep.

Chapter Two: Normal

School was easier than home. Sam never really had friends, so no one really knew how much more different he was now than the years before Imagia. Though the teachers were at first concerned for his different behavior, they quickly began to forget. After all, with so many students to worry about, the minor changes in an individual's psyche were not so easily noted. Besides, he had come home in the midst of a new school year to a teacher who was unfamiliar with Sam's peculiar imaginative traits.

This morning found Sam having a more difficult than usual time concentrating on the world around him. His thoughts were plagued by his previous night's conversation with Titus. He was mostly just staring at the reflection of his shoes in the worn, but well polished, linoleum floors. As he was walking down the hall to his locker, he almost ran right into a teacher that he didn't recognize. He barely took time to look up but mumbled an apology in passing.

Seventh grade was no different than any of the other grades before except he now had three teachers that each taught two subjects. Morning always ended with History – Sam's favorite subject. Thinking of past worlds and different ways of life always interested him more than the mundane repetitiveness of math and English.

Another detail that he kind of enjoyed, or rather, had gotten used to, would be Elizabeth Gibson. For so many years before, having to pair off for projects was annoying because no one wanted to work with him. This was now completely the opposite with Elizabeth.

When he finally made his way to his seat at the back of the class, Elizabeth was already waiting to greet him.

She had medium length brown hair that was nearly always up in a curly ponytail. But today she had it only halfway tied back. Her brown eyes were large for her face, but it fit her well. Though not tall, as far as girls go, she always managed to keep close to Sam in height. She had a kind face and a sweet disposition, but earned the title of 'shy' because she didn't have dozens of friends. Oddly enough, her number of friends seemed to drop the more time she spent with Sam.

She smiled at him. "Hey Sam! Did you study for the test last night?"

Sam snapped out of his stupor and grinned back. "Hey, Lizzy. Yeah…but it's gonna be an easy one. I'm not worried about it." He threw his book down on the desk and settled into his seat. There were still a few minutes before class started.

"Oh," Lizzy fretted. "Well…*I'm* worried about it. I never do well on Mr. Sanford's tests." She bit down on her bottom lip like she always seemed to do under pressure.

Sam shrugged and pulled out his pencil and notepad. Lizzy didn't seem to care how distant he always seemed to be, which was one of the reasons he didn't mind her friendship.

Lizzy yawned and then rubbed her eyes.

Sam noticed this because he'd seen her look this tired quite a few times since first meeting her. He knew exactly what she was about to ask him. He prepared himself for yet another brilliant weave of lies and deception. He asked her, "Didn't sleep well last night?"

"Nah. I had that weird dream again. You know the one?" She waited for a response but Sam only grinned and nodded quickly. "It felt so real. I mean…I know it's just a dream, but it still feels more like a memory. It's always the same too."

"Yeah," Sam said, "I know. Really weird stuff."

Lizzy's eyes were focusing on a scratch on the desktop as she reminisced about the dream. "I was following a unicorn…*my* unicorn…into some trees by my home and it was suddenly daytime. I followed it into the light. The place I went was pretty – so green. And the unicorn was so beautiful." She smiled. "And that's when it goes bad. Something terrible attacked me and then my unicorn tried to stop it. And that's when I first saw you. You took my hand and we ran. You told me to tell your parents that you were okay and then you pushed me back into the nighttime. When I turned around you were gone." She paused for a moment, somehow still saddened by what she remembered.

Sam knew what she was about to say next so decided to interrupt her thoughtful moment. "Lizzy, you know it's just a dream. Sometimes dreams can be really believable. Trust me. I've had some pretty vivid ones myself." He smiled to himself but also to ease her thoughts.

"But it's always the same. That dream never changes. Don't you think that's even just the *tiniest* bit strange?" She looked at him as if she was waiting for a confession.

He just shrugged. "Nah. Just a dream." He hated lying to everyone. But lying to Lizzy was never easy, especially because Sam knew the truth. She wasn't crazy and she definitely wasn't remembering some ridiculous dream. It was a memory that they both shared but could never talk about. The only trouble was that Sam knew more about Lizzy's "dream" than she did. He hated having the answers to her riddle but never being able to help her solve it. It was terribly annoying.

Lizzy was shaking her head grimly. "Dream." She snorted. "More like a nightmare. No matter how many times I have it, it's always really scary, you know? It always feels so…so…*real.* I still remember the first time I had that nightmare. I woke my parents up and swore that I saw you in the forest. I even gave them the message so they could tell your parents. That's how real it felt three years ago." Lizzy shook her head. "Still feels just as genuine now."

"I don't know. I don't think I've ever had that happen. Nightmares do funny things to you. Maybe you were sleep walking or something." More lies. And he had a sneaking suspicion that Lizzy could tell he was being less than honest.

She squinted her eyes at him and chewed on the inside of her cheek.

He recognized that look as well. He prepared himself for the next moment because it was inevitable. He sighed quietly.

Lizzy's brown eyes watched Sam as he fidgeted slightly in his seat. "I still think it's strange that you went missing right after that dream. It's like I predicted it or something." She hesitated for a moment and then asked the question that Sam despised more than anything. Not because it was Lizzy asking it, but because it was asked by nearly everyone that spoke to him. "You still don't remember what happened all that time you were missing?'"

Sam bit down hard and then started to grind his teeth as he controlled his frustration. "Give me a break, Lizzy. Don't you think that if I'd remembered something it would have been…I dunno…on the evening news or something? Sheesh."

Lizzy's face softened and she suddenly looked guilty. "I know, I know. I'm sorry Sam. I guess I'm just tired. Sorry. I won't ask again."

Sam grinned at her. She'd said that more times than he could count. "Eh. No big deal." The crisis was averted yet again. One more day and one more question answered and still no 'insane' label stamped in red across his forehead. He hated when his days began with a lie. Especially when he had to lie to his friend.

She went back to fretting about the test and Sam listened to all her concerns and answered a few questions she wasn't sure of. Once she began biting her nails, he knew she was in full-on concentration mode. He finally felt safe enough to go back to his own thoughts

Sam never thought Elizabeth would remember him when he got back to school after his disappearance. He didn't count on her remembering their chance encounter in Imagia so vividly. But when he returned, she quickly found time to bombard him with countless questions regarding his unexplained absence. At first he was miffed at her relentless questions, but soon grew accustomed to her companionship as the questioning started to turn into friendly chatter.

As much as he'd missed Imagia and the friends he'd made there, it made the sting slightly less when Lizzy was around. It was nice to have a buddy in this world too - even if he could never tell her the truth. He kept telling himself that maybe one day he could confess everything to her and maybe…just maybe…she'd understand and *not* think he's completely nuts.

Sam sighed and decided he'd better find a spare pencil for the test. As he was searching, his attention was suddenly shifted by the surprisingly loud sound of a book being forcibly dropped onto the teacher's desk.

Sam, as well as the rest of the class, looked up, startled.

A man, obviously not his normal teacher, Mr. Sanford, was standing silently behind the old oak teacher's desk with his hands folded behind his back. He was dressed in the darkest blue from head to toe and donned a black patch over his left eye. His hair was a little too long, perfectly messy, and jet-black, contrasting with his lighter skin. He stared at the class for only a moment longer before turning on his heel and scratching the letters "R-O-Z" across the blackboard.

He spun back around and placed his hands on the desktop. "Good morning, class." His voice was smooth and deep – quite pleasant, actually. "I will be your teacher for the next few weeks or until further notice. My name is Mr. Rozalam." He paused for few seconds while gazing with his eye across the questioning faces in the class. He turned one side of his mouth up in a half-grin and then said, "You can call me Mr. Roz."

The class seemed intimidated temporarily by his presence. But one of the girls at the front of the class raised her hand."

Mr. Rozalam turned his eye to her without moving any other muscles and asked, "Yes?"

She cleared her throat. "Um…excuse me, but where is Mr. Sanford?"

He grunted quietly and removed his hands from the desk. "I was not informed of his whereabouts. But I'm sure that he has good reason for his absence."

Sam and Lizzy exchanged confused glances. Lizzy whispered to Sam, "Did Mr. Sanford say he was going to be gone?"

Sam was about to answer her but was interrupted by the sudden sound of his name.

"Sam Little, I suggest if you do not wish to be moved, you'll do your best to refrain from speaking any further."

Sam, having not said anything yet, was taken aback for being singled out so suddenly. He was always so careful to stay low-key in school and could feel his cheeks growing hot. He started to shake his head nervously and then responded, "Sorry, sir. But I didn't say anything." Then he paused as he realized something. He didn't know why, but something seemed suspicious about Mr. Rozalam. "Wait. How…how did you know my name?"

Mr. Rozalam smiled again, a somehow intimidating gesture. He moved slowly to the front of the desk. Everyone in the room shifted in their seats and turned to look at Sam.

His cheeks grew hotter and he could hear a faint ringing in his ears.

Mr. Rozalam looked around the room and then his gaze fell back to Sam again. "My dear boy," he smiled again, "do you think I don't read the paper? Keep ear of the news? Sam Little. The boy whose mysterious reappearance was nearly as baffling as his disappearance."

Sam looked down at his desk. He felt like a fool. "Oh," he squeaked out.

With a sniff of a laugh, Mr. Rozalam tapped at a notepad on the top of the teacher's desk. "And it just so happens that a seating chart can hold such dazzling secrets as well."

The class laughed and Sam grinned too. With that, the air seemed to grow lighter.

"Now," Mr. Rozalam continued, "It seems we have a test to take and several chapters on American History that need to be covered in the next few weeks." He noticed the students' eyes fixating on his eye patch. He continued. "Of course, we'll never make it past the next hour unless I address the one question on everyone's minds." He tapped his eye patch lightly. "Let's get this out of the way. Yes. I wear an eye patch. No. I am not, in fact, a pirate. Yes. It's a perplexing tale indeed that requires books to be written to answer its mysterious nature." He paused for obvious dramatic effect. "And lastly, no. I have no plans to show you what lies beneath. I fear the nightmares it would give you would interfere with your test-taking skills." He smiled quite pleasantly as the class grinned and laughed. "Now, please take out your pencils and put away your study material." He glanced around the room again, his eye falling on Sam for a long moment before turning to face the blackboard.

Sam made eye contact with him. In that moment, he felt like perhaps Mr. Rozalam knew more about him than he should have. Goosebumps popped up unwillingly across his arms. He didn't like the sensation. And he most certainly didn't like this substitute teacher. He just didn't know why.

The test was easy, just like Sam predicted it would be. But then again, history came naturally to him. He actually had spent some of his evenings reading ahead in his history book after he'd finished all of his homework simply because he enjoyed it. By the time the last person turned their paper in to Mr. Rozalam, he had time to speculate several back-stories for their odd new teacher. When the bell rang, he was so caught up in his own thoughts that Lizzy had to nudge him back into reality.

He may not have allowed himself to use his imagination, but his mind was more than capable of finding ways to entertain itself. Lizzy waited while he gathered up his stuff. She had her faced pinched up with concern when she asked, "How do you think you did?"

Sam pulled one strap of his backpack over his shoulder and said, "I nailed it. It was a piece of cake." He was walking towards the door when he heard the sound of someone behind him clearing his throat intentionally. Both he and Lizzy turned around.

"May I have a word with you, Sam?" Mr. Rozalam asked kindly.

Sam turned back to Lizzy and she gave him a confused glance. He shrugged and waved to her. "I'll see you at lunch, k?" Lizzy nodded and left the room while Sam walked over to the teacher's desk. Avoiding staring at his eye patch, Sam asked, "What did you need to see me about, sir?"

Mr. Rozalam smiled up at him from his chair and then stood up. He looked down at the desk for a moment and then pointedly at Sam. "I just wanted to apologize for earlier."

Sam furrowed his brow. Confused, he said, "Um…I'm not sure I…"

Before Sam could finish his thought, Mr. Rozalam held up his hand to interrupt him. "I wanted to say sorry for when I brought up your…past situation. I should not have done that. It was inappropriate. I'm sure it was a very difficult time for you and I did not mean to upset you. I apologize." He smiled crookedly, but it was genuine.

Sam was taken aback. "Er…it's okay, sir. I'm used to it." He turned to leave, but Mr. Rozalam started to speak again.

"It isn't ok. But I appreciate you saying so. Oddly enough, I can identify with such a thing. I, too, had a difficult situation similar to yours when I was a child. Of course, I was unlucky enough to remember all the details of my circumstances." He grinned solemnly. "It's difficult being the odd man out. Thrown into the spotlight unwillingly, so to speak. I'm not sure of the duration of my position here, but should you feel that you need someone to talk to, I hope you don't mind me offering my ear to you."

Sam wasn't sure what to say. So he simply blinked and stared back questioningly. Mr. Rozalam was actually surprisingly nice. Apparently, his goose bumps from earlier were preemptive and off the mark. Which was completely normal. He'd developed a sense of paranoia ever since Imagia. If one thing was for certain, his stay in that world made him wary of dropping his guard. He smiled. "Thank you, sir."

"Please," Mr. Rozalam pleaded, "call me Mr. Roz. It's better. Don't you think?"

Sam grinned again. "Yeah. Thanks again." He turned and left the room, his mind whirling with a new range of scenarios of just what might have happened to his substitute teacher so many years ago.

* * * * * * * * * * *

Nearly a week had passed and Mr. Roz had quickly become a student favorite. For the first time in awhile, Sam was actually excited about going to school. It was Friday and he was looking forward to another history lesson. When he got to class, the words 'Homework: Essay – 5 pages', were scribbled on the blackboard. Each time someone walked through the door, it was quickly followed with an audible groan and slumped shoulders. Weekend homework. Never a favorite. Sam thought to himself that Mr. Roz was about to lose several students' approval ratings.

The class quickly settled and Mr. Roz began. "According to my lesson plans, a five-page essay is due on Monday." Murmurs of disappointment swept the room. "Your teacher would have you each write about the same boring subject, but as I do not wish to read the same information seventeen times, I am making a slight change to this." Several hopeful faces now looked back at him, Sam being one of them.

One of the girl students asked if this would make Mr. Sanford upset, to which Mr. Roz smoothly replied, "Well, Mr. Sanford isn't here to be upset by anything. Now, is he?" The girl blushed and didn't raise her hand again.

Mr. Roz continued, "I am going to personally assign each of you a particular historical moment or person. You are to give a brief description of your assigned subject, which should take up no more than a page. From there, you will explain something similar you've personally experienced in your life. If you've not had a similar incident, then you can describe exactly how you would have handled the situations that person or historical moment dealt with. I expect creativity here, children. There is no wrong answer. If you do it right, it should be fun!" He then turned and seemed to be speaking pointedly to Sam. "Imagination is key."

Sam's heart skipped a beat. He felt the hairs on his neck stand up. Though it seemed like his teacher's gaze was penetrating his thoughts, the moment was gone as quickly as it had come. Did he mean to look at Sam when he'd said the word 'imagination', or was his paranoia taking over again? Titus told him time and again that he was worried about Sam's paranoid behavior. Sam shook off the thoughts and chalked it up to coincidence.

Lizzy looked at Sam and mouthed the words, "You okay?"

Sam grinned and sort of half-shrugged and half-nodded at the same time.

Mr. Roz called out each student's name so that they could receive a piece of paper with their assigned subject on it. When it was Sam's turn, he reluctantly walked to the front of the class to pick up his piece of paper. It wasn't until he sat back down that he read what his subject was. Written in ink on a small rectangle of paper was:

~Christopher Columbus and his discovery of the New World~

Sam froze.

If ever there were a subject that he was all too familiar with, it was discovering a new world. And not just a new world, but a new world where the lands were wild and untamed and then taken over by someone that staked claim upon its soil only to begin waging war upon those that lived there before him. Just like Nadaroth. It wasn't just a familiar story. It was *his* story.

He looked up at his substitute teacher and sweat began to form around his hairline. His heart rate was climbing and it spiked about the time that Mr. Roz met Sam's stare. Even though they locked eyes for just a mere moment, there was a sly smile from his teacher that curled one side of his mouth into a peculiar grin.

The paper Sam held began to shiver just slightly. He looked back down at it and suddenly realized he was holding his breath. Even though he tried to convince himself that he was over-reacting, he realized one thing was happening that he didn't know how to control.

Sam was beginning to panic.

He'd been having some troubles during certain times of emotion since his return from Imagia. At times, when he was extremely afraid, upset or even excited about something, he found himself accidentally using his imagination. And one thing was for certain. He couldn't let that happen.

Not here.

Not now.

The panic was peaking and his mind began to whirl.

He vaguely heard Lizzy whisper to him, "Sam? Are you okay? You don't look so good."

Sam nervously wiped the sweat from his head that was inching towards his eyes. Then he did something he'd never done before. He stood up, the chair squealing harshly against the linoleum floor. He didn't look at anyone or anything as he almost ran for the door. He heard a few kids in the class whispering as he rushed past them.

Mr. Roz asked quickly, "Sam, is there a problem?"

He responded with the only thing he could think of. Just as he was out the door, he blurted out, "I don't feel good!" As the door closed, he started running full tilt for the nearest bathroom. The further away he got from his classroom, the more ridiculous he felt. That's when his embarrassment for how he'd just acted started to build on top of his fear for being seen as a freak.

Once he was in the bathroom, his fear began to take over his mind. He gaped at his sweaty, pale face in the mirror. He hastily looked at the reflection of the stalls behind him making sure he was alone. When he knew he was by himself, his mind raced with memories of Imagia and the forests that he'd become so familiar with – the secrets he knew he had to hide.

The mirror began to vibrate. Behind him, he could see things transforming. Leaves and vines began to cover the bathroom stalls as the room began to change into what he was seeing in his mind's eye. His emotions were spiraling out of control and he gasped. Titus was always there to help him calm down in these situations, but he was alone right now.

Alone and afraid of being caught.

A tree began to grow from the ground, creaking and cracking as the tiles on the floor began to shift and break. At any minute someone could come in the bathroom and find this happening. How would it look to them? He had to calm down. He had to stop this.

He tried to remember what Titus told him to do. He closed his eyes tight. As he gripped the sides of the now moss-covered sink, he inhaled slowly through his nose and pictured the bathroom how it was supposed to be. Sam pinpointed that single image in the sea of madness swirling through his panicked mind and focused on it.

In barely a whisper, he repeated to himself, "Just calm down. Just calm down, Sam. Just. Calm. Down." He tuned the world around him out and kept saying it over and over until he heard the door of the bathroom open and someone say, "Are you alright?"

Startled, Sam jumped back and let out a hiccup of a yell. It was Mr. Roz who was standing in the doorway with a look of concern on his face. Sam looked around the room frantically only to see that it was perfectly normal. There wasn't so much as a single leaf in sight. He hadn't answered Mr. Roz yet, which prompted him to speak again.

His one eye was wide when he looked pointedly at Sam. "Sam? Are you okay?" He waited patiently for a response.

Sam was finally calmed down and realized how insanely crazy he must have appeared at this moment. But one thing was for certain. The lie he was about to say would be quite believable with his pallid appearance. He stuttered just slightly as he said, "Yeah. I'm fine. I just…didn't feel very well. I think it was my breakfast." He tried to smile, failing miserably. "I think I'm fine now."

"Well," Mr. Roz began, "perhaps you should take a moment then. Return to class when you're ready." Then his teacher was gone, leaving Sam alone again.

Sam turned the sink on and washed his face with cool water. He closed his eyes for a moment and shook his head. He looked back into the mirror, finally composed. Who he saw staring back at him wasn't a boy who belonged in this world. Even though he knew it would never work, he quietly said, “I wish I could go back to Imagia.” He paused. “I just don’t belong here anymore.”

Slowly, he made his way back to class. This day was not going well. But a tiny thought lurking in the back of his mind told him that, for what it was worth, it could have gone a lot worse. Unfortunately, a somewhat larger thought tried to convince him that things were about to get very complicated.

He just didn’t know when.

Chapter Three: Complicated Truths

Going home was always a relief. Today was no different. In actuality, Sam was more relieved to go home than usual. His little loss of control in the bathroom made him not only tired, but also nervous. It would be nice to see Titus and talk with him before his mom got home from her job.

For two months after his return from Imagia, his mom wouldn't let him out of her sight. The first time she finally decided that he could be left alone, even if it were only briefly, he'd managed to destroy part of the house using his imagination. After that day, it took nearly two years before she would convince herself she could return to work part-time. This left him coming home from school to a nearly empty house. It worked out perfectly for Sam and Titus. It gave them time to be normal.

Sam was almost at a run when he got to the entrance to his cul-de-sac. He had his key ready to open the door and dropped his backpack on the ground in the hallway with a dull thud. He rounded a corner and called to his friend. "Hey, Titus! I'm home," he began. "You're never gonna believe the day I had."

Titus came trotting out of Sam's bedroom. "Hello, Sam. What happened?"

Sam proceeded to explain to his friend every single detail of his day. When he got to the part involving the bathroom, Titus' look became wary. As Sam came to a stop, Titus voiced his concern. "And you're absolutely certain that the teacher didn't see anything?"

"Yep," Sam assured him. "I mean, it was a close one. But, he didn't say anything at all and the bathroom was completely back to normal. I just feel like he's hiding something. I swear, Titus," Sam paused and furrowed his brow before continuing, "he knows something about me. I mean, Christopher Columbus? A discoverer of a new world? Come on! He kept looking at me funny."

Titus considered that for a moment. He'd gotten used to Sam's paranoid behavior. Something about returning home had caused him to be frightened and leery of anyone he didn't know. He nodded. "Yes. I'll admit it is a bit strange. But honestly, Sam, I don't think it's anything for you to worry about. You've felt this way in the past and nothing has ever come of it. There is no way anyone could know what you're hiding unless you physically tell them yourself. Your secrets are safe. We have other more weighing things to concern ourselves with."

"I dunno. It's different this time."

"Who do you think he is then? What are you afraid of?"

That was the question it always came down to. What was he afraid of? He stared down at the tabletop. As usual, Titus reasoned with him until he realized what fears were truly fueling his thoughts. He may have left Imagia, but his fears – his nightmares – still lingered. "I'm afraid that someone has seen me use my imagination. He could be a doctor. Or a scientist. Or someone that will take me away. Put me under a microscope…study me. When I got back…" he paused, remembering something uncomfortable, "there were so many people asking me questions. News reporters…doctors…police officers. I lied so much."

"Ah," Titus responded. "You see? You're feeling guilt for lying. You've always been afraid someone will know you lied. But you did what you had to do – for both of us. Taren warned you. He knew that this would be hard. We just didn't know how hard." He considered something for a moment. "No one could have predicted any of this. You just have to learn to control your fear. Which isn't simple after what you've seen and done."

San yelled out in frustration while slamming a fist down on the kitchen table. "I just wish I could go back! It's just too hard here!" Sam sat down roughly on one of the chairs.

Titus walked to him and put a paw on his thigh. He looked into Sam's eyes. "I know. But it's not happening. So we have to deal with each problem as they arise. Let's start with something simple. When is your report due?"

With an annoyed eye-roll, he said, "Monday."

"Wonderful. Let's get started."

* * * * * * * * * * *

Sam wasn't nervous anymore to go back to History class. The past few days had been very low key. In fact, he was convinced now that he had imagined Mr. Roz's suspicious behavior all along. Titus had been right again. So all he could think about now was how incredibly fascinated his doctors were going to find him this summer. That was, if he couldn't find a way out of that mess altogether.

Sam saw Lizzy sitting in her seat fretting about her homework, as usual. He sat down in the desk beside her. "Hey, Lizzy."

She popped her head up. She was chewing on a badly scarred pencil. She had it firmly gripped between her teeth when she answered. "Hey!" She spit the pencil out. "I heard that we're getting our papers back today. How do you think he graded them so fast? It usually takes Mr. Sanford two weeks to read all of them and we just turned them in three days ago."

Sam shrugged. His substitute teacher's ability to read at one-eyed super speed was the least of his concerns. Mr. Roz came in and the class quieted down. Lizzy stopped fretting and Sam yawned widely.

Mr. Roz taught the class again without any random concerning looks to Sam. It was a relief to not feel like the world was out to capture and dissect him. Class was nearly over and Mr. Roz pulled a rather thick pile of papers out of a cream folder on his desk. He passed them out and the room began to erupt in a series of hushed reactions to their grades. Some people were giving thumbs up to their friends while others were softly banging their heads on their desks in defeat.

Lizzy got hers before Sam and she squealed quietly when she saw the bright red "A" on the first page. Sam, on the other hand, was slightly nervous again. He had written his paper with Titus' help and wasn't sure if he'd written anything worthy of even a "C". If he'd written his true comparison to Christopher Columbus, he was quite certain he'd earn, not only an "A", but also an award for "Best Selling Fantasy".

The bell was about to ring as Mr. Roz laid the essay upside down on Sam's desk. He couldn't help but notice a slight frown on Mr. Roz's face when he walked back to his teacher's desk.

Curious as ever, Lizzy leaned across the aisle and asked, "How'd you do?"

Flipping the paper over, the first thing that caught Sam's eye was the bright red "D" scratched on the paper. Right below it, it read:

'Very disappointing comparison.
I imagine you could have done much better!
Please see me after school.'

Sam was busy trying to keep his composure together as he reread the note again. Lizzy sucked in a quick breath between her teeth. "Ouch. That's strange. You always get better grades in this class than I do. Why do you think he underlined 'imagine'?"

Managing to shrug slightly, Sam quietly said, "No idea." But, unfortunately, he did know. His suspicions weren't as wildly off the chart as he'd thought. This random substitute teacher knew something about Sam.

The panicking was starting to creep into his mind again. As he felt his palms go sweaty beneath the paper he was holding, he tried to remember what Titus said. No matter what happened, he needed to tackle one thing at a time. He looked to the front of the class, fearful for making eye-contact with his teacher. But when he did, Mr. Roz wasn't even there. The bell had rung and he had already left the room.

Now Sam was really worried.

The rest of the day went by too quickly. Sam tried not to let his concerns plague his mind, but as school ended and he started to make his way back to the History room, he couldn't help but to breathe a little faster and walk a little softer. At this time, he wasn't entirely certain what was about to take place. The best he could do was get ready to tell his finest lies and pray that he'd get away with it. When in reality, Sam just hoped that he was wrong and that, perhaps, he really did just write an awful paper.

The door was right there. He paused before he turned to go in. He looked down at his shoes and then closed his eyes. He inhaled deeply, and in his exhale murmured, "Everything's okay. One thing at a time."

Sitting at his desk, his back to Sam, Mr. Roz was gazing solemnly out the window. Sam tried to clear his throat, but instead it came out sounding more like a nervous hiccup.

Mr. Roz turned his head and smiled widely at Sam. "Ah! Sam! There you are."

Swallowing hard, Sam said, "Y-you wanted to see me, sir?" He couldn't miss the stammer in his words and grimaced internally.

"Yes. Yes, I did. I wanted to talk about your paper. Can you please shut the door behind you? Too much noise in the hall." He still had a smile on his face.

Sam hesitated at the request. Why did he need to shut the door? It wasn't that loud. And he wondered why he was so worried. What could possibly happen? He was at school and there were witnesses everywhere.

He shut the door.

The hair on the back of his neck stood up.

"Please. Come sit down." Mr. Roz was holding a hand towards the front seat in the classroom.

Sam didn't move. His knees locked. He felt like he was standing in front of the forest behind his house four years ago on that fateful day. Only, this time, he was smart enough to know what this knee-locking sensation was. It was fear.

Mr. Roz raised his eyebrow. "Are you okay, Sam? You look as though you've seen a ghost." When Sam didn't answer, he continued, "You're not in trouble. I was merely hoping to discuss your paper and give you an option to rewrite it."

Though the hairs on his neck didn't withdraw, he felt a sudden sliver of hope that perhaps he was over-reacting again. He found the nerve to move his feet. As he was about to lift his right foot off the ground, he stopped. Before he could move Mr. Roz did something unexpected.

He stood up quickly, held his hand out, gesturing for Sam to cease moving. In a quite demanding voice, he barked, "Stop!"

Sam's eyes went wide and neither person spoke for an awkwardly lengthy moment. It was no longer just the hair on his neck that was standing straight. His entire body went cold and he felt himself stepping back towards the closed door. Everything in his body told him to flee. He took another hesitant step back and grabbed the doorknob. He froze when he heard Mr. Roz speak again.

"Wait! Please don't go." He looked down and sighed.

To Sam, it was the sound of someone admitting defeat. Looking up, he saw his teacher turn to the window again. Sam suddenly felt a spark inside him that he hadn't felt in a long time. It was his sense of adventure. And it scared him. His adventures always seemed to end badly.

Sam took his hand off of the doorknob and waited cautiously. Mr. Roz shook his head, having decided something internally. In a hushed voice, he said, "Enough of this farce." He stood up, still looking away from Sam. "You're no fool to subtlety."

Suddenly, his teacher looked taller and much more intimidating. Sam couldn't help but to nervously glance back at the door and wish to have Titus standing by his side.

Mr. Roz turned around and took note of Sam's uncertainty. "Please, Sam. Even though you have every right to be fearful, know that I mean you no harm."

Sam opened his mouth to finally speak, "I don't…"

Mr. Roz raised a hand to stop him again. "No. Let me finish."

Sam scrunched his forehead up, confused.

Placing his hands calmly behind his back, Mr. Roz continued. "As I said, you are right to be cautious. I have lied to you from the moment I stepped through that door. I should have known better. But I assure you; you have nothing to fear from me. I have so much to discuss with you."

Sam feared the worst. Was he a doctor? Maybe he was a reporter. Did a neighbor see something he'd imagined and call someone to investigate? What did he know? He spoke up before Mr. Roz could say another word, anger touching the edges of his voice. "Who are you?"

A grin spread across his face, moving his eye patch up ever so slightly. "A friend – someone like you. Someone who's lost in a world that they don't belong in."

Sam's eyes went wide. He wasn't sure what he was hearing. "I…I don't…" Sam shook his head, trying to find the words. "I don't know what you're talking about."

Mr. Roz let out a short huff of a laugh. "My name isn't Mr. Rozalam. It's just simply Rozalam." He took one hesitant step forward towards the boy. Ducking his head down closer to Sam's level, he quietly stated, "I'm a Defender of Imagia."

Sam jerked backwards and gasped loudly.

Mr. Roz smiled again and said, "Sam Little, I've been looking for you for a long time."

Chapter Four: Impossible Possibilities

Torn in two directions, Sam couldn't figure out if he wanted to run from the room screaming or run to the self-proclaimed Defender and hug him. He was also torn between believing that this was real or that he had somehow fallen asleep in class and dreamt up this impossibility. At the current moment, he was leaning towards the dream.

Mr. Roz, or Rozalam as he called himself, stood perfectly still. It was evident that he was waiting for Sam to make the next move. When Sam failed to respond in any way, a level of awkwardness entered the scene.

So many things were running through Sam's brain. He didn't know if this was some form of trap or that he was actually standing in a classroom on Earth with an honest to goodness Defender of Imagia. But the more he considered the situation, the more he realized the obvious. There was no way anyone could have known details that he'd already revealed unless he had actually been to Imagia and seen its wonders. What Rozalam had told him with that simple introduction were three things.

First, by using the word 'Defender' rather than 'Protector', he disclosed that he was not only from Imagia, but also from the northern part of that world. When Sam had first been in Imagia, he'd met only Protectors. It wasn't until he'd reached the northern area that he'd learned that Defenders were essentially the same as Protectors, only from the north.

Second, He knew who Sam was. This could only mean that they'd been in Imagia at the same time.

And last of all, he trusted Sam. No one in their right mind would have spoken Imagia's name so straightforward to someone who hadn't been there. To speak of it so easily meant that he'd known Sam had been there and would remember.

As Sam finished processing these facts, his heart began to pound harder. Not a bad pounding, but rather an excited sensation that began to consume him. Through all the unease of the moment, he finally realized what was happening.

He was standing in a room with someone from Imagia.

He was no longer alone.

Rozalam noticed Sam's stance begin to shift. His body was no longer rigid and an excited grin started to turn up his young cheeks. New light sparkled in his blue eyes. Rozalam relaxed, shoulders falling ever so slightly and a smile touching his solitary eye. He broke the silence. "It's so good to finally tell you."

Sam took two steps forward, still worried he'd wake up from this dream. Quietly, he said, "You're real? I mean…really real?"

Rozalam nodded emphatically. "Yes. That I am. And we have much to discuss."

Still in disbelief, Sam couldn't manage to find the words that he needed to express his feelings. Part of him was elated while another part of him was scared. Strange things happened to him in his life. Ever since stepping one foot outside of the gateway to return home, he'd wished and hoped that there would be some way to get back to that world – his world – the world he really belonged in. Now, there in front of him, stood proof that it wasn't only possible, but a reality. Instead of asking the questions he should have asked, he blurted out the first one that his mind could successfully form into words. "If you're here, then does that mean we can get back to Imagia?"

Rozalam considered his question. "Hmm. I think that perhaps we should start with something a bit simpler. That can't be the only query that piques your curious mind, now can it?"

Sam tried to slow his thought process down a notch and then nodded his head twice. "Right. So how did you get here?"

Rozalam laughed heartily. "You didn't skip a beat, did you?"

He felt almost rude asking so quickly. But, after all of the years he'd been dying to speak to someone from Imagia, Sam just didn't care. He apologized half-heartedly. "Sorry, sir. It's just been forever since, ya know…since I talked to anyone from Imagia. I just…"

"No need to explain. And no need for apologies," Rozalam assured him. "I am just glad to finally stop hiding. Even if it's just with one person."

Sam knew exactly what he meant.

Rozalam sat down in his chair, a sigh of relief escaping as he relaxed into the seat. He gestured for Sam to do the same. "Please. We have so much to talk about. And honestly, I have no idea where to start."

The hallways outside were growing quieter by the minute and before long, it was just the hushed shuffle of a few people every so often that reminded them they were still at school. Sitting down, Sam looked to the closed door, a grin still on his face, and began his barrage of questions. "I thought that it was impossible for anyone to get back through a gateway once they'd become lost ones of Imagia. How'd you get here? And does that mean I can go back?" He paused to think but only for a split second. There was a greater question he had thought of that didn't make sense. "And how are you a substitute teacher? That doesn't make sense at all."

Rozalam nodded thoughtfully. Sam could see an internal struggle flash through his eye. Even though Sam's impatience for answers made him think hours had passed since he'd asked, the Defender began to speak, having made up his mind where to begin. "It's complicated, really." He took a deep breath through flared nostrils. "I'll get to that. No one really ever thought that people could get out once they lost their gateway. Actually, it was thought that it truly was an impossible feat. But, then again, you were considered impossible once as well." He smiled. "And I don't think I need to remind you that *you* were a lost one once. Yet, here you are." He held his palm up and towards Sam to reiterate his point.

Sam smiled back, a hint of red touching his cheeks. He looked down timidly.

"The story of your departure from Imagia is well known to all there. I fell into this world by accident. It was not my intent. But there is so much to tell you that I think we'd best start from a different beginning. There is a lot you don't know. And much of it is going to be difficult to hear."

"What do you mean?" Sam was nervous.

Rozalam stared at his hands that were folded on the desk. "When you returned to this world, word of your leaving spread far and wide. It reached me in Northern Imagia just days after you left. It didn't take long after that for things to get worse."

Sam scrunched his face up. He'd defeated Nadaroth. He asked himself how anything could be worse than that self-created nightmare. Though he was thinking this, he didn't speak his concerns aloud.

Rozalam continued without pausing. "This is going to come as a shock to you, just as it did to everyone else. When you killed that monstrosity in his shadowy lands, it was not the creature you thought it was. Some time after you left through that gateway, Nadaroth made himself known to many while they slept. Nightmares ran rampant for several days as he invaded dreams once again. He mocked Protectors and Defenders. Some even say they could hear his laughter on the breezes that came from the far north."

Shaking his head furiously, Sam couldn't find words. This made no sense to him. He wanted to scream – to wake up – because this wasn't possible. He'd watched Nadaroth fall to his death in that gaping inferno. Rozalam had noticed his disbelief and was waiting for him to speak. The silence was deafening. Still shaking his head, he finally said, "No. That has to be a mistake. I watched him die! I killed him!"

Sadness in his eye, Rozalam simply said, "I'm sorry, Sam. But it's true."

Sam felt sick. After everything he'd done and everything he'd suffered, for Nadaroth to have lived was absolutely horrible news. A strong mental image of Keesa, his friend and motherly-figure in Imagia, was vivid in his mind. Meekly, he said, "Then it was all for nothing. The pain. The…loss. What was the point?" His stomach churned again.

"No," Rozalam stated matter-of-factly. "Nadaroth isn't gone. But your pain and loss were not all in vain. He was weaker for all you did. It is thought that the creature you fought was actually a part of

Nadaroth – a single piece of the whole. When he…or it, I suppose…died, it was a severe blow to him. I don't know the details of what happened after you left, but another rumor is that he wanted you to leave. Some even say that it was him who made it possible for you to go." He half-snorted and smiled. "As for myself, I don't believe that. I believe Imagia herself let you leave, believing that she was safe. Who knows? Perhaps it was a display of gratitude."

Sam put his hands up suddenly and blurted out, "*She*? What do you mean 'she'? Imagia is a world. Not a person." He was incredibly confused and beginning to second-guess this so-called Defender.

Rozalam was nodding and smiling. "Ah. Sorry. There are some of us who believe that Imagia isn't just a world, but a life that sustains all other life. Which, if you think about it, really defines what a world is. There is no denying that Imagia is alive."

Sam thought about that. He remembered all the wonders of that world. He pictured the beauty and danger that it posed. There was no refuting the magic of the creatures he'd met along the way and how they felt as though they were actually connected to the world. Now that he was considering everything from that viewpoint, he couldn't help but to consider the possibility.

She.

The strangeness of that world never ceased to amaze.

Rozalam could see Sam's understanding. "There are many theories. But the point is, Defenders were still very much needed. Guardians remain in danger. Which is where I come into the picture. Your coming back to this world was a choice. Mine was a fluke." He shifted uneasily in his chair. "I had been tracking a fairly nasty creature through the woods when I heard a Guardian making its way to its gateway. Because I believed the creature wasn't too near, I stayed to watch from a distance. I had just come to the decision to stop the Guardian from leaving the gateway when I was proven how wrong I was.

"The creature was closer than I had thought. I shoved the Guardian out of the way and that beast ran into me, full force. I was thrown out of the gateway, the creature barreling through with me. I got up just in time to see the shock on the Guardians face as the gateway faded away. It was gone. As were my chances for getting back home."

His jaw agape, Sam let out a hushed, "Wow." He blinked as he thought. "What happened to the creature? How did it even get out?"

"Well," Rozalam started, "that's where it gets tricky. Anything born of Imagia can leave a gateway unnoticed. Or at the very least, unharmed. I am human. It was not. And we just happened to go through the gateway at the same time."

Sam thought of Titus. He wasn't born of Imagia, but he remembered being told that Titus could get in because he wasn't human. The gateway changed Titus when he went through, bestowing intelligence and speech to him. Now he wondered if a creature from Imagia would change as it came through to this world.

Rozalam answered that unspoken question for him. "The creature was…well…let's just say that it was very unhappy with its whereabouts. That's when things got even crazier. You asked me how I came to be a substitute teacher."

"Yeah."

"Were you aware that your teacher of this class was a hunter?"

Sam shook his head, confused at such a random question.

"He was hunting in the same woods that I just happened to be fighting the rogue creature in. Actually, Henry didn't…"

"Wait a sec," Sam interrupted. "Who's Henry?"

Rozalam lifted his eyebrow questioningly. "Your teacher of this class, of course. Henry Sanford. My goodness, Sam! Didn't you know your own teacher's name?"

Sam swallowed hard. He felt embarrassed. He'd never even thought about his teacher's first name. "No. I guess I didn't."

"Hmph. Strange. But nonetheless, Henry was there in the woods and had witnessed seeing me and that beast come flying out of thin air. There is a reason Guardians time leaving their gateways so cautiously. Grown men and women of this world simply do not understand. And Henry was in the wrong place at the wrong time."

As it is, most children think that teachers' lives outside of school simply do not exist. To them, the teachers eat, live and sleep in their classrooms. Sam was no different. He'd never pictured Mr. Sanford as anything more than his history teacher. He'd been naïve. In Imagia, he'd learned time and again not to judge something or someone so quickly. How could he have forgotten so easily?

All he'd heard awakened Sam's mind. The questions were forming a line. He wanted to know more. He didn't know how long Rozalam had been here and as his mind reeled, he considered the outcome of the creature's plight in the woods. Suddenly, he was very concerned about his teacher's well being. He sucked in a quick breath as he realized just how long Mr. Sanford had been gone from class. "Oh, no! So Mr. Sanford…he…he…"

Rozalam stopped him before he could jump to conclusions. He held up a hand with his eye wide. "He survived that encounter quite well. Oh, he was pretty stunned initially. But thankfully, he was hunting and well armed. To be honest, I'm not certain that I'd be speaking to you right now if it were not for him."

Sam's shoulders relaxed and he sighed. "Thank goodness."

"Yes." Rozalam said thoughtfully. "Thank goodness, indeed. It was a fast and dirty fight. The creature circled me and when I reached back to get an arrow, I'd discovered that I'd lost them when that blasted creature knocked me out of the gateway. Henry used his weapon and hit the beast. Of course, he angered it. I managed to distract it, jumping on its back. I'll spare you the details for now and tell you that in the end, it was Henry's steady aim that killed it." He laughed quietly as he thought of something. Sam looked at him, wondering what he was going to say next. "You know, I don't think that the beast was the thing that shocked Henry the most."

Sam narrowed his eyes. If it had been him, he'd be certain that any dark beast was enough to shock him. And he'd seen more than most people. He asked, "What do you mean?"

He snorted a quick laugh again. "Well, what do you believe any person here would think if you tried to explain to them that you'd come through a magic doorway from another world?" He watched as Sam smiled. "Yes. You see what I mean. He was hesitant to believe me, but after examining the creature he'd just killed, he was more or less convinced."

"Yeah. That would be hard to explain. I know. Trust me." The regret in those last words was difficult to miss.

"Mm-hmm. Well, that is how I came to be here. I'm afraid there's not much more to tell beyond that. I had no idea where I was. I'd not been in this world since I was a boy. Henry was kind enough to fill me in on all I needed to know." He smiled to himself. "Of course, I thought to myself that if I could find you, I'd be making some progress. When Henry brought me back to this town well more than a year ago, I planned on staying only long enough to learn how to survive this world."

Sam was confused. They'd been in the same town for so long and he'd never found him. He couldn't understand how this was possible. "How did it take so long to find me?"

Rozalam got up from his chair and walked to the windows in the classroom. He was staring outside for a long moment before turning to face Sam. Friend or not, this made Sam uncomfortable. Rozalam tilted his head just slightly and considered something. He turned back to face Sam again. "Sam, I wasn't sure I wanted to tell him everything. I wasn't even sure what to ask or even if I could trust him, to be honest. I decided to leave. In my travels, I overheard your name one day on a news program. It was on the television." He paused, remembering the moment. "Anyways, that was just months ago. I came back when I discovered that I'd been so close to you all along. I told Henry everything I could, and that's how I found out that, not only were you in the same town, but that Henry was your teacher. He was helping me find a way to meet you. He trained me and, though I'm sure he bent many rules, made it so I could be a substitute for him. The whole plan was almost complete when he heard of something attacking humans in the same area that we'd met." Rozalam turned back to the window and bowed his head.

Sam could feel a change in the air. He could tell that he was about to hear something he didn't want to hear. For a moment, he considered leaving. If he went back home, then he could just never know and count this as a good day in which he'd simply met a new friend. But the pull of curiosity – something that he'd not felt so strongly in a long time – was taunting him. He'd come this far. He had to hear the rest of Rozalam's story. Hesitantly, he asked, "What happened?"

Head still bowed, Rozalam replied, "Please understand that Henry was my friend."

Sam's heart flip-flopped.

Was. Rozalam had said '*was*'. "What do you mean *was* your friend?" Sam swallowed hard.

"I tried to tell him not to go. I told him that if something else really had come here from Imagia, that it was certain to be dangerous. But his life changed the day that he met me. He left. I stayed. I had to proceed with my plan to meet you. The next day, I was here. Teaching, I suppose you could say."

Sam closed his eyes. In barely a whisper, he guessed, "Is he…dead?"

Turning, Rozalam walked over and knelt down in front of the desk Sam was sitting at. Sam opened his eyes, dread overpowering the excitement. He smiled grimly. "I don't know for sure. But…he was meant to be home by now. I heard of another attack in those woods…missing people. My heart wants to believe otherwise, but…" he thought for a moment, "I'm just not sure. I've heard no word from him. I hope that he's alive. And sometimes hope is all we can cling to." Anger touched his previously cool manner. Biting the words off sharply, he said, "Henry was a fool to go! And he knew it."

"But, there's still a chance though. He could still be alive," Sam suggested hopefully.

The lines of Rozalam's face were concerned.

There was silence for a brief time between the two, the question lingering without an answer. Sam had just realized his world had shifted. He considered all he'd learned today. He'd finally be able to talk to someone besides Titus. Even though his dog was his best friend in this world, he longed to have someone else to share his real life with. Someone who would not only understand, but sympathize with him.

He grinned as he thought about telling Titus everything that had happened today. He guessed that his dog would be just as excited at the new prospects as he was. He suddenly couldn't wait to go spread the good news to his only recipient.

And just like that, Sam had an abruptly harsh awareness of the time. He jumped in his chair, nearly falling out of his seat and spun his head around to look at the clock.

Rozalam practically jumped out of his skin, thinking the worst and almost yelled, "Sam, what's wrong?"

"3:45! Oh no! I'm supposed to be home in ten minutes!" Sam began to fret aloud. "If I'm not home before mom, she'll freak out! I've gotta go or I'll never make it."

Rozalam, recognizing the situation's urgency, ushered Sam to the door, one hand reassuringly placed on the boy's shoulder. "I'm so sorry, Sam. I didn't think about the time. Please, go. We'll talk more later."

Sam was hastily fidgeting with the strap of his backpack, eyes wide. He truly hated to be leaving right now. He was precisely where he wanted to be and was being forced to go. Why it was always like this for him, he'd never know. His mind raced, torn between the trouble he would certainly be in if he didn't leave now and the amazing possibilities that he now knew were out there. He watched Rozalam open the door. He didn't know what to say, so settled for a quick smile.

Rozalam returned the gesture and said, "We'll talk again soon."

Sam nodded. He had just left the door and Rozalam was barely turned around to go back to his room, when his manners surfaced unexpectedly. "Oh!" Sam grabbed the door before it closed, surprising Rozalam again.

"Yes?"

"Uh, thanks. You know…for everything." His smile was ear to ear. "See ya tomorrow, Mr. Roz."

The man laughed genuinely. "You're welcome. And Sam?"

"Yeah?"

"Please, call me Roz." He hesitated, then added, "Except during class."

Sam's smile grew two-fold. He waved quickly and ran all the way home. He couldn't wait to tell Titus about his new friend, Roz – the Defender from Imagia.

Chapter Five: Revelations

Titus sat on his haunches, shaking his head slowly. The things Sam had just told him about his supposed substitute teacher were difficult, at best, to believe. Sam had mostly just bombarded him when he came running into the house after school. His mom pulled into the driveway mere moments after Sam had practically taken the doors off of its hinges in his excitement. He barely had time to get a rough explanation out before Sarah came inside. Sam was bursting to talk and told his mom, after a quick hello, that he wanted to take Titus for a walk. If they walked in the right place at the right time, no one would be around to hear them speak to one another.

And that is precisely what they had managed to do. In a secluded section of a park near their house, on a run-down, old walking path by the forest's edge, Sam had told Titus every unbelievable detail of his meeting with Roz. Now that Titus had soaked in all of the information, he was too stunned to respond.

Sam paced excitedly across the top of a fallen tree that had been cleverly trimmed into an extra wide bench. He was still explaining the possibilities to his friend when Titus finally found his tongue. "Not to be a consistent voice of reason, but are you certain that this wasn't a dream?"

Sam stopped pacing. He squatted down, his arms straight out while propped on his knees. "Yes," he said matter-of-factly. "I couldn't believe it at first either, but there is no way he's from here. No one could know the things he told me unless we'd been in Imagia at the same time." He jumped down from the bench and looked squarely at his friend. "It's real. We're not alone anymore!" He couldn't hide his joy.

Titus sighed, a touch of relief and joy somehow mixed into the sound. "Hmm," he considered his next words. "And you think we can trust this man, Mr. Rozalam?"

"Roz. And yeah." There was a too long second of hesitation. Titus noticed. "I mean, we'll be careful. I didn't tell him about you or my imagination still working. But if we can't trust someone from Imagia, then who *can* we trust?"

"Yes," Titus thought aloud. "This does change things. Perhaps in our favor, even." There was still uncertainty there, but he was warming up to the idea. Especially the idea of a change from the mundane life that this world offered a talking dog. "Nevertheless, we'd best get back home before Sarah gets worried. She's probably already on her way down the warpath as we speak." He grinned doggishly.

Sam agreed and they both headed back, new hope putting an extra skip in their steps.

* * * * * * * * * *

It was hard to believe that nearly two months had gone by so swiftly. Time seemed to pass at a steady crawl over the past years. But now that Sam had reason to be excited, it had done anything but that. He couldn't get away with staying after school daily, but he'd spent as much time as he could with Roz to talk about many things. There still had been no sign of Mr. Sanford, so the school had offered Roz an open-ended job until further notice. There was never a dull moment in Sam's eyes. His wonderment for hearing tales from Imagia sparked that familiar sense of adventure and curiosity that he'd nearly given up on so long ago.

The only problem with his new found obsession was that his parents had begun to question him. His sudden mood change didn't go unnoticed and Sam was under the hopeful impression that it would change things for the better. Perhaps he wouldn't be shipped off to those doctors anymore. Even Titus was hopeful.

Sam had finally convinced Titus to speak to Roz one day while they met up with him on their favorite park path. Even though Roz was pleasantly surprised, the shock wore off quickly when they all agreed that strange things were bound to happen after such an otherworldly experience.

But, despite their growing friendship with Roz, neither one of them had spoken a word about Sam's continued ability to imagine. Sam tried to convince himself that it wasn't a matter of trusting Roz, but rather trusting that he wouldn't be caught. It was too frightening of a thought to have someone see him do something so amazing in a world where 'amazing' labeled you as crazy.

Another tedious day of school had passed and Sam was just finishing his afternoon chat with Roz. They'd been discussing gateways and the prospect of finding one on their own.

Roz was idly tapping his fingers on his desk. "I remember being stuck in Imagia so many years ago and how I'd hopelessly wished to find a gateway back to Earth." He snorted softly at the irony. "Now I'm on Earth and even more desperate to find a gateway back to Imagia."

Sam smiled sadly. He knew that feeling all too well and he'd only been locked away from Earth for a brief time compared to Roz. He didn't really know what to say to his friend about this.

Roz saw Sam's face mirror his own feelings. "Strange isn't it? Living in that world changes you. It doesn't matter how long you're in Imagia. She becomes a part of you."

Sam nodded. He was never sure he could think of Imagia as a 'she'. But he did understand what Roz was saying. And it was one hundred and ten percent truth. Imagia had become a part of him just as much as he'd become a part of it. And that was why he couldn't cope in the real world.

The "real" word wasn't *his* real world anymore.

With that, Sam said, "I'd better go. My mom almost beat me home on Monday. She'd be super mad if I wasn't there."

Roz grinned. His cheek raised his eye patch slightly, revealing the hint of a silver-white scar. It made him look very dangerous.

"Well, if there's one thing that frightens me more than a pack of dragons, it's the wrath of an angry mother."

Sam laughed loudly. "No kidding!"

They both laughed and then exchanged good-byes.

Sam hiked his backpack up on his shoulder and began his afternoon walk home. He really enjoyed this time to himself. It always gave him time to relish all the new things he'd learned for the day – school subjects being nearly at the end of that list.

Today on his way home, he encountered a slight change of pace. As he turned off of the school grounds, he heard footsteps running up behind him.

"Hey, Sam!" It was Lizzy. "Wait up!"

Sam obliged. When she caught up, his smile was genuine when he said, "Hi, Lizzy. What's up?"

She was a little out of breath. "Nothin'. You sure do stay after school a lot these days. That must be a heck of an extra credit assignment you're working on."

He could hear the suspicion in her voice and swallowed hard. Through all his recent excitement, he'd done his best to not ignore his friendship with her, but was afraid she didn't think he was doing a good enough job. "Uh, yeah. It's been more of a research project thingy. Why'd *you* stay after school?"

"Detention. I got caught passing a note in math. Ugh. It wasn't even my note, but I got busted anyways." She rolled her eyes.

"That stinks."

"Yep. So, seriously though, is it really extra credit?"

Sam knew this was coming. She was bound to notice the changes. "Yeah. Why?" He knew why, but was hoping he wouldn't have to explain himself further. He hated making up lies as he went. It always made for a bad day.

Lizzy shrugged. "It's just that you've been like, I dunno, hanging out with Mr. Roz like he's your…" she didn't finish the thought.

Like always, Sam opted for fewer words and played dumb. "Like he's my what?"

She looked at him through accusing eyes then quickly looked back to the sidewalk ahead of her. She shrugged again. "It's like you're friends with him or something."

Part of him was angry at that accusation. He wondered what could be wrong with having another friend. Lizzy had other friends too and she didn't see him questioning her choices. He made sure to take an extra second to compose his emotions before he responded to her. "So? What's wrong with having a friend?"

"He's a grownup!" Lizzy could tell she was making Sam mad by the color of his cheeks. They were slightly redder than usual. She backed down. Being friends with Sam could be complicated and she'd accepted that long before now. "Sorry! Sorry. It's just kinda weird. That's all."

Sam didn't want to be angry with his friend. She didn't understand and part of the reason for her misunderstanding was really his fault. Keeping secrets had a price. He smiled and nudged her shoulder with his own. "Eh. No big deal. Weird isn't the worst thing ever. I just really like history and he's got a lot of pretty cool things to tell me about. He was kind of an explorer before he was a teacher." Part of that was truth, so it was easy to say. Roz really did have interesting things to say. They just weren't about Earth history.

Lizzy was apparently happy with that response. She grinned too. "Oh! Well, that's kinda cool, I guess."

"Yeah. Pretty cool."

They walked for a couple of blocks, Lizzy delving into further detail about her detention. Sam happily listened. Finally she said, "Well, I'd better get going. My mom's probably going to ground me for getting detention. See ya tomorrow!"

Sam waved and watched as Lizzy took off across the street towards her house. He let out an extra long sigh of relief. He'd left Roz's class early today so that he could take the long way home. Leaving Imagia had left him with a sense of adventure that could never quite be satisfied. He longed for the ever-green forests and the smells of the wild. The best he could replace it with was walking the paths and sidewalks that bordered the edges of the forest that he so desperately longed to venture in.

He walked by the towering wooded area. It was quiet on the half-trodden dirt paths that led almost too close to the trees. He was kicking at a rogue rock in the dust when something made him stop in his tracks. As he knocked it into the bushes, the sound of the rock hit a tree – and then a second rock hit something behind him.

The sound was just beyond the shadows. Something in Sam's gut told him to turn around. The hairs on the back of his neck started to prickle and he began to search the tree line. Something was off, because as his eyes scanned the quiet brush, he was abruptly aware that it was far too quiet.

A lone bird was calling from the shadows close by and was instantly hushed when the sound of something running across dry leaves made Sam gasp. He jerked his head to where he pinpointed the noise and saw a glimpse of a faint outline fading into the shadows of the trees. He nearly fell backwards in his haste to back away.

Something had been watching him.

He stood there and frantically looked around. He was completely alone and his realization of this caused dread to swell up in his chest. The panic caused him to think defensively, and the first thing that came to mind was a distraction. He didn't *want* to imagine something. He simply wanted to get home safely. He had no idea what could be in that forest, but he wasn't about to stick around to find out.

The ground vibrated softly under his feet. Ten deer, their fur a shade too silver and whose antlers were notably impressive, appeared out of nowhere and stampeded into the forest. Sam's hope was that it would distract whatever might be lurking there so he could get away unnoticed. With that, he whispered to himself, "Right. Run." His feet lifted off the ground with an extra hop. He ran as fast as he could go.

He was just about to leave the dirt path when something caught his eye. Stuck up against the remains of an old wooden fence, tangled in the thick growth no one had bothered to cut, was a piece of paper. He wouldn't have stopped if it weren't for the flash of the image that stared out from beneath the half-folded crease. No matter the fear that he felt, he stopped running and looked back to make sure he wasn't being followed.

Cautiously, he approached the paper and a faded image of a familiar green eye stared back at him. His heart was pounding mercilessly in his throat as he knelt down to pick up the too-worn, folded paper. Now his heart was throbbing in his ears. With shaky hands, he unfolded it. His eyes widened and he looked around the forest behind him, fear and disbelief fighting to escape him in a surge of emotions.

He stared back down at the picture in his hands. A much younger version of him stared back, a familiar hairy face smiling by his side. It was the picture of him and Yetews that he'd been so careful to never reveal to anyone. For a fleeting moment he wondered how on Earth he could have lost it without knowing. But that moment was shaken when he reached into his back pocket and felt the recognizable rustle of thickly folded paper. He froze before pulling it out. When he finally managed to move, he had the picture in his hand and unfolded it with trembling fingers. It was a perfect match. He'd only imagined two copies of this picture – one for himself, and one for his Guardian and best friend, Yetews.

It wasn't his copy of the picture he'd found.

It was Yetews'.

Something wasn't right. Panic, like he'd not experienced in some time, filled his core. Without pocketing the twin pictures, he ran full-speed for his house.

He needed to talk to Titus. And he needed to talk now.

Chapter Six: Dilemmas

Sam opened the door to his house, his heart racing. He burst inside yelling for Titus as he sped through the hall. "Titus! Titus, you aren't going to believe this! We have to…" He skidded to a sudden stop as he reached the kitchen. His eyes turned frantic. Standing there, with a look of agitation on her face, was his mom.

She had come home early today.

Titus came trotting out from behind Sarah's legs, panic taking over in his canine eyes. He looked from Sam to Sarah then back to Sam. His eyes trailed to Sam's hands where there were two distressed pieces of paper in broad daylight, impossible to miss. He looked at the paper meaningfully and then his eyes went wide and he whined low. There was nothing else he could do.

Sarah tapped her foot impatiently like she so often did when she was angry. Her arms were crossed and, by the look on her face, Sam knew that nothing that followed could be good. She flared her nostrils before she spoke. "Samuel Isaac. You have some explaining to do." She paused, waiting for a response.

Unfortunately, Sam was still in too much shock to say anything. He then did the one thing he shouldn't have. In an act of desperation, he hastily pocketed the two pictures.

His mom noticed.

She squinted. "I got off work early today. I thought it might be nice to take my son out and get some ice cream. But imagine my surprise when I walked in to find an empty house." Her voice was turning dangerous. "Where were you? And what did you just put in your pocket?"

Sam glanced to Titus who was doing his best to be a simple dog. "I…had to stay after school. For extra credit."

Not convinced, she responded angrily, "Ha! I don't believe that for a second. Your grades are perfectly fine. And could you please explain why you came in here yelling for Titus like that? I mean, honestly Sam. It's like you expected him to answer you. Are you talking to dogs now instead of people?" She didn't give him time to respond. "I come home to find you gone. And *then* I find you acting strangely again. And on top of everything, you're hiding something from me! What is going on with you? It's like you've been a different kid these past few weeks. Young man, you'd better tell me what's going on. Right now."

Sam was certain he'd never felt so flustered before this moment. The combination of concern for his recent discovery mixed with the emotional confrontation from his mother had made him temporarily lose his cool. He was so desperately convinced that he was dealing with an emergency situation that he didn't care what his next actions would spark. "I really am doing extra credit in History class. I just forgot to tell you. I swear!" His tone was meant to be one of urgency. But the only thing his mom heard was anger.

"Don't take that tone with me, young man! Extra credit or not, it doesn't explain why you came running in like a crazy person, talking to the dog. Now does it?"

He didn't have time to deal with this. Or at least, that's how he felt. Which is why what he said next was not thought through in the slightest. "I'm *not* a crazy person! I just needed to talk to Titus because…" As he heard himself say it, he realized what he'd done. He chewed on his cheek and swallowed hard. He tried to take it back, but the damage was done. "I…I mean that I…"

His mom looked back at him, exasperated. "You mean what?"

He looked down at his shoes and sighed. "Nothing."

"See? This is exactly what I mean." She held out a hand, palm up. "Give me what you put in your pocket."

Sam's eyes widened. He hesitated too long and watched as his mom's hand thrust out even further in expectation. He had no choice. Frantically, he searched his mind for an out. Those pictures were precious to him in a way she could never understand. He didn't want to lose them. He closed his eyes in concentration. He reached into his pocket and slowly withdrew one picture, hopeful that she wouldn't have noticed that there were originally two of them. As he opened his eyes, he handed her the folded photo.

She unfolded the picture. Her face scrunched up in confusion and she slowly began to shake her head. "What is this?"

"It's a picture."

His mom glared at his sarcasm. Angrily, she snapped back, "I know that. But I don't understand. Why were you trying to hide this from me?" She turned the picture around to reveal to Sam what he'd imagined in his mind: A picture of him standing next to a cow he'd once seen at a petting zoo when he was younger.

Sam could feel the relief in his chest. He'd morphed one of the pictures as he pulled it out of his pocket, unsure if it would work. He shrugged. At this point, silence was better than anything he could come up with.

Sarah sighed heavily. A hand went up to her face, her fingers rubbing between her worried eyes. "This is exactly the kind of thing we've been talking about." She shook her head, having decided something. "Your dad and I didn't want to tell you this yet, but we found a doctor. We're going to take you to him this summer. He's supposed to be very good at helping kids through traumatic situations."

Sam's eyes went wide again. "But mom, I'm fine. I'm not crazy! Please don't make me go to a doctor!"

His mom held up her hand, stopping him from continuing. "No. Sam, please. You need help that we obviously can't give you." She flashed him the picture. "You're hiding things from us. One minute you're impossible to talk to and the next you're suddenly perfectly happy. For heaven's sake, Sam, you're talking to the blasted dog like he's a person!" She threw her arms out in a gesture of total irritation.

He was desperate to avoid the doctor, angry at everything, and completely lost on what to do. So, he blurted out the only thing that came to his discouraged mind. "Stop calling him 'the dog'! His name is Titus. And *he* understands me!" He pointed at Titus while he spoke. Then he looked to his friend who was obviously struggling to stay composed. "Right, Titus?"

His mom looked at Titus, sadness now her main expression.

Titus cocked his head doggishly and woofed quite convincingly. When Sarah turned away, he looked back at Sam with disbelief evident in his face.

Sam knew everything that he'd just done and none of it was good. His shoulders slumped, giving up. "I know that he can't talk. He's just…easy to talk to."

Her shoulders slumped slightly as well, the hand holding the picture falling her to her side. They both stood there in silence for an extra long moment. Finally, she said, "Look. I love you sweetie. I wish we didn't have to do this. I wish whatever happened four years ago had never happened. But the truth of the matter is that it did. And we have to find a way past it." She walked over and kissed the top of his head and hugged him lightly.

Sam didn't say anything for fear of doing more damage.

His mom, her hands on his shoulders, looked at him with only concern on her face. "We'll talk about this later with your dad. Okay?"

He nodded, still looking at his shoes. As his mom started to walk away, he said, "Is it okay if I take Titus for his afternoon walk?"

She looked at both of them warily. "Yes. But no side trails. Got it?"

He nodded a bit too emphatically. "Okay. Can I have my picture back?"

His mom looked down at the random photo of her son. Shaking her head slightly, she handed it back to him. As a side thought, and mostly to herself, she said, "Strange. I don't even remember taking this picture."

Sam clipped the leash onto Titus' collar and they headed for their typical trail. As they went along, Titus was the first to speak. "What were you thinking back there?" There was a hint of anger in his hushed voice.

Sam felt genuinely bad. "I'm sorry. I don't know what happened. I just panicked. I guess I thought if you talked, that maybe she'd stop thinking I was crazy."

"You threw me to the wolves. What was I supposed to do? We both agreed that it was too dangerous to tell them."

Sam's eyes closed for a second. "I'm sorry,' he whispered.

Titus knew he was and that something must have been very important for him to come bursting into the house so carelessly – especially with the picture of him and Yetews in plain sight. "It's alright. We'll figure something out. We still have time."

Sam looked behind him, making sure his house was out of sight. "No. It's not okay. It's actually really bad." He proceeded to tell Titus about everything that had happened on his way home from school. He left no detail out as he pulled both of the pictures out of his pocket.

They'd reached their favorite secluded place, off the beaten path. Though one of the pictures was now different, he explained to Titus the significance of the situation. "See? Something's wrong. How did Yetews' picture end up back in this world?"

Calming Sam down seemed to be his new specialty and main focus these days. Generally, it was easy to see reason and sway his mind in the appropriate direction. This time, the situation was different. Titus was concerned with what he'd found. After hearing all of the facts, Titus finally added his take on the situation. "So you think something was watching you from the forest?"

"Yeah. And I don't *think* so. I *know* so. I heard it run off when I looked into the trees."

"Did it sound like a big and scary something or a small and harmless something?"

Sam was becoming alarmed by how long they'd been gone on their walk. His mom wasn't going to accept another unruly action today. He shrugged impatiently. "I dunno. It sounded like a person running across leaves. Freaked me out." He shuddered as he recalled the sound. "We'd better get back or mom's gonna flip out again."

Titus agreed. They headed back home.

Titus used his last free-speaking moments. "One things for certain. You should probably stay away from the forest until we figure this whole mess out."

Sam wanted to say something, but hesitated, fearful for sounding stupid. "What if…you know…it's Yetews? Watching me."

"He wouldn't have run from you," He added sensibly.

Titus was right. He felt stupid for even suggesting it. "I need to talk to Roz about this."

Titus had grown to trust Roz as well over the last couple of months, but he was cautious about Sam revealing too much to anyone. "I know you are in panic-mode right now. But it can wait until tomorrow. So don't even think about sneaking out tonight to go talk to him." He eyed his friend accusingly.

Sam didn't respond. He couldn't help but to think that Titus knew him way too well. He also knew that he was right. After the encounter with his mom, he couldn't afford to chance getting into more trouble. Not tonight.

The last thing Titus managed to say before he had to resume his most doggish behavior was, "Nice save, by the way. Morphing that picture was beautifully done."

Sam's thoughts went to the morphed picture in his back pocket. He couldn't help but to feel angst for what he'd done to his treasured keepsake. No matter how much wear and tear that picture had succumbed to, he'd not ever dared to change it.

Now it was ruined. Tainted by one careless moment.

He stopped walking just before they reached his driveway. Titus had already trotted ahead of him into the yard. He pulled out the picture he'd morphed. It was his copy that he'd changed. He looked at the picture, irritated for all he'd done to keep it hidden. He closed his eyes to block out the tears that tried to escape. Under his breath, he whispered, "Stupid picture."

He crumpled it up, threw it into street, and walked away.

Titus turned around and waited patiently for Sam to open the door. Despite his intelligence, he still lacked those useful opposable thumbs. He turned just in time to see the flash of white fall past the curb and out of view. He also couldn't help but to notice Sam wipe a sleeve across his eyes.

It was going to be a long night for them.

* * * * * * * * * * *

It was quiet in the room. The window was open and Titus took the opportunity to jump out while Sam was in the bathroom. He jumped back through the unscreened window just as Sam was opening the door. Perfect timing.

There was too much going on in his mind to notice much other than his own thoughts. He fell into bed, his quilt falling onto the floor. He sighed heavily. He pulled the picture he'd found on his way home out from between a rip in his mattress at the foot of his bed. It was weathered. Rained on, perhaps. He tried to figure out what this meant and ultimately came back to his own copy of the picture. Why did he have to morph *his* copy? And why didn't he just imagine a different picture altogether to hand his mom?

Quietly, Titus inquired, "Are you okay?"

Sam only half-heard him. "Hmm? Oh. Yeah. I just miss him. Sometimes, I wish that I could just forget everything."

Titus' claws clicked on the floor as he made his way to the bedside. He dropped something on Sam's bed. It was a crumpled piece of paper. He watched as Sam's forehead wrinkled with anger and then looked away. Sam may have said he wanted to forget, but Titus knew better. He slowly shook his shaggy head, tawny fur swaying. "No," he stated. "No, you don't." Using his nose, he nudged the crumpled photo that Sam had discarded earlier so that it was touching Sam's hand. Then he walked away to lie down in the cool breeze coming from the window, making a point to face away from his saddened friend.

Sam was upset. Too upset to see that picture again. He flicked it onto the floor and fell onto his pillow, a little too angry with Titus. He didn't want that picture. But that didn't stop him from staring at it. He fumed silently for a while, but the more he thought about it, the softer his expression became.

He waited and then looked over at Titus who was peacefully lying on the floor. He noted the slow, steady breathing. When he was certain that he was asleep, he leaned over the bed and quietly reached for the picture. Titus stirred and Sam grabbed his quilt off of the floor hastily, being sure to scoop up the picture with it. He flipped over, covering himself with the quilt and conveniently dropping the picture so that he could see it.

With as much stealth as he could manage, he flattened the picture out and closed his eyes, remembering exactly how it was before.

When he opened his eyes, he smiled. He looked over his shoulder at Titus. His smile faded as guilt sank in.

Titus grinned to himself as he heard the faint sound of paper rustling as it was being slipped back into the mattress.

Chapter Seven: When Adventure Calls

Sleep had evaded Sam through most of the night. What little sleep he did manage to get was riddled with unpleasant dreams and uncertainties. He got out of bed early, his hair tousled more than usual. He had barely wolfed his toast and orange juice down before he was out the door and off to school, his mom hollering a hasty goodbye as he went.

He'd made sure to tell Titus that he'd be staying after school with Roz and talked him into meeting them there. Titus had to pull a few degrading tricks to get left outside so he could manage his escape.

School was horrible. Sam wanted it to go fast, but it was like walking through mud with weights on. When history class came, Roz could tell that there was a sense of urgency in Sam's behavior. It made it difficult for him to teach and for either one of them to concentrate. As soon as the bell rang, Sam handed Roz a note, his eyes twitching with impatience.

By the time the final bell of the day sounded, Sam didn't think he could contain himself any longer. He met with Roz as soon as it was safe to talk. He nearly exploded through the classroom door.

"What is it?" Roz said urgently. "What happened?"

Pulling out both of his photos, now donning identical images again, he said, "You are never gonna believe what happened on my way home from school yesterday. Can we take a walk or something? Titus is supposed to meet us here." Roz agreed, gathered his things and Sam proceeded to relive almost every moment from the previous evening. He left out the parts where he'd used his imagination.

Underneath a large shade tree, Titus had met up with the two and listened patiently as Sam divulged all of his concerns and potential problems to their new friend. Roz was holding both of the photos in his hands, considering the situation. Finally, after deliberating for a quiet moment he offered his thoughts. "This is most certainly a strange, albeit intriguing, discovery. Short of the tales I'd heard of your Guardian, I didn't ever meet him. No word ever came our way of anything bad happening to him. And definitely no rumors of him returning to this world were ever mentioned."

"So how could it be here? I mean, it's just weird. First, you're here. Then there's something in the forest watching me."

"Possibly," Roz corrected him. "*Possibly* something watching you. You said you didn't see anything definite."

Sam gritted his teeth. Titus wasn't sure it was something watching him either. He hated it when he was doubted. "Yeah. I guess. But then I find this picture. It's just that a lot of weird things seem to have happened since you got here."

Roz's expression was pained. "Surely you don't think I had something to do with this? I didn't even know what Yetews looked like, Sam."

When he saw the look on his friend's face his eyes went wide. He didn't mean to offend him. It hadn't been his intent. "No! I didn't mean that. I just meant that it's been crazy lately. And now with my parents wanting to send me away, I just don't know what to do anymore." His shoulders slumped. "Me and Titus have been trying to think of something, but it's just impossible."

Placing a caring hand on Sam's shoulder, Roz questioned his words. "Sam Little using the word 'impossible'. Now that's a strange thing to hear, indeed." He smiled, his good eye twinkling.

"Okay. So, maybe not impossible. It just stinks. I don't want to go to a doctor. And I think they know I'm lying about staying after school for extra credit."

"Hmm," Roz considered something. "I might be able to help out with that. Maybe I'll pay your parents a visit. It might even help give us more time after school to talk."

"You'd do that for me?"

Roz grabbed his heart and feigned pain. "I'm hurt, Sam. But yes. I think we'd both do better to look out for each other any way we can."

Sam had a wave of honest guilt flow through him. Over the last couple of weeks, he and Titus had discussed the possibility of telling Roz about his imagination. The longer he kept that secret from him, the worse he felt about it.

As Sam was considering this, the lull in the conversation became too much for Roz to take. He elbowed Sam lightly in the side. "Hey. I was only kidding about being hurt."

Sam popped out of his thought and said, "Oh. No, I know. I was just thinking of something." He started to chew on his bottom lip and looked at Titus who gestured with a quick nod in Roz's direction. Titus knew that Sam was struggling keeping that particular secret.

The internal conversation that Sam and Titus seemed to be having did not go unnoticed this time. Roz's brow furrowed slightly. "What are you two not telling me? Is everything okay?"

Sam started picking at the dirt under his fingernails and looked down when he started to speak, afraid that Roz would be angry that he'd kept this secret so long. "So, you know how coming back here had a weird effect on Titus?"

"Yes. His speech. What about it?"

He fidgeted. "Uh…there's something else I haven't told you. But I don't want you to think that it's because I don't trust you or something. It's just because…I dunno. Because it scares me to admit it to anyone."

Roz didn't respond. He just listened with his full attention.

Sam wasn't sure what to make of his friend's silence, but continued anyways, butterflies fighting to leave his stomach. "The thing is…I can still use my imagination. I sorta found out the hard way." Before Roz could even respond, Sam suddenly blurt out everything about the moment he'd discovered his power was still there. "It was weird and scary and involved a big hairy beast that ended up falling into my elderly neighbors' pool and almost giving them a heart attack before I morphed it into a freakishly big deer." He grimaced and looked sideways at Roz, hopeful that he wouldn't be angry.

What Sam saw when he looked over was Roz silently chuckling, his shoulders bouncing up and down.

At first, Sam was confused. Then a hint of anger touched his thoughts. "Why are you laughing? Aren't you mad that I kept this from you?"

Roz started laughing a bit louder. Between his laughs, he said, "Can you imagine what your neighbors must have thought?" He laughed again and Sam's anger ebbed away. He joined in and started laughing too. Roz continued, "The look on their faces must have been priceless!"

When the laughter died down, Roz looked over at Sam and said something most unexpected. "Well, I suppose we're even then."

Sam didn't understand. "Huh?"

"All this time, I've been keeping silent as well and so here we are, both of us nervous to tell the other what we know. You see…I knew you still had the ability to imagine."

"How?" Sam asked, completely disbelieving.

"The bathroom."

All of a sudden, everything was clear. He hadn't fixed the incident in the bathroom quickly enough and Roz actually did see it. He smiled. "You saw that then?"

Nodding, he said, "I don't think I saw everything, but I was pretty sure that the toilets weren't normally covered in vines. Also, a branch slapped me in the nose when I opened the door. Actually, I had to sway a couple of older kids from going in by telling them someone was getting very sick in there."

Sam laughed again. He was about to ask why Roz wouldn't tell him what he'd seen. Then he realized that he'd probably kept it a secret for the same reasons that Sam had. But most importantly, he'd kept it a secret from everyone else. The feeling of having a person like this that he could trust was almost overwhelming. He almost forgot about the incident with the forest and the picture.

"Well," Roz said. "Now that we both have clear consciences, perhaps you and Titus should get home. Angry mother: round two, does not sound like a good idea." He grinned widely.

"No kidding," Sam agreed.

Titus looked around cautiously before speaking. "As much as I don't relish the idea of endangering you, Sam, I would like to go past the forest on the way home. Maybe I can smell something from yesterday."

Roz nodded. "I think that's a good idea. Just don't linger. If something really was watching…well…let's not take any chances. I'd rather not be stuck in this world completely alone," he smirked.

Sam smiled. Then his mind wandered to the forest and what they might find on their return trip home. He stopped grinning and they said their goodbyes.

They'd reached the same spot that Sam had experienced on his previous encounter and Titus took a couple of wary minutes to sniff around the place. He shook his shaggy head doubtfully. "I don't smell anything out of the ordinary. I smell," he sniffed the ground again, "deer. Lots of deer."

"Uh," Sam hesitated. "Yeah. That was sorta me. I panicked. I forgot to tell you. I kind of imagined some deer that stampeded through the forest. I thought it would help chase away anything. Give me a head start." He said those last words in the form of a question.

Titus smiled. The kid really could take care of himself if push came to shove. "Where did you find the picture?"

"Up the path. By that old wooden fence."

"I'll check there too. You ready?"

Sam was staring into the trees. He felt really silly for his freak out yesterday. He may have found the picture, but now he was starting to think it had all been in his head. If something otherworldly had been in that forest, he was sure Titus would have smelled it. He scuffed the dusty ground of the path. "You go ahead and check it out. I'll catch up, k?"

Titus nodded hesitantly. "Remember what Roz said. Don't linger."

Sam didn't say anything. He simply nodded and slowly started to walk along as Titus ran ahead of him and out of sight around a curve in the path.

As he turned to catch up with Titus, he was abruptly aware of the hair on the back of his neck again. This time, there was no sound to alert him. He didn't know why or how, but he felt that strange sensation of being watched. Again.

Fear did strange things to him. His knees locked. His skin prickled. His stomach was alerting him that it wasn't pleased with lunch. He looked into the forest, squinting his eyes. He thought about running again. It was ridiculous to feel the kind of fear he felt yesterday. And to feel it again after Titus had just checked it out was even more absurd. If he were in Imagia, he could understand it. There was always something to be leery of in those mysterious woods. He suddenly felt like a great big chicken. Instead of running, he pushed past all of those feelings. He reached down and picked up a rock. He pulled his arm back and launched it as hard as he could into the trees while saying, "Stupid forest."

The rock disturbed a small group of birds into flight and Sam watched them flutter out of the trees and into the sky. They cooed and squawked as they went. When the hushed sounds of their fluttering wings disappeared, he swore that he could hear a faint whisper – a hushed voice.

And it said his name.

He gasped and stepped back, nearly tripping over his own feet. He turned and was about to run when something froze his feet to the ground. He knew Titus would be back in a matter of minutes. But something sparked in him that he hadn't felt in years.

He wanted to know – no – he *had* to know what was in that forest. He pulled out his copy of the picture of him and Yetews. He thought to himself that it was probably nothing. But then again, what if it *was* something?

What if it was some*one*?

Without another thought, he pulled his feet out of their stupor, and quietly took a forced step into the tall grass that led into the dense, darkened forest.

It was hard to be quiet in the thick brush and overgrowth. His heart was pounding – mostly in fear – but partly in excitement. He was in the forest now, the shade almost overpowering his senses. He hadn't gotten far into its depths when his foot came down and snapped a twig loudly. He closed his eyes, frustrated at his clumsiness. It was a small twig, but the sound was loud in the quiet of the forest. There were trees surrounding him now.

He knew he should turn around. He should be running back home with his tail tucked firmly between his legs. But the feel of the forest and the smells that permeated him reminded him of Imagia.

It reminded him of home.

As the sound of the snapped twig finally stopped echoing like a beacon in the dark, he looked down to make sure he didn't repeat the mistake. While examining the ground, he heard a sound not of his making. Another whisper.

There was no mistaking it this time. Something was in here with him and his sudden comprehension of this reality stopped him dead in his tracks. What had he done? He thought about yelling for Titus. But would he even hear? His breathing was too fast and his heart was practically beating its way out of his chest. He backed up slowly, desperate not to make another sound. His shoulder bumped into something and it made him jump and turn around. A little squeal of fright escaped his mouth before he realized it was only a tree. He sighed in relief.

He only made it one more step when he heard the sound of dry leaves crunch right behind him. He didn't even have time to yell as someone grabbed him from behind. Sam was helpless as a hand firmly covered his mouth, cutting off his impending scream.

Chapter Eight: Trust

There is only so much that can be done when fear takes over and survival instincts kick in. After a year in Imagia, Sam had kept some of those rudimentary survival skills he'd learned from Taren. Though it had been several years since then, for some reason he couldn't explain, he could remember almost every detail of his stay there. So as the hand clamped down over his mouth, cutting off his scream, he could only think of one thing to do.

Fight.

Generally, he'd fight with his mind. But this attack was so sudden that he couldn't even think straight. As a next best move, he did the only thing he could think of – start struggling. He brought his arm up as far as he could. With as much force as he could muster, he brought his elbow back and made contact with a ribcage.

There was a subtle "oomph!" that escaped his captor, but he didn't loosen his grip on Sam regardless of the blow. The whole ordeal had only lasted a few seconds before the person whose hand was muffling him used his other hand to force Sam to turn around.

The muffled sounds of Sam's screaming suddenly went silent. His eyes widened and he stopped struggling to escape.

The man standing before him, still holding a hand over Sam's mouth, held one finger up to his lips, urging him to be quiet. When the man was sure that Sam understood him, he gently took his hand away from the kid's mouth and smiled largely.

Sam, eyes still wide in shock, squeaked in disbelief, "Garrett?!"

The Protector from Imagia, a man Sam had met and befriended, quickly responded, "Shhh!" He brought both hands up, palms open, and Sam realized he was speaking too loud.

Quite a few decibels lower, but with equal excitement, he said, "Garrett! Is it really you? Are you really here?"

The Protector was tall and muscular; his shoulder-length blonde hair was tied halfway back and he had joyful eyes. A smile took over his entire face before turning serious. He lifted one eyebrow sincerely. He ran a finger over a jagged, silvery scar that stretched from brow to chin. "It's a nice scar, isn't it?" he asked.

Sam remembered the first time he'd seen that scar and the story that went with it. He was having trouble holding in his excitement, but quietly responded, "But scars from dragons never stop burning! It *is* you!" With arms opened wide, he rushed at Garrett who was smiling at Sam's response. He threw his arms around Garrett in a hug of true friendship and said in a muffled voice, "Oh my gosh! I can't believe it!"

Garrett had to step back to counteract the force of Sam grabbing him suddenly and he laughed quietly as he returned the hug. "It's good to see you too, Sam. See? A scar never lies." There was hesitancy in his voice. "And so, speaking of scars, would you mind showing me one of yours?"

Sam broke off the hug, eager to ask a million questions, but confused as to why Garrett would ask that. But when he looked into his eyes, he realized that there was nothing but sincerity there. He tried to think straight but his mind was jumbled. He tried to form a coherent question. "Er...which scar do you mean?"

Garrett noticed his puzzlement. "Your worst one."

A flood of memories came back to Sam. He'd spent a lot of time with Garrett after the battle with Nadaroth and they'd enjoyed a good time together comparing battle scars. He remembered the one that hurt the most and the one that even his parents had seen since returning. It was one reason why they were truly afraid of what had happened in Sam's absence. They'd even taken him to a couple of doctors to have it evaluated.

Sam reached a shaky hand to the collar of his shirt and pulled it sideways as far as it could go, revealing a thickened and quite jagged scar. Its pale, white color stretched the width of the heavy knife blade that had been stabbed into his shoulder by Ognotz, the collector, and then twisted to open the wound even more.

Garrett's smile returned and he pulled Sam into his chest to finish the hug he'd interrupted. "Like I said – a scar never lies." He tousled Sam's hair. "Sorry Sam. I had to be sure it was you."

They stepped back from each other and Sam gathered his wits. "Why wouldn't it be me?"

His eyes darted around the forest as he replied. "That's a question for later. I'm just happy that we've found you."

Still trying to keep his voice low, he excitedly said, "I can't believe this. I can't believe you're actually here. This is amazing!" His smile was ear to ear.

Before Sam could start questioning him, Garrett looked down at him, false seriousness as his expression. "It most certainly is amazing. And you've grown!" He paused, nodded his head to the side and jokingly added, "Not much, mind you. But you're most definitely taller than the last time we met." He broke the serious look with another dazzling smile.

Though he was nowhere near offended, Sam replied with a simple, "Hey! I've grown a lot! I'm a teenager now, you know?"

Garrett laughed. "Too true, my friend." Through his smile, there was something uneasy about the way his eyes scanned the forest around them. "And speaking of friends, where is Titus?"

As if speaking his name acted as a summons, a low growl broke the silence of the shadowy trees. He jumped through a series of bushes and tall grass to land between Sam and Garrett. His teeth were bared as he landed but upon seeing the stranger he'd meant to threaten, his growl was cut off.

"Titus!" Sam yelled too loud. "It's okay! It's Garrett!"

But by the time he'd gotten the words out, Titus had recognized who it was and had already backed down, his hackles still slightly puffed up from the ordeal.

Titus sat back on his haunches and cocked his head. "Garrett? How is this possible? I don't smell a gateway anywhere."

"It's good to see you too, Titus," Garrett snipped. "As I said to Sam, this is a question best explained later."

"Why later?" Titus asked.

"It's complicated."

Sam was overwhelmed. During the lull in questions forming in his busy mind, he managed to speculate. "Is Yetews with you then? Is that why I found this?" He pulled the tattered photo out of his pocket and held it out for Garrett to see. "Where is he?" He looked around the trees, hopeful that his best friend was waiting to pop out of the nearest shadow to surprise him.

Noticing Sam's eagerness to find his friend, Garrett felt inclined to stop him before he got too excited. "No, Sam. He's not here. But that picture is definitely the one we had. We lost it yesterday. And now I know why we couldn't find it."

Even though he was excited to see Garrett, his shoulders slumped slightly upon hearing this. Garrett was great, but he wasn't Yetews. Then, as if he'd just actually heard what Garrett was saying, he scrunched his face up and said, "Hold on a second. You said 'we'. If Yetews isn't here, then who is with you?" Titus looked between both of them, just as eager to hear the response, and started to sniff the air. He picked up on a faint scent and a low growl began to rumble in his chest.

Garrett stepped between Titus and the direction that he picked up the scent and said, "Whoa there! Calm down." He sighed. "I suppose this would be the best time for introductions." He turned around and addressed an especially shadowy area. "Come on over. It's him."

Somewhere high, up on a branch, the leaves shuffled and a silhouette of something jumped down to the ground. It wasn't very big, but looked somewhat familiar. A creature, standing about two and a half feet tall, walked towards them. He may have been small, but he exuded confidence as he strode up. He was rodent-like, reminding Sam of his friends Iggy and Arty. But unlike them, this creature was more muscular, much taller, and looked more like a cross between a beaver and a kangaroo.

It walked erect and was dressed in the rustic clothes that were common in Imagia. On his back, the handle of what looked to be a short sword stuck up just right to be grabbed on a moment's notice. Around his neck hung a leather-pouch that he clung to with one hand-like paw as he approached. Despite his size, Sam couldn't help but to feel intimidated by this creature. He fell into place at Garrett's side and in a gruff, heavily accented voice, asked, "Are you certain it's him?"

Sam, not expecting such a voice to come from him, could only manage to stare. He waited for Garrett to introduce them all and silently wondered who this creature could possibly be and why he was with Garrett outside of Imagia.

Garrett looked at the creature. "Yeah. It's definitely him. And it looks like we found out where that picture went as well." He pointed at the picture Sam was holding. Then, without any further explanations, he simply said, "Sam, this is Foo. He's a Guardian." Then, smiling, he looked at the Guardian and said, "Foo, I'd like you to meet Sam Little. And you've heard me speak of Titus." He pointed at the dog whose look was complete suspicion. "So you can both stand down. We're all good guys here."

Realizing who all was standing here with him, Sam grinned and said, "Hi, Foo. Nice to meet you."

Foo simply grunted and crossed his arms, finally removing his grip from the pouch he'd been clinging to. "So, what now?"

After a frustrated sigh, the Protector apologized. "Sorry about Foo, here. He may be a Guardian, but I assure you that he has no need for a Protector. He doesn't mean to be rude. He's just on the defensive right now. This world is a strange place."

It was hard to believe that this world would be considered strange to anyone. But it was all a matter of perspective. Sam remembered how strange Imagia was to him from the very first moment he'd set foot in his gateway.

"It's okay. I get it," Sam replied. He couldn't stand the pressure of the questions forming in his mind. He was torn between being overwhelmed with excitement and overpowered by confusion for what was transpiring. "Garrett, what's going on? Why are you here? No, wait." He paused and reformed his question. "Forget why. *How* are you here? And how did you find me?"

"Now, just hold on a second! Let's tackle one question at a time, okay?" He looked overwhelmed as well. Quietly, he added, "Taren warned me that you'd be full of questions." There wasn't even a chance for Sam to ask anything else before Garrett, a little louder this time, said, "And before you go asking about Taren, he's not here either. It's just Foo and me. Okay. Let me start with how we found you. And trust me, it was no simple feat."

Sam nodded emphatically. "Okay. So how did you do it?"

Garrett leaned up against a tree. Sam noticed how tired he looked and wondered if he'd been able to sleep at all since getting here. The Protector started by gesturing to the forest around him. "Forests are one of the most common places to have a gateway open because it provides excellent camouflage. We knew several details of your location. And we knew that if we found a forested area, that we'd be more inclined to find you. We went through many gateways before we found one in this part of the world. Many Guardians, including Yetews, helped."

The sound of hearing Yetews' name gave Sam butterflies. He wanted so badly to see his best friend and Guardian. The hope had been little to none for so long. But with the events happening lately, hope was rising in him and today he was most optimistic of all.

Garrett continued, "The process of getting here is…well…complicated. So if you don't mind, we'll delve into that later." With a nod from Sam to affirm this, he kept going. "You see, Foo is an excellent tracker. It's more or less his specialty. His child imagined him that way. That's why we were so lucky to gain his aid. Yetews loaned us your picture. We knew that you'd look older by now and needed something to look at for comparison.

"When Foo tracked us to this village, we had no idea how we were going to find you. Needle in a haystack, so they say." He grinned widely. Sam grinned back. "So in answer to your question, it was all a matter of luck. We each took shifts sleeping and looking around the forest edges. It wasn't me who found you. It was Foo."

Foo grunted again in affirmation. His look hadn't softened at all, but he began to explain his part. "Yes. It was merely a rush of dumb luck that I just happened to be looking out at the same place where you were walking yesterday. I saw you and couldn't believe my eyes. I'd never met you, of course. So I needed to get a closer look. That's where things went awry. You were looking away from me and I needed to see your face. So I threw a stone in your direction to get you to turn around. You looked right at me. I didn't want you to see me before Garrett if it was, in fact, you. I was only mostly certain I'd found you. I decided to get Garrett. Apparently I'd frightened you. I had no idea you were going to react so violently."

Sam interrupted him. "Violently? I didn't react violently. All I did was try to get away."

Garrett was hiding a grin behind his hand. "Well, in Foo's defense, he did almost get run over."

"Run over!?" Foo blurted out. "More like trampled to death! Have you ever tried to run for your life as a herd of silvery beasts stampede over you? I think not."

All of a sudden, Sam felt guilty. He didn't know who had been watching him, but now that he recalled the situation, it had been fairly dangerous to anyone in the deer's path. "Sorry," he said. "I didn't mean to hurt you. I just wanted to get away."

Foo nodded. His expression actually softened a bit. "No permanent damage done. But I lost the picture in the stampede. It must have blown down the path where you found it."

That explained the picture, at least. But it left so many other questions unanswered. Titus sat next to Sam, taking all of the information in as well. He finally spoke up with a question of his own. "How did you know Sam would return to this place?"

"We didn't," answered Garrett. "But it was the best place to start. If it was indeed him, I knew that he'd have a hard time staying away from here with questions unanswered. And it looks like I was right." He winked at Sam. "Some things never change."

Excitement and relief was running high through the four of them. Now that they'd found each other, it was time to move on to far more pressing matters.

Garrett started to change the subject. "Now that we've found you, we have a lot to discuss. First of all, how old are you now? You have to be, what? Fourteen?"

Sam smiled. He hadn't had his birthday yet, but this would definitely be his best birthday present of all. He shook his head. "Not yet. I'm –"

He was cut off by something he hadn't experienced in many years. Titus jumped up, ears laid back and growled low. Garrett jerked around and drew his bow. Foo pulled the short sword from its sheath on his back and took a very impressive fighting stance.

Someone was coming towards them from the same place that Sam had entered the forest. The sound of dry foliage crunched beneath their feet. Sam's heart began to pound a little harder. What would this scene look like to an unsuspecting person?

Garrett whispered loudly, "Sam, get behind me."

He complied without question.

It was only a moment later that whoever it was made himself known. In a quite threatening voice, a man said, "What have you done with Sam?"

Sam knew that voice. It was Roz. He jumped out from behind Garrett. "I'm here!"

Garrett whipped his head around and stared at Sam with wide eyes. He was so surprised by Sam's sudden movement that he stuttered when he said, "What are you doing? Get back!"

Roz ignored Garrett and directed his concern to Sam. "Are you alright?"

Sam nodded, eyes darting between both fretting parties. "Yeah. I'm just fine." Suddenly aware of the seriousness of the situation, Sam took a moment to soak in what was happening. Everyone had weapons drawn and pointed at someone else, including Roz. No one was willing to withdraw out of fear for his own safety. There was only one thing that he could do. He ran between them all and put his arms up to halt the unnecessary protection. With an arm held out to each side, he said, "Stop! Nobody needs to kill anyone. I'm fine!"

Garrett was the first to anger. "Sam, stand down," he growled. We don't know who this is. Get out of the way." His voice was harsher than Sam thought possible.

"This is Roz. He's my friend."

Garrett narrowed his eyes, hesitant to back down. "How do we know we can trust him?"

Before Sam could get any words out, Roz blurted out, "I might ask you the same thing!" His eye darted to Sam and he asked, "Can we trust them?"

Sam nodded forcefully. "They're friends."

With a swift nod of his head, Roz lowered his bow and sheathed his arrow. He eyed Garrett and Foo, waiting for them to return the gesture. "If you trust them, then that's good enough for me." He smiled at Sam, but kept a watchful eye on the weapons still being aimed at him.

Though he still seemed hesitant to lower his guard, Garrett made up his mind and in a jerky movement lowered his bow as well. He, however, kept them at his side, ready to aim in a heart beat if need be. He looked down at Foo and jerked his head slightly, signaling for Foo to stand down as well.

Once again, Foo had his hand grasped tightly to the pouch around his neck and Sam wondered what mysteries lie inside that would cause him cling so desperately to it. He sheathed his sword and exchanged a harried look with his Protector counterpart.

Now that everyone was finally calmed down, Sam introduced them in hopes of easing the thick tension that muddled the atmosphere around him. He sighed, relieved that no one was trying to kill each other any longer. “That was fun,” he said sarcastically.

Titus trotted over to Sam’s side. He looked up at the boy and muttered, “Well, you did want adventure back in your life.” They smiled grimly at one another.

Sam turned to Roz. “What are you doing here?” Now that he’d thought about it, he had no idea why Roz would be here and even more confused as to why he’d be armed. He’d never seen the Defender with a weapon. But it would make sense that he’d have one with him somewhere. He did come into this world fighting a creature.

Roz’s eye went wide. “Sam, are you even remotely aware of how long you’ve been here?”

As if a bolt of lightning struck beside him, he jolted to the side and looked at Titus. “Oh no! The time! I forgot about the time!”

Garrett asked, “What are you talking about?”

Ignoring Garrett’s question, Roz walked over to Sam, concern thick on his face. “I went to your house to talk to your parents about you staying after school for a research project we’re working on. Remember? And when I got there, your mother was in hysterics. Your father was also there and getting in his vehicle to go search for you. When I told them that I would help find you and that I hadn’t seen you since school was out, your mother broke down in tears. She’s waiting at home to see if you’ll return. But I didn’t tell them where I was going.” He shook his head disbelievingly. “I knew you were coming back to this part of the forest. But after what you told me you thought you saw here, I was afraid you were in danger. I feared the worst.

"I went to get my bow and headed straight here. I followed your tracks and when I saw that they went into the trees, I thought you'd been captured by something." He waited for Sam to respond.

Slapping a hand on his forehead, he started to panic. "Oh man! I'm in so much trouble! What am I gonna do?"

"Can you fake an injury? I can take you back home and tell them I found you and that you couldn't walk. Perhaps a sprained ankle?" suggested Roz.

Sam was already nodding frantically. "Yeah. But..." he looked back at a very confused duo. Garrett and Foo were completely lost as to what was happening. He was having trouble coming up with a way to make this work.

Finally tired of waiting for an explanation, Garrett asked, "Can someone please tell me what is going on?"

Foo seconded that question. "I'd like to know that too. Surely one of you can explain."

And just like that, Sam knew what to do. "I've got it! Titus can lead you two through the forest to where it meets up with my house. I'll tell my mom that Titus got off his leash and I tried to find him but fell and sprained my ankle. Roz can take me home." He turned and directed the next part to just Titus. "Can you do that?"

"Yes. Excellent idea." He trotted over to a still very confused Garrett.

"Awesome." Sam grinned at his plan. Then he added, "Garrett, Titus can explain everything to you on the way. And when the light goes off in my room tonight, that will be your signal that all's clear and he can bring you to my window. You'll have to be careful not to be seen by my parents though."

Sam could see that Garrett was about to protest the whole idea and that he wasn't happy about the situation they were in, but there simply wasn't enough time to argue about it. He turned to leave with Roz.

Before they parted ways, Garrett got one last thought in. "Sam, please understand that finding you is of great importance. We need to talk soon."

"K. Sorry. But I have to go. Titus will explain everything. I'll see you soon. Promise." With that, he and Roz started to jog out of the trees and head for home.

As soon as they stepped onto the dusty path, Roz said, "Can you imagine a swollen foot or something?"

He thought about it. He'd never tried morphing his own body before. He didn't even know if he could do it. Closing his eyes, he tried to imagine his foot to match what he remembered a sprain would look like. When he opened his eyes, his foot was completely unchanged. He looked up at Roz apologetically. "It's not working."

"Hmm. Hold on." He took his bow and quiver of arrows off and disappeared into the forest again for a moment. "Best not walk up to your mom fully armed." He smirked. "Might not go over so well. You'd better start limping and lean on me. We've got to make this look real."

He leaned on Roz and did his best to look injured as they took the path to his house. Chewing on his cheek, Sam was instantly aware that his life was about to go from mundane to complicated. He just wasn't sure he was ready for it.

Chapter Nine: Collateral Damage

Limping up the driveway, Sam looked up to see the front door to his house swing open and hear his mom yell his name loud enough that every neighbor was sure to hear her.

"Sam!" She ran to him. Her arms were around him instantly, a motion that both hugged him and checked for injuries. Her eyes were red and swollen.

Sam felt like crawling under a rock and hiding. He couldn't have felt guiltier about what he'd just put his parents through. "I'm fine, mom," he managed to squeak out. He added, "I'm really sorry. It was an accident."

The worry lines in her face were deep. She was trying to be patient, but there was a hint of anger at the edge of her reply. "What happened?" She also managed to look at Roz like he was just as guilty as Sam was.

"I was taking Titus for his walk and he saw a rabbit. The leash broke and I ran after him. But I tripped in a hole and hurt my ankle. I tried to hop home, but kept getting tired. Mr. Roz found me. He helped me get back."

Sarah squinted her eyes, the look almost lethal. But then she turned and wrapped her arms around Roz, shocking both him and Sam. She hugged him tight and whispered, "I don't know how to thank you enough."

While she was hugging him, he looked down at Sam and gave him a sideways victory grin. When she pulled back, Roz simply said,

"I'm just glad he's alright. I'd hate to lose my best student and research partner."

She sighed a heavy breath of relief. "Let's go inside and call your dad. Then we can all talk about this and perhaps find out what this whole research project is all about."

Sam thought for a second and decided to make the situation more believable. He put on his most worried face. "But, mom! What about Titus?"

She stopped and brushed the hair out of his face lovingly. "I'm sure he will find his way home. Sometimes I think that dog is a lot smarter than we think he is." She put an arm under Sam's and positioned herself to help him walk inside.

Sam's eyes flicked to Roz for a short moment as he fake winced. He had a hard time keeping a straight face. Especially after Roz had to turn away so that Sarah wouldn't see him smiling.

* * * * * * * * * *

"Thank you for your time, Mr. and Mrs. Little," Roz shook hands with Sam's dad and nodded courteously to his mom. "I think Sam will do amazing things one day. I hope this project will help take him even further."

Sam's dad grinned and said, "Thank you for finding him. And also for giving him something to be excited about. He seems happier these days. This project seems to really be helping him."

"And," started his mom, "it's good to finally find out what he's been doing at school. Perhaps you can teach him how to stop keeping secrets like this from us." She sent an accusing look in her son's direction.

Sam leaned on the old crutch that his mom dug out of the attic and looked down at the floor guiltily. Of course, she had no idea what he was actually feeling guilt about. And he was more than okay with this. He looked up as he heard his parents say goodbye and headed for the door. Before his mom had a chance to close the door, he blurted out, "Mom, can I go talk to Mr. Roz for a minute? I need to ask him a couple of questions. It's about the research we did yesterday."

His parents exchanged a glance and his dad nodded to her. He always seemed to be more easygoing with Sam than his mom did. Her worry lines started to show again, but she agreed. "Alright. But don't put too much weight on your foot. You need to rest it."

Sam hobbled out the door with Roz as his parents went into the kitchen, most likely to discuss the happenings of the afternoon. He watched them turn the corner and then he shut the door. When he was certain it was safe, he and Roz started to laugh. Sam looked up at his friend and said, "You were awesome! I can't believe I got away with all of that!"

Roz was impressed as well. "*I* was awesome? What about you? That move with the 'I lost my puppy' face was pure brilliance."

Sam was elated. He hadn't felt this alive since Imagia. "Holy cow! I can't believe how well that worked. That was just too cool." He held out a closed fist towards Roz.

Cocking his head, Roz looked at it, confused. "Um, what are you doing?" He was staring at Sam's waiting fist.

Realization hit him. He understood how strange that gesture might look to Roz. "Oh! Well, in this world, something we do when, I dunno…something is really awesome or cool, is we do a fist bump. It's kinda like a high five."

"Ah," Roz said. "I see. Teach me."

"Well, you just put your fist out like mine and then we bump them together."

Roz's lip turned up at one corner and he held out his fist as well.

Reaching over, Sam bumped his fist into Roz's and said, "See? Like that."

"I think I've got it." He reached his fist back out and they both bumped them together again. He grinned again and said, "I think I like that gesture."

Sam sniffed out a laugh and shook his head. Sometimes he forgot how different their two worlds could be. And with that thought, he remembered who was waiting in the wings of the forest just behind his house. In all the craziness, he'd almost forgotten the reason why he'd gotten into this predicament in the first place. Titus had probably already reached the edge of the forest with Garrett and Foo. He turned his head towards where he assumed they'd be waiting. "What's happening? Why are so many from Imagia finding me?"

Roz looked towards the forest as well and thought to himself for a moment before answering. "Imagia. She's as mysterious to you as she is to me. Perhaps you'll find out more when you speak to your friends."

Sam whipped his head around and furrowed his brow. "Just me? Aren't you coming too?"

"Perhaps. But later, I think. I have a feeling that your parents will not let you out of their sight today. You should go speak to them after school tomorrow and then we'll find out what comes next."

"But you should be there too." Sam wasn't happy about Roz not being involved.

Considering this, Roz made a decision. "I don't think your friends trust me. But I'm sure if anyone can change their mind, it's you." He smiled. "For now, I think it best that you sort things out with them by yourself. Protectors. Defenders. We are not always the most trusting of lots."

Sam agreed with this plan. He said, "Okay. Then I'll see you tomorrow at school." He turned to go back in the door, but was stopped when Roz spoke his name.

"And Sam?"

"Yeah?"

"You really were impressive today." He held out his fist, a sideways grin taking over his face.

He was beginning to like his new friend more each day. He reached over and bumped Roz's fist.

And today was a good day.

* * * * * * * * * * *

The evening had been long. It had also been the exact opposite of Sam's good day. He had spent most of his evening pointlessly resting and icing his foot. He had to work pretty hard to convince his mom that he didn't need x-rays.

By the time his parents finally let him escape to bed, he'd talked more about school and his research project than he'd bargained for. Making up a project wasn't hard. He merely needed to sound excited about it to be convincing. Meanwhile, Titus had returned and his mom fretted about the grass and twigs stuck in his fur while his dad watched the evening news.

An anchorman was talking about the most recent attacks in Colorado. They were only a state away from the forest they talked about. For some reason, Sam found himself making a mental note of that.

Thankfully, he'd finally gotten to bed. His parents, having had a long day as well, also turned in early for the night. Sam couldn't have been happier with this seemingly perfect timing. Titus had told him that when all the lights in the house were off, Garrett would meet him at his window.

The last light went out and the house was quiet. Even though he expected it, Sam flinched at the quiet rapping on his window. Trying to avoid the squeak of his bedsprings, he managed to get to the window and open it without making more than a whisper of a noise.

Garrett had decided to leave Foo in the woods in case anyone might be peering out a window nearby. Sam reminded him that if anyone was doing any sort of peeking, that they'd be just as concerned about a grown man sneaking around his house as they would a strange, furry creature wearing clothes.

For the first time, Sam actually noted that Garrett was genuinely concerned about the situation. Whispering, he said, "I can't talk for long. I never know when my mom is going to sneak in here and check on me."

Garrett nodded seriously. "I understand. It can wait until tomorrow. Titus says that you will have a good amount of time after your schoolings tomorrow. We can talk more then. But I do want to warn you of two things."

"What?" Sam asked, slightly uneasy about Garrett's uncharacteristic seriousness. He was so used to him being the happy-go-lucky type.

He turned to look behind him briefly before answering. "I don't think I need to warn you that the ability to leave Imagia has changed drastically. Otherwise, I would not be standing here speaking to you." He waited for Sam to nod his head before continuing. "The truth is that Imagia's laws didn't change. We simply found a way around them. I'll explain more to you tomorrow. But because of this, we fear what other things may have found a way to bend the rules as well. So please be careful. In other words, don't go gallivanting into the forests alone anymore. It might not be safe." He raised an eyebrow accusingly.

Sam felt suddenly anxious. His eyes wandered beyond Garrett and into the depths of the darkness beyond his backyard. As he thought about what might be out there, his heart jumped. He'd just remembered something – the news.

He gasped. "Oh man."

"What is it?"

"There have been these stories on the TV."

"What's a Teevee?" He pronounced the vowels too long.

Sam scrunched his face up, confused. He remembered Garrett telling him that he'd only been a Protector for twenty-two years. Surely he remembered what TV was from his time here as a kid. But maybe he was wrong. He tried to think of how to explain it but decided to just take a different route. "Um, it's a thing that tells you about news and stuff."

"Ah. What about it?"

"Well," he started, "there is a forest not far from here that people have gone missing in. Some people are swearing that there is *something* in there attacking them."

Garrett went silent, deep in thought. At last, he said, "Then we'd better be on guard. There is one more thing." He paused, hesitant to continue. "I know that this will come as a harsh shock, but Nadaroth…"

"Is still alive. Yeah. I know."

Garrett, obviously confused, stuttered, "H-how did you know that?"

"Roz told me everything," he answered without skipping a beat.

Garrett ran his fingers through his hair, thinking cautiously. "Look…about Roz…are you sure we can trust him? It's very strange that he happened upon you before we did."

Sam turned defensive, but tried very hard not to raise his voice. "He's my friend. And I trust him just as much as I trust you. I hope that clears things up."

Sam looked angry and Garrett noticed. He put his hands up in defeat, smiling. "Okay, okay! I get it. I have always trusted your judgment before. We're all just a little jittery these days. You'd understand if you were still in Imagia. Trust me."

Sam couldn't resist the innocence of that reply and the genuine smile on his friend's face. He regretted his anger, but was happy to make his point known. He was about to say something else when he was interrupted unexpectedly.

The sound of Titus' nails clacking on the wood floor as he jumped to attention startled both Sam and Garrett. He whispered fiercely, "Your mom! She's coming!"

Sam's heart sped up and he ran to his bed as quickly and quietly as he could. He was about to tell Garrett to hide, but noticed that he was already gone. He pulled the covers over his shoulder just in the nick of time.

The door to his bedroom clicked open and a small beam of light from the hall bathroom streamed in hitting Sam square in the eyes. He feigned innocence and sat up, looking towards his mom. He squinted at her and said in his best sleepy voice, "Mom? What's wrong?"

She looked startled and slightly guilty. "Oh. Nothing sweetie. I just wanted to make sure your…ankle wasn't keeping you awake with pain."

Sam was certain that both he and his mom were equally guilty of lying just now. He played along. "No. It feels fine."

"Alright. Goodnight, sweetie."

"Night, mom." He flopped back down onto his pillow as she shut the door, once again leaving him in the comfort of the dark. When he was sure it was safe, he went back to the window and whispered into the night, "Garrett?"

He'd been hiding off to the side of the window. "I'm here. But that was a bit too close." He had a fat, yellow fluff ball in his arms. It was Sam's cat, Cooper. Garrett stroked his back as he purred. He handed him through the window to Sam. "Nice creature you have. Came out to meet us earlier. He won't leave Foo alone." Sam took Cooper before Garrett finished and said, "Let's talk tomorrow. We'll keep watch from the trees tonight."

Sam agreed and slipped back into his bed, a yawn escaping him. It had been quite the adventurous day. He welcomed sleep as dreams of Imagia drifted through his mind the entire night

* * * * * * * * * * *

School dragged along at a snail's pace. And for the first time in his life, Sam actually considered skipping class. Knowing that there were no less than two individuals from Imagia waiting to meet with him made waiting practically unbearable.

During History, Roz could tell that Sam's patience was wearing thin. Unfortunately, there was nothing either of them could do but wait. Even Lizzy managed to poke Sam's leg and whisper, "What the heck is wrong with you today?"

His creativity had run dry for the moment. All Sam could come up with was a mediocre shrug and a mumbled, "I'm just ready to go home."

Lizzy wasn't about to push him. She knew better. She merely replied, "Must be a Friday thing."

By the time the last bell of the day rang, Sam was already out the door and gunning for home at a steady jog. He made sure to go past Roz's room to remind him to meet up at their agreed time and location for one of Titus' walks. When he put his mind to it, he could get home in impressive time. Today was one of those days.

He dropped his backpack on the kitchen table and then double-backed to pick it up. If his mom came home early and saw his backpack then she'd know he wasn't at school. He and Titus flew through the back gate and into the depths of the forest within no time. Garrett and Foo were patiently waiting for them in a small clearing that was warmed by the sun filtering through the canopy.

Garrett had brushed away his previous night's worrisome demeanor and was wearing his staple grin. "I swear that time moves slower here. I feel like we've been waiting for two days." He leaned on a tree, one leg bent against it for support and his arms crossed. "So. We've got a lot of catching up to do before your mother returns."

Sam nodded, eager to hear everything.

Foo was standing close by. "Honestly," he said, "I think this conversation would be better discussed on the way home."

Home. Sam knew what Foo meant by that. But he didn't know what he meant by 'on the way'. Were they going somewhere? His look of confusion apparently needed no words, because Garrett responded immediately.

First he sighed and pinched the bridge of his nose. But then, without any hesitation, he said, "What my impatient little friend here meant by that statement is simple. I won't beat around the bush with you Sam."

There was a little spark of fear behind his response. "What is it?"

Three heartbeats later, Garrett stated, "We're here for one purpose. To find you and bring you back to Imagia."

Sam had a sudden desire to sit down. But with the hope that he wouldn't appear weak, he locked his knees and stood his ground. He'd wanted this for years now. He'd wished on every falling star and hoped on every dream that he could go back to Imagia. He had been so certain that it was what he needed to make his world right side up again.

Now that the answer to his heart's desire was staring at him right in the face, he wasn't sure he was really ready for it. He'd not responded to Garrett yet and the silence had become deafening. Sam began to notice. He tried to shake his mind out of the pit it was in. He finally sputtered out a question. "I…I don't understand. How is this possible?" It only took that one coherent thought to open the floodgates of questions he had. "How did you get here? How are we supposed to get back? I don't see a gateway anywhere. Where is it? And how the heck am I supposed to just *leave*?" The pitch of his voice kept getting higher with a hint of hysteria mixed in.

For a moment, Garrett hung his head. After composing himself, he tried to answer Sam's questions. "You know that Nadaroth is alive. But what you don't know is that he's waging war upon the Guardians. And the truth of the matter is that we don't stand a chance against him without your power to help us. He can build an army with his mind. And I can guarantee you this: For every ten of his creatures, we have one ally to fight it. And that's *if* we're lucky! Those, my friend, are not good odds."

Sam was still in shock, but not so much as to lose his train of thought. "Okay. I still don't understand how we get back though."

Titus sniffed and nodded. "Good question."

Garrett continued, "Rumors began a year ago. A spy discovered that Nadaroth was going to try to open a gateway so he could send out something to hunt you down and…well…kill you."

Sam's stomach flip-flopped.

"His plan is to destroy all Guardians. He knew that if we could find a way to bring you back, that we would do it without hesitation.

It became a race. Who could find a way to get Sam Little first?" He was shaking his head solemnly. "Now I think that it was a trick. With our close relationship with Guardians, he knew that we'd be able to work with them. We did all the work for him and now we're paying dearly.

"You have to understand that we did what we did to give Imagia the best chance – and Guardians as well. We worked with new Guardians until we discovered a way to bend the rules of gateways. Needless to say, it worked. And here we are. If you decide to come back with us, I can tell you all the details."

Taken aback, Sam said, "If? What do you mean *if* I go back?"

Foo snorted and Garrett threw him an annoyed glance. "Look, Sam. We can't force you to come. It's a major decision. And it's a choice, much like one you made four years ago, that only you can make." He paused, giving Sam time to think. Then he added an afterthought. "But we don't have much more time. Foo is a Guardian and Imagia has opened a gateway to let him back in. He can feel it. And the longer that gateway is open, the more chances Nadaroth has to let loose every creature he can muster in order to hunt you down and kill you. We have to close that gateway soon."

Sam couldn't think straight. Too many things were happening too quickly. He looked back through the forest at his home. He thought about leaving his parents again. He thought about the pain they'd go through. Then there was Lizzy. How could he just disappear like that and not tell her why? It was a lot to consider. So he asked, "How long do I have to think about it?"

"Think about it tonight and tomorrow. We'll see where that takes us. If you need another day, we'll figure it out. Does that sound fair?" asked Garrett.

Sam looked at Titus questioningly. When he dipped his shaggy head once in approval, Sam answered, "Yeah. Okay."

In an oddly human gesture, the mighty Protector rubbed his belly. "Good. Now, you wouldn't by chance have something to eat, would you? I'm starving. And so is my furry comrade, here. Finding food in this forest is difficult at best."

Though he had no idea what they'd find to eat in this forest, Sam could only imagine that it wasn't very tasty. His mouth turned up in a grin and he said, “Of course! My mom keeps the fridge stocked. She says I have a hollow leg.” He snickered.

Foo’s face wrinkled up in confusion. “Why would your leg be hollow? Is it made of wood?”

Everyone laughed, which made Foo grumble something angrily to himself. The only thing Sam could make out was, “sensible enough question.”

They were all just about to head towards the house when something could be heard coming towards them. The grass and brush were being shoved, rather clumsily, out of the way by whoever it was. They heard a stick crack and a voice yell out, “Ouch! Where on Earth did that come from?”

Sam knew that voice. He spun around, wide-eyed, and stared at everyone in the clearing. “Oh, man!” He whispered harshly. “It’s my neighbor!” His mind searched frantically for an idea. He looked at each of them and realized that the hardest thing to explain would be Foo. His eyes settled on the small Guardian. “Foo, you have to lie down on the ground and pretend you’re dead, right now!” he demanded.

Taken aback, Foo snarled, “What? Have you lost your mind?”

Sam looked back. He could make out the silhouette of his neighbor. He’d be upon them in less than ten seconds. He flipped back around to Foo and pleaded. “Just trust me. Lie down and…and look dead.”

Foo looked at Garrett exasperated. But Garrett simply shrugged and motioned him to do as Sam said.

They couldn’t have timed it better. When Sam’s elderly neighbor, Mr. Irving, came upon them in the clearing, he stopped dead in his tracks and gawked at the scene. After a long judging look at Garrett, he finally focused on Sam. “What is going on here, Sam? I saw you and your dog running into the forest. When you didn’t come back out, I thought I’d better make sure you were okay. Does your mom know you’re out here?”

It was a lot of questions and Sam’s mind raced to find a believable story. He put his hands in his pockets to hide their shaking. “Hi, Mr. Irving. Yes. My mom knows. This is my…cousin, Garrett.”

Mr. Irving furrowed his brow and looked between the both of them. “Cousin?”

Sam's heart sped up. He'd never had to think this quickly before. "Um, yeah. Distant cousin. Like second or third cousin or something. I forget. He's a hunter and he was showing me some tracks in the forest before he goes back to get the deer he killed."

Mr. Irving scowled and crossed his arms. "You know it's illegal to hunt within shooting range of housing areas around here, young man."

Garrett didn't skip a beat. He politely answered, "Yes, sir. I was quite deep in the forest when I killed the beast. I simply came to meet Sam before taking it back to my cottage."

Sam cringed at the word cottage.

Mr. Irving didn't miss it either. "Cottage? Where exactly are you from, son?"

A little too quickly, Sam blurted out, "The Netherlands. He's visiting with his uncle."

Though he had to think about his response momentarily, Mr. Irving nodded twice. "Well, you should be careful. I've seen things moving back here."

Unexpectedly, a woman's voice interrupted them all making everyone jump. "Honestly, Harold! Don't be ridiculous! No more monster movie marathons. The only thing moving back here is your imagination." It was Mrs. Irving. She'd followed her husband into the woods.

"Martha! You scared the lot of us! I told you to wait at the fence."

She merely rolled her eyes and came to stand next to him, taking in the scene as well.

As if he didn't care what she said, Mr. Irving continued. "Either way, you'd best be careful."

Garrett glanced to Sam and nodded to Sam's neighbors. "Yes, sir. I'll do that. Thank you. Now if you'll excuse me, I really must finish teaching Sam about tracks before it gets too late." He managed to make his brilliant smile look respectful.

Mr. Irving eyed Garrett for a moment longer before he responded. For a just a moment, Sam was convinced that he was in a heap of trouble right now and that Mr. Irving was two seconds away from dragging him back to his house and calling his mom.

Then Mrs. Irving tugged on her husband's arm and said, "Come on, Harold. Let's leave these young men be so they can finish their lesson. We need to go or I'm going to be late to my knitting club!"

Mr. Irving sighed and nodded. "Well, you be careful, Sam. You should –" He stopped mid-sentence as his eyes fell on Foo's limp body. "What is *that*?" He said, eyes wide and pointing to Foo.

Sam and Garrett exchanged quick, nervous glances and then both let their eyes fall on Foo as well. Sam's heart sped up significantly. Even though there was hesitation, he managed to answer fairly quickly. "It's a badger." He silently thanked his mom for all the wildlife books he'd read as a kid. Foo didn't fit the description perfectly, but it would do.

Garrett gracefully turned to walk past Sam and Foo at just the right angle so that he could mouth the word, "*Badger*?" questioningly without being seen by the Irvings.

Sam shrugged slightly, eyes on the edge of frantic.

Mr. Irving scrunched up his face. "A badger? Is it dead?"

"Yes. Quite dead," Garrett answered.

"Huh." Mr. Irving scratched at the stubble on his chin. "Why is it wearing clothes?"

Garrett, realizing that he had no answer to this, stuttered out a half response after looking to Sam for help. "Well, you see…"

Sam interrupted suddenly. "Taxidermy!"

Mr. Irving took his eyes off Foo and looked at Sam, one eye-brow up. "Taxidermy?"

Garrett was looking him with eyes wide, a grin fighting to show. He cleared his throat in attempt not to laugh.

Sam was either getting very good at lying or was experiencing a moment of ridiculously perfect dumb-luck. "Yeah," he answered. "Garrett's uncle is a taxidermist. Has a shop and everything in the Netherlands."

Mr. Irving's eye-brow didn't seem to want to go back down. His eyes went from Foo to Garrett a couple of times before he asked, "Aren't they supposed to dress them *after* they stuff them?"

"Well…" he paused as his heart skipped, "he wanted to surprise his uncle and send a picture. He's hoping to take over the family taxidermy business." Sam ran over what he'd just said and how silly it sounded and then simply smiled up at his neighbor.

Mrs. Irving tugged lightly on her husband's arm again and Mr. Irving shook his head and pursed his lips. "Well, don't touch it Sam." He sniffed the air once. "It smells terrible. And it looks like it probably carries disease."

"Yes, sir."

"Good evenin', Sam. And you," he directed at Garrett, "be careful with those weapons, young man."

Nodding once respectfully, Garrett said, "Yes, sir. Thank you, sir."

"Night Mr. and Mrs. Irving," Sam said. As he watched them turn around and leave, he felt his shoulders relax and a breath left his mouth as though he'd been holding it in for ages.

As the two left the forest, they could hear Mr. Irving say, "That boy is so strange, Martha."

Mrs. Irving, now a faint voice in the air, said, "Yes. Odd boy."

Without warning, Garrett started laughing quietly.

"What?" Sam asked.

Looking at the boy, eyes wide, "Taxidermy?" he smirked.

"Sorry. It's the best I could come up with."

Foo, who'd just done the best dead badger impersonation he'd ever hoped to do, got up and brushed himself off. Between the four of them, he was the only one who did not look amused by the situation. As he picked at some leaves on his arms, he muttered, "Disease. Ha! Not likely."

Sam, Garrett and Titus all exchanged smiles and Garrett reassured Foo. "Ahh…don't take it personal, Foo. You haven't taken a bath in weeks. It's been rough."

It was obvious that Foo didn't think this was funny.

Trying not to get the Guardian too upset, Garrett decided to redirect them all. "I think it best that we discuss things further at a later time. That was too close of a call. I'd rather not repeat that situation. Perhaps you'd best be returning home before your mother is the next to come find you."

Titus, always worried about being caught in a situation like this, agreed with him. "It's getting close to time for your mom to get home anyways. We have much to consider."

Everyone started to walk to the forest's edge so that Sam and Titus could return to the house. Foo, still agitated at his humiliation, fell into place between Garrett and Sam.

Foo shook his head and thought for a moment. Then he sniffed beneath his arms. His ears laid back against his head and he quietly snarled to himself, "I don't smell anything. And I do *not* carry disease."

Sam looked down at the Guardian and then back up to Garrett who winked at him. Then they both started to laugh again.

As they pushed their way through the last bits of thick growth, the three non-creatures made their way towards Sam's house, leaving Foo behind to watch from the safety of the trees. Before they left earshot, Foo hollered through the brush, "It's not funny, you know. Maybe it wasn't *me* they were smelling!"

The only reply Sam and Garrett could offer was the laughter they couldn't contain.

Chapter Ten: Choices

The day was drawing to a close. Sam needed to spend this time thinking about his choice. Going to Imagia the first time was easy. He didn't even realize he'd made that choice until he was already there. Staying in Imagia was not what he'd originally chosen to do. But undeniably, it was still a choice when he pushed Lizzy back through his gateway and stayed locked inside the strange world. But the most obvious choice was when he took that first step through a gateway to go back home. It was the hardest decision he'd ever made in his life.

Until tonight.

Sam had barely eaten dinner. He had spent the evening poking the food around his plate and pondering what he was going to choose to do or say the next day when he'd speak to Garrett again.

His parents were barraging him with questions about how he felt or why he wasn't eating. They asked if he was sick. He opted to tell them he was tired after yesterday's crazy events and blamed his lack of appetite on residual soreness in his ankle. He'd never used the crutches and his parents were simply amazed at how quickly he was walking on it again. His mom gave his teenage hormones credit for the speedy recovery.

Usually during school, the time seemed to stop just to be annoying. Now, with such a drastic decision weighing on him, it decided to double in speed. Every moment Sam looked at the clock, all he could see was how little time he had left to choose. And he had absolutely no idea how he was going to do it.

He blinked and the house lights were off and he was staring up at his ceiling, wishing for an answer to somehow appear in the patterns of the tiles. Garrett didn't even bother visiting tonight. Sam figured it was to give him time to think. Titus jumped back through the window and confirmed this.

"I took them the food you saved. They said thanks." Titus yawned.

Sam blinked, waiting for more. "And?"

Genuinely innocent, he asked, "And what?"

"And what else did they say? Did they ask if I've decided what to do yet?" His voice indicated he was frustrated in some way.

With a heavy sigh, Titus merely said, "No." He saw Sam's face fall. He didn't want to rush his friend's choice either. Finally, he said, "I believe we all know that this decision isn't an easy one. They aren't pushing. You have to make this decision on your own. No one can make it for you."

"And what about you. You think I should go. Don't you?" Sam didn't mean for his words to be accusatory, so he hesitated only for a moment before adding, "Sorry. I didn't mean it to come out like that."

Titus, ever understanding, shook his shaggy head. "It's okay. No harm done. It's a lot to think about. But in the end, what I think doesn't matter. As I said, the decision is purely yours." He turned to gaze out the window.

Sam could see the longing in Titus' eyes. There was no hiding the desire to go back to a world where he'd belong again. He got out of bed and walked over to the window. He could feel it too. Somewhere out there, a gateway was waiting; a world where he didn't have to hide anymore was calling to him. Standing by his friend, he whispered, "It's not making the decision I'm worried about."

Titus looked up at him. "Oh?"

Sam didn't break his gaze from the silhouette of the gently swaying forest. "It's living with the consequences that come after."

* * * * * * * * * *

It was obvious by the end of the day that Sam's thoughts were nowhere near the real world. By the time afternoon had rolled around, he'd stubbed his toe on the end of his bed, tripped over more things than he'd cared to count, knocked over a fifth grader carrying his lunch, spilled pop on his pants, and elbowed poor Lizzy in the head – twice.

When school let out, Lizzy let him have it. She may have been shorter than Sam, but when she puffed her chest out and stood on her tiptoes, one finger poking Sam in the forehead, she could be quite intimidating. "What the heck is wrong with you today, huh?" She stopped poking him. "I mean, seriously! You'd think you suddenly went blind or something! Did you forget to sleep last night or are you just genuinely trying to annoy every person that comes in contact with you?" She had one eye slightly squinted and her arms were crossed, waiting impatiently for his answer.

Sam felt terrible. He had more reasons to feel bad than Lizzy could understand, but he didn't quite know how to explain to her why his head was in the clouds. Part of him wanted to simply walk away and ignore her tantrum. The more logical and friendly side stood his ground. For a fleeting moment, he wanted to take her aside and tell her all the thousand thoughts in his head – spill the truth into her lap and hope for the best reaction. He wasn't sure if he'd really meant to go through with that plan on some level because he was suddenly aware that his mouth was hanging open as if the words were fighting to get out. He closed his mouth with an inaudible pop and his shoulders fell.

"I'm sorry, Lizzy," Sam started. There *was* something he could tell her. It was something he'd wanted to talk to another person about for a while. Hopeful that this might be enough, he said, "Look. I've got a lot on my mind today. With summer just around the corner, I've had some things happen that I just don't know how to handle anymore."

Lizzy's expression abruptly softened. "What happened?"

"Things are," he paused to form the right words, "not easy." He shook his head and hiked his backpack onto his shoulder. "Wanna walk with me?"

Now her face was concerned. "Of course." She pulled her backpack on and they started for home.

As they started walking, Sam disclosed more to her than he'd planned. Even though what he talked about wasn't the biggest part of his disconnect today, talking to her was actually taking a lot of weight off of his chest. He felt good. He'd told her about how his parents never felt like he's healed from his disappearance and that he was going to have to see a doctor over the summer. He told her that a lot of pressure had been on him to go back to normal and that he wasn't the same person he was before he'd left. He finally finished with, "So I just don't know what to do. I have all these…things…to worry about, and I just don't know what to think about it anymore."

They both stopped walking because they'd reached the intersection where they had to go their separate ways. Lizzy, completely intent on listening to his every word, did something Sam didn't quite expect. She reached up and hugged him. She held him tight and softly said, "I'm sorry, Sam. I had no idea. You're such a strong person." She pulled away. Looking into his wide, blue eyes, she continued, "Even if you *are* a little weird."

They both chuckled and Sam squeaked out, "Thanks."

"I just wish I'd known sooner. Maybe we could have figured something out that would help. Is there anything I can do?"

As he looked at her genuine concern, for the first time in a long time, he felt like he might just make it in this world. For the tiniest instant, he forgot the looming choice he needed to make. Sam didn't answer her as quickly as he should have and just like that, the moment was gone. Guilt returned and he broke his gaze away from Lizzy's eyes much too suddenly. He practically stuttered out, "No. Just listening to me…" he trailed off.

Trying to get him to look at her again, she gently asked, "Just listening to you, what?"

Sam didn't know why, but part of him was scared to look at her face again. There was something so satisfying about divulging that secret to her. It became overwhelmingly appealing to him. He was certain that if he looked at her again, that he'd blurt out every secret he'd ever kept from her. All the pain and frustration that he'd been holding in all of these years was welling up in him. His heart began pounding too hard. What was happening to him? All of a sudden, he didn't know where to look. He wanted to look down at his shoes but he'd somehow forgotten where they were. He wanted to run for it.

Lizzy made it worse. She could see the all too familiar look she'd seen in him before. It was as if he was battling something in his mind. She wanted him to know it was okay to just be there. She reached over and took his hand in hers.

Sam flinched slightly. She'd never done that before. Against his own judgment, he stopped fighting and turned his head to look into those big, brown familiar eyes. She was smiling, but it was a worried look.

Lizzy repeated gently, "Just listening to you, what?"

He knew what to say now. Smiling, Sam answered, "It helps. Listening to me helps. More than you could ever know."

She gave his sweaty hand a gentle squeeze and smiled back. Then, catching Sam completely off guard, she reached up on her tiptoes and gave him a quick kiss on his cheek. "Anytime." She let go of his hand. "Give me a call if you want to talk more. K?"

He barely managed a nod. His cheek felt warm and his stomach fluttered strangely for a moment. When she started to walk away, he wanted to call her back and tell her how important she was to him. But by the time the thought could form into words, she'd waved goodbye and Sam was left standing on the sidewalk, unsure of what just happened, but somehow…happy.

* * * * * * * * * * *

Sam looked at the clock, exasperated. He couldn't believe that it was already evening. The sun was still high enough that it could be considered late afternoon, but there was no denying the time. There was also no denying that Garrett would be waiting for his answer. In fact, he was probably sitting just at the edge of the forest staring at the house, wondering.

Suddenly, Sam felt self-conscious. He moved away from the back screen door to his house and tried to look busy. His parents weren't home. His dad had to work the Saturday shift and his mom left to go to the grocery store for her weekly shopping trip. She'd promised to pick up a pizza on the way home. As Sam recalled this, he realized something completely ridiculous: There was no pizza in Imagia.

That thought made him laugh. Titus looked up from his water dish and asked, "What's so funny?"

Still chuckling, he responded in between laughs, "Here I am…trying to make this *huge* decision…and all I can think about…" he started laughing harder, "is how there's no pizza in Imagia!" He doubled over, and held his stomach. When he finally started to regain his composure, he wiped away a tear from his cheek and flicked it across the room. All the while, Titus stared at him in a most confused way. "Ahhh," Sam sighed. "That felt good. I haven't laughed myself to tears in a long time."

"Are you finished then?" Titus asked.

Sam simply shrugged and mumbled the word 'pizza' under his breath as he grabbed a banana to eat.

A sharp rapping at the backdoor made Sam gasp, spin around, and drop his banana on the floor. Staring back at him through the glass of the door was a very guilty looking Garrett. He mouthed the word 'sorry'.

Garrett was looking back towards the forest when Sam opened the backdoor for him. He hesitated to come inside, one hand calmly placed on the sheath of the knife he wore on his hip. Sam didn't give him a chance to start. Nervously, he said, "What are you doing up here? What if my mom was here?"

"She's not. I saw her leave awhile ago." Garrett replied. He'd been watching the house just as Sam had thought.

"Yeah. But I have no idea when she'll be back. What's wrong?"

Before answering, Garrett looked to Titus. "Can you go see Foo? He's waiting for you. We need you to check something out."

"I'm on it." He bounded off without hesitation, almost eagerly.

Sam frowned. "What's going on? Did something happen?"

Garrett shook his head. "No. Have you decided what you'll do?"

Sam was taken aback. He was sure he had until nightfall to give his answer. He cleared his throat. "You need an answer right now? It's just that I kind of thought I had until tonight." His palms started to sweat like when he'd gotten a pop quiz at school. He noticed that Garrett looked a little nervous as well.

Nodding slowly, he glanced back again at the forest, Titus already out of sight. "I understand. But something's come up. We think there might be something in the forest."

"Something. What you do mean?" Now Sam's forehead felt clammy.

"We aren't sure. But it's big. We think we found a footprint." Garrett paused dramatically and added, "A *big* footprint."

"What do you mean you *think* you found one?" Sam's mind raced. This was the kind of discussion that didn't belong in this world. "So…it might be nothing?"

Garrett stood in front of the door thinking. He looked like he was trying to convince himself. "No. I don't think so. The problem is that we only found one print."

Now he was confused. "How is that a problem?" Sam wasn't a Protector. Once upon a time, he'd hoped to be one himself. But he couldn't deny that when one of them had a hunch, it's best not to ignore it.

"It's a problem because whatever it is has been covering its tracks. So it's either not alone, or something even worse." Placing a hand on Sam's shoulder, he looked at him quite seriously and said, "It's smart."

Big and smart. That was almost never a good combination.

Either realization of the potential situation or plain and simple fear fueled his response. He shivered noticeably and asked, "How big?"

Garrett thought for a moment. "Well, I'm not sure what kind of things you would normally find in your forests here, but lets just say that it's…well…Imagia big."

All of a sudden Sam felt like the floor had dropped out from beneath him. He was sure his stomach was sitting right atop his shoes. He couldn't hide his stutter when he said, "Are you s-sure? I mean – is there any chance you're wrong?"

Garrett let out a slow, unsure breath, cheeks puffed up and eyes to the floor. He opened his mouth to answer but was cut short.

An angry voice from behind Sam said, "Who are you?"

Sam jumped and flipped around only to meet eyes with his very angry mom holding two pizza boxes. Her eyes were deadly and Sam yelped, "Mom!" He wanted to tell her that he could explain everything and then give her some cleverly designed story about research partners and important projects. But the only thing he could sputter out was, "What are you doing home so soon?"

Wrong answer. Sam knew it before the words left his mouth.

His mother, on the other hand, seemed to know exactly what to say. She glared at Sam for a split second, enough to send a chill through him. She turned to the stranger standing in her kitchen and simply said in a most deadly tone, "I don't care who you are or what you're doing here. Get out of my house."

Sam did the worst thing he could do. He said, "But mom, I can explain! He's a friend!"

"No!" his mom shouted. "He's twice your age! Fourteen-year-old children do *not* have friends twice their age. I don't care who he is." She spun on her heel and directed her anger towards Garrett again, who had only taken a step back and was looking to Sam. "Get out! Now!"

Sam was about to protest again when his mom slammed the pizza boxes down onto the counter. "You will leave my house now, sir, or I will call the police." She turned her glare towards Sam and ordered, "As for you, young man, we need to talk. Sit down." She pointed to one of the kitchen chairs.

Sam turned to apologize to Garrett. He didn't really know what to say. He was in deep trouble and quite flustered. Sam went to open the door for Garrett, hoping his mom would see it as a display of good manners and Garrett pat Sam on the back and whispered, "Keep your ears open."

Another small shiver ran up his back as the door shut and Sam went to sit in the chair, awaiting his punishment. He knew speaking would only make this worse, but he had to try. He begged, "Mom, please. If you will just let me *try* to explain, then – "

"Sam, stop!" She didn't like yelling, but a mother's temper can only be pushed so far. "Honestly, I am so mad right now that I don't want to hear your explanation! I thought you might like some dinner before I got my shopping done and came home to find you fraternizing with some random person that I've never seen before. What do you expect me to do? Be happy?" She didn't wait for his response. "Because I'm anything but happy! I want to trust you, but the secrets are getting out of hand."

Now Sam didn't want to say anything. He felt bad. Very bad. He looked at his mom's face as she put her hands over her eyes in frustration.

She was giving up on him. He didn't want to make her feel this way.

When she spoke again, her voice was slightly muffled through her hands. "Dr. McKinney is a good doctor. Your dad and I talked to him and you'll be starting sessions the first week of summer vacation. You have to stay there for two weeks for evaluation and then he'll decide what kind of treatment program is best for you."

His mom talked a lot more over the next half-hour. He didn't say much to her. She explained all the programs and the different methods Dr. McKinney used. Through an array of emotions, she told him all of her concerns and all the things that she wanted to fix and how she wanted her little boy back from years ago.

Now Sam wanted to give up too. The world was topsy-turvy. But it didn't matter anymore. He swallowed hard and looked to her, half-heartedly pleading. "Mom, you don't understand. There is nothing that I can tell the doctor that you don't already know."

"Doctors have ways to get you to remember. You have to know this is what's best for you."

Looking into his mom's tired eyes, he thought what this could mean for him. As he considered everything, he heard a faint sound from outside. Someone was hollering his name. His eyes fell on his mom.

She'd heard it too.

She scrunched up her face. "Is someone calling your name?"

They heard it again; only it was getting closer and more frantic sounding. Sam recognized the voice. It was Titus. He must not know his mom was home. Panic started to take over and then he heard his friend yell again. This time he yelled, "Sam, it's coming!"

Sarah looked at her son, completely confused. "Did someone just say 'it's coming'? What on Earth –" She took one step towards the door but stopped when the floor began to quiver.

Sam felt it too. He stood up fast, his chair flying out from behind him, and spun to look outside. Titus was at a dead run for the house from just beyond the back gate. He could see Garrett standing at the forest's edge, bow in hand and aimed.

The floor shook again, this time the table rattling along with it.

His heart pounding like thunder in his ears, Sam looked frantically between his mom and Titus. He had no idea what would come of this situation, but he knew it was going to be a defining moment – for everyone.

The ground shook even fiercer and Sam's mom screamed out, "Oh my Lord! It's an earthquake! Sam, get under the table!"

Of two things Sam was certain: This was not an earthquake and he wasn't going to be able to keep anything secret anymore. He closed his eyes hard, if only for a single breath. As his mom desperately reached for the kitchen counter, Sam realized he needed her full attention. "Mom! Listen to me!" Her wild eyes searched his face.

The ground trembled harder. It was getting closer.

Sam ran up to his mom and grabbed her arms, forcing her to pay attention. "Mom, I'm so sorry. Sorry for everything."

"What are you talking about, Sam? What is going on?" Her voice was panicked.

"You have to do what I say. There's no time to explain. I'm so, so sorry!" He turned and ran to the door. "You have to get out of here!" he ordered her as he swung the door open.

Exasperated, she shook her hands wildly and screeched, "Sorry for *what*? You're not making any sense!"

Sam didn't look at her as he said, "I'm sorry because your whole world is about to change."

Titus burst through the door, hackles raised. Whether he'd seen Sam's mom or not, he didn't hesitate when he yelled, "I got here as fast as I could, but it's fast! You don't have much time!"

Sarah gasped and jumped back, slamming herself hard into the counter. She was trying to say something but the only thing that came out was a series of stuttered consonants as she pointed at Titus.

The house was trembling; pictures fell off the wall and shattered on the floor. Sam ignored his stammering mother. "Titus, get mom out of here. Now!"

Titus nodded.

Before Titus could say anything else, Sam turned and stood tall. "Mom!"

She looked her son in the eyes, terrified.

"Mom, I'm *not* crazy. Titus *can* talk. And it's *not* an earthquake." He didn't wait for her response. He turned and put his hands out, eyes closed.

The sky outside darkened and thunder clapped.

Then the entire kitchen side of the house ripped off through the sounds of a deafening roar.

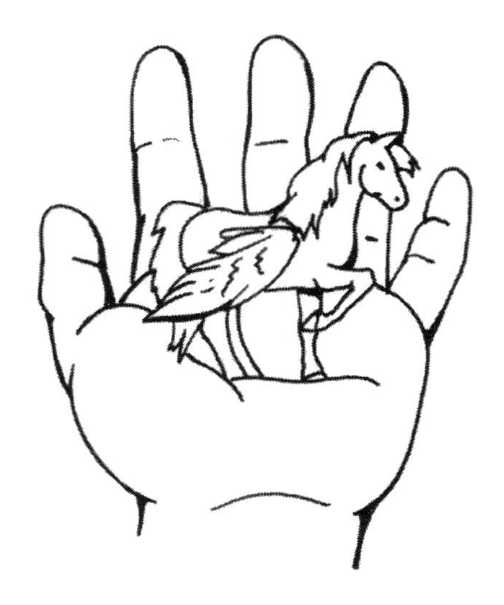

Chapter Eleven: Truth Will Out

Sam scrambled to his feet. The force of the kitchen wall being ripped off had thrown him to the ground. A board from the ceiling had fallen, nicking his temple, and then landed on his chest. He threw it off, took a very fleeting look back towards his screaming mother and ran into the backyard. As he ran, he imagined the thickest, black smoke rising from the ground. It enveloped the massive beast, confusing it long enough that Sam could put distance between it and himself.

The shroud of smoke didn't work long, but Sam had gotten his bearings. He imagined a colossal rock wall that shot up from the ground all around the monster, caging it in the strong stone. The barrier shuddered, rock fragments showering the ground. Whatever this creature was, it was strong. The wall wouldn't hold long.

Garrett and Foo had reached Sam. Garrett yelled through a clap of thunder, "I hope you can do better than that, my friend."

Exasperated, Sam said, "Give me a break! I'm a little rusty at the whole battle thing." Before anyone could say another word, Sam's eyes closed and the ground started to quiver yet again.

Stampeding from the forest came a colossal rhino-like creature. It may have looked like a rhino, but it was three times the size, had extra large horns, and was jet-black. At the same time that it barreled through the back fence, the trapped creature burst through its rocky prison and snarled. It was taller than the house, covered in shimmering, gray scales, and had firelight where its eyes should have been.

The rhino-beast dipped its head and both creatures clashed. The sharp horn of the rhino-beast pierced the belly of the enemy, but just barely. Its scales were strong. Both beasts were locked in battle and tumbled across the backyard, destroying everything in their path. They were heading for the forest.

Garrett was grinning. "Not bad for a rusty half-pint." He slapped Sam on the back heartily. "But we can't let it get away. Let's go!" Garrett took off at a sprint towards the battling monsters.

Sam had already started following suit when he heard is mom screaming for him. He turned around and saw Titus standing between her and the rubble of the house. He was barking orders at her. "Sarah, you have to trust me. Sam knows what he's doing. I have to get you to safety!"

There was no time to explain. He shook his head and took off at a dead run. Titus would take care of his mom for now. He looked up at the sky and tried to concentrate his thoughts on the clouds. It suddenly grew twice as dark and a fog set in. His house could no longer be seen.

Garrett stumbled slightly as he turned to see the quickly approaching fog behind them, shock on his face. Bow drawn and aimed, he let an arrow fly. It hit the enemy square in the back of the head, but then plinked off and fell to the ground. He huffed sarcastically, "Oh great." He looked at Foo and said, "We have to find a weakness."

The beast dodged Sam's creation and twisted around, one clawed hand reaching desperately as it ran. It was aiming for Sam. Before it could reach him, the rhino-beast hit its back, puncturing the hard scales and driving it face-first into the ground.

The enemy wailed and turned fast, kicking the rhino-beast off. Both the beast's fists went up and then back down with frightening speed. It delivered a deadly blow to the back of the rhino-beast. A dull cracking sound told them that its back had been broken. Falling to the ground, it trumpeted in pain. Before Sam could do anything to help, the enemy beast grabbed the head of its fallen foe and twisted sharply. Another cracking sound and the rhino-beast went limp.

Furious, Sam held his hands out slightly towards the ground and when the beast turned and roared triumphantly, the earth began to crack below it. A fissure opened in the ground and the creature fell backwards into it. It wasn't deep, but that wasn't important. As it struggled to get up again, the ground became alive around it. It was as if the roots of the entire forest had a mind of its own. They began twisting around the creature, trapping it in a web of sinewy wood.

The creature fought as the sounds of snapping wood shattered the air around them. It fought frantically against the wooden web, but it wasn't fast enough. The roots entwined its arms and legs. Then the beast let out another roar, only this time, it was one of pain.

Garrett looked on, bow still aimed. He realized that the roots weren't just around the creature, but growing *through* it. He turned to look at Sam. But Sam didn't notice Garrett's incredulous look. He was deep in concentration, all focus on the roots that were devouring the beast before them.

When the roots finally stopped growing, Garrett went up to the whimpering creature and stood looking down into its fiery gaze. Foo joined him, and without any word, lifted his sword above his head and aimed for the eyes.

Just as Foo was about to strike, the beast did something that no one expected. It spoke. A rough and eerie voice said, "We will find him. We will take him. We will never stop." It took in a loud, painful breath and gurgled, "We are not alone."

Foo looked at the creature in disgust. He stared into the red eyes and his sword lowered hesitantly for a split second. He growled and raised his weapon, bringing it down into the creature's eyes. The light left the beast in a wisp of smoke. The fight was over.

In one lasting moment, the ground swallowed the creature up as the roots returned to their underground domain. The dead rhino-beast shimmered and turned into a million fireflies. The sky lightened and the fog faded like smoke in the wind. Sam fell to his knees, trembling and suddenly out of breath. His heart was racing.

Garrett ran over to him and took a knee beside him. He looked over to Foo and said, "See? I told you he could handle it."

Sam sat down and then fell onto his back. He closed his eyes and tried to make the world stop spinning around him.

* * * * * * * * * * *

His mom had spent a long time in hysterics. Sam was losing track of just how long it had been at this point. Between her frantic attempts to make sense of the situation and her uncontrollable outbursts of confused questions, Sam hadn't managed to get a single word in.

Truth be told, he wanted her to get as much out of her system as possible. He also needed to regain his own composure. He hadn't imagined this hard since Imagia and his mind was still reeling.

In between all of the craziness, their party had grown by one more. Roz had shown up. His mom was in such a tizzy that she either didn't notice or chose to ignore it. Between the house, Sarah, and a quiet look from Sam, Roz didn't need to ask what had happened. He knew the details would come later.

Finally, after a very long bout of 'someone needs to explain' and 'I must be crazy' remarks, Sarah covered her eyes and hiccupped. She took a loud breath through her nose and shook her head slowly. "This isn't happening," she whispered.

Sam took advantage of the moment of calm and reached out to his mom. He put his hand on her shoulder. "Mom, this *is* happening. Maybe we should get dad." Her wild eyes searched her son's face. "I'll explain everything – to both of you."

* * * * * * * * * * *

George and Sarah Little were having a night that they'd never forget – no matter how hard they might try. George came flying into the house at record speed and quietly panicked when he saw the kitchen wall. His eyes were frightened, but he managed to keep much calmer than his wife. Since calling his dad home, Sam had finally managed to get his mom to stop flipping out and now both of his parents sat across a rubble-covered table from two total strangers, a talking rodent, and their quite verbal dog.

Sam was sitting next to his parents trying to explain what had happened, why it was possible, and where he went all those years ago.

He wanted to think that this would be easy now that the cat was out of the bag and he had a company of friends to back up his otherwise insane sounding story, but it was anything but.

Sarah kept shaking her head randomly; her eyes were still wild and confused. George, on the other hand, was sitting there, mouth slightly ajar, and not saying a word. Silent shock was what Sam assumed was happening. Though only twenty minutes had passed, time felt as though it was dragging as he waited for his parents to say something. Finally, as Sam was about to try explaining his power to imagine again, his dad spoke.

"So you're telling me that you wished to go to some other world, developed a superpower, got trapped in said world, defeated some evil monster, and randomly showed up over a year later by chance. *Then*, after a few years, a bunch of your friends from that world came here to find you, brought a giant creature with them, which ripped my kitchen off and threw it into the backyard, and then you just *imagined* some way to kill it and then, poof! All is back to normal?" His voice was getting noticeably higher. "Except, now my *kitchen* has an elephant sized natural air conditioner, the *dog* is telling me everything's okay, and your *mother* has gone catatonic! Does that about cover it?" Somewhere in his rant, he'd stood up. This was about as hysterical as Sam had ever seen his dad. It was a bit frightening.

Sam glanced at his friends. "Well," he started, "my friends didn't bring the creature with them. But, yeah. That about covers it."

George nodded several times, quick and sharply. "Right. You have to understand, Sam, that this is all a bit tough to chew. Imagination as a power? Dark creatures? Another world? I mean, how am I supposed to just believe all of this."

Sarah, for the first time since George came home, moved on her own and spoke. She looked at her husband and shook her head. "We *can't* believe it. It's *not* possible."

Sam looked at his mom. He felt a mix between relief that she was talking, anger that she couldn't believe her own eyes, and hurt that she would not believe him. Struggling with the right words, he started to open his mouth to speak when Roz spoke for him.

"With all due respect, Mrs. Little, I can't understand how you could possibly think that. You see your house. You heard Titus speak.

You even witnessed his powers of imagination. How can you say such a thing?"

Sam's mom stood up suddenly and shot a dangerous look at Roz. "You have no right to speak here," she hissed. "I have no idea what I saw and I refuse to believe that any of it was a result of some *power* that you claim my son has!"

"Sarah," George pleaded gently to his wife, "please calm down. Sam said he'd show us when he could. We have to believe him. He's our son, for Heaven's sake. For years now we've wanted answers and like it or not, I think we are finally getting them." He held her hand gently and watched as she closed her eyes, took a calming breath, and sat back down.

Ever grateful for any support, Sam smiled weakly at Roz. Hesitantly, he placed his hand on his mom's shoulder. She flinched, which hurt Sam inside, and he quickly removed his hand. He hadn't used so much of his power willingly since Imagia and he could feel the exhaustion in his mind. After the fight, he couldn't have even imagined a rock if he tried. But the weight had lifted enough that he knew it was time to try again.

Titus could see the look on his face before anyone and encouraged him. "Go ahead, Sam. Show them."

Garrett, Foo, and Roz all sat a little straighter in their seats as they waited for what was to come next while Sam, as gently as he could, said to his parents, "Mom, dad, please just watch the table and then…well…just watch."

Sam focused on the middle of the table, his thoughts went out before him and he imagined the very first thing he had ever tried to imagine – a richly colored flower like none on Earth. First, a crystal vase appeared and then a sapphire flower with wide, fragrant petals.

Sarah and George both gasped and pushed back slightly from the table.

Sam didn't stop there. He made the green leaves multiply and vines grew from the stem in elegant spirals over the top of the table. The flower petals began to open wider and the middle began to gently glow brighter and brighter until tiny glowing lights began rising into the air. Soon, the whole kitchen was alight with the magical lights floating around everyone. Sam stopped concentrating and looked at his parents. They were both standing and looking around in wonderment, the disbelief beginning to shift in their eyes.

His mom cautiously reached out to touch one of the lights and Sam concentrated once more. One of the lights floated onto her hand and took the shape of a miniscule, prancing pegasus that glowed brighter than the rest. The corner of her mouth turned up in a hesitant smile and she tenderly stroked the tiny horse with her pinky. It gave a short, tinny sounding whinny, shook its mane and flew out of her hand.

A muttering of approval was heard around the table. Sarah turned around. There were tears in her eyes. Only this time, she was smiling. Sam smiled crookedly at her and shrugged. She rushed to her son and threw her arms around him, holding tightly. She buried her face in his messy hair and said the few words that made Sam's heart fly: "I'm so sorry, Sam! I believe you."

Sam hugged her back even tighter. Another set of arms wrapped around them both and Sam heard his dad whisper, "Me too." There in the otherworldly glow of his normal kitchen, Sam felt peace in his heart. The truth was out and he'd never been so thankful for anything in his whole life.

Chapter Twelve: A Bump in the Plans

The hours that had passed since Sam gave his testimony to his parents were long, but much needed. Between Sam, Titus, and the occasional added commentary of the rest of the Imagia crew, nearly everything necessary had been disclosed to his parents. Even though they were still struggling with their own belief of the situation, there had finally been an understanding between them all.

His mom had even offered up the pizzas she's brought home. At first bite, Garrett was shocked. "This is the most delicious thing I've ever tasted!" he exclaimed.

Foo, on the other hand, sniffed it carefully and pushed it away. When Garrett pulled out his third piece and devoured it gratefully, Foo finally picked up his piece and ate it. He never admitted it, but the look he was trying to mask was enjoyment. Sam smiled and gave a piece to Titus while wolfing down his own.

Sam had regained his mental footing and offered to fix the house in a spectacular display of his power. But his dad strongly refused. He said that they'd tell everyone it was an earthquake and get it fixed the right way. How no one in the neighborhood had managed to see what happened was a miracle. Many of their neighbors were retired and traveled a lot.

Occasionally, Foo or Garrett would leave with Titus and make a round or two through the nearby woods to check for other potential problems. Sam's mom would get noticeably nervous each time they left and his dad would hold her hand or pat her leg reassuringly. The atmosphere proved to be one of caution, everyone seeming to be a bit on edge.

Sam, on the other hand, was very much at ease. He'd revealed many things to his parents, cleverly leaving out many of his injuries and pains in a desperate hope to ease their minds. He'd described everyone: Yetews, Taren, Keesa, Iggy, Arty, Enoch, Orga, and even Warg. He'd just begun excitedly trying to describe Yetews for the third time when he slapped his forehead and said, "I can't believe I didn't think of this before. Here!" He held out one hand in front of him and concentrated his gaze on his fingers. A piece of glossy paper materialized in them and he grinned. Turning the paper over, he revealed a very detailed photo of everyone he'd just finished describing. He pointed out individuals and spouted off their names.

When Sam got to Yetews, he reached into his pocket and pulled out the picture of him and his Guardian. He tapped the picture and laid it on top of the group photo. "This is me and him. Ya know…before I came back."

A look of realization came over his mom then she sighed apologetically. "Oh sweetie. I've seen this before, haven't I? Only it was different."

Sam nodded. "Yeah. I changed it before I handed it to you. Sorry."

His mom didn't say anything further on the subject. She pat his hand and smiled sadly.

As if a great weight had just lifted from him, Sam fell into a chair across from his parents. "So, that's what happened," he said in conclusion.

His mom was absentmindedly shaking her head when his dad stated, "That's what happened then, but you haven't explained why this lot," he poked a thumb towards the guests at their table, "is here now and sitting at my table…*not* in that other world."

For a moment, Sam considered lying. With the truth, he knew that it didn't matter how this conversation ended. Someone was going to be upset. Lying would make what he had to do easier. But then the moment was over and he knew that he owed his parents an honest response, if nothing else.

Sam looked between Garrett and Roz and neither of them gave any sign as to what he should do. Rather, they seemed to be equally as curious for what might be said. The weight that had lifted started to bear down on him again. He swallowed hard and then spouted out exactly what none of his friends had expected. "They came to take me back to Imagia."

Sam's mom jumped up from the chair and screeched, "*What*!?"

Sam felt his face flush. She didn't punch him in the gut, but it had definitely felt like it. He didn't expect that reaction. Apparently his dad didn't either, as his mouth was trying to get words out to calm her and they only came out in a slur of nonsense. Sam cowered slightly. He repeated himself, a little less confident this time. "They need to take me back to Imagia. It's not just about them. You saw the creature that was sent after me. They won't stop."

Garrett added, "He's right. And it not only puts him in danger, but you and the rest of this world along with it. It's more dangerous for him here in this world right now than it would be in Imagia where we are ready to fight."

Sam could see she wasn't convinced and softened his tone as he pleaded with her to understand. "Nadaroth didn't die. He's destroying everything, mom. People…Guardians…the whole world is being hurt because of him."

"I don't care! That world can take care of itself. I am not about to let anyone take you away from us again." Her tone was threatening, as was her stare at Garrett and Foo.

Garrett dared to speak. "Mrs. Little, you must understand what is at stake here. Not only is Sam powerful, but there are those – some of them right here in this room – that would die to protect him and stand by his side through it all. Our world is dying and we are desperate for any chance to save it."

"I don't care! That world means nothing to me!"

"But it does to Sam. He has friends there. And what about his Guardian? Surely after everything we've told you, you can understand how important Yetews is to him. He's your son. Certainly what is important to him is important to you." Garrett was getting angry as well.

Sarah stood a little taller. "How dare you," she hissed at him. "Of course I care about what my son cares about. But he's a child!"

Garrett pounded a fist onto the table. "You underestimate your own son! You have heard the general story but you do not know the full details of what he has been through and done. Your son is a hero and a brave young man, child or not. You, madam, give him very little credit!"

Foo elbowed Garrett sharply. He scowled up at him and in a hushed tone said, "Enough, Garrett."

Sarah looked as though she might actually explode. Her husband recognized the silence before the storm. "Sarah," George calmly cooed, "please calm down."

She looked at her husband, tears threatening to spill, hands shaking slightly. "No, George. You can't sit here and tell me that you're going to let this group of strangers just whisk our son away into some horribly dangerous place and leave us here to worry and cry about it...*again*."

He nodded. "You're absolutely right. I won't." He stood up and hugged his distraught wife. When he pulled away he met her gaze and said, "Because he won't go alone. I will be going with him."

The whole room lost control. Garrett stood up, shoving the chair into the wall behind him. Foo jumped up and tried to talk him down. Roz was helping out by trying to explain that Sam needed to straighten this out without the commotion and that it was making things worse. Titus was arguing to Sam about what this could mean and Sam's mom was yelling about how ridiculous the whole thing was as his dad was trying to explain how it was the best thing for everyone.

Sam stood there in the middle of the chaos trying to figure out what had just happened. Everyone was fighting and yelling and all he wanted to do was run away from it all until he didn't have to deal with anything stressful anymore. The voices around him began to muffle and he heard ringing in his ears. He closed his eyes and his heart started beating faster. He didn't want this. He tried to calm down and thought of the green forests of Imagia's southern lands. It was quiet –

peaceful. The sun filtered down through the lush canopy while birds fluttered by and he could almost smell the fragrance of exotic flowers. It was the place where his first gateway brought him.

He felt himself calming down as he completely tuned the voices of anger out around him. But then he felt a pair of hands shaking him hard. “Sam!” It was Roz. “Snap out of it!”

Sam’s eyes burst open and all around him the forest in his mind was in the process of taking over the room. He gasped and concentrated on reversing the damage. Just as quickly as the room changed, it returned back to its original state. Though it wasn’t his intent, what happened had done one good thing. The room was quiet. Granted, they were all staring at him. His dad was protectively holding his mom and both of them looked at Sam as though he were trying to hurt them.

Sam looked down at his shoes. “I’m sorry,” he squeaked out. “I was so mad. I…I just wanted everyone to stop fighting and I got lost in my own thoughts.” He looked over to Roz who was smiling crooked. He’d seen this before. Sam then directed his next words at Garrett and Foo. “It’s been happening more. My power has gotten…” He trailed off, not sure how to finish his sentence.

Titus finished it for him. “His power has gotten much stronger. Sometimes he loses control like that when his emotions are high.”

George went over to put his hands on his son’s shoulders. “I know it will be a lot to take in, but I’m going with you. Regardless of what you’ve been through, I am still your father. I’m not asking permission.”

Sam was touched. But he knew the truth of the situation. As if mirroring Sam’s own thoughts, Garrett walked over to them – much calmer.

Garrett squinted thoughtfully and took a deep breath. “Mr. Little, I get what you want, but you need to understand something very important. You can’t –“

Sam interrupted him, eyes wide. “No! My dad said he’s going and that’s the final word on it.” He turned where his face couldn’t be seen by his parents and gave a very meaningful look, hopeful that he was understood. He knew why his dad couldn’t go, but his dad didn’t. And Sam wanted to keep it that way.

It took a moment, but Garrett understood. He looked at Sam, nodded once, and then nodded at George. "Very well. We'll need to leave soon. The morning after next." He was fairly certain that Sam knew exactly what he was doing and hoped that was the answer he needed to give.

With a solemn smile, he agreed and turned back to his dad. "Ok?"

The smile his dad gave back was lacking confidence, but he tried. "Agreed. I'll get everything worked out for your mom and be ready by then."

Sarah sobbed loudly. "No!" She shouted. "You're not leaving me behind. No husband and no son? No. I'm going too!"

Sam could hear Garrett sigh and was certain he heard Foo use some rather unfriendly language.

Just as Sam was sure things were about to get crazy again, his dad put a stop to it instantly. There were no harsh words. He simply walked up to her and rubbed her arms lovingly. "Honey, you know you can't. It's not safe for you in your condition."

Sam heard those words and he simply said, "Condition? What condition? Mom, are you okay? Are you sick?" The worry was heavy in his voice.

Both his parents turned to him and the whole room was thick with concern. His mom's lip started quivering. George saw this and started to answer for her when she put her hand out and squeezed his fingers. "It's okay," she said. "I'll tell him."

Sam was worried. "Tell me what?"

"Well," she began, "we didn't want to tell you yet because we weren't sure how you'd take it. Sam, sweetie?" She reached out to him, holding his hands. "You see, the thing that we want to tell you is that I'm pregnant. You're going to be a big brother."

She smiled at him, tears forgetting their boundaries now.

Sam's stomach did two back-flips and then somersaulted across the room. His smile wouldn't stop growing.

This changed everything.

Chapter Thirteen: Efficiently Inconspicuous

The words, 'big brother', kept flying through Sam's mind as he walked Garrett and the others to the borders of the forest. He couldn't have heard news so amazing. All his life he'd wanted a brother or sister and now it was really going to happen. His mind was racing. He was also quite silent.

His parents had agreed to let Sam walk his friends to the forest. His mom had suggested they all sleep inside, but it was decided that it was safer to keep watch through the night from outside. Sam's silence was unreadable by the others. So when they reached a safe distance into the forest, far from the sight of others, Garrett turned to Sam and simply said, "So?"

Sam set the lantern down that his dad gave to him and replied, "So what?"

He raised his eyebrow and waited.

"Oh. Sorry. It's been a long day." After an understanding nod from Garrett, he said, "It's simple, isn't it? I'm going back to Imagia with you."

Garrett exchanged a concerned look with Foo. He shook his head slowly and cautiously began, "It's not that, actually. About your father…"

Sam cut him off quickly. "I know he can't go."

"Then why did you tell him that he could?"

Sam simply said, "Because *he* doesn't know that." He turned around and walked to the nearest tree, sliding down to the forest floor with his back against the trunk.

"Sam," Garrett started, "I don't think your dad is going to understand any of this. Do you really think that he will just miraculously change his mind in two days?"

Titus walked up to Sam and agreed with Garrett. "He's right. You know you have to tell him the truth."

Roz chimed in next. "Even I know that this trip will end with only one human returning to Imagia."

He didn't want to hear any of this now. Four voices began to discuss the finer details of why and how. But Sam already had the answer. Suddenly, he blurted it out, silencing everyone instantly. "That's why we aren't leaving in two days. We're leaving tonight."

Four sets of questioning eyes were staring at him now. He had gotten their undivided attention.

Garrett started a small fire while Sam explained everything. They all sat around the warm glow in the cool night air, listening intently. It was fairly simple, but required good timing.

Sam explained that when his parents went to sleep, they'd leave within the hour after. They'd meet up in the forest and head towards the place where Sam had heard of on the news with the mysterious disappearances. It was their best bet and seemed to be in the right direction that Foo was feeling pulled towards.

The problem wasn't making the plan. It was executing it. Everyone voiced their concerns on being able to do this without his parents knowing and Garrett kept bringing up the fact that Sam had just gotten some very emotional news that might make him not want to follow through.

Despite what anyone said, Sam was certain that everything would go fine as long as they trusted that he knew what he was doing. And as far as his 'emotional' issues went, his only reply was, "I know what I'm doing," said in frustration.

The forest was quiet around them. Sam had promised his parents that he wouldn't be more than an hour away from the house. Despite the happenings of the evening, it was more than obvious that both his parents had reservations about the company that their son was keeping and what they wanted with him. There was some quiet conversation happening between the others as Sam merely sat in silence, thinking about what was about to happen. He was wondering if Garrett might be right. What if in the end, he couldn't follow through? What if he chickened out? Either way, someone was going to get disappointed.

On the first hand, going to Imagia meant that his mom and dad were going to be heartbroken to find him gone in the morning. He was going to do everything possible to make it easier for them, but how could they not be devastated again? The only comfort Sam had in the sea of his worries was the fact that they wouldn't be alone this time. Soon there would be another kid for them to love and take care of.

Another child.

His replacement.

That thought stung. He didn't want to dwell on it anymore.

So he thought of his other option – staying. Imagia had barely a chance as is. Nadaroth wouldn't give up until Imagia was completely under his control. Yetews would be hurt that Sam chose to stay, but he'd understand. At least that was Sam's hope. The whole world of Imagia had risked so much to bring him back. How could he let them down and send Garrett and Foo back empty handed? Given enough time, Nadaroth would destroy every Guardian – Yetews included. Staying home would be a devastating blow to an entire world.

Sam furrowed his brow. He couldn't help but be angry. They put their hope in him. And he was just a kid. Was it really his fault if they were foolish enough to base the fate of a world on him? He didn't ask for this. As his thoughts went down this road, he could feel himself grinding his teeth. He slowly relaxed his jaw and decided that he was done arguing with his own thoughts.

As if having a conversation with someone else, he pushed himself off the ground and muttered, "It doesn't matter. The decision's done." He brushed the forest off his pants and said louder, "Come on, Titus. We'd better head back."

Titus had been in the midst of conversation with Garrett and Foo at the time, but got up without any hesitation. Roz also joined them, as he had to go and retrieve the rest of his stuff for the journey.

Before they headed back towards the house, Sam turned and reminded them, "Don't forget. As soon as I send Titus, be ready. It'll be a few hours, but we can't wait or this won't work." He waited for a nod from Garrett and left, Titus trotting just ahead of him and Roz at his side.

They had just left earshot of the others when Roz looked down at Sam. Sam could feel his eye on him and looked up and grinned half-heartedly. He'd gotten to know Roz really well by now and knew what he was thinking. Before he could utter a word, Sam said, "I know. This is crazy, right?"

Roz chuckled. "You said it. Not me."

"Yeah. But it is."

Roz pat Sam on the shoulder and grinned. "As long as you are doing what you know is right by you, then I don't think it's crazy at all." He chuckled again. "Of course, that is being said after a psychotic creature ripped your house apart and tried to kill you while you used a mystical power of imagination to fight it in the wrong world."

Sam laughed too. He wasn't sure what it was about Roz, but it was very easy to talk to him. He didn't feel like he needed to hide his thoughts when he was around. The house grew closer and Sam slowed to a stop. When Roz turned to him, Sam scrunched his face up and asked, "I am doing the right thing. Right?"

Thinking for a second, he simply said, "Right for one may be wrong for another. So you just have to ask yourself, is it right for you?"

For a moment, he stood in silence. Thoughts of Imagia in ruin ran amok through his mind. His parents had always taught him that even when it hurts to do it, you should always do the right thing. He nodded slowly and looked at his friend. "Yeah. It is."

Smiling, Roz replied, "That's all that matters." Roz clapped him on the shoulder again. "Now," he went on, "I'd best get my things." He walked off, but turned and said, "Oh, and Sam?"

"Yeah?"

"I know time is short, but I think you have a friend at school that would appreciate knowing that you will be leaving."

With that, Roz left and Sam suddenly remembered Lizzy. He started running towards the house. He had something he needed to do.

* * * * * * * * * * *

Sam ran into the house, and the back door fell completely off the hinges, clattering to the ground loudly. His dad came running into the kitchen, eyes wide, carrying the lamp that had been sitting next to the TV. A look of relief washed over him when he saw his son. “Oh geez, Sam.” He lowered the lamp. “I thought…” he trailed off, rubbing a hand over his chest nervously.

Sam knew that none of what had happened over the course of the day could be easy on his parents. He glanced quickly to his dad’s hand and could see it shaking slightly. Suddenly, he knew that his dad being left behind was a good thing. It was a sign of his dad’s nature that the only weapon he could muster was a small lamp that would barely do damage to a cat if thrown.

“Sorry, dad.” His dad put the lamp down on the counter. “It was an accident. I should be able to fix the house soon. I’m just a bit tired still. Been a long day, I guess.”

At first his dad seemed angry at this. “What did I tell you? We’ll take care of it the normal way.” His dad grinned when he saw that Sam was concerned. “Don’t worry about it. Nothing a good hammer and nails can’t fix.”

“No. I meant that I could –“

“I know what you meant,” he interrupted a bit harshly which Sam winced at. “I’m sorry. It’s all…a bit much to take in. I’m sure I’ll get used to it in Imaginatia.”

Sam snorted out a laugh.

Confused, his dad asked, “What?”

“Imagia,” Sam corrected him. “You said it wrong. It was just kind of funny.”

“Oh. Sorry. As you said. It’s been a long day.” He smiled back. “But I’ll get it right next time.”

Sam’s face fell slightly. He didn’t catch himself fast enough and his dad noticed. Next time was never going to happen and the realization was barely starting to hit him.

“I know you’re worried about me coming, Sam, but I can’t let you go alone. Not this time. You came home to us broken. I will make sure that we both come home again safely to your mom.”

"But dad, what about mom and the new baby? Don't you think someone needs to be here for them?" Sam asked this hopefully, wanting to find some way to convince his dad to stay.

His dad shook his head. "She won't be alone. We've talked about it and we're going to arrange to have your aunt Josephine come and stay with her. She isn't married and her job will allow her to work here. We're going to tell her that we have to take you to a special doctor in another country that can help you remember what happened to you. It's all planned out." There may have been a crooked smile on his dad's face, but Sam knew that he had his own reservations about the whole idea.

That settled it. There was no way Sam was going to be able to convince his dad to stay here unless Sam agreed to stay as well. Instead of fight against this, Sam knew that it was best to just let it go and move forward with his own plan. He put on his best fake smile and tried not to sound over excited. "That will work great. And then maybe by the time we get back, I'll have a new baby brother…or sister."

"Brother."

Sam stopped short. "Wait. What?"

His dad was beaming. "We weren't sure if we were going to say anything until he's born, but the circumstances being what they are, you might as well know. We found out early. It's a boy."

Whatever Sam was struggling with didn't seem to matter for the moment. "A brother! That's awesome, dad!"

"I know! We never thought we would have another child, but your mom always wanted to try. It's been rough, but she's doing good now." He looked behind him cautiously and then said, "And just between you and me, that's part of the reason she's been a little crazy lately."

Sam grinned. His joy was genuine. But it was abruptly shelved when his dad mentioned leaving again.

"Hopefully we won't miss him being born, but your aunt is really good with this stuff. And your mom is actually kind of excited to have her here."

"Yeah." Sam felt sick inside. The way they were talking was as if they were planning a full itinerary for a vacation that was certain to only take a few months. He wanted to say, *'Because obviously, this is just a quick trip. Run to Imagia, defeat the bad guy, and be home in time for Christmas.'* But he didn't. He just smiled and it was enough to convince his dad.

"Sounds good." He rustled Sam's hair. "I think we'd better all turn in." He yawned loudly and stretched his arms over his head. "I've got a lot to do tomorrow to get ready."

His dad was half way through the door to the living room when Sam quickly asked, "Hey, dad?"

He turned back around and raised his eyebrows questioningly.

"If I leave a letter for Lizzy, do you think that mom would take it to her when I...er…we're gone?"

"Of course she would. Now you'd best get to bed. We've got a lot to do if we're leaving in just two days."

Something gut-punched Sam. Or at least it felt like it had. And this, he was sure, was his conscience. Guilt was never fun.

* * * * * * * * * * *

Sam had been lying in his bed, fully dressed, for at least an hour. He'd occasionally glanced out his window, straining his eyes in the dark in hopes of seeing the fire's glow somewhere in the woods. In between his nervous glances to the door and his impatient lying on the bed, he would take a glimpse towards the desk in his room that had two envelopes on it with the name "Lizzy" scribbled across the top one. The second letter lay hidden beneath the other, the envelope blank.

The letter to Lizzy was the easier of the two to write. He wanted to call her or go to her house and talk to her face to face, but ultimately, he knew it wasn't going to happen. It wasn't feasible. He got out of bed and sat down at his desk. He opened the letter to reread it again, making sure it was good. He just hoped that it explained enough without scaring her:

Dear Lizzy.

Hey. I know you probably are going to end this letter with more questions than answers. but it's the best I could do. I guess when you read this. I won't be there for you to punch me in the arm. (which kinda hurts. you know?) and so I'll just come right out and say it. I've been lying to you since I came back. The truth? I never lost my memory. I remember everything. But what I remember sounds crazy. Especially if I try to explain it all in a letter. Really I just need you to know that the place I was at all those years ago...well...I have to go back. I'm not crazy. I'm sure you'll think I am. And that's ok. Something happened today and my mom and dad know everything now. Well, almost everything. I'll make sure they answer your questions if you want to know more. Mostly, I just wanted to say goodbye. You deserve that. You're a good friend and I'll miss you. I hope to see you again someday, but I don't know what's going to happen. This letter is pretty lame. Sorry. I just can't write everything down and chance that someone else will read it. It wouldn't be ~~smart~~ safe. Just remember one thing. No matter what anyone says, you aren't crazy. You never were.

The truth is, the place I went to is amazing! But now they need me back. I'll be okay. Promise. I have to go. A lot of friends are depending on what I can do. I wish I could say more but I have to leave now. If I ever come back home again, I hope you don't hate me. Thanks for everything.

Bye Lizzy,
Your Friend,
Sam

As he finished reading it, he grabbed the pen off his desk. It wasn't enough. She had to know one more thing. He started scribbling.

P.S. You know your dream about me and you? It wasn't a dream. It was real. That's where I was and it's time for me to go back.

He put the piece of paper back in the envelope and pulled out the other letter. This one was harder to write for him. He would never admit it to anyone, but signing this letter was one of the hardest things he had to do. He hadn't reread this letter yet. His hands were shaking and Titus noticed.

"Sam?" he asked cautiously. "Are you alright?"

He hesitated a moment too long to be convincing. "Yeah. I hear dad snoring. It's time." A shaky breath and then he whispered, "Go."

Titus didn't move towards the window, but rather closer to Sam. "Are you sure this is what you want?"

Closing his eyes tight, he merely nodded. If he tried to speak again, words might fail him.

Against his better judgment, Titus put a paw on Sam's leg and nosed him gently in the arm, rubbing his head affectionately next to his hand. Though Sam knew his friend meant well, he was sure that if he reacted more, he'd fall apart. He scratched behind Titus' ears. "Go. I'll be there soon." His voice cracked on the last word.

With that, Titus disappeared through the window and into the night. Sam looked at the letter and began to read.

Dear Mom and Dad,

I know that when you get this letter, you're going to be really mad. It's okay. I understand because I'm kinda mad at myself. But you have to let me explain. I didn't want to do this. I wanted to give you hugs and tell you I'd be ok. But this was the only way. You wouldn't have let me go if you knew the truth. Dad, I know you wanted to come, but the truth is...you can't. I wish you could, but a gateway will only let one person through and then it will close. It's impossible for you to go with me. That person that goes through has to be me. There's no other way. I'm sorry I didn't say anything to you, but you were so cool to want to come with me and...I just didn't have the heart. Sorry.

Mom, I know I'm only fourteen (almost). But if I told you everything I've seen and done...you'd know that I can do this. Kids aren't meant to stay in Imagia for as long as I did. When you're there for too long, Imagia has a way of changing you. I wish I could explain, but I don't know how. But please know that I'll be ok. I have a lot of friends there. They'll watch out for me. I promise to be careful. I wish you both could understand how big this is. It sounds crazy to say this about myself...just some regular kid...but I'm important to them. You've seen what I can do. I don't know how or why, but it happened to me. And now a whole world is dying and I might be the best chance it has. I wish there was another way, but there isn't. The truth is, that being gone from Imagia is almost harder than being gone from here. Hiding like I've been has been hard. I think I might be dangerous in our world. Something happened to me when I was there. Even if that world wasn't in trouble, going back feels...right.

You both taught me that no matter how much it might hurt, you should always follow your heart and do the right thing. So that's what I'm doing. I hope you understand. I'm sorry for all the times I lied and for leaving like this. Don't try and find me. You won't be able to. I'll be in Imagia by the time you get this. Please tell my new baby brother that his big brother loves him. I love you both so much and I'll miss you. I have to go now. Imagia needs me.

Love,
Sam

P.S. When this is done...I will never stop trying to come home to you. I promise.

P.P.S. Please give Lizzy her letter and answer all her questions. She deserves to have answers. You can trust her.

P.P.P.S. Titus is coming with me. I think he's just happy that he doesn't have to eat dog food again.

As he finished reading, his eyes lost focus as they began to tear up. Though he knew it was the right thing, it was harder than he'd thought. Whether because of embarrassment or pride, he didn't want to cry. But what no one could see wouldn't hurt anyone. He blinked hard, allowing two tears to fall onto the letter. Wiping his eyes with his sleeve, he folded the paper and slipped it into the envelope. He took the pen one last time and wrote "Mom and Dad" on it.

His backpack was shoved under his bed so his parents wouldn't suspect anything. He yanked it out and set it down. Leaving for Imagia would be different this time. He'd had time to pack his essentials, some food he'd managed to sneak out when his parents weren't looking, and a few things that would remind him of home. He grabbed the blue worry-stone off his nightstand. His mom had given it to him a couple of years ago to help him when he struggled with everything. He slipped it into his pocket with the pocketknife that his dad gave him last year on his birthday then slung his backpack over his shoulders.

He picked up the letters and took one last look around his room. His heart was heavy, but he was ready. Now it was time for his last goodbye. It was risky, but he'd never be able to do this without trying.

Careful to avoid every creak and groan of the floor and doors, he tiptoed through the house to his parents' room. The door was closed. He put his ear up to the wood and listened. He could hear two distinct snores. Though the snoring had always annoyed him, he was thankful for it tonight. Closing his eyes, he imagined. The door disappeared and he walked through to his sleeping parents. Making no noise, he stood over his mom and dad and smiled. Through the dark, he concentrated on their faces and memorized every detail from their messy hair to the drool slipping out the corner of his dad's mouth.

This was it. Carefully, Sam placed the letters next to his mom's reading glasses and imagined a picture of the three of them together, smiling. He propped it up next to the lamp and closed his eyes again. He could feel the tears threatening to form. He took one more risk and leaned over his mom, gently kissing her on the forehead.

It hurt. He didn't think that it would hurt so bad, but his heart beat in his ears and without warning, the tears that threatened, became reality and one slipped out, splashing onto his mom's cheek.

He gasped quietly and stepped back as she stirred.

Blinking, his mom sat up with a small jolt and stared directly at where Sam was standing.

Sam didn't budge. He barely breathed. They were making eye contact, but only Sam knew this. He'd imagined an invisible wall in front of him that only he could see through. It blocked out everything around her so that all she thought she saw was the room around her, just like normal.

After looking around for a moment, sure she'd been woken by something, she rubbed her forehead, yawned loudly, then laid back down. She poked his dad in the side, turning him over to stop the snoring, and quickly fell back to sleep.

Sam dared not make a sound as he backed out of the room slowly. When he got through the door, he whispered, "By mom. Bye dad. Love you." Then he imagined it back to the way it was with one change. Next to the letter, he made a planter out of which grew three of his sapphire flowers – two large and one smaller. He navigated through the dark and left through the rubble of the kitchen.

He was halfway through the backyard when he stopped suddenly. Despite what his dad said, he placed all of his concentration on the house. The rubble moved silently around and shifted and morphed until the house was perfect – inside and out. It was as if nothing had happened. He smiled – a bittersweet gesture – and then turned on his heel, running full tilt towards the forest.

Through the dark, he felt his life in this world fading away. There was no turning back now. Four years ago, his feet glued to the ground in fear of going into this same forest. If he stopped now, he was sure the same would happen tonight.

The world blurred around Sam as he ran, the only noise in the spring air being the sound of his breath. Suddenly the tall grass shifted and trees were towering on every side of him. Just as Sam was realizing that he had no idea which direction to run, a voice on his right startled him. "This way, Sam."

Turning to the voice, Sam saw Roz holding a flashlight that was pointing into the trees. The glow of the light that reflected off his face showed the dark of his eye-patch.

It barely took two minutes to reach the others. Roz, despite being taller and older, was having difficulty keeping Sam's hurried pace. Both huffing from the effort, they reached Foo, Titus, and Garrett who were all patiently gathered around the dying embers of the fire.

"You made it!" Garrett cheerfully chimed. "Were there any problems?"

Sam was clutching at a stitch in his side, wincing. "No. But we need to leave. Now."

Everyone could sense the urgency in those words. There were no objections. Foo kicked dirt over the remains of the fire and each one picked up their meager belongings, indicating they were ready to go.

Garrett addressed Foo. "Which way do we go?"

"North from here. Follow me."

Titus trotted to Foo's side and stated, "We'll need to keep good speed so we can be sure George and Sarah can't follow behind."

Foo grunted his agreement and began to lead the party deeper into the woods. He didn't get far before Sam stopped cold. "No," he said. "We'll use the night as cover. We can get there a whole lot faster if we fly."

With a questioning look, Garrett was about to ask how, but ended up standing there with his mouth ajar as the whooshing sound of feathers on air filled the forest around them. Three falcons roughly the sizes of small cars were expertly navigating through the canopy and then landed on the ground next to everyone. They lowered themselves to the ground, waiting for their passengers.

Not a word was spoken through the silent awe as they each in turn scrambled atop the feathered backs. Each bird had a leather harness to hold onto. Titus opted to ride with Roz, while Foo sat with Garrett. Sam rode alone. As if a whisper on a breeze, they were gone. Sam hollered to Foo, "You lead the way. We need to make it to the forests in the Rockies before the sun comes up." Foo nodded and urged his falcon to fly faster.

Now the trio of unearthly sized falcons flew northward in silence. Sam looked behind him and strained his eyes. For a moment, he saw the lights from his street illuminating his house, the smallest point of light in the dark. And then it was gone.

All of a sudden Sam was thankful it was dark and that he was riding alone. At least no one could see him cry.

Chapter Fourteen: A Familiar Fight

It had been a long night, but the falcons were true to their calling and made it to the Rocky Mountain Forest just as the sun was peeking over the horizon. Foo had no way of honing in on his gateway from the skies and needed to get to the ground to feel which direction he was being pulled in.

Once they had landed in the forest, Sam managed to morph the falcons into smaller versions of themselves so as not to freak out anyone who might come across them. As the sun rose above the mountains, they were forced to figure out which way might be the best direction to go next. Foo could feel a gateway calling to him, but found he was strangely being pulled in two separate directions. He was getting frustrated and everyone could sense the situation becoming more urgent for him.

Sam was the first to make a suggestion that only half of them agreed was a good idea. Eventually, they decided their next course of action, hopeful that they'd get a better idea which direction to go. None of them had thought much further than actually reaching the forest, as they'd been nearly certain that Foo wouldn't have a problem finding the gateway.

Sam, being in a new state and far from familiar territory, convinced the others that they should go to the town from the news story he'd heard on the radio. If the hikers that had gone missing were related, (as they thought was the case) then it was their best bet to find the gateway. Garrett was hesitant. In fact, Sam actually thought he looked a little afraid at the prospect of going into civilization. Though, he couldn't understand why.

Roz, on the other hand, was quite happy to proceed. He had become very comfortable traversing this world and wasn't afraid to look for answers with the people in the town. He'd admitted to Sam how much he'd truly been enjoying many things like TV and junk food.

In the end, for obvious reasons, Foo stayed in the forest, well hidden from any wandering passersby. Titus made sure to keep track of the scent trail of each of them so no one would get lost and then the four of them set out into the town and began searching for clues.

The town was quaint, with shops of all kinds down the main street. It obviously relied heavily on tourists, as every shop had magnets and coffee mugs with the town's name plastered on them.

They'd just spent several minutes talking to an elderly couple about the missing hikers. It had been just fifteen miles east from this town where the last reports were. After thanking the nice couple, Sam looked fairly relieved when he said to the others, "I guess Foo got us pretty close after all. Cool."

Garrett, still looking more nervous than necessary, looked around cautiously and said, "Good. Let's get back to the forest and start looking. I don't know how you could feel comfortable here. I feel like something is watching us." He looked anxiously behind him at a shop that was stuffed with t-shirts bearing wildlife of every kind.

Sam rolled his eyes and wondered how long Garrett had been away from this world. He could kind of understand being uncomfortable, but replied anyways. "You're just like that because you had to leave all your weapons with Foo so that we won't look like crazy people."

Titus, who had to remain quiet for this part of the journey, glanced around. When there was no one within earshot, he quietly said, "Follow me. We aren't that far from Foo."

The sidewalk that they were on was at an incline and the road in-between was narrow and busy. They waked quickly, Sam trailing in the back while Titus and Garret led. Sam, having not been to Colorado since he was seven years old, was enjoying sightseeing. He stopped to look into a window that had intricate woodcarvings from ceiling to floor in the shapes of trees, animals, and everything in-between.

The others were in the process of crossing the road. Roz called back, “Come on, Sam! Need to keep moving!”

“Coming!” Sam hollered back. As he passed the alley to his left, he caught a glimpse of something out of the corner of his eye and stopped. The alley was dark and had several stacks of crates next to a large garbage bin. In the darkest shadow at the back of the alley, there was a shadowy figure. When Sam squinted, he saw it move. He stepped back suddenly and gasped.

The shape was familiar to him in a way that made his stomach flip-flop. As he watched it, he took a hesitant step forward and saw the distinct outline of two humps, each covered in dark hair. Another step forward and the shape began to move towards him and two eyes met with his own. He couldn’t believe what he was seeing. It was Yetews! He was certain of it.

Sam took another step into the alley and was just about to disappear into the shadows when he heard Garrett yelling at him in panic.

“Sam! Get back!” Garrett shouted, franticly trying to cross the street through the busy cars.

Sam watched him, confused. Then he heard the three words that he’d heard before during his days in Imagia.

“It’s a trap!” Garrett vaulted over a car that nearly plowed over him only to be stopped by another screeching to a halt.

For him to risk such a move Sam became genuinely concerned and suddenly his stomach stopped flip-flopping and simply dropped. The hairs on the back of his neck prickled uncomfortably and he turned back around to Yetews. Several emotions tore through him in a very short time. He felt stupid for putting himself in a familiar position, embarrassed that he could think this was anything but fake, and most importantly, terrified beyond measure.

Whatever he foolishly had assumed was Yetews, was most definitely not him. It must have sensed that its prey was about to escape. It launched itself at Sam who managed to leap sideways out of its path. It tumbled into a small outdoor souvenir display. Postcards and trinkets flew everywhere.

The creature was the same shade of black as Yetews, but now resembled an oversized bear that had several otherworldly qualities about it. For one, it had a pair of ram-like horns that twisted down each side of its head. It also had a set of bony plates running down its back that reminded Sam of a stegosaurus.

Having missed his target, the bear-beast tumbled awkwardly into a parked car setting off a high-pitched alarm. By the time it gathered its senses, Sam was already up and running full tilt down the sidewalk. He had no idea how fast the beast could run or if it was gaining. He just prayed madly that Garrett and Roz were close behind to help him.

People on the sidewalk were screaming and running hysterically away from the wild animal. While some were simply screaming in terror, others were yelling, "Bear!" Sam had no idea where he was or where he was going, but he saw a sign ahead of him that read *Ultimate Outdoorsmen* and he made for the door. He jerked it open and burst through, hopeful that the creature wouldn't know how to open doors with its bear-like paws. He ran through the aisles, now void of people, of what was thankfully a fairly large hunting and camping store. He ducked behind a huge tent display and tried to catch his breath.

A loud shattering sound echoed through the shop. Sam muttered sarcastically to himself, "Great! It doesn't *need* doors, Sam. You idiot!" What few customers and employees that had been in the store had already ran out in sheer panic towards any exit they could find, fearing for their lives.

The store was empty and Sam bit his cheek, attempting to not utter a sound. He could hear it sniffing and grunting, probably trying to pick up Sam's scent. He was waiting for it to let loose some spine-tingling roar, but it never came. There was no real way to know where it was.

All the while wondering where his counterparts were and why they weren't in here kicking this creatures butt, Sam unfroze enough to look through a small crack in the display of tents. He could see the beast and it was still close to the shattered window. The usual creatures Sam had battled were mostly the same, brute force always their main weapon. This beast, on the other hand, was stalking slowly, watching for movement. It was listening. This creature was smarter than the others. It was downright frightening.

Sam looked around, desperate for anything. He saw a group of rocks that were making up a fake campfire next to him and he cautiously picked one up. He took a deep breath and hurled it as hard and quietly as he could across the store, willing it to hit something breakable. To his relief, it made direct contact with a display of outdoor cookware, knocking loudly into the metal.

It worked. He watched the creature bare its yellowed-teeth and then plow loudly through the store, knocking everything out of the way as it went. Sam was just about to run towards the door when he heard the tinkling of a bell. Someone had walked through the door. He peeked out and saw Garrett and Roz.

Thankful as he was for seeing them, he also realized how defenseless they all were. Unfortunately, the creature didn't care whether or not they could defend themselves. It b-lined straight for them. They scattered, both running in separate directions. The beast chased after Garrett.

Sam took the opportunity amongst the chaos to run towards Roz, who spotted him and motioned for him to follow. They both leapt over the front counter and ducked out of view. Now Sam was worried for Garrett. He whispered, "We're in a hunting store. Where the heck are all the weapons to kill this thing with?" he asked exasperated.

Roz gave him a strange look somewhere between confusion and dumbfounded.

"What?" Sam hissed.

Shaking his head disbelievingly, he whispered back, "You have the power of imagination, Sam." He raised his eyebrows, his one eye waiting for Sam to catch on.

He slapped himself in the forehead. "Oh geez. Sorry! Not my best day."

They both heard the sound of Garrett yelling out followed by the sound of several displays being loudly knocked around. Both Sam and Roz's faces went a shade paler and they both looked at one another. Roz pointed up, indicating that they should peek over the counter and Sam nodded in agreement. Roz held his hand up and counted off on his fingers: One, two, three.

Both noiselessly peered over the counter but neither could see the beast. Roz whispered, “Where did it go? Do you see Garrett?”

Sam merely shook his head and shrugged.

“Okay,” Roz whispered, “imagine me up something good. I’m going out.”

With a quick look of concentration, a sturdy bow appeared with a quiver of silver tipped arrows and then a hilted sword joined the pile. Roz grinned widely. “Very nice.” He lifted the sword and shifted it in his hand, feeling the weight and balance of the blade. He sheathed it, strapped it around his waist, and threw the quiver over his shoulders. Grabbing the bow and one arrow, he nodded once to Sam and his mouth turned up at one corner in a nervous grin. He said, “Watch my back,” and then leaped the counter stealthily.

Being in this situation was a small reminder to Sam of what he was going to be up against when he got back to Imagia, and it made his nerves prickle. Though, he couldn’t tell if the prickling was for excitement or fear. He watched as Roz treaded lightly through the upturned store. There was still no sign of the beast.

Sam, feeling a little braver, stood up and decided to follow Roz. A beast that size couldn’t have been missed. It was a bull in a china shop. If it was after Sam, then there was a good chance that it went out the backdoor thinking that Sam wasn’t there any more.

He started zigzagging through the maze of upturned displays when he saw Roz drop to the floor unexpectedly. Sam stopped. Roz had found Garrett unconscious on the floor and hollered, “It’s Garrett. He’s knocked out, but okay.”

Sam blew out a sigh of relief, but it was short-lived. Without any warning, Roz leapt at Sam and yelled, “Above you!” He hit Sam directly and knocked him out of the way just in time. The beast had dropped from where it was clinging to the wooden rafters on the ceiling. It had been camouflaged in the wood and shadows. In landed right where Sam had been standing. It was completely unconcerned with Roz and bared its teeth, rumbling low when it spotted Sam on the floor.

Roz pulled back the string of his bow, aimed and then let loose an arrow that hit the creature in the front flank. It howled in pain and redirected its attention at him. The two of them began to circle, Roz aiming to shoot again and the beast planning to dodge the shot. Three arrows later, the beast dove at Roz, missing him but managing to disarm him of the bow. A glint of light on metal shone bright as the sword appeared. Roz took his stance and stepped forward.

As if the sword was a stick, the beast swat it out of Roz's hand and it flew across the store, Roz flying backwards with it. Sam was getting closer to the two. He watched as the beast leapt, mouth open and ready to kill. Sam stopped dead in his tracks and screamed, "Roz!' As the word left his mouth, an enormous boulder materialized and dropped out of midair, landing on the beast, its back breaking with a sickening crack.

Roz was hastily scooting away from the still chomping jaws of the creature. Shock was his only expression. A quick sense of relief swept over Sam and he imagined another sword next to Roz's hand. When his hand met the cool steel of the hilt, he wrapped his fingers around it, stood up, and rushed the creature, impaling it without a second thought.

Sam bent over, put his hands on his knees, and relief washed through him. He only took a moment and then ran over to join his friend.

They both looked down at the dead beast. Sam looked at Roz. "You saved my life." There was a hint of surprise in his tone.

Roz shrugged as if it was no big deal. "Of course I did. That's what friends are for, right?" Spoken as if it was the most obvious thing in the world.

Sam laughed quietly. "Yeah."

Roz then said, "But while we're on the subject," he pointed at the impressively sized boulder and pointed at it, "that was…well…epic!"

Such a word coming out of a Defender from Imagia made Sam laugh out loud. "Thanks!"

"I think this requires one of these," Roz said as he held up a closed fist towards Sam.

Sam beamed. He held his fist up and they bumped them together. After that, he looked over at Garrett who was groaning and stirring. "Is he okay?"

"Yeah. I'll go help him up."

The whole ordeal hadn't lasted more than five minutes. But that was all it took for police sirens to start wailing in the distance. Sam went cold. He looked around the store and then at the creature. He had to do something quick. Scrunching his face up in deep concentration, he began to morph the scene. It shivered and shifted then suddenly the bear-beast was simply just a bear and the boulder was a small rock.

The sirens were getting closer.

Out of nowhere, Titus came running up to them and barked, "The police are just down the road. We have to get out of here!"

Roz held a hand out for Garrett and helped him off the floor. "You alright?"

Holding his head with one hand, he answered, "Yeah. I've had worse."

"We have to get out of here before the police see us," Sam ordered.

Though Garrett looked a bit confused, they all agreed and ran through the back entrance marked 'fire exit only' and headed as fast as they could towards the forest.

Sam only hoped that his grizzly bear was convincing enough. He also wondered if grizzly bears were even native here. Either way, he was sure this was going to be on the nightly news. He'd be lucky if his parents didn't put the pieces together when they saw it.

If things weren't dire before, they were now. They had to get to Imagia – fast.

Lungs burning, sides aching, and gasping for air, the four of them made it into the shadows of the forest, running desperately for their Guardian comrade. Titus led, picking up Foo's scent effortlessly.

Once they were all reunited, they paused briefly, safely away from the eyes of the city. All of them, tired from the ordeal, took a few moments and looked guardedly around.

Sam, clutching at yet another stitch in his side, complained, "Man! This is *not*…how I thought…this trip would go!" He couldn't seem to catch his breath yet.

Foo was demanding that someone explain what happened. Garrett, still dizzy from being knocked unconscious, tried to fill him in regardless of the world spinning around him. "We were attacked." Garrett watched as Foo's eyes went wide. "It was waiting for us. Rather, it was waiting for Sam. I know this sounds crazy," he said as he cast a sideways glance at Sam, "but I could have sworn it knew that Sam was going to be here."

"Wonderful." The others couldn't miss Foo's obvious sarcasm. "This just keeps getting better and better, doesn't it?" He threw an almost accusing look in Sam's direction that didn't go unnoticed by him. "Then what happened?"

Rubbing at the small, tender knot on the back of his head, Garrett simply pointed at the others and said, "You'll have to ask them. I was…well…slightly incapacitated." He chuckled darkly.

For some reason, Sam had an overwhelming need to justify what had happened. If not for nothing, then at least he wanted to prove that this wasn't his fault. And certainly, he hadn't planned things to go so badly; despite what Foo might be thinking. The pain in his side was mostly gone so he filled in the rest of the details quickly. "Pretty much, whatever that thing was, it looked like Yetews when I saw it at first." Before anyone could make him feel bad about this, he quickly added, "I *know* that was stupid so you don't have to say anything."

Everyone except Foo was shaking their heads, ready to reassure him that this wasn't their thought, but Sam ignored them and went on. "Obviously I was wrong and after it attacked, we had a little mishap with Garrett getting knocked out. Whatever it was, it was smarter than the other things we've fought. I dropped a giant boulder on it and morphed it into something a little less out-of-this-world and we took off to find you." He pointed to Foo. "Other than the fact that we totally trashed that store," he grimaced guiltily, "I think we are ok."

Roz noted, his voice grim, "I think we know what happened to all of those missing hikers."

Sam felt his stomach churn. His thoughts went to his missing teacher. "At least it's dead now."

"True," Titus agreed.

Garrett changed the subject with urgency. "Unfortunately, this means we need to get to your gateway now, Foo. If that thing was here, it had to get out of Imagia somehow. We need to get that gateway closed as quickly as possible before anything else has a chance to escape."

This was not something that Sam wanted to think about. He looked at the others, a half-grin on his face in an attempt to lighten the mood, "Well, at least we're safe." He thought for a second and then added, "For the moment."

Everyone laughed quietly. But their laughter was cut short. Something was racing towards them through the woods, its feet heavy but fast.

Foo cursed under his breath as they all frantically grabbed their weapons and started to run. He hollered to them, "The gateway is this way!" He started running. Foo was unexpectedly fast for his size, and everyone fell in behind him at a dead run.

Whatever this new threat was, it was fast and gaining quickly. Sam could hear it getting closer. His heart was pounding painfully fast. If it weren't for the fear driving him forward he would have been certain that he'd fall over from exhaustion at any moment. He could only vaguely see the others running in his peripheral. He chanced a quick look behind and regretted it instantly. It was the same bear-beast from the town. Or at the very least, it was another one just like it. Sam saw Roz's face and knew that it mirrored his own look – disbelief.

It roared and stopped all of a sudden. Sam saw Garrett skid to a stop and turn, bow aimed. He slowed down as well, desperately trying to think of something to imagine in defense. Too much was happening and he was far too out of practice for battling. That, combined with his dizzy head from the constant running, was making it hard to concentrate creatively. Knowing it had worked on the last beast, he quickly imagined another boulder dropping from the canopy of the trees above.

It fell deftly towards the beast. Sam grinned smugly but the look was wiped clean off his face as the beast stepped to the side, the boulder just missing him. The sound of rock hitting ground echoed around them and everyone was standing in shock of what had just happened.

The beast's lips curled over its teeth. It was smiling wickedly and looking directly at Sam.

The soft twang of an arrow being released was an encouraging sound until the bear-beast skillfully dodged it as well.

The feeling of shock was almost palpable. Garrett looked over at Sam and yelled, "Sam, go! Follow Foo!"

He almost fell over backwards as he started to run but he regained his footing and dodged through the trees and bushes, desperately trying to keep sight of Foo while not hitting anything.

Foo was leaping around the forest floor as though he was one with the trees. The white stripes of fur on his back were blurring in and out of Sam's field of vision as he tried to keep up. He was falling behind. Sam risked a quick peek behind him to see how far away the creature was now. In doing so, he didn't notice the giant root jutting out of the ground in front of him. His foot caught and he went tumbling down.

In the short time he'd fallen and gotten back up, he'd lost track of Foo. He opened his mouth to yell for him but was interrupted by the howls of the bear-beast getting once again too close for comfort. Without thinking, he took off again, running in the last direction he'd seen Foo go.

He ran full tilt, constantly looking around him for any sign of the Guardian that he'd lost sight of. Out of the corner of his eye, he saw a flash of fur. Sam turned his head and yelled out to him, "Foo!" Then instantly, as though someone had opened a window on a hot day, the air around him changed. He skidded to a stop. Not only was the air warmer, but the sun too bright – the trees too green.

Sam spun around and saw what his eyes and heart could hardly believe. He'd run straight through the gateway without even realizing it.

He was back in Imagia.

The gateway itself was just a few feet away, glimmering and revealing the darker forests of the Rockies just beyond it. He saw Garrett running vaguely in his direction and then spotted Foo running to meet him. Roz and Titus fell into sight quickly after. There was no sign of the bear-beast. Sam walked to the edge of the gateway, careful not to cross again, and hollered at them. "Hey guys! Over here!"

The others saw him, mixed looks of concern, relief and shock sweeping between them all. They were walking towards the gateway and Sam noticed Foo was intensely explaining something to Garrett. Roz was pointing at Sam, arguing about something. As they got within better earshot, Sam chortled, "Looks like I found your gateway, Foo!" He bent forward, putting his hands to his knees to better catch his breath.

Foo cautiously approached the gateway, carefully taking in the scene. "Sam," he hesitated, "that isn't my gateway."

Sam's eyes went wide and his face turned whiter than normal. "Wait. What do you mean?"

"I *mean* that my gateway is just ahead over there." He pointed towards his left. "I can see it."

Sam swallowed hard. In his poorly timed state of inobservance, he'd just managed to get completely separated from everyone. Instinctively, he stepped towards the gateway to rejoin his friends and Roz held up a hand and nearly shouted, "No! Don't come back through until we figure this out." Sam obeyed, taking a tentative step back.

Sam watched as Garrett turned to tell Foo something that he couldn't hear. It was fairly obvious that mild panic was setting in on both sides. He decided to go back through the gateway. Two steps were all he managed when a massive, hairy hand grabbed him around the waist from behind. He yelled out, causing Garrett to spin on the spot.

Roz yelled, "Sam!" at the top of his lungs.

The creature was apelike, but carried a look that showed it was semi-intelligent at the very least. It towered over Sam by several feet with muscular arms as thick as Sam was wide. Its bottom jaw jutted out, two yellowed, dull tusks sticking upwards towards its beady, black eyes.

Sam had only struggled for half a moment when a human stepped up to him. Dressed in black, with dirty blonde hair that hung just below his ears, the man was intimidating at first glance, but somehow familiar. Sam didn't have time to see much else. The man waved casually to the creature holding him and barked, "Do it."

One giant fist flashed up and hit Sam square in the back of the head. The next thing he knew was pain. His head was spinning and his eyes fluttered. The man in black got very close to his face and said in an almost bored, but very polite tone, "So sorry. But we can't have you imagining something, now can we?"

Sam struggled to grasp what was happening. Everything was moving so fast. He watched as the man held up something in front of him. He held it by a pair of shimmering wings. Through his stupor, Sam recognized it as small fairy, barely the size of a sparrow. It was shining like a bright star and looked terrified, struggling madly to escape.

Sam's vision was blurring and his head was whirling as he tried to see past this stranger. He was having trouble holding his head up and it swayed as he tried to regain control. He heard Garrett yell something, though he couldn't understand because of the ringing in his ears, and he thought he could see him running towards the gateway. But the man in black blocked his vision again as he dangled the helpless fairy in his hands and said in that same polite tone, "I guess we won't be requiring your services any longer, Guardian." The last word was spoken thick with disgust.

Sam vaguely watched as the man tossed the little Guardian into the air across his field of vision to another creature he'd not noticed before. A large set of teeth flashed as the fairy Guardian flew towards it and then disappeared.

The throbbing pain took over now and Sam's body went limp, still held up by the arm of his enemy. The gateway shimmered, dark shapes blurring together. Sam's head flopped forward and then nothing but blackness followed.

Chapter Fifteen: Wrong Way

There was something oddly comforting about being knocked out. At least, this is the vague feeling that seemed to surface as Sam floated about, trapped in his own mind. He felt heavy, as if he were tied down to something and unable to move. There was a certain familiarity to the feeling, but he couldn't put it together. He thought about trying to move, but couldn't remember how. That's when he heard the muffled voices. There was no sense in them at first. But then the fog began to lift.

A voice somewhere close beside him said, "He looks dead."

The voice was recognizable, but Sam couldn't place it. More than just his ears began to work and he was mildly aware of something poking him in the shoulder.

This time, a different voice answered, "Would you stop pokin' him? For cryin' out loud!" Sam felt the same about this voice, but he still couldn't get his body to react. Somewhere in the back of his mind he wondered if perhaps the first voice was right. Maybe he *was* dead. The second voice interrupted this thought. "He's not dead, you moron. He's breathing!"

The first voice muttered, "Well…he sure *looks* dead."

"Do dead things breathe?" The second voice sighed heavily. "Honestly," he continued, "how have you survived this long?"

Now the voices were becoming even more familiar to Sam and he wanted nothing more than to prove that he wasn't, in fact, dead at all. The fog that seemed to push him into the ground was nearly gone and he became harshly aware of his body. His head was heavier than normal and there was an aching pain that enveloped his skull. He pushed through as hard as he could but the best he could muster was a pathetic sounding moan.

Suddenly, the second more reasonable voice became quite serious. "Hey! I think he's waking up!"

There was a scuttling of noises. Feet were moving near him and Sam could feel the presence of a third body very close to him. This new voice sounded extremely concerned when he said, "Sam? Sam can you hear me?"

This voice, Sam knew. However, he'd not heard it in so many years that the only explanation was that he was dreaming. Or was it? He just couldn't figure out what was happening. Regardless, he wanted to answer the third voice. He tried, but only managed to groan again. The pain in his head wouldn't allow him to do more than that.

The third voice responded to his pathetic noises and Sam felt his shoulder being shaken slightly. "Sam?"

He tried to move his hands, a motion to wave off the worried voice so he'd stop fretting. But his hand felt like it was stuck in the mud. He had so many questions. Why was he lying down? How long had he been sleeping? Why did Roz and Garrett allow him to fall asleep when they had a gateway to find?

That's when the floodgates in his mind opened. Like a movie in fast-forward, he remembered the gateway. He remembered the bear-beast and the events that led him back to…

Sam gasped and sat upright incredibly too fast. His eyes went wide as he yelled, "No!" His head protested this movement instantly and his arms, no longer jelly, reached up and clawed at his skull as he shouted out in pain. A pair of strong arms pushed him back to the ground carefully.

"Whoa there, kid!" He continued to help Sam back to a lying position. "You need to take it easy. You're safe now."

Still cradling his head between his hands, Sam managed to open his eyes. As they focused in the bright daylight, he saw the face of a friend half-heartedly smiling back at him. Taren, not a day older than when he'd seen him years before, was looking down at him. Though Sam's head throbbed painfully, he managed to finally get words to form. "Taren?"

Taren smiled wider, his teeth showing between the short, scruffy beard he now wore. "Yeah. It's me. You got quite the bump on your head so just try to relax, ok?"

Sam didn't want to relax. He wanted answers. "But…how? How are you here? What about the others? What happened? How did you even – "

But he was cut off before more questions could form. "Still the same old Sam. A hundred questions before I can answer one." He grinned again, a little of the worry dissolving from his eyes.

When Taren stopped smiling, Sam noticed that there was some difference in his face. Though still as young, worry lines seemed to touch his eyes.

For the moment, everyone seemed to be safe. No crashing trees or angry roars filled the air around them and Sam tried to take a moment to make sense of the situation. He'd had years now of practicing to calm himself and took a deep breath in through his nose. The panic began to fade. Still holding his head in an attempt to alleviate the relentless pain, he kept his eyes closed and calmly asked again, "What happened? The last thing I remember is some man…dressed in black. He was holding a fairy…" He paused as his memory returned and then finished, "and then he…"

The hazy memory became crystal clear as he struggled to make sense of it. The look that came over Sam's face must have been pretty grim, because Taren put a careful hand on his shoulder.

His words almost venomous, he said, "Your memory is accurate. The fairy was the Guardian of the gateway that you came through."

"Was?" A knot formed in his throat.

Taren's scowl was more than simple anger. There was regret in his voice. "We were too late to save her."

Sam tried very hard to contain his emotions, hopeful to mirror Taren's control. But sudden realization for the day's events hit him like a ton of bricks. Not only had he just witnessed a Guardian die, he'd also managed to leave all of his friends at home without even saying goodbye.

One human. That was the law of gateways. Only one human could enter the gateway and it was a law that couldn't be broken. Sam knew when they set out on their journey to the gateway that Roz wouldn't be coming with them. Though unspoken, it was always the plan. But if all had gone right, then Sam would have at least been able to say goodbye and thank him for everything.

He now had to come to accept that he'd never see his friend again. On top of all of that, he was worried about the rest of their group. Would Titus get back? Did the bear-beast get killed or would it stop them from getting back through Foo's gateway safely?

Taren was right. There were too many questions. But in actuality, all he really wanted to do was yell at something. He settled for a half yell – half growl and then shouted, "This was not part of the plan!"

Suddenly, though completely forgotten until this moment, the two other voices Sam had heard before spoke again, startling him.

"Well, if your plan was to get back to Imagia, then I'd say you most certainly succeeded," the second voice said.

"Too right!" chimed the first voice that'd been certain of Sam's death.

Despite the pain in his head when he turned to look, his heart made a little leap in his chest. Sam smiled when he put names to voices. "Iggy! Arty!"

Both ferrets were standing, in their anthropomorphic state, just as impressive as they were the last time he'd seen them. Arty, always the more sensible of the two, simply grinned back and punched Iggy in the shoulder saying, "See? Not dead." His chocolate brown fur and white chest and paws were exactly the same. Right down to the notch out of his ear, battle damage from years before.

Iggy shrugged, smiling as well. "I was only joking." Arty rolled his eyes but he ignored him. "How many years has it been? I mean, judging by your size, you're what now? Thirty? Forty?" His sable fur and black-masked face was exactly the same. He'd always been the bigger joker of the pair.

Sam smiled genuinely, rolling to his side and regretting the movement instantly. He rolled back and winced.

"Come on, now…hugs all around!" Iggy announced as he went to hug Sam around the neck. He pulled Arty over with him and they all embraced one another, old friends reunited at last.

"It's great to see you two!" Even though his head was splitting and his day had gone from bad to worse, he really was happy to see them again.

Taren shooed the two off of Sam. "Alright, you two. Break it up. Sam needs to rest this off so we can rendezvous with the others back at Orga's." Sam's face flashed to Taren as he said this. "There will be a lot of excitement when everyone hears the good news." He smiled down at him. "Sam Little is back in Imagia."

Sam grinned up at his old friend. "Yeah. I guess I am."

Taren, kneeling next to him, surprised Sam. He said, "It really is good to see you, kid," then reached down and pulled Sam into a tight hug. He accepted it with open arms. It was like he was hugging a big brother who'd been away at school for a couple of years, and pushed past the pain. He simply enjoyed the moment.

"It's great to see you too."

Sam wasn't sure, but when Taren pulled away, there seemed to be a significant amount of moisture built up in the Protector's eyes.

"Well," Taren sniffed a little, making sure to remove any weak emotions from his face, "now that we've all be reacquainted, I need to go speak with Zaru. We need to make rounds to check for any stragglers that Gabriel left behind. Can you two manage to keep an eye on him for a bit? I won't be long."

Iggy and Arty stood tall in mock attention, saluted Taren and said in unison, "Aye, aye Captain!"

Rolling his eyes, he muttered something obviously insulting and then left. The place they were at wasn't exactly fully forested. Situated in a small glade, the view beyond was stunning. There were trees, thick and emerald, stretching beyond sight while a small crystalline lake sat at the base of the hilly forest beyond. The sky was clear blue and the grass was tall around them. Sam wasn't completely concealed, but he was fairly sure that he was more than well protected for the moment. Taren wouldn't have left him if he were in imminent danger.

Just as he'd promised, Taren wasn't gone long. Iggy and Arty had begun a potentially lengthy explanation about certain situations that they'd been in since they'd last seen Sam, but were stopped short when Taren forced everyone into silence. Reasons for such an order were directly related to Sam's pale-faced grimace at the slightest of movements. The two ferrets sulked off, disappointed.

Sam, eager as he was to ask his million questions, was actually, for the moment at least, grateful for the peace. As much as he hated to admit it, he needed to sleep this off. Unfortunately, he didn't feel very tired. So many exciting things were happening and he feared sleep would evade him. His thoughts didn't take much pushing to stray to Yetews. Before really attempting to sleep, he grabbed Taren's boot as he walked past. "Is Yetews at Orga's?"

He'd paused before responding, as if considering his words carefully. "Yes."

Sam noticed. "Is something wrong?"

"No." Taren knelt down. "But there will be if you don't try to get some rest." Cautiously, he lightly tousled the top of Sam's hair and grinned. "Now," he stood back up, "sleep. We'll be right over there if you need anything."

Sam did just that. He closed his eyes and drifted off. The thoughts of seeing Yetews eased the pain in his head. Soon, he'd be reunited with his Guardian and all would be right again.

* * * * * * * * * * *

Imagia dreams were different. Not only were they more vivid, but there was also always something more to them. Sam became aware he was dreaming as he left the in-between – the place between awake and dreaming where the conscience can still have control. Vaguely, he could hear Taren, Iggy, and Arty's voices trailing away.

Strangely enough, Sam's dream led him exactly to the place where he least expected to be – right smack, dab where he'd fallen asleep. There was no difference between where he was lying on the ground before he fell asleep and where he was currently standing. The only thing that didn't match was the rather relieving fact that his head didn't hurt. It was nice. This is where he stayed for a long time in his dream.

After a long while, he was thinking that this was one of the more pleasant dreams that he'd had. It was probably where he'd made his first mistake. He'd never had good dreams before in Imagia. Why start now? As if a little bird had already alerted him to Sam's return, Nadaroth appeared in front of him.

Years before, Nadaroth would appear as a being so frightening that Sam would wake up screaming in terror. Today, Sam merely thought how annoyed he was that Nadaroth had to show up and ruin his pain-free escape on his first day back. Whether it was because he'd already fought face to face with him before, or because perhaps he was older now and not as easily impressed, Sam sighed heavily, shoulders slumping, and said, "I'm not afraid of you, ya know." He turned away from Nadaroth's dark, motionless form and began to walk away. He grinned. He felt in complete control of this dream.

Barely having taken a few steps, he heard Nadaroth's hissing voice in his ear and the hair on the back of his neck prickled. "They lie," his voice echoed through the trees.

It was the last thing he wanted to do, but Sam gave in. He turned and squinted at the smoky, cloaked figure. It was black as night with eyes a fiery red. It was a strange thing to hear. Sam's natural curiosity took over. "Who lies?" he asked.

Though he couldn't be certain, a slight change in Nadaroth's pose gave Sam the eerie impression that he was actually smiling somewhere in that darkness. A wispy, bone-thin hand pointed towards a place in his dream that wasn't there before. A part of the woods had become overly darkened, dead trees forming an arch to the center of the place he was meant to go.

For a brief moment, fear touched Sam's senses. Then he remembered the most important thing: This was a dream. It wasn't real. He glanced back at Nadaroth who still hadn't moved. Rolling his eyes, he said, "Whatever. You can't hurt me here." Deciding that he wasn't falling into this trap, he regained his senses and began walking away from the darkness. As he did, Nadaroth hissed again, louder than before, "They lie." Just as the words stopped echoing, another voice rumbled from the shadows. Though the words would never have been understandable by anyone but him, Sam distinctively heard the voice hollering out for him. Sam immediately translated them in his mind. *Sam, no!*

Yetews.

There was no hesitation. Sam ran, point-blank, into the darkness. His sleeves caught on the dead branches like fingers tearing at his skin while he desperately fought to find Yetews in the ominous shadows. He could hear his friend crying out in pain and it made his footsteps fall faster. He came upon a scene, but he couldn't run further. Something invisible stopped him and he was forced to merely look on in horror.

Yetews was there, chained to a damp cave wall, his head slumped over as he was forced to remain upright by the manacles around his front wrists. He was breathing hard, his breath coming out in visible puffs in the cold air. His fur was matted and below his feet there was a thick, dark puddle of something that looked suspiciously like blood. Sam shivered and pounded on the invisible barrier. "Yetews!"

Pounding until his fists became numb, Sam shouted for Yetews over and over. On the last slam of his fist against the barrier, a crack formed, fracturing away from the point of impact like a spider web. Sam stepped back, trying to figure out how to get in. Then Yetews, weak with tears in his eyes, slowly looked up. But he wasn't looking at Sam. He was looking past him and fear took over his every expression. He fought against the chains and Sam became desperate to reach him. He backed up and ran at the glass. He put his arms over his eyes and jumped.

There was no impact. Laughter, familiar and frightening, filled his mind and he slowly slid his arms away from his face. Yetews was gone. Now he was back in the woods, but oddly enough, sitting high up on the branch of a tree. The laughter faded away, ending in a single whispered word. "Lies." The word lingered until it, too, was gone and left Sam in silence.

He looked around. Nadaroth was gone. New voices now met his ears. He looked down from his strange vantage point and saw that he was back where he'd started. Not far below him, he saw Taren, Iggy and Arty sitting around a small fire. They were talking very seriously about something. Sam strained to listen.

Iggy's voice met his ears first. "…not the best idea. He's going to find out one way or the other. I say it's best to tell him now."

Taren looked upset. "No. We have no idea how he'll take it. We also don't know how badly hurt Sam is. He needs time to heal before we tell him about Yetews. He's been through enough today. Let him sleep. Let him heal."

Arty growled, "I think you're making a big mistake. If we don't tell him everything soon, he's going lose trust in us. And I think you know that."

Sam watched Taren hesitate then shake his head. "No. We are under orders from Orga. He knows what he's doing."

"Well then," Arty stood up and pointed at Taren, "you're *both* making a mistake." He paused to look at Taren. "And you know it. Don't you?"

Taren opened his mouth to answer, when his eyes unexpectedly met with Sam's. Sam gasped and nearly fell out of the tree. Taren stood up and had his bow in his hand quicker than lightning. Arty spun around, Iggy following suit quickly after. They were now all three looking right at Sam, and for reasons he couldn't understand, he was terrified that they could see him.

Taren aimed his arrow straight at Sam and growled, "A spy!"

Sam yelled, "No! It's me!" But he was too late. The arrow came right at him and he reached out in a frantic attempt to block it.

Right when the arrow was to have hit him, Sam opened his eyes, waking instantly. He sat upright so fast that he forgot for a moment that he'd been lying down. He yelled out again, "No!" He was gasping for air as he looked around in utter panic. He was on the ground in the exact same place he'd fallen asleep. He could see Taren and the others running towards him and he began to steady his thoughts.

It was a nightmare. Despite how hard he'd convinced himself that Nadaroth couldn't scare him, he'd been wrong. He was terrified and the speed of his heart proved it.

"What happened?" Taren was worried.

Trying to make sense of everything he'd just seen in his nightmare, he shook his head, the pain of it waking him further. "I…I don't know. I saw Nadaroth."

"But how?" Iggy asked. "He can't possibly know you're here already."

"I don't know. But he knows. He kept saying, 'they lie' and then…" Sam trailed off as he looked cautiously around his surroundings.

Taren fidgeted, "No. Are you sure it was him? I killed the spy before it could get away." He didn't wait for Sam's response. "Gabriel. Of course." He cursed quietly. "Are you okay?"

Sam tried to focus on answering him, but his mind wouldn't let him get past what Taren has just said. "Did you say you killed a spy?"

"Yes." Taren pointed back towards where they'd come running from.

Lying there on the ground was a dead bird. It was black, resembling a crow in an otherworldly way. It had an arrow sticking straight up through its chest. Tracing where it might have fallen from with his eyes, Sam saw that it was right beneath the tree that he'd been perched in just a moment ago in his nightmare.

Shaking his head again, Sam tried to discount what the facts were adding up to. "No. It's not possible." He was now sure that, somehow, he'd been the bird in his dream. He'd been the spy, hearing everything that the others were saying. His mind kept going back and forth. He pieced together what Nadaroth showed him and what he heard the others talking about. They were staring at him as he muttered to himself.

"Kid, you're not making any sense." Taren put his hand on Sam's shoulder in attempt to get him to lie back again.

Shocking everyone, Sam shrugged off Taren's hand angrily and shouted, "Let go of me!" Anger flashed in his eyes. "It was you."

Taren stepped back. "What are you talking about?"

"You're the ones lying!"

"What?" Taren was genuinely confused.

"Nadaroth told me you lied and I heard you talking in my dream. You were talking about Yetews."

"Whoa, now. Just calm down. There's something you need to know about Nadaroth. He can –"

"Don't lie to me!" Sam's head was pounding fiercely, but he didn't care.

"Sam! You've got to listen to Taren!" Arty was standing between them, hands raised in surrender.

Wild and irrational were Sam's thoughts. But he was among friends. He tried to convince himself to slow down and think. His anger didn't cede, but he waited for Taren to explain. He also became aware that he was now standing, but he couldn't remember getting up.

Taren quickly explained. "Nadaroth doesn't just get in our minds to scare us when we sleep anymore. He does everything he can to use our dreams against us as a weapon. He's been trying to turn us against each other. He doesn't seem to do it often, but it's driven some nearly mad. When they wake, they can't tell dreams from reality."

Sam took in what Taren said and it sounded right. He wanted to trust his friends. Why was he so quick to discount all they'd been through after one dream?

But it nagged at him. He had to know. This time more calmly, he simply asked, "Yetews. Where is he?"

Iggy and Arty looked up at Taren. There was more to their looks and Sam wasn't about to fully dismiss it. But he waited and listened.

Without so much as a blink, Taren answered. "I've already told you. I didn't lie. I swear it. He is at Orga's."

He wasn't lying. Sam could tell. He calmed down. Whatever had just happened made him realize that two things were certain. First, he was most assuredly back in Imagia. And second, things were different than they were three years ago. He also realized that his head was not throbbing nearly as bad as it was before he'd slept. It still, however, didn't feel good at all and he sunk back down to the ground in defeat.

"I need to see Yetews, Taren."

"I know. Tomorrow. I promise."

Sam nodded. "Ouch."

Taren sighed. "Sleep. It will help."

A strange sense of guilt washed over Sam. He never wanted to get angry with his friends. He felt horrible. Barely able to look them in their eyes, he said, "I'm sorry. I don't know what came over me."

Reaching over to pat Sam on the knee, Iggy smiled and chimed, "Welcome back to Imagia." He grinned and Sam chuckled lightly.

Reluctantly, he laid back. His eyes wandered to the dead bird and upwards to the branch. His stomach gave a small lurch. Thoughts began to simmer in his mind again, but quietly this time. He fell back into a very restless sleep, hopeful that it would be nightmare free this time.

Chapter Sixteen: The Madness

Sleep had helped. Sam woke up feeling better. His head hurt. There was no denying that fact. But the rest that he'd had decreased the throbbing. More than anything, he felt as though he had a very bad headache that was made worse if he turned too quickly. As promised, Taren had preparations ready for their journey to Orga's home by the time the sun rose on the following morning. Sam was very grateful for this, as he was eager to be reunited with Yetews.

It was later revealed that there had been a few others in the forest around them after Sam's rescue from the man that was called Gabriel. Though no major details of this man or his party of miscreants was explained, it was obvious to Sam that they were bad news, no matter how one might look at it. Vague as his memories were from his capture upon entering the gateway, there was no denying the things that he remembered. Anyone who would so easily extinguish the life of an innocent Guardian could be nothing but evil.

There had been two Protectors and two others that Sam heard the names of. Whoever Zaru was, he must have been important, as Taren met with him twice more before they left for Orga's home. Sam made his friends promise to tell them everything about these hidden friends in the forest later. Taren agreed, but in haste. Sam wanted to push for answers, but his mind was set on getting to Orga's as fast as possible. His head also hurt so bad that he didn't honestly want to talk. Sam failed to mention this little detail in fear of Taren putting off leaving for another day.

The trip, also as promised, was not that long. It was oddly convenient that the gateway that Sam had accidentally happened upon was so close to Orga's home. This was a fact that the others were very vocal about. It was too close for anyone's comfort and efforts had been placed to ensure that the enemy was far away before returning.

Once the all clear was given, it took the majority of the day of traveling by foot to reach the familiar clearing that served as Orga's home. Three years had passed since he'd last stepped foot onto these familiar grounds. Sam's heart fluttered and his stomach welcomed a drove of butterflies as he neared the friendly sight of the underground dwelling. It may have been a long time, but everything looked almost exactly the same. Sam stepped over the last of the thick underbrush and into the clearing. By the looks on the others' faces, he was totally aware that he must have been grinning like a fool for at least the last half hour.

Taren was grinning as he walked beside Sam. As he gazed down at him, Sam met his stare and asked, "What?"

"Nothing." He seemed to be sizing Sam up for a thoughtful moment. "It's just that I was trying to figure out how much you've grown since I last saw you."

"Ha!" Sam blurted out. "My mom said I must have eaten magic beans for breakfast one year because I started growing so fast. I've grown almost ten inches since my eleventh birthday!" Sam was very proud of this fact and it showed. He'd puffed his chest out slightly when he talked about it. "I'm still not super tall, but I finally outgrew a lot of the girls in my class. Lizzy was actually taller than me until last year when I had a growth spurt."

"Lizzy?" Taren asked.

"Yeah. She's…well…my friend from back home." He thought about that for a few seconds. A sudden realization came over him. Four years ago, he'd pushed Lizzy through his own gateway out of Imagia. Taren had been there on that fateful day. There was a good chance that he might even remember her. "Actually," he started, "do you remember Elizabeth? You know, the girl that I sent through my gateway that one day?"

"Yes." It dawned on him rather quickly. "Oh! You mean that's the same girl?"

"Yep."

"Does she…you know…*know*?"

Sam honestly didn't know how to answer this. He wondered if his parents gave her the letter yet. Perhaps they thought it best not to give it to her. Perhaps she was sitting at school wondering what horrible thing might have happened to her friend now. These thoughts were a fast way to spiral into a bad place for Sam. He diverted his train of thought. "I never told her." He lied. It was better than explaining everything. Perhaps another day, he thought.

Finally, they had reached their destination. The grassy slope that led to Orga's door was well traveled. Barely anything was growing in the middle, indicating heavy foot traffic. Sam looked around, waiting for Warg to eagerly greet them hopeful for some scratches and moldy mushrooms. He didn't see Orga's over-sized salamander-like pet anywhere and assumed that he must be inside keeping Orga company. He started to walk down the path when something held him back.

Taren was holding onto his shoulder. Iggy and Arty had already gotten halfway down when they stopped as well. Their faces showed just as much concern as Sam's face showed confusion. Why he was being stopped so close to the door, he simply couldn't fathom. He watched as Taren and the ferrets exchanged anxious looks. "What's wrong?"

Taren was at a loss for words. So Arty spoke in his place. "The thing is, a lot has changed since you left. We don't know who all is going to be in there and…well…"

"We just don't want you to be overwhelmed," Taren finished for Arty.

"I don't care who's there. I just want to see Yetews."

Iggy and Arty turned quickly and began to descend to the door. Taren pat Sam heartily on the shoulder and asked, "Are you ready for this?"

Sam started walking again and grinned. "I've been ready for this for three years." He didn't have to reach in his pocket to pull out the picture of him and Yetews that he faithfully carried. He was just glad that it was no longer going to be the closest thimg he had to seeing his Guardian again. All that stood between them was a door. He reached up to knock, but Taren beat him to it. He knocked quickly three times. And then twice again, only much slower. There was a scuffle of noise on the other side followed by silence.

Taren surprised Sam when he clearly stated the words, "Sapphire, right shoulder." He grinned guiltily at Sam, knowing full and well that at least ten questions had just popped into his mind.

The door swung open and a man that Sam didn't recognize stood there, burly and heavily muscled. He was beaming. Reaching his arm out eagerly, the two clasped hands and shook them. This man's dark skin was a heavy contrast to Taren's and he was at least a half a foot taller. His deep voice welcomed them. "Taren! Good to see you!"

"And you, Hasani. It's been awhile, hasn't it?"

Hasani nodded enthusiastically and then looked straight at Sam. "And who is your companion?"

"This, old friend, is Sam Little."

"Sam Little?" His enthusiasm quickly changed to shock. "But how? Where are Garrett and Foo?" He looked beyond Taren expectantly only to see no one else and concern touched his deep brown eyes.

"That's a story indeed. Let's just start by saying that through a series of very strange events, Sam arrived unexpectedly."

"Mmhmm," Hasani pondered that briefly and then held out his hand to shake Sam's. "Well, then! Fantastic to meet you, Sam!" He laughed.

When Sam shook his hand, he noticed how strong he was and automatically assumed that this must be another Protector. He casually wondered what his story was as they were welcomed inside Orga's home. He made a silent note to be sure and ask him later.

The room that Sam remembered had changed more than the outside. There were several chairs around the old table and dishes littered the surface. Maps, most likely drawn by Taren, had been pinned up to the walls with cryptic symbols and writing on them. Even the smell was different. There was a heavy scent of leftover embers from a dying fire, some sort of bread cooling, the musky smell of earth, and an almost overpowering scent that reminded Sam of too many people packed in a warm room. The other strange sight was that of many unfamiliar faces. Beside Hasani stood two other men that had stopped mid-conversation to stare at the new arrivals and a tall creature standing next to a brunette woman that Sam vaguely remembered seeing once upon a time in the Village of Exile. Four unfamiliar faces were all staring at him, and exactly zero of them could he put a name to.

Suddenly, Sam felt very out of place. He began to fidget to which Taren immediately noticed. He smiled reassuringly at him and then asked Iggy and Arty to go and get Orga.

It only took a moment for them to scurry off into the maze of chambers that was Orga's home and even less than that for them to come running back in. Orga came into view shortly after and Sam's face was beaming. The sight of his old friend was overwhelming and he didn't think before he reacted. He rushed up to Orga and threw his arms around him. "Orga!" Sam hugged him, and the Old Guardian returned the gesture, wrapping his long, mottled-brown arms around him.

Chuckling from the unbridled show of emotion, Orga said, "Welcome back, Sam. I never thought I'd see the day!" When Sam stepped back, Orga's beetle-black eyes twinkled and he motioned for Sam to sit at the table. "Please, you must be starving after your journey. We have plenty to eat."

Sam shook his head and waved off the offer. "Actually, I want to see Yetews first. Where is he?" He looked around for some sign that his Guardian was going to step out of the shadows and surprise him with a welcome like no other.

But silence followed. It took too long for Sam to notice. No one, not even Iggy and Arty, were saying anything. Orga and Taren were simply just staring at one another, some unspoken conversation making the now uncomfortable silence almost deafening. Visions of his nightmare came flooding back into his mind. Something was wrong. The room began to shrink and Sam's headache began to tap a new level of pain. Sam spun too fast on his heel and pleaded with Taren. "You told me he was here. Where? Where is he, Taren?"

Arty, anger in his words, said, "Alright. We're here now. You can't keep it from him any longer. Tell him now, or for the love of Imagia, I will!"

Sam, expecting the worst, couldn't seem to stand. He sunk into the nearest chair and spurted out the only thought that he could form. "He's dead. Yetews is dead."

Instantly, Taren dropped to his knees and snapped Sam out of this before it was too late. "No. No, he's not dead, Sam. I told you he was here and that is the truth. But…" he struggled to find words and looked at Orga.

Orga, standing beside Sam, placed a hand on his shoulder, his overly-long fingers squeezing reassuringly. "Tell him everything, Taren. He's ready."

"Ready for what?" Now Sam felt even more confused. He kept picturing Yetews strung up on a cave wall, eyes sunken in despair. He shuddered.

"Okay." Taren pulled up another chair and all eyes in the room, familiar and not, were upon Sam's face. "To begin with, we didn't tell you this yesterday because we needed you in a safe place so that if you imagined something or if something went wrong, we could be sure you were able to see him with your own eyes to believe us."

Sam's face scrunched up in confusion. "If he's not dead, then just take me to him. I don't understand what's happening!" His head throbbed harder, making his vision blur slightly. Sam didn't feel very well.

"Get on with it!" Arty ordered. "Before he passes out."

Taren flashed a glare at Arty, but continued. "Alright. When you left three years ago, things stayed very quiet in Imagia for nearly a year. We didn't even have residual battles happening. It was as if your destruction, or supposed destruction, of Nadaroth, completely destroyed all things tied to him. We got worried.

"We began to send out tracking parties, trying to get a feel for what might be lurking in the shadows. When nothing seemed to show, we let Guardians become more integrated back into the world. That was our first mistake. Nadaroth was waiting for us to get comfortable – to slip up. We still kept watch, us Protectors, over Guardians, but we weren't nearly as vigilant as before.

"One night, when we were sleeping, many of us had the same nightmare. Nadaroth simply led us into darkness and we watched as Guardians were taken, dragged into an abyss. By the time we woke up and realized what was happening, it was too late. The damage was done. Nadaroth wasn't showing us what could be, he was showing us what he'd already done. Guardians all over were being taken."

Sam's stomach churned, his face turning ashen gray.

Taren stopped, hung his head and pulled his thoughts back together. He stuttered when he began again, his voice cracking. "I…I let Yetews go into the woods alone that morning. We still struggled with some communication, but I knew that he needed to revisit some places that reminded him of you. He'd been hidden for a very long time. I barely hesitated when he left. But…it was all my fault." Seeing the pained look on Sam's face caused far more hurt to the Protector than he expected. He didn't want to finish, to shake his world any further, but he pushed on. He had to.

"Yetews was captured."

Sam's entire face winced in pain completely unrelated to his head injury. He whispered, "No."

"I tried, Sam. I tried to find him!" He punched the table, causing everyone in the room to jump. He was angry with himself. "I searched for a week on my own, but couldn't find anything. We rallied together, Protectors, Defenders and other Guardians like Foo. We sent search parties out that were gone for months but there was no sign of him. We feared the worst.

"Nadaroth was back. He invaded our minds with…terrible things. I will not speak of them again, but Yetews' face flashed in my dreams one night and I knew. I don't know how I knew, but I did. He was alive. We doubled our efforts. Between the battles that we were facing on Imagia's good lands once again, we knew our mission was to get him back. For you.

"Word came to us from one of our spies in the North of a Guardian that was being held in a cavern. We weren't sure it was him until the spy said that this Guardian was being held for information regarding you."

Sam bit his lip, fighting back the rage and pain that flowed in his blood.

Lowering his voice slightly, Taren continued. "It'd been nearly a year and a half since he'd been taken. We had no idea what we'd find when we got there. But a large group of us set out to rescue him. The tip we'd gotten was true. It was him. And he was heavily guarded. It wasn't easy, but we found Yetews and brought him back here, to Orga's."

Swallowing hard, Sam fought to get the words past his lips in something louder than a whisper. He couldn't bring himself to look up from his feet when he asked, "Where is he? I want to see him."

"Sam," It was Orga this time, "we will take you to him, but you need to understand something."

"What?" He didn't mean for the words to come out so angry, but they did regardless.

"Please remember that we may have found ways to communicate with Yetews before he was taken, but since he came back, there has been little we can do to get him to even so much as try. Because of this, we have no way of knowing exactly what happened to him or why he is…well…the way he is. We only know one thing for certain."

Sam began to tremble, partly from fear for what he was about to hear next and partly because he was feeling anger unlike any he'd felt before. Taren stopped Orga with a raised hand. Reaching his strong, steady hands over to Sam and placing them on his shoulders yet again, he silently hoped to give him his own strength. Taren cautiously finished what Orga began.

"They tortured him."

Sam couldn't take it. Before another word was spoken, he leapt out of the chair, throwing it backwards onto the floor. "Stop!" As he jumped, he gasped in pain and grabbed his head. The sudden movement was excruciating. He fell to his knees, his vision blurring even more.

Taren rushed to Sam's side and helped Sam get back to a chair. He wasn't just worried about Sam's feelings anymore. His eyes went to Orga who was confused as he watched Sam hold his head. Taren quickly explained to the old Guardian. "Gabriel found Sam first. And he suffered a very bad blow to the head." He tried to hide just how concerned he was and then said, "It's not good."

Taren pushed on as soon as Sam regained his focus. "I will not tell you any more details of that day. Not unless you ask. But understand that he is here now. Before we take you to him – because I know we can't stop that from happening – you need to be prepared."

Sam saw the pained look in Taren's eyes. Shame for his outburst sunk in. He knew that Taren didn't do anything wrong and that the only blame belonged to Nadaroth alone. He calmed himself, looked up at his friend and apologized. "I'm sorry. I didn't mean to –"

"It's okay," Taren stopped him. He didn't need to hear the rest. With a pitiful smile that didn't touch his eyes, he said, "I know you're upset. We all are. But as I said before, you need to prepare yourself. Yetews isn't himself. He's angry, pacing all day long. He barely comes out of the room. He's been grumbling things over and over, but we can't understand him. We've tried to talk to him many times but it always goes badly."

"What do you mean by 'badly'?"

Iggy surprised everyone by answering. "He flips out! He's gotten his strength back. Which makes him dangerous." He approached Sam, more serious than he'd ever been before. "We know he's your Guardian. But he's hurt others before. He might hurt you too."

"That's right," Arty agreed. "If you go to see him, we can't leave you alone. It's not safe, my friend."

Sam was already shaking his head before Arty could finish. "No. He's my Guardian. He's my best friend. He would never hurt me. I can understand him." He flashed everyone a confident smile. Deep down, there was a miniscule voice that told him to be careful, one of doubt. But it was so insignificant that Sam merely shook it out of his mind and stood a little taller. Yetews existed because of him and they were connected on a level no one else had. "Once he sees that I'm back, he'll be fine." He said the words, but they felt like lines from a book as he spoke them. "Take me to him."

There was no arguing with Sam about this and each of his friends in the room knew it. Taren led the way. They walked down the corridors that branched off of Orga's main home. They went past several rooms that each held memories from Sam's old life in Imagia. They approached the place that Sam was most eager to see. It was his room. The very one he'd spent many nights in, the memories still vivid as ever in his mind.

There was one difference. It had a door. And it was a very heavy one at that. There had never been doors on any of the rooms that'd he'd seen. He lifted his hand to feel the cool, rough wood. Set unevenly in the top of the door was a window much like the one on

Orga's front door. It was covered in filth as if someone had thrown mud or food at it. Which is exactly what Taren reassured him of.

"He, uh, doesn't like us bringing him food all the time."

"Why is there a door?" Sam asked, afraid of the answer he'd get.

With all sincerity, Taren stated, "For safety."

Sam squinted up at Taren. "His or ours?"

"Both." He put his hand on the door handle. "Are you ready?"

With a deep and slightly shaky breath, Sam answered, "Yeah. But I have to go alone."

Iggy and Arty began to object and Orga stopped them. "No. He's right. We'll be right here if something goes wrong. Taren and Hasani, be ready just in case he needs to get out quickly."

Hasani acknowledged with a simple nod and he and Taren's stance became alert and rigid.

Taren hesitated and looked to Sam once more. "He's not the same Yetews that you left behind three years ago. Be careful. He doesn't trust anyone." The door handled clicked loudly and Taren nodded to Sam. "We'll be close."

Sam returned the nod, indicating he was ready. "He won't hurt me." Though he didn't know how this could possibly go wrong, his stomach flipped as the door swung open. He tried to convince himself that the feelings he had were excitement, but he wasn't entirely persuaded.

The door swung open just enough for Sam to squeeze through. The room was darker than the hall, only one oil-lamp illuminating it from a corner. As his eyes adjusted to the dim light, he was met with a disturbing sight. His bed that he'd imagined was upturned, as well as all the furniture in the room. It smelled strange and in the furthest corner, he could see why. Rotted food sat in a pile, flies buzzing around it.

Away from the light, huddled in the corner opposite of him, he spotted Yetews. He was facing the wall, his head swaying to and fro, eyes closed. Sam strained to listen and could hear low rumbling. Yetews was grumbling something too low for him to understand. His once shiny black hair was now dull, matted, and sticking up in strange places. He could see the large ape-like hands on the floor, and they were filthy.

Sam wondered how Yetews had failed to even try and look up when he entered the room. He tried to call out to his friend, but the words were stuck in his throat. His stomach did another flip. Digging deep for the courage to speak to his Guardian seemed like a ridiculous thing to need to do. His voice came out louder than he'd planned. "Yetews?"

Yetews went stiff, his head no longer swaying, and his eyes opened. He still didn't turn, but Sam could see that he heard. So he tried again. "Yetews? Buddy? It's me, Sam." He swallowed hard. "I'm back." He took a couple of steps closer to his friend.

Though he didn't move, he did grumble something. It was much louder this time and Sam understood perfectly.

"No. I'm *not* going to get out. I just got here! Look at me." He got another two steps closer.

Yetews growled this time, a menacing sound and quite unlike his friend. His body tensed even more and his hands curled into fists. He grumbled again. Sam translated the word in his mind. *Lies*.

With shaky hands, Sam reached into his pocket and pulled out his picture of him and Yetews. "No. It's me, Sam. Would you just turn around and look at me and I'll prove it." He held the picture out, ready to show his Guardian.

For a moment, Sam didn't think Yetews was going to move, but then he turned his head and looked into his eyes. Sam smiled.

Yetews frowned. His eyes were filled with a madness that was frightening.

Sam didn't mean to, but he took a step backwards and Yetews began to turn. This time, in a confused tone, he held out his hands and said, "Yetews?"

Yetews repeated himself only he bellowed it and punched the ground with his fist causing Sam to gasp and flinch.

Lies! Yetews didn't believe him. He growled again and Sam heard what he said too late. His eyes went wide, barely having time to react. Yetews growled and charged. Sam jumped out of the way, but Yetews caught him on the shoulder with his powerful arm and he fell hard to the ground. The picture dropped out of his hands onto the floor. In a blur, Taren and Hasani were there and pulling him out of the room. Sam's shoulder ached, but not nearly as much as his heart.

His and Yetews' eyes met as they rushed him out of the room. Something in the madness faded for that moment and his green eyes were his again. The tortured Guardian looked on in horror as he watched Sam being taken out, hurt and confused. Their eyes met – Sam's filled with pain, and Yetews' with regret. But the moment was over, the madness returned, and the door was closed. Yetews roared angrily and something heavy hit the door.

Sam was only half aware of being led out of the hall and back into the main room. He could feel someone guiding him, but didn't know or care who it was. Voices were rushing around him and he couldn't decipher the words. When they reached the old wooden table, he felt hands push him down gently into a seat, and he simply sat there, his mind replaying this waking nightmare repeatedly. The words around him started to form.

"I told you it was too dangerous!" Taren was livid.

Orga argued with him. "If anyone can snap Yetews out of this, then it is his child. Sam is his best chance. You can't deny that!"

Others joined in, unfamiliar voices that Sam couldn't care less about at the moment. Coming back to Imagia was a choice he'd made. But, as nothing good was coming from his arrival, the doubt lingered. Sam merely wanted to wake up from this nightmare and it was becoming more and more obvious that this wasn't possible.

The arguing escalated quickly, Sam's name being thrown around constantly. What had he come back to? Why was it happening? Why was he still here listening to this?

And just like that, he ran. It happened so fast, that everyone stared at the gaping door in shock.

Orga sighed sadly, "Taren, go after him."

In a flash, Taren was up and gone.

Sam scrambled up the worn slope, running for the woods. He didn't know why he was running, as it would accomplish nothing. And moreover, he had no idea where he was running to.

Taren called out to him.

Somewhere in the back of his raging mind, Sam could hear him. But he blocked it out.

Leaving was all he could do. He had to get away from the eyes of those watching him in that room. He couldn't let them see how angry and devastated he was. Nothing was going as planned. Sam started to wonder if he'd made the biggest mistake of his life choosing to come back. In a matter of two days, every expectation that he'd had for his return was wrong and spiraling completely out of control. His entire world was turned upside down.

His footsteps slowed dramatically when he became aware of a burning sensation in his chest. The forest around him was spinning. He recognized the feeling. He was hyperventilating. He'd had many bouts of this after returning back to his home. Slowing his breathing, he saw the images of his nightmare. Yetews' torture, the tree branch he perched atop, and the words, still clear in his mind, from his friends. Nadaroth wasn't giving him a nightmare, he'd placed Sam's mind in that of the bird spy.

Head pounding, blood boiling, and heart broken, Sam spun on his heel as Taren came up behind him.

"Kid, you gotta stop! It's not safe out here by yourself," Taren pleaded.

He was so angry. His emotions were spinning wildly out of wing. He needed someone to blame for this mess. "You rescued him from torture just to lock him in another prison!"

"You can't really believe that."

"He was shut up in that room like a prisoner!"

"Yes, but *he* built the door! He knew he was a danger. You don't have the full story."

"Lies! Nadaroth showed me the truth. You *lied* to me!"

Taren became suddenly tense. He held his hands out in front of him and walked slowly towards Sam. "No. Think back. No one lied. We told you what you needed to know at the time."

Sam's fists balled up, the knuckles turning white. He wanted only one thing right now and it was to be alone. And Taren was standing in the way of that desire. He yelled, "Just stop it! Leave me alone!" He concentrated on Taren and for the first time since returning, he imagined. A large deer like creature materialized in front of him, rearing up to strike the unsuspecting Protector. Taren fell back, covering his face in a desperate attempt to protect himself from the blow that never came.

Instead, the creature faded as quickly as it had appeared and he was met with the sound of Sam screaming out in pain. When he looked over at the distraught kid, he saw him down on his knees, holding his head, screaming out in agonizing pain.

Immediately, Taren jumped to his feet and ran to Sam. He couldn't pry his arms away from his face, but kept trying. "Sam! What happened? Sam! Look at me!"

Rocking back and forth, his head covered, he repeated the same thing over and over. "Help! It hurts!"

"Look at me, kid. I can't help you unless you tell me what happened." He tried to speak calmly, though he looked around for help that wouldn't come.

Sam stopped rocking. He was trying to regain control, but the pain was overpowering. His head hurt so badly, worse than yesterday. But as he quieted himself, it began to subside. The piercing pain became dull. He didn't look up. He remembered what he'd just done. He imagined something that almost hurt his friend. He whispered, "I'm so sorry, Taren. I…I don't know what came over me. I was just so…"

Taren squeezed one of his shoulders lightly. "You were upset. I know you didn't mean to." There was something in his voice that made Sam wonder if he really meant that. But he let him finish. "Nothing has gone right. I'd like to say I'm sorry we brought you back into this mess, but I'm not. Maybe I'm selfish, but we need you here. Besides, Imagia just wasn't the same without you."

Upon hearing the grin that was obviously on Taren's face after those last few words, Sam opened his eyes and looked up at him, wincing from the fresh ache that touched his head as he moved. What he didn't expect was Taren's sudden sharp inhale. He was looking at Sam in shock.

"What's wrong?" Sam asked.

His eyes wide, he said, "Your nose is bleeding."

Wiping the back of his hand across his nose, he felt the warmth instantly. They both put it together at the same time, but neither of them actually said the words. Sam had just tried to imagine something and it caused him pain. Now he was bleeding.

There was no hesitation from either of them as Taren helped Sam up. Sam asked, "What's happening to me?" He felt weak and shaky.

Pausing a moment too long, Taren shook his head. "Come on. We have to get you to Orga."

Chapter Seventeen: Unexpected Company

Orga rushed over to Sam and Taren as fast as his feet could go, which was not a very impressive speed. "What happened? Were you attacked?"

"No." Taren helped Sam into a chair, as he was actually having a hard time seeing for the moment. Sam's vision had been getting fuzzier as the day grew on and this new development didn't help matters at all.

Orga looked Sam over carefully as he questioned them both. "Noses don't generally bleed unless something hits them. Taren, you, of all people, should be plenty familiar with that."

Taren didn't show any amusement to Orga's quip. He glanced over at Iggy and Arty and insisted that they go and get an array of herbs and flowers that Orga grew just outside of his home. They didn't refuse. They also didn't crack any jokes, which was the first thing that led Sam to believe that this was more serious than he hoped it was.

Except for Hasani, all of the others who'd been in the room before were gone now. He helped Taren move the table closer to the best-lit area of the room. Once it was situated, he indicated that Sam should get on the table and lie back.

"Tell me exactly what happened," Orga insisted.

Sam got on the table carefully. A fleeting memory came to him. The day he'd injured his knee was one of his first painful memories in Imagia. He remembered sitting here years ago while Orga attended to his wound. The table seemed so much smaller now. As he laid down, someone put a rolled up piece of cloth under his head. It felt good to lie down and he welcomed the softness of the cloth as he rested his head. If everyone weren't watching him with such concern, then he might have even been able to fall asleep.

Taren tried to explain what happened, hoping that Sam would fill in the gaps that he couldn't. "I sure hope you have more information than I do, Sam."

Orga gave him a confused look, waiting for something more concrete.

"Really, nothing major happened. There wasn't an attack of any kind. Sam was upset, understandably so, and the best I could tell is that he tried to imagine something." Sam was silently grateful that Taren left out the details of what that 'something' really was as he continued to explain. "What he imagined only materialized for a brief moment then faded almost instantly away. By the time it was gone, I looked over to see him kneeling on the ground, holding his head, and screaming out in pain. Did I miss anything so far?" He was looking at Sam when he asked.

"No. As soon as I tried to imagine, my head felt like it was going to explode. Way worse than yesterday even. It was horrible."

"So then when the pain seemed to get better, he looked up at me and that's when I saw his nose bleeding. Do you think it was related to imagining?"

Stroking his large jowl, deep in thought as he looked at Sam's face, he finally said, "Yes. I do. I don't know if this was Gabriel's intent, but there is a possibility that the head injury that was inflicted could have caused enough trauma to his mind that using his imagination may have been affected. Though it seems a bit strange, to say the very least."

Orga prodded gently on the back of Sam's head where it was the most tender. "Just relax and try to hold still for a moment." His voice was kind and filled with concern. Though his long fingers were gentle, Sam winced enough times that Orga thought it best to not continue.

Arty came through the door, flustered. "Here they are. Iggy's tryin' to dig up the dolostia root." He handed several strange plants to Orga who took them and began to chop and mix them in a pot over the fire.

Sam had no reason to question or be concerned with what the old Guardian might be doing, but he still made a point to ask anyways. "What are you making with all of that stuff?"

"Well, pending that our small friends find the dolostia root, I'm making a tea of sorts. It should take away a significant amount of your head pain."

"Oh."

"You don't sound very eager. Is my cooking so bad?" He turned enough to flash a small, encouraging smile.

"No, it's not that. I just don't like tea."

Orga chuckled. "Well, I'm not making it for a celebration."

Sam wanted to laugh, but his head hurt too badly. He'd suffered many an injury upon his last stay in Imagia. He was fully aware of the array of plants and minerals that proved useful in aiding the healing of his many cuts and bruises.

It didn't take long for Iggy to return, dragging a set of large, woody roots behind him. "Sorry about the dirt," he apologized as he dragged the roots along then tossed them up for Orga to catch.

A smell that was most unappealing filled the room as the mixture brewed over the fire. Sam kept thinking that if the mixture tasted as bad as it smelled, then he was in for a very long night. The tea mixture, when finally ready, had the consistency of tea, but was dark gray and very pungent.

"Drink up, Kid," Taren said as he handed the cup to Sam.

Quickly sniffing it, Sam wrinkled his nose and groaned. "Oh man! This smells like death! Remind me why I have to drink it?"

"Because you don't want to have a raging headache for the next week." Taren grinned. "And trust me, from first hand experience with this stuff, you're going to want to hold your nose."

"And we'll be sure to hold our noses when we're around you," Iggy chortled.

With a roll of his eyes, he plucked up his courage and pinched his nose. “Can’t be worse than mom’s meatloaf. Oh well. Bottoms up.” Eyes tightly closed, he slurped down the tea as fast as possible. When the taste hit his tongue, he gagged and accidentally dropped his empty cup. It shattered as it hit the floor. He gagged again, forcing himself not to throw up the concoction. His face screwed up, distorted from his effort.

Most in the room held back their amusement with Sam’s reaction, but not Iggy and Arty. Both ferrets began slapping their knees and laughing loudly. Iggy pat Arty hard on the back once and blurted out, “Did you see his face? Didn’t I tell you he’d gag?” He then went into an over-exaggerated replay of Sam’s reaction.

“Shut up, you two, or I’ll pour a little down your gullets for good measure.” Taren threatened them, but it wasn’t very convincing with the poorly concealed grin he wore. “You alright, Sam?”

“Ugh,” he groaned again. “Never mind what I said. It’s worse than meatloaf.”

Taren couldn’t resist a small snigger after that. “It tastes terrible, but you’ll be happy you took it in a few minutes.”

“Oh he’ll be happy alright,” Iggy smirked. “He just won’t remember why.”

The taste lingered on his tongue. Orga handed him some water in a new cup. By the time he’d started drinking the water, a dazed feeling washed over him. The pain in the back of his head went from a loud roar to a dull mumble. The only problem was that he couldn’t seem to see straight. “I feel strange.” His words were slurred.

“That’s normal. Taren, you’d better help him to a bed before he falls over.”

Nodding to Orga, the Protector put an arm under Sam and led him down the hall. “Come on, kid. Better sleep this off. You’ll feel better tomorrow.”

Sam looked up at Taren and suddenly started giggling. “Do you know something?”

“What?”

“I think I’ll grow a beard like you.”

“Why’s that?”

"Because…" Sam starting giggling again, "I'd look all strong and manly-like!" He giggled again which was abruptly interrupted with a loud burp.

Taren wrinkled his nose at the smell. "I'd definitely say the root tea is working."

"Hooray! The toot tea is working!"

Arty and Iggy burst out laughing at Sam's reaction to the tea and slip of the tongue. Even Orga quietly joined in.

"Yes," Taren agreed. "The *toot* tea is working. So, time to take a nice nap." He was trying desperately to not laugh at Sam as well, but it wasn't working.

"Yep! Nap to take a nice time." His words became more slurred as a fresh round of laughter broke out behind him.

As Taren helped him lie back on the bed, Sam began humming a song quietly to himself with his eyes closed. It didn't take long for the tea to take full effect. The humming continued as Sam tried to remember what exactly he was doing and where precisely he was. A vague thought came to him. He was quite certain that his mother would not have approved of whatever drink he'd just had. The humming came to a full crescendo before it finally died out and Sam drifted off in one of the most peaceful sleeps he'd ever had.

* * * * * * * * * *

Dreamless sleep was always the best kind of sleep in Imagia. No dreams meant no nightmares and that meant peaceful resting. Since Nadaroth's return to power, bad nights were far more common than before. Some had taken to using the root of the dolostia plant for calming their minds before sleep, but its side effects were well known and not many used it often.

The combination that Orga had given Sam was not as common. Several herbs had been added to relieve his immense pain. The reaction he had was normal, but Orga had made it slightly on the strong side making his reaction more exaggerated. He, as well as the others, was concerned with Sam's condition. Taren knew that Orga could help ease a majority of the pain, but just how far the damage went, no one was certain.

In his medicated state, Sam slept well through the night and late into the next morning. When he finally started to feel the fog lift, he chose to remain still for fear that his headache would come back in full force. Careful not to move, he focused his ears on listening, hopeful to hear something interesting.

He was alone in the room, which by the looks of it likely belonged to Taren. In passing, he mentioned to Sam that he'd been staying with Orga more than any of the others had. The old Guardian's safety was one of the highest priorities. At least one Protector was always with him at all times.

The room was mostly empty. Protectors rarely had need for personal belongings outside of their choice weapon. There was a bow leaning against the wall, an empty quiver beside it. What might possibly pass as an armoire was open and had a few changes of clothes stacked inside. There was a chair next to the bed, roughly hewn, but comfortable looking. A pair of boots was the only other thing on the aged wooden floor.

In the main room, there seemed to be an awful lot of commotion going on. There were certainly more than just five voices that could be heard chattering away. Curiosity was getting the best of Sam by this point. Straining to put names to voices was impossible. There were too many other noises to drown them out. The most prominent sound was that of dishes clanking together. Dishes could only mean one thing – food.

Sam's stomach responded right away. It had been a long time since his last real meal and the growling of his stomach reminded him how starved he was. Something smelled delicious. He moved his head cautiously from side to side and there was no significant pain. He took a deep breath and the rich smell of bread and meat filled his nose. The bed, though not overly comfortable, was hard to leave. Carefully, he sat up, dizziness sweeping over him briefly. It passed and he noticed there still wasn't much pain. Taking it one step at a time, he made his way out of the room.

He turned into the corridor and stopped when an odd feeling overcame him. He felt as though he was being watched. Turning the opposite way he was headed, he spotted the closed door of the room that once belonged to him. It was just two rooms down. In the murk of the window he saw a green eye. Yetews was watching him.

Something far greater than curiosity took over. A deep instinct was telling him to go to the door – to go to Yetews. The other noises and the smells of promised food could wait. He needed to go to his Guardian.

Before Sam could even take a full step, a voice from behind startled him.

"You're up. I was just coming to check on you."

Sam jumped and spun to meet the voice. "Taren! You scared me." He was surprised, but the sudden movement only caused a dull ache in the back of his head and not the blinding pain he expected.

"Sorry."

"No biggie."

"How's the head?"

"Good…I think. A little achy, but a lot better. What the heck was in that stuff?" He was referring to the tea he drank yesterday.

Taren chuckled. "Ah. I take it you slept pretty well."

"I'd say! I don't even remember getting into bed."

"Well," Taren started, "you were pretty out of it. It was actually quite amusing, truth be told."

Sam's cheeks flushed. He didn't know what happened, but he preferred not to hear the full details at the moment. Whatever it had been, he was certain it was embarrassing.

"Are you hungry?"

"Starving!" He followed Taren, looking back once. Yetews was no longer watching.

"And just so you know, there are some individuals out here waiting for you."

"Who?"

"You'll see." Taren put a hand to Sam's chest, stopping him.

"What's wrong?" There was something strange about the way that Taren was looking at him.

"Look." he glanced over Sam's head toward the room Yetews was in. "I know what it's like to lose a Guardian, but having yours so close, but…broken…" Taren was trying to find the right words. He didn't want to hurt Sam further. He just wanted him to know the seriousness of the situation he was in. "I can't imagine that kind of pain. I know you want to go to Yetews, but you have to be careful. He *will* find his way back. I know he will." He gave a lop-sided grin. "Just be patient. Okay?"

Sam thought for a moment. Seeing Yetews in that dangerous frame of mind was scarring. He didn't want to risk being killed by his Guardian. Not just because of dying, but also because of the pain it would cause Yetews once he realized what he'd done. But the pull that he felt to his friend was very strong. He needed to tell someone so they'd understand. "I've been waiting three years. I can wait a little longer. But…" he realized that it was hard to explain, but dug for the words, "it's like he's calling to me. I can't explain it because it's a feeling. It's just like…like…the first moment that I came into Imagia. Know what I mean?"

Taren didn't speak. He merely nodded, empathetic to what Sam was feeling. He jerked his head towards the main room and said, "C'mon. They're waiting."

"I know word travels fast, but who could –" As Sam came out of the corridor, he nearly choked on his own words. Sitting at the table were a group of faces that he was almost certain he'd not get to see again for a very long time, if ever at all. "No way!"

The buzz of conversation went silent and everyone turned to look at Sam. Sitting at the table were Garrett, Foo, and Titus. The shock seemed to glue Sam's feet to the ground. In no scenario that had ever been played out in his head, would he have gotten so lucky as to see all of these faces again in Imagia so soon.

"Garrett!" Sam was elated and it showed.

The three new arrivals all left their meals and went to greet Sam, though Garret was the only one to grab his hand and shake it enthusiastically. Whatever weight he had been struggling with when he'd found Sam back home was now gone and he was his old bright self again. He was beaming when he said, "I'm so glad that you're okay! Though, I hear Gabriel gave you quite the bump on the head." Anger quickly flashed in his bright eyes. "I'm very sorry about that."

Sam impulsively touched the goose egg that had settled on the back of his head. It was still sore to the touch. "It's alright. Really. I'm just glad that you guys made it to Foo's gateway. I was really worried."

Foo, still as irritable as ever, had his arms crossed when he acknowledged Sam. "Hello, Sam."

"Hey, Foo!" Really, I'm so sorry for all the trouble I caused. I swear I didn't plan it like that."

Sam was surprised to see him grin, even if it was small. "All's well that ends well. Besides, it was worth it."

That was a compliment in the highest regard coming from Foo. Sam took it very seriously, feeling honored for such a thought. He knelt down and Titus instinctively trotted to him. Throwing his arms around the shaggy, familiar neck was extremely comforting.

Titus, relieved at last, said, "I don't think I'd ever been so worried about you. When Taren informed us as to what happened, I was infuriated."

"Seriously, I'm okay. Just sore, that's all." When Sam stood up, he looked somber. It showed. There was one missing from their party and now that they were all reacquainted, he had to ask. "Did…did Roz say anything to you? I didn't get a chance to say goodbye."

Garrett jumped like he'd just received a small shock of static electricity. "Sam, Roz is –" The door opened, interrupting whatever he was about to say.

Hasani came in first, speaking with whoever was following behind him. The voice that responded was agreeing with him. "That is most assuredly an understatement, to say the least."

When Sam heard this voice, his heart jumped and his eyes went wide. At first, there was doubt. He could hardly believe his eyes when he saw who walked through the door next. He glanced around for a second and made a mental note that no one else in the room seemed to be concerned, so it had to be real. Before this person had a chance to see Sam, or walk in the door for that matter, he blurted out, "Roz? Is that really you?"

Roz shouldn't, according to the laws of the gateways, have been able to return to Imagia. When Titus had first come here, the first image of him had been a trick. It was perfectly reasonable that this was also a trick, so Sam didn't rush over to Roz like he wanted to. He quickly tried to think of a way to know, without a doubt, that this was the real Roz. But, his friend managed to prove himself genuine before he had a chance to come up with something.

In complete sincerity, Roz stated, "Well, the thing is, I remembered that you hadn't turned in your latest history assignment in class and…well…what kind of teacher would I be if I didn't make sure you got it done? I wouldn't want to have to flunk you." He followed with a crooked grin that pushed his eye patch just slightly askew. It was the perfect response, and he knew it.

Sam was already halfway across the room by the time Roz assured him, "You didn't think I'd let you fight this battle alone, did you?"

The two threw their arms around each other enthusiastically for a quick moment and then Roz held a fist out to Sam. The fist bump sealed the deal. It was definitely Roz.

"But *how*? I mean, was there a third gateway?" Sam, still beaming, asked his questions, not really sure that he cared how Roz got here. He was just glad that it happened.

Roz, on the other hand, looked confused. "What do you mean by a third gateway? I came here through Foo's."

Wracking his brain, Sam couldn't figure out how this was possible. "No. The rule is just one human." He looked between Garrett and Roz, trying to see what he was missing. "If Garrett is here, then you shouldn't be."

Orga, who had been standing quietly for so long, interjected at this point. "Ah. I think maybe I can clear up this confusion."

Sam looked back at him, eagerly listening.

"Garrett isn't human." He watched Sam look at Garrett in complete confusion and clarified, "Well, essentially he's human for what you see. Remember that gateways don't recognize anything born of Imagia. And Garrett was born here, in the Village of Exile, to be precise. So technically, he isn't human."

Shock was about the only expression that Sam could manage as he stared at Garrett.

Garret, looking a bit guilty now, had never realized that everyone didn't know this information. He'd never kept it a secret, but it was also not something that came up in conversation on a regular basis. "I'm sorry, Sam. I guess I thought you knew."

"But," Sam started, still trying to work out the details, "but you're a Protector."

He smiled and looked around at the others who were also sharing what Sam thought looked like an inside joke. "You don't have to lose a Guardian to choose to protect them. It's not a right of passage. It's a choice."

Sam slowly sunk into the nearest chair as he processed the new development. Before he had left Imagia the first time, he was sure that his destiny would travel down the same path as Taren. He wanted to become a Protector. He hadn't lost Yetews and still knew that he would dedicate his life to the protection of other Guardians. For some reason, he'd always believed that he would be the first person to choose this path with his Guardian still by his side.

As he thought back, he remembered now. There had been others with Guardians that he'd seen; Protectors that hadn't lost their counterparts. He saw Garrett differently now. He understood the joy that flowed from him. He'd never lost a Guardian and was never trapped here. Of course he was happy. Sam felt dumb for never even considering this possibility. His next words came out in a sigh. "You never had a Guardian." It wasn't a question, but a revelation.

"No. Well, not technically anyhow. One *did* sort of latch on to me though."

Sam immediately glanced at the only possibility that could come to mind. "Foo?"

Foo scoffed. "Ha! Not likely."

"No," Garrett sighed. "Should I have had Foo as my Guardian, I'd likely have given up on Protecting altogether."

"I don't need a Protector. I'm more than capable of taking care of myself."

Iggy and Arty both managed to roll their eyes at the same time. In unison, they both muttered, "Here we go again."

In a nasally, mocking voice, Iggy said, "If I had to rely on Protectors to save me, I'd be dead."

Arty, also mocking Foo, "Protectors need me more than I need them!"

Foo looked murderous, but there was also something else; perhaps it was embarrassment. "Shut up, the both of you. Why don't you go out and steal something."

Iggy and Arty were amused, feigning hurt feelings. They walked past Foo. Iggy made sure to pat him on the shoulder as he passed. "Ah, don't worry Foo. I'm sure someone will try to do you in soon and you can save yourself yet again!"

Calling over his shoulder, obviously trying to poke Foo just a little more, Arty called, "And if not, we know a guy who owes us a favor."

"Too right, Arty. Too right!"

Foo brushed off Iggy's paw and skulked off, his fists balled up in frustration. He was muttering something that was certainly unfriendly. Especially coming from a Guardian. He disappeared from the room. The obvious discord between those three must not have been anything new, as everyone went back to eating without another thought on their little spat.

The volume in the room doubled now that everyone was enjoying the food and conversation. Sam's head, though still achy, felt much better and he was enjoying everyone's company. Each one in turn, gave their own accounts as to what had happened, filling in the missing gaps over the last couple of days.

Garrett, Foo, Roz and Titus had managed to get to their gateway fairly easily. Apparently, the bear-beast had vanished through Foo's gateway before they could kill it. This was slightly disconcerting, as it meant that somewhere in this world, there was a somewhat intelligent creature running amok that wanted to kill them. Though now that it was back in Imagia, Sam was actually a bit relieved to know that it wouldn't be able to hurt anyone else back home.

Titus had no trouble getting back through the gateway. He and Foo walked in last side by side and the gateway was none the wiser to his arrival. Titus did mention that the relief he felt coming back to Imagia was almost overwhelming. Sam had always believed that Titus' return home was harder on him than he'd ever let show. A talking dog simply didn't belong on Earth.

Roz had expected to leave them at their gateway, and only then did Garrett reveal to him that they could both go through. As the conversation lingered on this subject, Garrett brought up an interesting point. He asked Sam, "If you thought I was human, did you think that I wasn't returning to Imagia as well?"

To which Sam replied, "Actually, yeah. I just thought it was some grand sacrifice or something weird like that. If it makes you feel better, I feel about as dumb as I can get." They all shared a good chuckle about the situation.

As the day drew on, stories were shared and order started to be formed from the disarray that Sam had arrived to find. When the talking died down and everyone began to settle in, Sam was left to contemplate all that he'd been through in such a short time. His musings eventually led him to the one thought that he'd been trying so desperately to keep silenced. He was thinking of home.

It was a terribly annoying thing to think about something that brought out such feelings. Being nearly fourteen years old, Sam was already dealing with so many emotions, anger being one he couldn't seem to control very well. Fearing that he'd break his brave façade in front of his group of friends, he decided it best to move to somewhere more private. He excused himself, playing off of his injury. No one suspected anything. In fact, Orga agreed that Sam needed some quiet time alone to continue his rest.

Before heading down the darkened corridor to his new temporary room, Roz caught his arm.

"I haven't got to speak to you alone. I imagine you've been dealing with quite a bit." Roz looked around and lowered his voice even further. "Are you alright?"

"Yeah. Really, it's just a bump. Orga thinks I'll heal up just fine."

Raising the eyebrow over his good eye, he quietly said, "I'm not talking about your bump."

Roz knew. Sam had been wrong. All the time that he'd spent back home with Roz was starting to show. He was a really good friend and Sam couldn't hide from him his real reason for needing to be alone. Partly, it felt good to have someone there that knew him so well. But the other part just wanted to slip away, no one any the wiser for his reasons.

"I'm okay. Yeah. Just…ya know…need some time to process stuff." He tried to smile, but it mostly just came off as an awkward lip twitch.

Roz didn't hold him back any longer. He nodded. "You have a lot of strength. But…if you ever need to talk." He didn't have to say anything else about it. "Now I think I will go familiarize myself with the grounds. Imagia and I have some reconnecting to do."

As Sam made his way slowly off to the room, his thoughts went to his parents and Lizzy. He hoped that they were okay and tried to picture what their reactions would be to his letters. His heart, now that he was letting them back in, ached nearly as much as his head. In just a couple of short weeks was his birthday. And by the end of the year, he'd be a big brother. He'd always wanted a brother and now he would most likely never see him.

Before he turned into the doorway, his eyes glanced to the door of his old room, hopeful to catch another glimpse of Yetews' green eyes. But none were there to meet him. It'd been a long day already. Even though things were significantly better after being reunited with his friends, the madness that had taken his Guardian was still a heavy burden on him. Yetews was a major reason that he'd wanted to return.

This room was dark, stale, and unwelcoming – not like his old room had been some years back. Sitting on the bed, Sam contemplated what he should do. The longer he thought, the more his head ached. He most definitely wasn't going to let anyone know how badly it was really hurting. They'd probably make him drink more of that dreaded mind-fogging tea. He rubbed the back of his head involuntarily and felt the pull again.

Yetews might have attacked him once, but he was sure that there was a moment when he really saw Sam and knew what was happening. Despite the lumpiness of the mattress, lying back on the bed felt good. He cleared his mind of all thoughts but one.

Yetews was calling to him.

Reluctant to sleep, he focused on the how and the when. Tonight, when everyone was sleeping, Sam was going to try again. Dangerous and foolish as it might be, no one had to know. If he could sneak out of his own home, right under the sleeping noses of his parents using his imagination, then he could easily do the same here.

He had the plan and was ready to go. Now it was time to wait until the perfect moment. Whether he was tired or not, his last thought as his eyes focused on the dusty domed ceiling was clear. He was going to get Yetews out and regain his trust soon. It was a call he couldn't ignore. In the quietest whisper, he promised, "I'm comin' Yetews," and then succumbed to a nap, hopeful to quiet all the aches a little more.

Chapter Eighteen: Broken Mind

It'd been almost two weeks since the return of Garrett and the others. It had also been as long since his silent promise to release Yetews from his self-made prison. It may not have been a prison to the others, but to Sam it felt an awful lot like one. He knew that Yetews was in there for not only protection from himself, but also from Sam.

Several of the nights since his return, Sam would feel the otherworldly pull to go to him. Two days after his promise, he sneaked to the door when he was sure no one was watching and tried to go inside, convinced that doing so without the watchful gaze of the others would prove less of a threat to Yetews. His attempt, though led from good intentions, did not go as unnoticed as he'd planned. When he'd finally gathered the courage to pull the door open, a voice from the shadows made him jump.

"You might want to reconsider that. He just had a pretty nasty meltdown." Taren was leaned up against the wall, barely visible in the shadows of the night.

Sam hadn't expected anyone there. He just knew that he needed to see Yetews. It was getting harder to be separated from him the longer he was back in Imagia.

Taren knew the toll it was taking on Sam and understood. He wasn't without compassion as he remembered all too well the pain of being without his Guardian. Sam had much more invested in his relationship with Yetews than many others ever dreamed of having with theirs. He shook his head slowly. "I know it's hard. But he's dangerous to you."

Sam sighed sadly. He put a hand on the door, trying to send his feelings inside, hoping Yetews would find a way to understand him. "I know. I just wish…I just wish I knew what happened."

"If Nadaroth had anything to do with his torture," Sam winced at his words, "then I'm sure you, or something that looked like you at least, were involved. It's the only thing I can think of that could explain him attacking you. But we won't know unless he can tell us. Which doesn't work unless you're listening and can translate."

Sam didn't respond. He hated this. Visions of Yetews being tortured ran through his mind and he squeezed his eyes shut, his forehead now against the door.

"I know that if anyone can get through to him, it's you." Taren had come to the door and looked through the window. "I can tell you that he's been much quieter since he saw you. Maybe…"

Sam looked up at Taren, hopefully.

Taren didn't finish his thought. But smiled sympathetically. "We'll try again. Soon. But…promise me you won't try to go in without us."

Sam nodded. "Okay."

The days that passed after his failed attempt seemed slower somehow. The need never dulled to see Yetews, but Sam knew that it was folly to try and go to him again. Too many eyes were watching. When it didn't hurt to use his imagination again, nothing could stop him from trying.

He'd used his imagination accidentally one day, when his mind began to wander after a long, restless night's sleep. Sitting at the table during breakfast, he'd nearly fallen out of his chair in agony as the pain in his head spread like lightning through every blood vessel in his head. Roz happened to be standing close by and caught him before he could fall and hit his head again.

After that, it was decided that Sam needed to stop imagining, or try to stop at the very least, until he'd given his mind a significant time to heal. The bump on the back of his head was still quite swollen and Orga wanted Sam to rest his mind until the swelling was gone. The pain was significant enough that Sam was all too happy to agree. Unfortunately, he'd never realized how reliant he'd become on using his imagination and it added more to his already frustrating situation.

Many things seemed to upset him easily these days. Things were boring. During the long days, and even during some of the nights, many others had come to Orga's home. Some were hoping to see with their own eyes that Sam had indeed returned to Imagia. Others were there purely on business. This was quite usual, as Sam came to realize. He had returned to a broken world. And the innocence that he'd felt the first time he'd been there was no longer present.

Many that came were Protectors, coming to report on situations around the world. Some had even come from places that Sam hadn't even known existed. Imagia was bigger than he'd ever believed. He felt naïve thinking that he'd explored the entire world in the single year he'd traveled Imagia's paths.

In fact, there were several people that came who looked very exotic. One woman who'd come just yesterday, was dressed in heavier clothes, all lined with tan fur. Though she had to remove much of her outfit to accommodate for the warmth of this climate, she was very comfortable in her surroundings. She'd come from a place in Imagia that was much colder. When Sam approached her, she welcomed him with a warm smile and explained that she lived in a mountain range where it was not unlikely to see snow on most days.

Another Protector, still paired with his Guardian (which once again reminded Sam how ridiculous he'd been to think this wasn't possible) was wearing a necklace made of odd seashells that shimmered against his heavily tanned skin. Before leaving, he tugged a shell from the leather string and offered it to Sam, wishing him well. His Guardian, though human in figure, was reptilian. His face had the subtle likeness to that of a sea turtle. Obviously the Impossible Way was not the only watery lands. This Protector came from an island back home before being trapped here.

One thing was very similar about all of them. Each Protector that came knocked on the door and spouted odd combinations of colors and different body parts. Finally, after the latest guest knocked and answered with "Crimson right ankle", Sam pulled Taren aside.

"Okay. What's the deal with the colors and body parts? I know it's a password or something like that. But do you mind telling me more?"

"It's not really a password, but rather a code, I suppose you'd say."

Sam raised his brow.

Taren did something unexpected that made Sam feel a bit awkward. He lifted his shirt up, exposing his muscular back so that Sam could see his shoulder blade. Tattooed on his skin was a flower, just like the one he'd imagined so many times before. The petals were a brilliant sapphire color. It wasn't large, only a few inches from petal to stem.

Pulling his shirt back down, Taren smirked. "Every Protector who walks through that door has one. If they don't, then they'd better have someone with them that does. Each has a color and a specific place that it's located on their body. We memorize them. That way, we know that whoever we are talking to is one of our own and not an imposter. Which, as you can imagine, has happened before."

Taren wasn't the least bit surprised at the words that came out of Sam's mouth and chuckled when he asked. "When do I get one?"

"I thought you'd ask. Soon enough, I imagine. It does sting a bit, though."

"I can take it."

"I have no doubt in my mind."

Sam thought for a moment and looked over at Roz, who was deep in conversation with one of the more recent visitors. "Roz'll need to get one too then. He's a Defender, you know."

A strange look came over Taren. "Yes, well, about that..."

The door opened quickly. Hasani, standing in the arch, looked distressed. He didn't say anything. But apparently no words were needed. Taren rushed over to him and they both disappeared outside. But before shutting the door quickly, Taren said, "Enforce precautions." And then they were both gone.

Those Protectors that remained inside moved around anxiously, looking through the small window on the door as they each passed it. Sam walked over to Roz, who looked just as confused as he felt.

"What do you think is going on?" Sam asked him.

"Good question. The Defender in me is screaming 'imminent attack'. But before we get too worried, let me go see if I can find out what's happening." He grinned cautiously and crossed the room to talk to Garrett. Sam decided to follow him, not wanting to be left out of the loop.

Garrett, the only one not pacing about, was sitting with his bow in hand, running a leather cloth over the string. He saw Roz and Sam coming and smiled warmly at them. "I know what you're going to ask, and I can't really answer you. All I can tell you is that when we say to enforce precautions, that means no one gets in without proper identification."

"The flower thing?" Sam asked.

"Ah. Taren told you then."

Roz raised his good eyebrow. "Care to share?"

Sam explained what Taren had revealed earlier about the tattoos and then added, "I told Taren you'll need to get one of those soon." He pat Roz on the arm. "Hope they let me get one too."

Roz eyed Sam, surprise on his face.

"What?"

"I have a feeling your mom would be extremely thrilled."

"Ha!" Sam started laughing. It was so different with Roz. Everyone avoided the subject of his parents. Most would go out of their way to not mention them. Roz, on the other hand, seemed perfectly at ease about the subject and it was oddly refreshing. In a way, not talking about them seemed more damaging. Even Titus refrained from talking about them, which was surprising as they were just as big a part of his life as Sam's.

Garrett looked apprehensive about the subject and went back to tending his bow.

"Well," Roz went back to the subject at hand, "my guess would be something ominous is afoot."

"Generally, that's the case," Garrett agreed, eyes still on his bow.

About thirty tense minutes passed before there was a knock at the door. One of the recently arrived Protectors cautiously approached and waited. Sam couldn't make out the muffled words that followed, but knew that it was a friend, as the door was opened. Taren came in, alone this time. He crossed the room and disappeared into the hall leading away from everyone, not missing Sam's curious expression. Something in Taren's manner told Sam that something was amiss.

Garrett tried to explain what he could so as to keep the new comers somewhat informed of the situation. "Looks like he's securing Orga's Safety right now. There must be something coming this way."

"Something bad?" Sam asked.

Garrett shrugged. "Hard to say. Generally it's nothing too serious. Precautionary, really. You know how us Protectors can be. Let's find out, shall we?" He said this as Taren reappeared.

In a very serious tone, Taren began to brief everyone. "Something is in the forest, not far from here, but getting closer. "Everyone needs to go to the clearing and fan out. There are enough of us today that we shouldn't have a problem keeping whatever's out there from breaching the set perimeter. It's most likely some stray scouts, but it's best to be prepared just in case it's a bigger threat. Garrett, you're to remain outside the door. Arty and Iggy, you'll stay at the top of the slope as lookouts for him. Roz, Titus, and Foo, you'll be with me. I'll show you the protocol for these situations." They nodded in agreement. "Sam?"

Sam's heart gave a little lurch, part excitement and part nervous. "Yeah?" he said eagerly. He'd been keen to try out his imagination. Everyone had told him to bide his time, hoping for more healing before he attempted to use it again.

Taren seemed to know exactly what Sam was thinking. "Sorry, kid. You're staying in here with Orga."

"*What*?!" Sam took a step forward. "No way, Taren! You brought me here to help! What good is that gonna do if I'm stuck in here?" He was infuriated.

By this time, nearly everyone had already left the home, but Roz and Titus hesitated shutting the door, both turning to listen. Taren glanced back at them momentarily, defiant. When he faced Sam again, he paused, thinking. Lowering his voice slightly, he pointed out the problem. "Look. The last time you imagined, you fell to the ground and had a nosebleed. You haven't even tried to imagine so much as a blade of grass. You aren't ready for a fight." He could see the cogs working in Sam's mind and before he could get a word out, Taren added, "I think you know that, too. We didn't risk everything to bring you back here just to see you get killed or captured after a few days."

Sam knew he was right, but that didn't change how mad it made him. "Oh, come on! This is stupid. If you just let me –"

"No. Look, I'm sorry." Taren looked to the others and then back at Sam. "There may be a lot of us here today, but we can't afford to have to protect you as well if you get in trouble. We'll see how you've healed soon. And though I'm sure you will more than likely be okay, now is not the time to have you incapacitated."

Sam sighed angrily. He wanted to protest this further. But he also knew that Taren wasn't going to change his mind on the subject. Instead of arguing, he quietly growled. "Fine." Roz gave him a look that told Sam he understood the irritation he felt, but also that he regrettably agreed with Taren. Sam spun on his heel and went to the table, sitting down heatedly. The door shut and he slammed a fist into the table, releasing some of his anger.

It was quiet inside. Every few minutes, Sam would go crane his neck up to the window in the door and see if there was anything happening. So far, he could just see Garrett pacing calmly. Once, Garrett even met Sam's eyes and winked. He hated it, but Garrett's attitude was always uplifting, even when Sam just wanted to stew in his own anger. Finally, he decided to just go and sit patiently until something more exciting happened.

Patience was harder than expected. Peeking once more through the door and seeing that nothing had changed, Sam decided to use the absence of the others and sneak down to Yetews' door. After Taren's warning, he knew it would only cause more problems if he tried to enter the room unattended. But he'd hoped to look in the window and maybe see his best friend.

What he forgot to take into consideration was that Orga was still inside. Just as Sam had managed to find something to stand on, as he was too short to reach this particular window, a soft voice called to him from a room just down the hall.

"Sam, will you join me please?"

Thwarted again, Sam put away the crate he'd found to stand on and joined Orga.

This room was the most unfamiliar to Sam. It was Orga's room and he'd never felt comfortable, not even years ago, to go inside. Orga, his large body and heavy tail not capable of using a chair, was squatting next to a roughly hewn table that was covered in old scrolls and parchment that had maps on them. It looked as though every map from every Protector was stacked haphazardly on the table.

Orga watched as Sam eyed them. “Maps from the Protectors. I’ve been spending a lot of time with them as of late.” He sighed and placed the map he was holding into the stack.

“Why?” Sam looked around the room. It was cozier than he’d ever thought possible. But he had to remember that Orga had lived here for most of his long life. There were many curious items stacked up and placed around the room. Maybe one day Orga could tell him about some of the odd things he was seeing for the first time.

“Well, I suppose you could say that I have my reasons.”

With that, Sam turned around and pretended to be looking at something by the doorway. Really, he was trying to hide his annoyance at yet another thing being kept secret from him.

Orga had a strange way of knowing exactly what Sam was thinking a lot of the time. He reassured this with his next words. “I know you’re upset that so much seems to be kept from you right now. But I promise that all will be explained to you soon.”

Sam turned back to him, hopeful. Orga was smiling at him, his large jowl turned up at the corners and his beady eyes twinkling. “Sorry. I guess that I just expected things to be different. I’m not a little kid any more.”

“We know. That’s what makes this harder.”

“How?”

Orga made his way to what could only be his bed. Or something like a bed, at least. It was mostly upright in the fashion of a chair, and covered in a rag quilt. It accommodated his features well as he settled into the cushions. “It’s difficult to explain.”

“Try me.”

Smiling again, “Alright. The last time you were here, you were so young, yet experienced an incredible amount of pain and suffering. For many, it was difficult to witness.” Sam assumed he meant Taren. “But you recovered. Children amaze me. They can bounce back so fast if given the need. Years have passed and we knew that you’d be growing older, wiser to the world. But you being absent from us for so long, no one knew how you’d grown. To us, you see, we still saw how you were. Small and young. Innocent.”

"Yeah," Sam interrupted him, "I get it. But I wasn't so innocent. I saw horrible things. Orga, I *did* horrible things. You know that."

He was nodding. "Yes. But when you came back, in our minds we still see you as the same Sam Little that left years ago. People want to protect you from the horrors of reality."

Sam let out a little snort at that.

"What is it?" asked Orga.

"It's nothing. Just…you know…reality. I'm not sure that word holds much meaning to me anymore."

"I can see your point. Nevertheless, you need to switch perspective for a moment. You came here with certain expectations, yet are seeing so much has changed. You expected Yetews to welcome you with open arms, unchanged from the years separated from you. You expected Taren to be the same as before, but war has hardened him. You expected everyone to be right where you left them, frozen in time." He watched as Sam's attitude shifted and softened. His comparison had worked. "You understand."

Sam didn't say anything. He just nodded. The truth was, not much was frozen in time, as Orga had said. Everyone, even Iggy and Arty, were different now. There had been suffering at the hands of strife in the world; there was loss. Sam's mind strayed to thoughts of his first time visiting Orga's home. A warm welcome was given to them from Warg, Orga's portly, crocodilian-like pet. This memory of him jumped out in his mind. It was the thing that made Sam realize that Imagia was not the same place he'd left all those years ago.

"Warg," he said sadly.

Orga's face fell slightly. "What about him?"

"That's when I knew it was different. You're right. I thought everything would be the same. I pictured coming to see you and seeing Warg rush at us, ready for a treat from Taren. But…he was…" Sam couldn't form the words he needed to say. He'd found out quickly why Warg wasn't there to greet them. About a year ago, Taren had taken him out in the forest to let him run and forage for his mushrooms when a rogue beast – one of Nadaroth's creations – attacked them. Though Taren did all he could, the beast reached Warg first. He'd never had much in the way of bravery, and tried to run. Warg didn't make it home that day. Sam continued without finishing that particular thought. "I just don't think I've really accepted that it's this bad. You know?"

"Mm-hmm. And I can see that in you. But you're stronger now. I can see your mind working when you think no one is watching. You're angry. Confused. The others see it too, they just don't know how to help and it frustrates them just as much as it does you. So please be patient. You've grown up, Sam. They know it. And part of them fear that it means you will now bear even greater burdens."

There was an awkward silence that followed. The wisdom that Orga held was always comforting. At least that hadn't changed.

Sam decided to fill the awkwardness with a subject change. "So, how about telling me about those maps now?" he asked.

Orga chuckled. "Always curious. Some things never change."

Sam laughed quietly too. He felt his spirits rise, even if it was just a little.

"I've been trying to piece the maps together in hopes of finding Guardians."

"Guardians?"

"Yes. Eleven of them, to be precise."

Sam started to move towards the maps so that he could get a better look at them. His interest was piqued. But just as he picked up the first one, there was a loud bang on the front door of the home. It startled both Sam and Orga and both of them exchanged a worried look.

Another bang, louder this time.

Sam rushed to the hallway, Orga slowly following. He ran down to the end and cautiously listened. There was commotion outside, a lot of yelling and a strange howling sound pierced the air somewhere close by. Sam inched closer to the door.

BANG!

Something heavy slammed against it. Garrett was yelling at someone.

In a hushed voice, Orga called to Sam. "Sam! Get away from the door. Come with me! Quickly!"

Sam turned and looked at Orga for a moment but then there were several loud bangs on the door and the hinges groaned with the pressure. Then suddenly all went quiet. Garrett was no longer shouting. Sam decided to go to the door. He needed to see if Garrett was okay.

He didn't make it there. Instead, the door came crashing in and tumbled heavily across the room, just missing Sam. A hideously ugly creature, wrinkled and muscular, fell into the doorway holding Garrett by the throat. Its tufts of wiry hair were intermingled with scaly skin. It had elongated arms and legs that both ended in claws. Menacing yellow eyes stared at him above its razor-sharp teeth. Sam had a sudden thought of werewolves, only much uglier.

Sam unfroze and ran towards the table, hoping to shield himself from the creature. As it stood up, it threw Garrett across the room and he landed heavily, gasping for air. The creature targeted Sam instantly. It leapt across the room, screeching and snarling. Sam ducked under the table as it flew at him.

He ran across the room as the beast recovered from the miss. The creature lunged again and again, but Sam was wiry. He dodged the attacks over and over, ducking under and around things as the beast turned the place upside down. The sounds of wooden furniture breaking and things being tossed across the room filled the air. Fear took over Sam. Adrenaline had kicked in and he was trying to get out of the house. He had to lead the creature away from Orga – away from Yetews.

Sam had ducked just in time to miss a chair flying over his head and he leapt over it, right towards the door. He knew there was no way he was going to outrun this beast. Even if he did, he had no idea what he was running into in the clearing. This monstrosity had gotten past Garrett which means it had gotten past several other well-armed Protectors.

Something heavy hit his leg as he scrambled up the grassy slope and he flew forward. He flipped onto his back and saw the yellow eyes emerging through the door. He pushed off the ground and ran again, ignoring the fresh pain in his leg. All of a sudden, he felt the heat of the beast as it stealthily jumped over him and landed ten feet away. It was blocking the top of the slope. That's when Sam realized that it wasn't trying to kill him. It was trying to capture him.

There was no choice. Sam had to use his imagination. It was now or never. There was a split second of hesitation in fear of what may happen when he tried. He reached his arm out to help him focus on the spot he wanted his image to appear, his eyes wide. He imagined thick wooden spikes on both sides of the underground slope. As he did this, a faint image of the spikes flickered into view but then disappeared in a ghostly fashion.

At the same time that he pictured the spikes, his head erupted into pain so horrible that he grabbed madly at it and screamed out, his eyes closed tight. He didn't care about the creature anymore. He didn't care about anything. He just wanted the pain to stop. He felt something warm on his upper lip and the metallic taste of blood hit his tongue.

Sam was on his back on the ground now, still clutching his head. The creature was closer, as Sam could hear it howl out. Two other howls returned the call, but further off in the distance. He couldn't open his eyes, the pain still so bad that he was sure his skull was cracking open. He was about to yell out for help when the howling sound stopped and was replaced with an ear-piercing screeching sound.

Something of substantial size just barely grazed the top of Sam's head as it leapt over him from behind. It landed in front of him, the ground quaking beneath him as it hit. Then, it let out a most furious snarling roar. Strangely enough, the sound didn't frighten him.

He forced his eyes open, blinking hard in the sunlight. Towering above him was a mass of long, black fur. It slammed a heavy hand into the ground, roared again, and it threw itself at the attacking beast. Sam tried to watch, his eyes watering and blurring in and out of focus.

There was a blur of black as it reached the gray beast. Then two powerful arms pulled Sam's attacker into a chokehold. It grabbed at the snapping jaws and pulled them in opposite directions. There was a loud cracking sound as the attacking beast's jaw broke. Its jaw now dangled oddly, but it jumped to attack this new foe again, screeching loudly. But it was futile. It stood no chance against the raw muscle of this new creature. There was a dull, nauseating crack as its neck snapped and the wrinkled body of Sam's attacker fell limp to the ground.

Sam's vision was starting to stay in focus, but the pain in his head hadn't left. He watched as his rescuer turned around, terrible and beautiful. Two cow-like, emerald green eyes looked back at him, a hint of madness still around the edges. Yetews stood before him. He was breathing hard, anger on his face, teeth bared. As he looked at Sam, their eyes locked.

Sam couldn't believe it. The shock was greater than the pain and he was almost certain he was dreaming. "Yetews?" He could barely get the word out.

Yetews looked at Sam heavily. There was a very powerful inner struggle happening in those big, green eyes.

He was fighting the madness.

He was winning.

Sam tried to get up. He tried to run to his friend. But when he moved the world spun around him and he fell back to his hands and knees. A drop of blood landed on the back of his hand. A huge ape-like finger touched the blood and Sam looked up again.

Yetews looked at the blood and then made a fist. He pounded the ground in front of him, the dirt flying out in a small cloud. His eyes and face screwed up in pain and he snorted loudly, baring his teeth. He was breathing heavy, fighting again.

Sam watched, a new pain added to his head and leg. Now his heart hurt as he watched his Guardian struggle. But then, Yetews opened his eyes. And the madness, though still there, was softened. He looked at Sam again and reached out with his huge hand.

Although he didn't mean to, Sam flinched. Yetews pulled back for only a moment and then continued to reach towards him. The warmth of Yetews' large knuckle brushed Sam's cheek. Sam leaned into it slightly. In his other hand, he held the tattered photo that Sam had dropped in the room.

One side of Yetews' mouth drew up in a weak smile. The world seemed to stop moving. A sensation like that of several electric sparks traveled up Sam's spine and spread through his body, a new and welcoming warmth. All the pain, though still there, didn't matter at this moment. He threw himself at Yetews and two hairy arms wrapped around him.

For a moment, Sam was ten years old again and finally seeing his best friend for the first time. And even if was only for that moment, Imagia felt right again.

Chapter Nineteen: Trust

Quickly approaching the slope into Orga's home was the sound of several hurried footsteps. Yetews turned to see who was approaching, worry now mixed into his already troubled mind. Sam could hear the voices that belonged to some of the footfalls and knew it was friendly company, but he could also see that Yetews looked upset. There was some concern now about what kind of reactions would take place – from everyone.

Yetews, still purposely placing himself between Sam and everyone coming, had taken a very tense defensive stance. When the first of the approaching party broke the rise of the slope and saw the scene unfolding, weapons were drawn all around. The first to the scene was Taren. His bowstring was pulled taught and aimed at the dead creature on the ground. Everyone fell into place around him and Taren immediately looked to Yetews.

The arrow's target changed. It now threatened the Guardian, who snorted angrily in return. Steady hands held their ground as Taren demanded answers. "What happened here? Where is Sam?"

"I'm right here!" Sam slipped quietly around Yetews, careful to ensure no one was startled. "I know this looks bad." He took a moment to take in the whole picture himself. The body of the deranged looking werewolf creature was severely mangled and lying in an awkward position about ten feet away from him. The door to Orga's home was missing, wooden splinters lying chaotically about. Garrett was gone. And to add to the chaotic mess, there were several pieces of plates and chairs littering the ground behind them. He shuddered to think what the inside of the home looked like.

Taren was angry and asked loudly, "Who are you?"

Sam was taken aback. "Er…Sam. It's m-me. Sam." He couldn't stop the slight stutter, as Taren looked more frightening than he ever had before.

"I wasn't talking to you."

All weapons were pointed at Yetews now. Sam jumped in between them, hands raised and face bloody. "Whoa, whoa, whoa! Guys, what are you doing? It's Yetews!"

"Sam, Get out of the way! This isn't Yetews. When we prepare for a time like this we lock Yetews in the room for his protection. And I have the only key. So this is an imposter!"

"No! He saved my life. It's him! Put your weapons down!"

Taren hadn't truly taken time to really look at Sam. His eyes flashed to the blood, still wet on his face, dripping slowly off of his chin. He let his grip loosen, trying to make sense of what he was seeing. Everyone stood their ground. As Yetews had yet to show any sign of attacking, no one else made a move towards him. Worry touched Taren's eyes now and he was just about to ask what proof there was that this was, in fact, Yetews. But he was interrupted.

Edging out of the door, stepping over the random pieces of his home, Orga cleared his throat. "Stand down. Everyone. It really is Yetews. I can explain."

Taren showed no signs of relinquishing his weapon or his aim on Yetews. "Proof," is all he said.

Orga sighed. He pointed at Taren first. "Sapphire, right shoulder." Then he pointed at Garrett. "Purple, back." He proceeded to point out three more tattoo locations before Taren lowered his weapon, breathing a sigh of relief. Everyone else followed suit.

Orga explained everything to the best of his ability. Pointing towards the corridor leading off of the main room, he said. "Really, all the proof you need is right down that hall. Where there was a door, there is now none. Or rather, none attached at the very least. But I will explain further."

When the attack had happened, Orga, despite his pleading, couldn't keep Sam in the room with him. Unbeknownst to either of them, Yetews had been watching. As soon as the creature knocked in the door, the locked Guardian began throwing himself against his own door to get out. Orga, having no key, was unable to help him and was forced to sit by on the sidelines and watch as it all unfolded.

At first, Orga told them he was concerned about what was motivating Yetews. But when Sam yelled out, he seemed to double his efforts to escape. The pounding became frantic and he started to throw his entire body up against the heavy wood. It was then that he realized that Sam being endangered was driving Yetews to fight past the madness and save his child. At the very least, this was his highest hope. He hadn't got to watch the entire event progress. He'd remained hidden under Taren's orders, but he could most certainly hear much of what was happening just beyond his front door. Or rather, what was left of it.

As soon as it was clear that Yetews was not an imposter, Taren asked, "Where is Garrett? And what about Iggy and Arty?"

Arty spoke up from behind him. "We're here." He was holding a piece of cloth above his eye and Iggy had an arm under him to help hold him up.

Everyone looked down at them. Sam's heart skipped. He gasped. "Arty! Are you okay?"

"Yes. Just need a rest, that's all." He jabbed his thumb towards Iggy. "Makin' this lazy bag of bones pull his own weight for a change…or my weight. Whatever." He gave a feeble grin in attempt to ease Sam's worried expression, but it had the opposite effect. Sam was now more worried.

"Garrett's another matter," Orga announced. "He's inside and needs attending to promptly."

Hasani, Taren and a woman Protector Sam didn't know the name of rushed past Sam. The others remained outside and began to fan back out across the clearing so as to make sure there were no other threats.

Only Roz and Titus remained. Roz began to walk towards Sam when he was stopped in his tracks by a rather menacing growl from

Yetews. Sam wanted to stop him and tell him about Roz, but was too concerned for Garrett to say anything just yet. He turned and ran inside, worried about the damage that the fallen Protector had taken.

When he reached the others, they had already moved Garrett to the table. He was unconscious and very battered. The scar that ran the course of his face was now hidden in the swollen bruising of his eye and bloodstained cheek. He looked terrible and Sam feared the worst. He looked dead. He squeezed up to the table, desperately watching for the rise and fall of his chest. He had to count at least six breaths before he sighed in relief. He was alive.

"Will he be okay?" Sam fretted.

The woman was checking him all over. She was currently feeling Garrett's tender throat. It was easily the most bruised area. She glanced up at Sam and reassured him in a honey-sweet voice. "I think so. There doesn't seem to be too much internal damage. But he'll probably have a bit of a headache when he wakes." She pulled up the sleeve of his arm, revealing a deep cut. It also looked very swollen by his hand. As she pushed around his arm gently, Garrett let out a low moan. She placed his arm down gingerly saying, "And I think his wrist is fractured. That's what the swelling is from, I believe."

As she continued to work on Garrett, he began to come around. When his eyes fluttered open for the first time, he groaned and tried to speak. The words came out harshly, his throat swollen from being choked. "Now that's a face I'm happy to wake up and see." He flashed a weak smile at the woman and her cheeks went pink. She seemed momentarily distracted, but as soon as he moved to try and sit up, she pushed him back down gently, "Oh no you don't. I can't fix you if you don't sit still."

Garrett moved his good arm, palm out, in a sign of easy defeat and winced. "You're the boss."

Sam watched the two interact. The woman was very careful with him, but moved like she had experience in this sort of situation. She had long, dark brown hair that she wore in a heavy braid down her back and very dark eyes that looked even darker by contrast to her skin. She worked in near silence, but kept looking at Garrett anxiously as he rested.

Taren noticed that Sam was trying to figure out who she was. "Come on, kid. Let's take a walk."

They left the table and walked out the door, Taren leading Sam away. Yetews was no longer anywhere to be seen and he instantly felt worried that he'd imagined the whole thing. "Wait a second," he stopped walking. "Where is Yetews?"

Taren looked around too and caught sight of his tail disappearing down the hallway as they stepped outside. "It looks like he's going back to his room."

Turning on his heel, Sam intended on going to him, ignoring the initial tug on his arm. Taren jumped in front of him when he didn't stop. "He'll be fine. He just had a major breakthrough and I imagine he needs a moment. Give him space. He came to you. Let him work this out on his own time."

Craning his neck around Taren, he watched as Yetews turned into the room, disappearing from sight. His heart sank as he watched the tail vanish. That one moment when the world felt right again seemed to be fleeting now. Sam didn't mean for the words to come out so harsh, but he agreed. "Sure. His own time."

"That's not what you want to hear. I get it. But let's take a walk and I'll fill you in on what's happening. Sound good?"

"Yeah," still too harsh. He forced the next words to come out softer. "That sounds good."

"Good." They walked up the slope leading away from the chaotic mess, Taren stepping over the broken body of their enemy. Sam kicked it– on purpose – as he walked around it. Taren asked, "Feel better?"

"Not really. No." He thought for a second and looked back at the creature. "But it's a start." They walked past Roz and Titus. The moment Roz saw them, he jogged over with Titus by his side to ask what was going on.

Sam smiled seeing his friend approach. He hadn't had enough time with Roz since they'd been reunited. He'd tried to speak with him several times, but was constantly interrupted. They found it difficult to just get a word in with one another.

"Well *that* was a fun little adventure." Roz's sarcasm was thick, but Taren frowned as Sam grinned widely at his quip.

"I think," Sam began, "you might have a warped sense of what the word 'fun' means." They both laughed.

Pulling a piece of cloth out of his pocket, Roz handed it to Sam. "Here. Clean yourself up a bit. You look terrible! Looks like you ran head first into a tree."

He'd completely forgotten about his nosebleed. It had finally stopped flowing, but the blood was still fresh on his face. It was only then that he realized that his shirt, one of his favorites from home, was tainted with the drips of blood. His head was still hurting, but it was a dull throb and easily manageable now that the original brunt of the pain had subsided. He also became aware of a different pain, a burning sting on the back of his calf. He wiped at his face as Roz pointed out the back of his leg.

"It looks like you took a hit there as well. How bad is it?"

Sam shrugged. "Burns a little, but I'm not sure. I almost forgot with everything going on."

Taren was instantly crouching behind Sam and rolled up his pant leg. "What happened?"

Sam jerked his leg when Taren touched it. "Ow! Dang!" he lifted his leg, trying to see what the damage was, but it was in an awkward place. "I don't know what hit me. But I think that *thing* threw something at me."

"Well," Taren finished looking at it, "it's not terribly deep. But you'll need to get it cleaned."

Roz was just about to say something else when Taren stopped him. "Actually, I needed a word with Sam. If you don't mind."

His forehead wrinkled as he eyed Taren. A moment crossed between them, both seeming to struggle with how to react. Roz nodded curtly and turned to leave. Titus watched both of them and hesitantly said, "I'm glad you're ok, Sam," and trotted after Roz, leaving them alone.

Taren's gaze followed Roz for a fleeting moment and then he started speaking. He could see the bewilderment on Sam's face, but sidestepped it and brought up the first subject. "First, I thought you might like to know about Maggie."

"Maggie?"

"The Protector helping Garrett."

"Oh. Yeah…are they…you know? Together?"

Taren knew that Sam noticed how the two looked at each other, even if it was only for a moment. "You caught that, huh?"

"She blushed. And she looked really worried about Garrett."

Taren had to give Sam some credit. The ten year old that he used to be would never have noticed a romantic relationship. He'd done a lot of growing up since they'd last been together. He had to mentally remind himself that Sam was a teenager now. He also had to remember that hiding things from him wasn't an option. "Yes. They're together. Kind of." He rolled his eyes slightly. "It's complicated."

"How so?"

"I think I'll let Garrett finish this conversation at another time. To be honest, I'm not really sure how to answer it."

"So what else do you want to talk about that Roz can't be here for?"

He definitely wasn't going to be able to hide anything. That was even more obvious by the expression on his face. He sighed, not wanting to make things worse. "I suppose I'll just come right out and say it then. I'm concerned about Roz. I know how you met and I'm grateful that he was there for you during such a hard time. But, the truth of the matter is that we have no idea where he is from or what his intentions are. I just don't know how much we can confide in him."

Sam could feel his temper flaring and it was growing with every word that came out of Taren's mouth.

His agitation didn't go unnoticed as it grew in Sam's eyes. He tried to ward off what was coming. "I know he's your friend and I'm not saying that he's not a good person, but we have to be very careful who we share certain things with. If the fate of this world didn't rely on it so much, perhaps I wouldn't be so concerned."

Sam was biting his tongue. So many moments flashed through his mind and with each memory, came more anger. Finally, he couldn't hold it back any longer. "You don't trust him."

Taren let his gaze flick to Roz who was on the opposite side of the clearing. "Truthfully?"

Sam didn't answer. He scowled and crossed his arms.

"Okay. Truth. No. Not really. No. I've been around a lot and I know that we've met other Defenders, but something about him makes me cautious."

Sam shook his head, exasperated. “Keesa. Iggy. Arty. Enoch.” He kept his voice low, restraining himself from yelling at Taren. “No one wanted to trust them. You’d think that after so many times, maybe you’d just learn to trust *me*. I haven’t been wrong yet, have I?”

“No. You haven’t. But –“

“No buts! He saved my life!” Taren looked shocked at this information. That gave him a little jolt of satisfaction. “Yeah. That’s right, Taren. He did. Back before we returned, things got bad and Roz saved me. Would someone we can’t trust save me? Because I don’t think so. Not only did he save me, but he put his own life in danger to do so.” Sam started to turn, ready to storm off, but stopped to add more. “He’s my friend, Taren. Friends trust each other. I trust him with my life just as much as I trust you or Garrett.”

Taren held out his arm to stop Sam before he could walk away. “Okay. You’re right.” Sam stopped, but Taren noticed that he didn’t stop scowling just yet. “Look. We’ve been at war. Trust isn’t always easily earned. That doesn’t excuse me, but you have to understand how careful we have to be. We’ve lost friends from putting our faith in the wrong people. I don’t expect you to understand, but maybe that’s where you’ll just have to trust *me*.”

Jerking his hand out of Taren’s grasp, he snapped, “Everyone keeps saying that I won’t understand. Just stop it! I’m not a little kid anymore! I understand a lot. I especially understand the difference between a friend and an enemy. An enemy doesn’t save your life.”

This time Taren was angered. “Now hold on just a moment! You act as though I’m attacking you when I’m just being cautious. Do *not* be so quick to judge me and my actions. You have been gone a very long time. You have no idea the things that I’ve done. We’ve all done things and seen things we regret. But they were necessary!”

“I have regret too, Taren. So don’t you forget that either.” With that he began to storm away.

Before he was out of earshot, he heard Taren plead, “Sam, wait.”

Sam paused and half-looked over his shoulder to say, “Maybe it’s not *me* who can’t understand,” and then headed back inside. He didn’t have time to argue about who could or couldn’t be trusted. As far as he was concerned, there wasn’t a single enemy amongst them. Even if he was angry with Taren, he knew that somehow it would get worked out. For now, the one friend that he needed to be with was alone and confused, fighting a battle in his mind. And there was one thing that he did understand: Friends don't let friends fight a battle alone.

Sam walked past everyone, ignoring their stares and muttered concerns, and turned the corner into the dark room that once belonged to him. It was time to show everyone the true meaning of trust.

Chapter Twenty: Fourteen Candles

Being in Imagia the first time was hard. It was not necessarily based solely on the fact that Nadaroth was trying desperately to destroy all that was good about the world, but also because being ten and potentially forever separated from his parents was devastating. Being in Imagia for the second time was equally hard. Only now it was for much more complicated reasons. And on a completely different level was the simple fact that returning to Imagia a second time was, until now, unheard of.

Sam knew what it was like to deal with loss. He was familiar with how to handle pain and suffering. He was even well equipped to deal with fear on levels that no one should have to experience. One long year in Imagia, separated from his parents and fighting daily to harness a strange power was bound to teach him how to cope with such things. But the one thing he'd never learned to deal with was losing a Guardian.

He'd come close to such a thing twice. First, when Yetews was feared dead during the last battle with Nadaroth and second, when he had to say that fateful goodbye three years ago. Yetews was not lost to him on a physical sense. But as matters of the heart go, his Guardian was teetering on some dangerous edge that Sam was trying very hard to pull him back from.

A breakthrough was what Taren told him Yetews had experienced. And for that one fleeting moment, Sam was inclined to believe him. To make matters worse, Taren had just pushed Sam into proving himself. Perhaps it wasn't Taren's intent, but choosing not to trust Sam's judgment regarding Roz drove him to a very rash decision. When walking towards Yetews, Sam had a level of confidence that he didn't normally have. Walking into the room was easy. Pulling Yetews from whatever mental abyss he was trapped in was anything but.

Now that he'd reached the dark, musty room, Sam felt a familiar fear grip his confidence and squash it like a bug. Too late to turn around, he knew that he had only one path to take and it was forward.

Adjusting his eyes to the darkness, he finally spotted what he was looking for. Back in the corner where he seemed to frequent, was Yetews. He was huddled in a corner just like before, sitting with his back turned. Other than the slow rise and fall of his chest when he breathed, there was no movement. He wasn't swaying back and forth like before, but he still held the same posture of someone fighting inner demons.

Sam wondered what he was waiting for. "Yetews?" he quietly called out.

Yetews' back stiffened slightly. Sam noticed.

"Okay." Sam took a cleansing breath. "Here's the deal. I know that things are…well…pretty bad. Nothing is going the way it was supposed to go. It's like Imagia is broken. Shoot. *I'm* even broken." He sighed heavily. "I don't know what happened to you, but Nadaroth showed me –" He stopped. A shiver went up his spine as the images of that first nightmare swam through his thoughts. Staring at the dust around his shoes, he struggled to put his thoughts into words. There was a small part of him that was worried about what might happen if he said the wrong thing. But there was no door to stop him from running should things go south. So he sputtered out some words and hoped they wouldn't make things worse.

"I guess I don't know for sure if what that monster showed me was the truth, but I think it might have been. I saw you being…*tortured*." He still didn't look up from his shoes, but noticed that there was no sound of Yetews moving towards him – or moving at all, for that matter.

But Yetews did move. When he heard the word 'torture', he turned his head, peering sideways at Sam, his eyes pained for what Sam might have seen.

A long time seemed to pass as they both stood there in silence, Sam reaching for words and Yetews waiting. Finally, Sam tried again. "I don't know what he did to you. But I know that it must have been really horrible if it made you attack me like you did. He must have broken you pretty badly. I guess that makes us both broken."

Yetews looked away, back into the corner again, but his face was determined. He grumbled something very low, but Sam heard him clearly this time. Though his Guardian spoke in a series of grumbles and growls, Sam could understand them just as easily as if he were speaking to anyone else. It was a special bond between them that even he admitted might not have been the best situation for those around Yetews. Sam looked up, surprised to get a response and answered his Guardian. "Why wouldn't I forgive you?"

Though he didn't answer right away, his head hung a little lower and his eyes closed tightly when he growled back to Sam.

"What do you mean you don't trust yourself?" Sam's heart almost broke as he listened to the pain in those growls and grumbles that followed, sounds he'd long since wanted to hear. But now the sounds were not what he expected. Sam listened as his best friend told him that he'd never earn Sam's trust again after what he'd done and he tried to reassure him. But before he spoke, he knew that it would take more than words to convince Yetews' broken mind.

A reunion with a Guardian is meant to be a joyful occasion, and Yetews had anything but joy in his words. Hesitating only for a moment, Sam set himself, straightened his back and decided that no Guardian of his would live with such an idea. Without another thought, he lifted one foot off of the ground and walked towards Yetews.

The closer Sam got, the more he took in. Yetews' massive hump above his shoulder where Sam would frequently ride years ago was missing hair over a spot that looked scarred from what could only have been a burn. The ape-like hands were balled up in fists and the knuckles were covered in thick, unsightly scabs. A part of his right cow-like ear was missing the tip, looking perfectly sliced off somehow. The smaller hump that sat above his brows was uninjured, but the hair on it no longer looked sleek and long, but rather jagged and unkempt. He looked thin. His eyes were closed, hiding any madness he was fighting, but his head was leaned up against the wall, a saddening sign of defeat.

He didn't look at Sam when he approached, but Sam was definitely looking at him. There was only one thing he wanted. He was much bigger now, being nearly fourteen years of age, so sitting atop Yetews' great shoulders was no longer an option. His Guardian couldn't support him like that. But there was one thing for certain: Sam was certainly going to support Yetews – whether he liked it or not.

Speaking softly, he started by repeating Yetews' question. "How could you ever be trusted again?" Yetews didn't budge, simply sitting there; his head leaned hopelessly against the cold wall. Slowly, so as not to startle him too much, Sam reached a wary hand out. He inched closer to Yetews, not quite touching him. Sam closed his eyes. He thought of all the pain and loss, all the complications, all of the moments that led up to this one pivotal point in his life. Finally, he placed his shaking hand on Yetews' soft, fleshy muzzle. It was warm and whiskered, just like he remembered. Goosebumps tingled on his arms as he whispered, "Because I'll never give up on you."

Something in that one innocent touch and spoken promise set off a spark. Yetews' eyes flew open and Sam's did the same. Something stirred deep within the tortured Guardian. They locked gazes and Sam watched as Yetews fought against all the pain, all the suffering. He watched the green of his eyes brighten and the pupils shrinking as they focused on him. Instantly, the two connected. Their minds joined on a level beyond understanding, each seeing the other's thoughts. They both stood there watching and listening as they shared the past three years of memories without a single spoken word.

The connection was electric and neither could pull away. Neither wanted to. The memories came fast, almost in a blur. It started to hurt. Sam's mind was reeling with what he was seeing. Visions of Yetews' torture, the pain he'd had since Sam's departure from Imagia. The moment his gateway closed and Yetews knew he was alone. Yetews saw Sam's fears and his family as he fought against using his imagination around them. The joy he'd felt when finally sharing his power with his parents – the baby brother he would never see. Meeting Roz and every hopeful moment with Titus.

The entire thing barely lasted a minute, but it finally brought Sam to his knees, his head pounding and his heart racing. He didn't realize it at the time, but he'd started yelling out before the bizarre phenomenon was over. The world around him came back in a rush of senses and the first thing he heard was a familiar voice.

"Sam? What's going on?" Taren had followed after him. He sounded extremely concerned as he stood in the doorway looking upon what could only be a very peculiar scene.

Opening his eyes and regaining control of his lungs, two strong, ape-like palms reached down to him and helped him off of his knees. Each one, a Guardian and his child, looked at each other with understanding and forgiveness in their hearts. They both smiled.

Sam turned to face Taren. For a second, he forgot that he was angry with the Protector. "I have no idea what just happened. But I think," he turned to look at Yetews who smiled again and nodded once, "that things are okay now."

Taren looked confused. He kept glancing between the two. "What happened?"

Sam felt a bit queasy after whatever he'd just experienced. He rubbed at his stomach. "Actually, I have no idea. But it was really weird. I think maybe we'd better go talk to Orga."

Taren didn't have a chance to respond. Sam and Yetews walked past him and they headed straight for Orga. Hopefully, the oldest Guardian of Imagia could shed a little light on the situation.

* * * * * * * * * *

"To be honest," Orga admitted, "I haven't any idea what it was."

Sam sighed. He'd just finished explaining – or rather, attempting to explain – what him and Yetews had just experienced. "You don't have any of your theories popping to mind?"

He chuckled. "Unfortunately, no. Not this time."

"Well," Sam sat back heavily in his chair, "that sucks."

Orga tapped his spindly, brown fingers on the table as he considered the newest development. After a moment, he rubbed his large jowl, considering something. "This entire situation is unique in its own right. When you were originally trapped in Imagia, you were with Yetews the whole time. That in and of itself is an unnatural thing. Rare, in fact. The bond between those that still remain with their Guardians is a strong one. Ask any of them and you'd see."

"What does that have to do with what just happened?" Sam pushed.

"I'm not sure I know. But, since children have been trapped here, I only know of a small number of Guardians who spent such a significant time with their child and then be separated from them in the end. Two of them are right here in this room."

Sam looked around, trying to figure out who he was referring to, when they both said in unison, "Guilty as charged." Iggy and Arty, who were standing on the table, each raised a paw in the air.

Iggy crossed his arms, looking quite set in his response. "But as you know, we didn't exactly end on good terms, if you'll remember."

Sometimes, it was easy to forget that Iggy and Arty, both of which were more likely to whip out a wisecrack than show any sign of being noble, were actually Guardians. But the pained look that betrayed their cool exterior was very hard to miss. Their child had deceived and tried to kill them when he became a collector too many years ago. Though it was no excuse for the darker dealings in their past, it was definitely a big part of the situation.

Sam asked them, "So what about you guys? Any ideas?"

"Nope." Arty shook his head.

"Not a one," Iggy agreed. "But, uh…being separated from your child after so much history isn't exactly like flyin' through a rainbow on the back of butterfly."

Orga reflected again before adding another thought. "I can't speak from experience. But I can agree that it would have lasting negative effects. I can only think of one other example, but he didn't spend more than his ten days in Imagia. He did lose his Guardian though, becoming trapped here."

A feeling much like that of having something heavy sitting on his chest, came over Sam. "Nadaroth," he guessed.

"Yes." Orga was still mindlessly stroking his jowl. "You are the first child to be separated from his Guardian for a long period of time and then be reunited with him again. This has never happened. Maybe Imagia has given you both a gift."

A gift. It was a strange way to look at the situation and Sam wasn't the only one to think this. Many of the others had doubtful looks on their faces that mirrored Sam's own.

Sam felt a shiver building and tried to push it back down. "Some gift," he said, sarcasm thick. "Now I get to watch my Guardian being tortured any time I want. Oh. And the pain part was pretty awesome too."

Roz snorted and joked, "Well, nothing says "good gift" like a good old fashioned nosebleed." The others in the room gave him disapproving looks. But Sam's lip turned up at the corner. Taren was scowling rather harder than the rest and Sam was suddenly reminded that he was mad at him.

The discussion didn't last much longer after Roz's poorly timed joke. Sam knew that answers were unlikely. Instead, he walked past Roz, reaching his balled up hand out to him. They bumped fists as Sam passed. Yetews following close behind as he left. In a completely unexpected sign of approval, Yetews pat Roz on the back heartily and grinned appreciatively. Sam's memories of Roz were all good, and Yetews was grateful for him.

Taren noticed. All of a sudden, he was forced to rethink his opinion of the strange Defender.

* * * * * * * * * * *

Yetews hardly left Sam's side now. Sam would sit in a corner or outside under the shade of the trees (well guarded by a barrage of Protectors), and tell him of all that had happened in the three years since they'd said goodbye.

Of course, Yetews knew it was mostly pointless since their memory sharing, but he was happy to listen. He knew Sam needed to tell him these things with his own words. Some memories weren't nearly as vivid as others and hearing them from Sam's point of view was almost like hearing new stories. Yetews, on the other hand, didn't seem to share much of anything past the occasional memory prior to his capture.

Sam was aware of his lack of sharing, but knew that it was for good reason. Neither of them needed to relive those memories. So he just let it slide. It wasn't the thing Sam was concerned with, truth be told. Every so often, when Sam would lose himself in a story, he would glance up into Yetews' eyes and see a glint of the madness that he was still trying to fight. Those green eyes couldn't lie. Not to Sam. But he refused to mention it. He was afraid of how Yetews might react. He'd come so far to fall backwards again.

It wasn't just his eyes that showed the madness at bay. His hands would involuntarily clench into fists, knuckles white. His ears would droop and the crunching sound of teeth grinding together could be heard as his mind fought to quietly keep himself in check. It was tough to watch, but even tougher to ignore. Sam did his best on both regards and so far it seemed to be working.

Another week passed. During its passing, tension seemed to be growing. Even more new Protectors were coming and going. So many, that Sam eventually stopped trying to keep track of all their names. Most of them only stayed briefly, speaking with Taren or Hasani, who both seemed to be the ones in charge. Sam, though still having not completely forgiven him, knew that if a leader was chosen amongst the Protectors, they couldn't have picked one more fit for the task than Taren.

By week's end, Sam had eased up on his cold-shoulder routine with his friend. Taren's attitude had changed as well. He was no longer looking at Roz like an imposter and had even hinted that he would need his own tattoo sooner than later so that he could enter Orga's home without constant accompaniment.

With that, Sam figured it was time to forgive and forget. He didn't have to actually say anything. Taren glanced his way one day and Sam nodded once. Just like that, all was back the way it should have been.

Now more concern could be addressed to the fact that Sam wasn't seeing any major kind of move that would indicate something important was about to happen in the fight against Nadaroth. He decided it was time to figure out what exactly the future held for him. After all, he was brought here to help bring Nadaroth down for good this time. Shouldn't they be doing something about it?

Taren and Orga could see Sam coming a mile away. The look of determination on his face could only mean one thing: He had questions. Both of them exchanged a knowing look. Orga inhaled deeply and curled his fingers over Sam's shoulder, squeezing once, and said, "I'll let you two talk."

As Orga waddled away, Sam watched him, perplexed. How that old Guardian was able to recognize Sam's needs before they were addressed always bordered on unnatural.

"Before you can ask, yes. He knows you want to know what the plan is." Taren redirected Sam's thoughts. "Strangely enough, we were actually just discussing when we should catch you up to speed."

Sam shook his head quickly, trying to refocus on his original purpose for approaching Taren. It didn't take much to remember. "I guess there's no point in beating around the bush, then. I know the first goal was to get me back here. But since things didn't go the way you wanted, what's the big plan now? I mean…I'm kind of useless now."

Sam's mind being somehow damaged during his first minutes back in Imagia had been a significant setback. Even though the others were optimistic that his imagination would return, Sam wasn't so sure. The pain he would experience when trying was debilitating at best.

Taren started to disagree with the use of the word 'useless', but Sam stopped him fast. "You can disagree with me all you want, but it's the truth. If you'd known that my imagination was gone, you'd never have risked so much to bring me back here."

Taren could see the disappointment being poorly masked on his face. "Well, I suppose that's right."

Sam hadn't expected that. He raised an eyebrow, intrigued by Taren's honesty.

Walking over to the nearest chair, Taren sat down heavily, the weight of the world seemingly on his shoulders. He motioned for Sam to sit across from him and he obliged. Taren sat back, carefully considering his next words, with his arms crossed against his chest. "Tomorrow is an important day. Did you realize that?"

It was an odd change of subject, but Sam thought hard. The only conclusion that he'd come up with was that he'd been in Imagia for almost three weeks now and that a lot seemed to be happening that he wasn't being included in. In an attempt to not sound like a whining child, he settled on a weak shrug.

The Protector's face wrinkled slightly as he frowned empathetically. "I guess I hadn't realized how consumed you were with everything going on around here that you'd forgotten."

"Forgotten? What are you talking about?"

"Exactly four years from tomorrow is the day you first came to Imagia." He watched Sam's face come to realization. "If I'm not mistaken, that would make tomorrow..." Taren paused dramatically, waving a hand towards Sam, waiting for him to finish the sentence.

Sam's eyes went wide. He couldn't believe he'd forgotten. "My birthday." If there was a person alive that felt dumber that him, Sam would have been surprised. He lightly bit down on his bottom lip and felt a surge of embarrassment. He flopped back in his chair and rubbed his cheeks, beginning to laugh. "Well," he started, "I feel like an idiot…again. I forgot my own birthday." He didn't say it too loudly, as he didn't feel like drawing attention to his blunder.

"Yes. I suppose you didn't know this because you weren't around. Do you remember that we were planning on celebrating your eleventh birthday?" He waited for Sam to nod. "Well, after you left, we still celebrated it."

"You did?"

"Mm-hmm. We did. Orga even found a way to make a birthday cake like you described. Well, something like it at least. I'm sure it wasn't the same as you'd have wanted. But it was very good!"

Sam listened, feeling honored and saddened at the same time. He remembered looking forward to that day. He'd never had a birthday party surrounded by friends as he'd never really had any until Imagia. It was one of the most bittersweet moments he'd had when he returned home. Celebrating his eleventh birthday with his mom and dad was good, but his heart had longed for the friends he'd left behind.

"I'm sure it was awesome." Sam was being completely honest.

"We've celebrated your birthday each year since."

Nostalgic feelings washed over him as he remembered the past. But despite it all, he still wondered what good he was to Imagia without his imagination. "That's actually really cool. But it doesn't change anything. I wouldn't be here right now if it weren't for you needing my power. Which I don't have now."

"First of all," Taren corrected him, "it's not that you don't have it. You do. You just can't use it at the moment." He watched Sam roll his eyes and stopped him before he could interject another opinion on the matter. "Argue all you want, but when you try, it's not that nothing happens. It's just weak. Your mind is a muscle. You simply need to strengthen it. Second of all, you have assumed something quite incorrectly."

"What?"

"That we knew you had imagination before we went to find you."

Sam hadn't actually thought that through. How could they have possibly known that he would retain the ability to imagine after leaving? Once again, his naivety was showing. He decided to hear Taren out – without the eye rolls this time.

"Truthfully? The idea of trying to leave Imagia and find you was not a popular opinion in the beginning. Our list of supporters was small. Eventually though, as Nadaroth grew in power, we ran out of options. Others joined our cause and it became the best option we had. There are still those that think we made a mistake. But I know that you'll prove them wrong in the end."

That sort of optimism was one of the things that used to drive Sam crazy when he was younger. Now that he was older, he understood it. Sometimes clinging to a foolish hope is all anyone has to remain grounded. Too many times, the foolish hope of returning to Imagia was what got him through his hardest times back home.

"So, what now? What if my imagination never really works right again?" Sam wondered aloud.

Taren's eyes glanced behind Sam, which made him turn around, curious. Orga was busy working on something near the rudimentary wood stove. As he watched the old Guardian he asked, "What's he doing?"

Taren chuckled. "Making you a birthday cake."

Whipping his head around, Sam had a strange feeling that he knew exactly what they were thinking. "Now hold on just a second. I don't know if I'm thinking what you're thinking, but I think getting a wish granted is sort of a one time deal. I don't think blowing out birthday candles will work this time."

Grinning wide now, Taren raised an eyebrow. "Couldn't hurt."

"Um…"

Yetews, who Sam had almost forgotten was sitting quietly behind him, put a hand on Sam's shoulder. He grumbled something, gesturing to Taren.

Sam considered what he said and blew out slowly. "Yeah. You're right. Even if it doesn't work, at least we'll have something to celebrate. Okay, Taren. You win. Bring on the candles. Let's see what happens."

* * * * * * * * * * *

Orga spent almost the entirety of the previous day making what ended up looking nothing like a birthday cake at all. It was thick and rectangular, but muddy brown and had nothing that looked like frosting on top of it. Instead, there was a thick, pale goop that dripped haphazardly over the edges. Poking awkwardly out of the cake were fourteen thick candles, yet to be lit.

Sam stared at the messy creation, his mouth slightly ajar. Yetews poked him in the ribs and grumbled low. They exchanged a look and shrugged. Each of them got their noses close and sniffed it when Orga wasn't looking.

Surprisingly, it smelled delicious. Sam cast a quick glance over his shoulder to make sure no one was watching and poked at the goopy glaze. It was thick and sticky. He looked at Yetews. "Well, mom always said homemade is best. Don't knock it 'til you try it, right?"

Yetews grinned crookedly. Orga sidled over and said, "I know it's not what you expected, but it's actually really good. If I do say so myself."

Sam said, "I'm sure it's great. Thanks for making it."

"I've made it every year since you left. I think it gets tastier each time."

Sam got the feeling Orga was defending his creation. He didn't know what to say, so changed the subject. He prodded at the candles. "I'm not sure I can just blow out the candles and get another wish granted to return my powers. I don't think I feel it like I did when I was ten."

Orga's beady eyes went wider than normal, showing a little more white around the edges than usual. He didn't say another word. He pat Sam heartily on the back and turned to address those in the room.

There were quite a few there today. Taren, Hasani, Maggie and Roz were there along with several other Protectors that Sam was having trouble remembering the names of. Iggy and Arty were enjoying a conversation with Titus. Foo, who had managed to keep mostly to himself for the last couple of weeks, had returned. He was keeping Garrett company. It was the first time in a week that Garrett was up and around, looking more his normal, cheerful self. His arm was still healing, but he didn't look nearly as pale. He kept smiling across the room at Maggie who kept blushing. It was the fullest that Orga's home had ever been. But it had helped to have so many there to fix it up after the clash with the werewolf beast.

The hushed chatter went silent as Orga began to speak. "Today, as you all know, is a special day. In Imagia, birthdays are not celebrated as often as they should be. But today is different. Four years ago on this day, a special boy with a unique ability came into this world and brought a light with him that shone bright in the darkness. Though the light only shined briefly, we were and always will be ever grateful to him for giving us the one thing we needed most: Hope. Today we celebrate the fourteenth birthday of Sam Little."

All eyes in the room went to Sam and everyone clapped. Sam felt himself grow hot in the face. He'd not been expecting a speech on his behalf. He'd really just expected to blow out the candles and move on. Roz pulled out a chair at the table, his eye motioning for Sam to sit. Taren walked across the room and ushered him over.

"Come on, kid. You're the guest of honor today," he whispered through the clapping.

Never, in all of Sam's birthday experiences, had he ever felt more emotion than he did today. He sat down, trying not to make direct eye contact with anyone. He did catch Roz's glance and saw him wink, which was extremely impressive with just the one eye.

The clapping fizzled out and Orga continued. "Sam, we hope you know that here, amongst your friends, we can never tell you how grateful we are that you have sacrificed so much in your young life for a world that was not your own. Today, we celebrate your birthday, but more importantly, we celebrate you. Taren?"

Sam heard the scraping of metal across the table. He hadn't noticed the several cups sitting there, all filled with something that had a faint sweet odor to it. Everyone was taking a cup. He looked to Taren who was now grinning proudly down at him, his cup in hand. Goosebumps started to grow on Sam's arms. His eyes were now on the man that, in many ways, Sam felt was a brother.

Taren cleared his throat. "Well, kid. What can I say that Orga hasn't already mentioned?" He paused for a moment, his emotions showing. The room was quietly attentive. "You changed our world the day you came here and changed it even more the day you left. I know that it hasn't exactly been the easiest ride, and certainly not painless. And I believe we all know how painful it is to answer your never-ending questions." Low chuckles broke out. Sam smiled sheepishly. "But I am blessed to have been there with you for the journey. I, uh…I never had a brother. But I hope you know that you will always be one to me."

In the pause of clapping that followed, Taren smiled at Sam. Those words created a lump in his throat that forced Sam to swallow hard.

Taren raised his cup in the air and everyone in the room followed suit. He finished what was obviously a toast. "As Orga said, you sacrificed so much for a world that was not your own. But if one thing has proven true, it is that when you left, a part of Imagia left with you. Imagia is, and forever will be, your world. I think everyone will join me in saying that we are glad you're back. Happy Birthday, Sam! And welcome home."

It was the loudest happy birthday he'd ever received in all his fourteen years. There were more pats on the back, 'hear, hears', and cheers than he'd ever experienced. And most importantly, more friends than he could have ever hoped for.

But, he missed his parents. A fleeting thought went to a future where he was wishing happy birthday to his little brother. But he pushed it back down, not willing to let that pain roam free right now. Sam was too happy at the moment to worry about what might never be. At least that's what he told himself.

Roz tapped Sam on the shoulder and handed him a cup of the sweet-smelling drink. "You might want to drink it slowly," he suggested. "It's got a kick to it."

Sniffing the drink, Sam thought it smelled a bit like apple juice, only sweeter. Most everyone seemed to be enjoying it and so Sam figured it couldn't hurt. He took a gulp and instantly started coughing. More rounds of laughter broke out when Sam wheezed, "Woah! What *is* that stuff?"

"Remember the fruits from the tree? The ones that spin down when they fall?" Taren had knocked them down when Sam was especially hungry once upon a time. Sam had compared them to maple tree seeds that he called helicopters. When Sam nodded, Taren said, "They make an excellent drink if you age it right."

Sam suddenly had the strangest inkling that he might be drinking something a little stronger than apple juice.

"Whaddya say?" Arty asked. "Ready for a bit of crake?"

"Too right! Bring on the crake!" Iggy cheered.

Foo, who had been the quietest of them all, growled at them. "It's not *crake*, you idiots. It's *cake*! Geez…"

The two shrugged and started pounding their small cups on the table. "Cake! Cake! Cake!" They kept repeating it, getting a few others to join in.

Orga returned to the table, his cake creation in tow, and placed it in front of Sam.

Taren exchanged a look with Orga. Sam was quick to notice that the candles weren't lit. It got very quiet in the room, all eyes on him.

Sam awkwardly waited for someone to light the candles, ready to wish for the second time in his life. But no one was lighting the candles.

"Go on, Sam," Orga urged him. "Blow out your candles."

Thinking this was some strange miscommunication of worlds, he tried to explain without hurting their feelings. "Well, the thing is," he gestured to the unlit candles, "generally the candles are lit before you blow them out."

Orga's heavy jowl turned up at the corners in a devious sort of grin that took Sam by surprise. "Are they, now?"

All of a sudden, Sam realized what was happening. He wasn't supposed to blow the candles out to make a wish. He was supposed to *light* the candles with his imagination. It was his birthday and what he wanted most right now was to imagine again. Even if it was just something small, it would be the hope that he needed. Orga said he brought light to the darkness once. Perhaps it was time to bring the light back again.

"Well," he started as he looked at all the hopeful faces in the room, "I guess, what's a birthday cake without candles?"

Sam inhaled deeply and blew out his breath shakily. He was nervous, but thought back to his tenth birthday. He closed his eyes, shutting out the tense silence around him. He felt Yetews' hand squeeze his shoulder once to reassure him, but then blocked that out as well. He remembered the gift that his wish brought to him. Faces flashed in his mind's eye, friends and family alike. He wanted this.

Though his eyes were closed tight, he saw the cake in his mind. It was clear and wonderful. He filled his lungs once more, held it for a moment and then let out his breath in a steady stream. Instead of picturing blowing out flames on the cake, he imagined flames appearing as he blew.

He let the world around him back in and opened his eyes. Fourteen candles now held fourteen perfectly flickering flames with no sign of disappearing. Sam didn't glance around the room. But if he would have, every face would have been smiling back at him.

Sam took another breath and blew out the flames. As the smoke curled up towards the ceiling, more than candles were lit that day. Hope was rekindled. And it burned brightest in Sam's eyes.

Chapter Twenty-one: Brothers Broken

"Again!" Taren bellowed.

Sam let out a half-growl, half-yell, throwing his arms in the air in frustration. "It's not working!" He started to walk away from Taren. They'd been attempting to strengthen Sam's mind with daily imagining exercises for the past two weeks. It hadn't been going nearly as well as any of them hoped, but no one was more irritated at the outcome than Sam.

Still focusing on the positive of the situation, Taren stopped Sam from leaving. "Come on, now. Don't give up like that! I think we can all agree that you've come a long way." The best he could do daily was try to keep Sam's spirits high by pushing optimism.

Unfortunately, it wasn't working today. Sam spun on his heel and his hands became very animated in his extreme annoyance. "Ha!" he yelled, sarcasm thick. "Oh yeah! It's going *fantastic*! I can finally imagine a flower. A *flower*, Taren! I was imagining flowers in my *sleep* when I was ten years old. This is a joke." He spun back around and stormed over to the nearest tree. With an over exaggerated movement, he slid to the ground and locked his hands around his bent knees. He leaned his head back against the rough bark and sighed angrily.

Hesitant at first, Taren joined him. He sat down, cross-legged, next to Sam in the afternoon shade of the tree. They didn't say anything to each other for a long moment. Sam ran his fingers through his sweaty hair, making it even messier than usual. He plucked a weed out of the ground and started tearing it apart absentmindedly.

"Look," Taren started, interrupting the silence, "I know this isn't going the way you wanted it to."

Sam tutted. "You can say that again."

He chose his next words carefully. "At least the nose bleeds aren't as bad."

"Well, I guess that's something."

"It is." Taren reassured him. He poked Sam lightly in the ribs with his elbow.

The exercise they'd been working on today had involved setting flame to a pile of wood. He was to try and create a ball of fire and send it to the woodpile in an attempt to control his powers in motion. The majority of his attempts were just a few wisps of pale smoke. In fact, the only thing that had yet to fade was a small flower that was nowhere near as brilliant as the ones he was so famous for creating.

The fire, on the other hand, was proving to be impossible. He had managed to create one ball of fire that floated in the air before him, but it fizzled out before it even had a chance to get to the target. The rest of his tries were even worse.

Sam was getting tired and his head had begun to throb again. He rubbed at his temples, eyes closed tight.

There was a rustle of leaves as heavy boots made their way over to them. Sam opened his eyes and the blurriness cleared. It was Roz.

"I think it's time for a break. He looks like hell." When Sam returned with a weak smile, Roz added, "No offense, Sam." He held out a hand and Sam grabbed at it. Roz pulled him off the ground and Sam brushed the forest floor off of his pants.

Taren also got to his feet, politely rejecting Roz's outstretched hand. "I suppose you're right."

"Orga sent me anyways. He's got some lunch ready. Boy, does that Guardian enjoy cooking."

Taren nodded. "He's always been like that. Ever since I've known him."

Over under the shadows a large, black shape moved. It got up, stretched loudly, and then shook all over. Leaves and grass fluttered down around Yetews as he joined the others. Iggy and Arty were hanging on Yetews' curly horns, having been watching the exercises as well.

They all started walking towards the sloped entrance to Orga's home. Taren hollered over to Foo. He'd been keeping watch from a low branch in one of the larger trees. "You want some lunch, Foo?

"Not hungry," he grunted.

Just loud enough for the others to hear, Iggy muttered, "Course he's not hungry. He just finished devouring all the joyful feelings in the forest."

Sam shot him a reproachful, yet mildly entertained look.

Taren, though, shushed him. "I'll have someone bring you something later." Foo was in a very grouchy mood as of late because he was ready to do something more useful than sit in a tree.

"Thanks," he said.

Lunch was normally unproductive, much like Sam felt his training sessions were. But he looked forward to it, nonetheless. They would take the time and discuss plans for the upcoming journey to Exile. Exile was a town that Sam held with high respect. Lost children went to live there if they'd been unlucky enough to become trapped in Imagia. The town was impressive and Taren had a home there as well.

From what had been told so far, Taren's home had become somewhat of a second headquarter for the Protectors to convene and bring news. Other than Orga's home, it was the most important place for those fighting to save Imagia. It was also highly guarded. As of yet, Nadaroth had not attacked the village. Its inhabitants were growing wary, constantly on their guard.

Many precautions had been taken to ensure the safety of the village and the people that called it home. Exile wasn't the only village in Imagia, but it was easily the largest and most populated. Sam had learned much about the efforts of everyone in the last weeks. There were spies on both sides. Some of their own spies were actually spreading false information and trails that kept both headquarters as secret as possible. It was proving to become increasingly difficult as Nadaroth kept invading minds in the in-between in hopes of finding more definitive information. Fortunately, he had yet to find a mind that was important enough to reveal anything to help him.

As it were, Nadaroth didn't seem concerned about the locations of the Protectors. In fact, there had been a sudden decline in attacks for several months now. Taren was worried most about this, certain that it was because Nadaroth was holding something even more dangerous at bay. He referred to it as the quiet before the storm.

From all the information that had been gathered thus far, activity from Nadaroth's land was waning. He hadn't imagined anything in the form of a large army. Instead, he had been gathering as many marked beasts as possible from collectors.

When Sam heard about this, his thoughts saddened as he remembered Keesa. She was a marked beast. Most targets were powerful creatures that could be controlled easier than others. Collectors had been gathering them for years in an attempt to fill Nadaroth's lands with as many as he could command. Keesa's death still stung when Sam thought about it. She was the kindest soul he'd known who could become instantly terrifying when anyone threatened those she cared for. And she had cared very deeply for Sam.

Lunch conversation today was mostly just going over their plans for travel. Exile wasn't very far from Orga's but travel through the woods would be slower than usual. They needed to backtrack and leave false trails in case they were being followed.

The main question on Sam's mind was voiced at the first moment of silence. "So, I know everyone has been talking about this journey, but who all is coming?"

"We will have Iggy, Arty and, if he feels he's ready, Yetews," answered Taren.

Sam had just assumed that Yetews was going. It hadn't occurred to him that there was a possibility that he might not come. He'd just gotten his Guardian back and wasn't about to go anywhere important without him. Sam jerked his head around. The look on Yetews' face was all he needed for reassurance, but the extra nod helped. Sam relaxed again.

Taren continued. "Foo has offered to come." When Iggy and Arty both rolled their eyes at this, he ignored them. "We've also had a few volunteers. Pax, Hawke, and Arthur." He pointed at each of the volunteers. Pax was a strong, somewhat severe looking woman who wore her hair tightly braided. Her skin was nearly as dark as her hair. Hawke was a tall, burly man who seemed to mirror the same severe look as Pax. If Sam hadn't seen him laughing earlier with the man called Arthur, he would have been quite intimidating. Arthur was the opposite of both Pax and Hawke. He was short, wiry, and full of optimism. His sleek, black hair was pulled back in a nub of a ponytail and his eyes almost disappeared when he smiled. He was the only one who spoke when Taren introduced them.

"I'm honored to be part of this journey and to protect you, Sam."

"Er…thanks." As nice as that was meant to sound, it really just made Sam realize how pathetically helpless he must be to need so much protection. He looked to Taren with his next question. "Is that everyone? I'm sure Roz is going with us too. Oh. And you forgot about Titus."

An uncomfortable silence crept across the room and Sam was instantly aware that he didn't know as much as he thought he did. That little flicker of anger that always seemed to hover at the edges, started to grow again.

"As for Roz," Taren began, "I didn't want to speak for him, but I assumed he would want to be there with you."

"Of course!" Roz assured everyone. "I wouldn't be back in Imagia if it weren't for Sam. I owe him one or two already."

"Alright. And, I know this may seem a bit unexpected for you, but Titus isn't coming to Exile with us."

"Wait. What?" Titus always went with Sam. This was not something he was prepared to hear. He shot an almost betrayed look across the room at Titus who looked away guiltily.

"Garrett, I think you'd better take it from here."

Sam turned to where Taren was looking. He didn't realize that Garrett was in the room. He'd been spending most of his time healing from the run-in with the werewolf beast. Though a bit thinner and a shade paler than usual, he looked mostly like himself again. His bruises were faded, his arm was no longer in a sling and he looked as happy as he ever was.

"Hey there, Sam! Long time no see. As you know, I've been a bit indisposed. But now that I'm mostly on the mend, I have a task that needs to be attended to. And it would go much smoother with the help of another good tracker. Which is why I was hoping that you'd understand if Titus went with me."

"What task?" Sam was more curious than upset now. After not being able to help Garrett during the fight, he'd felt guilty that he'd gotten so badly hurt. It helped seeing his friend feeling this well.

"Well, this is where it gets a bit complicated, I'm afraid."

"I can keep up."

"Oh, I have no doubt." Garrett winked. "Do you remember much about the man that attempted to capture you when you got back to Imagia?"

"Not really. I didn't have much of a chance to see him before I lost consciousness. He was dressed in black and looked kinda familiar for some reason. He reminded me of someone…I think. Or something like that anyhow. The only other thing I remember is how…well…polite he was. It was really strange."

"Yes. That is Gabriel. Politely wicked. He'd rip your hand off without blinking, but apologize for it. And you know what? I think he really means it when he says sorry." Garrett laughed darkly.

"Gabriel. I remember hearing Taren use that name. So what about him?"

Garrett pulled up a chair, his smile faltering. "I honestly have no idea how to sugar coat this so I'll just come right out and say it. Gabriel is my brother."

"Your *brother*?" Sam's eyes went wide. He hadn't seen that one coming at all.

"Yes. That's probably why you thought he looked familiar." He poked his own nose. "Same nose. Though, I do think I pull it off much better, don't you think?"

As Sam looked at Garrett, the memories of those first moments back in Imagia clouded his vision. He could see it now. They could have been twins if it weren't for the fact that he knew Garrett so well. And of course, Garrett donned a large scar down his face that set them apart instantly.

When Sam didn't respond to his making light of the situation, Garrett cleared his throat. "Yes. Well, I suppose it is a bit of a shock. Gabriel is my older brother. We were barely two years apart in age. We did practically everything together as children. But one day, I noticed that the things he began doing were unsavory." He noticed that Sam was listening intently. Garrett grabbed a piece of bread off of the table and took a large bite before continuing.

"I suppose my father saw it before I did. But that's a different story for another time. Let's see…we were about nineteen when everything happened all at once. I had decided that I wanted to become a Protector, despite my brother's constant frustration with them. I could never understand why it bothered him so much. But now I know it was because we never had Guardians. Orga and I both think he was resentful for it.

"It wasn't until he woke me up in the middle of the night and asked me to come with him, that I knew he'd taken things too far."

"What happened?" Sam asked.

"He took me to a cave that was near our home. He'd captured a Guardian. He'd been holding it captive for weeks, torturing it. He'd heard Nadaroth was looking for collectors to bring him marked beasts and destroy Guardians. He was trying to get the Guardian to tell him how to find gateways."

Sam stopped him. "Can Guardians even do that?"

"No. But Gabriel wouldn't believe the poor thing. I was shocked…devastated. I couldn't believe what he'd done. I threatened to tell our parents, but that didn't do anything but force him to go further. He tried to convince me that what he was doing was right. That Imagia had been trapping kids here and Nadaroth was right to claim the broken lands. I didn't know how I hadn't seen this side of him before. I knew I had to tell our mother and father. But, I loved my brother. I couldn't go through with it. I still had hope that I could change his mind. I was just as young and naïve as he was.

"Hindsight is a funny thing. I know now that I should have turned him in. It could have prevented many things; which includes our current predicament. I think that Gabriel knew exactly what he was doing when he had you knocked out. Especially from what you've told us."

Sam shook his head as he thought it through. "How could anyone have known that hitting my head would cause problems with my imagination? It's impossible."

Holding up a finger, Garrett corrected him, "Improbable, yes. Not impossible."

"I don't understand," said Sam. "How is that different?"

"You're in Imagia. The only thing I think is impossible is that something *is* impossible. Was it impossible that he took out your imagination with one cleverly placed blow to the head? No. The probability was not good, but it was surely possible."

Sam wanted to hear more. "So you never turned your brother in?"

Something flickered in Garrett's eyes before he answered. In that one brief moment, there was a sadness that surfaced, blacking out the joy he normally wore. But it passed just as quickly. "No. I didn't have a chance to. The guilt weighed too heavily on my heart. However, I couldn't stand by and let that Guardian be tortured any longer. If I did, I might as well have been doing the torture myself.

"That night I decided that I would go free the Guardian when Gabriel left the cave. I pretended to be asleep and heard him leave. I waited just long enough that he wouldn't catch me following him. I was rather good at tracking." Garrett puffed his chest out and smiled proudly. "I waited for a long time, dreading what horrible things he must be doing to the poor soul for such a long time. Well, he finally left and I went in the cave. It was barely alive when I cut it down. I tried to help it out of the cave. But I didn't make it very far before my brother came back in.

"The look of betrayal on his face was…hard to see. But I tried to explain that what he was doing was wrong. He never raised his voice. Not even when I told him I had no choice but to tell our parents what he'd been doing. He simply walked up to me, pat me on the shoulder with a smile, and imbedded his knife directly into my stomach."

Sam gasped. There was no way that he would have seen this coming. "He tried to kill you? Your own brother?"

"Yes. I don't know how I didn't die." Garrett lifted his shirt, revealing the large silvery scar. He looked down at it and shook his head. "Not as good as my dragon scar, but it's a beauty, isn't it?" When he noticed that Sam was more shocked than entertained, he pulled his shirt back down and continued. "I still believe that he knew exactly where to aim so as not to kill me, but wound me just enough that I couldn't stop him.

"As I lie there bleeding on that cold cave floor, I watched him kill the Guardian, helpless to stop him. Of course, before he left, he looked back at me and said, 'Sorry, brother. But I'm afraid you're wrong. You've put your trust in the wrong side.' And then he was gone."

Sam was aghast. "Your mom and dad must have been devastated when they found out."

Garrett sighed sadly. "I wouldn't know. Gabriel killed them that night. I found them the next day when I finally dragged myself home."

"Oh my gosh, Garrett. I'm…I'm so sorry."

He smiled, surprisingly. "It's not your fault. It wasn't even mine. Though I did blame myself for a long time. But Nadaroth has a way of setting his roots inside of a person. They grow and grow until they take hold. I still have hope though."

Sam couldn't believe his ears. Garrett noticed the confusion before he had a chance to voice it.

"He is my brother. No matter how difficult that is. He kept me alive when he could have killed me. And for years there was no sign of him. No word. I thought he might have died as well. He has become Nadaroth's most prevalent pawn at the moment. It's my task to find out what his next move is. And maybe…just maybe…"

Garrett trailed off, deep in his own thoughts. Sam wanted to ask what 'maybe' meant, but something in him told him that he shouldn't ask. He, as well as everyone else, let it go.

There wasn't a word spoken in the room as Garrett finished his story. Most already knew everything. But respect was given. Sam had always seen Garrett in a positive light. There was no way that he, or anyone who'd met him, could have known that there was so much sadness in his past. There was a reason he was so highly regarded by everyone. To have dealt with so much and come through the other side with a smile was one of the strongest things Sam had ever seen.

When Garrett finally regained his composure, he stood up. "So, now that I've completely drained the happiness from the room, I think I'll go start making my preparations. And with your blessing, Titus can prepare as well." He paused as he watched Sam consider what it meant. "I promise you that I will protect him with my own life, if need be. Gabriel is difficult to find. He's clever. I could use Titus' talented nose. Two trackers are better than one, I always say." He chuckled, attempting to lighten the mood in the atmosphere.

Titus trotted over to Sam. The wisdom that had grown in his eyes over the years was hard to ignore. He put a paw up on Sam's knee. "I want to help him. You know that I can. And, to be honest, I really don't think I'll need 'protecting'," he said with an eye roll. "I'm fairly certain I can manage to keep myself alive and well."

Garrett retorted, "He's right you know. I just said that because I thought it sounded impressive."

Titus gave a lop-sided doggy grin. "We all have a part to play in this battle. Besides," he looked around the room, "I think you'll have quite the party to keep you company while you're away."

With that, Sam had no choice but to agree. He opened his mouth to speak, but couldn't figure out what words would work. So his mouth closed with an inaudible pop and he nodded.

Titus returned the nod and not another word was spoken. He'd have plenty of time to find the right words. Until then, there were other plans to be made. Today wasn't the day for goodbyes.

Chapter Twenty-two: Matters of the Heart

The collective mood at Orga's home was quite somber. Preparations were complete and those leaving were ready to embark upon their set tasks. The only thing left was to wish each other well on their journeys.

Sam agreed that it would be good for Titus to go with Garrett to find Gabriel. Garrett, still feeling somewhat connected to his brother, stood the best chance of not only finding him, but also discovering whatever information he knew regarding Nadaroth's plans. In the past years, Garrett had had more than a few run-ins with his estranged brother. Despite the fact that he had tried to kill Garrett once, Gabriel had never tried too hard to dispose of his brother.

Orga knew that Garrett was hopeful that he could change his brother. But he also believed that Gabriel felt the same way about Garrett. Which would explain their inevitable inability to destroy one another. Either way, it was a strange relationship that had proved useful for finding out information. Whenever anyone asked about their relationship, Garrett's only response was, "It's complicated," and then left it at that.

Several Protectors were remaining with Orga. He wasn't about to leave his home. Sam had also been told that a few extra reinforcements were to arrive before they left in order to establish a further radius of protection around his borders. When he asked who was coming, hopeful that perhaps his old shrinking dragon friend,

Enoch, might be one of them to return, something important came up and the subject was dropped. Enoch was the only friend that remained unseen since Sam's return.

Maggie was one of the ones remaining with Orga. Zane was another that showed up to help. It only took a moment for Sam to recognize him when he arrived. He'd been the first Protector to greet them in the Village of Exile all those years ago. He was ecstatic to see Sam again, shaking his hand vigorously when he arrived.

The rest of them were going to Exile. There, they would meet up at Taren's home and lay out their plan. Which Sam still had no idea what that meant. Even though they talked about it frequently, no real details of what this trip entailed was ever given. After awhile, Sam decided to just roll with it and stop letting it bother him. Taren and the others had good reason for their secrecy. At least that's what Sam told himself. Otherwise he would just get upset at his lack of knowledge.

The sun was just rising enough that the light began filtering through the canopy, casting a bright green glow across the clearing. Everyone was outside, the warmth of the early morning a refreshing change from the inside of Orga's home. A light rain from the night before wet the ground, which Titus said would make things difficult for tracking. But the damp air felt nice. Sam noticed he wasn't the only one breathing in the smells.

Taren was looking into the trees, a slight air of impatience to his stance. Then suddenly, his body relaxed slightly and he turned to address everyone. "Alright everyone, listen up." the crowd quieted, all eyes on him. "Now that the rest of our reinforcements are here, it's nearly time to go on our ways. Orga has asked to address us before we leave." Taren stepped back and all eyes went to Orga who was standing near the top of the slope into his home. He never ventured too far, rarely having left the confines of the clearing.

Orga gazed around at everyone before speaking, his eyes falling on Sam last and the longest. He smiled somberly and then spoke. "Sometimes, in the face of adversity, leaving behind those we love and call friends can be the most difficult thing we do. Not a one of you is unfamiliar with loss or pain. In times of turmoil, when the world is at battle, the one thing that is constant is fighting for what is good. And each of your sacrifices, no matter how little they seem to be, will not be in vain.

"I can't say what tomorrow will hold for any of you. But I can say that here, we are amongst our friends. I hope that all of your journeys are productive and that each of you remains safe. Before you leave, remember this," Orga's eyes locked with Sam's now, "Nadaroth will try to break you all. He is trying to break all of Imagia. When in doubt, trust in your friends." His eyes began to scan the crowd again. "Sometimes, the choices we make are all that we really have to call our own. Choose your paths wisely. It is time to say your farewells. Be safe everyone." With that, Orga turned and began to descend back into his home.

The crowd dispersed, many words of well wishing being muttered. Sam watched Orga leaving and rushed to follow him. As Orga isn't known for his speed, Sam caught up easily.

"Wait!" Sam called to him.

Orga turned and gave him the same somber grin he'd seen earlier. He didn't answer; he merely raised his brown brow slightly.

"I want to ask you something before I go."

"You want to know if I think bringing you back was a mistake."

Sam was taken aback. He swallowed, looked at his feet for moment and then said, "No." He shook his head quickly. "I mean yes. Or…kind of. I don't know. I just," he tried to choose his words carefully, "I'm not very useful right now. And," he lowered his voice, "everyone has so much faith in me. What if…" Sam blew out a defeated breath. He didn't finish his thought.

"What if they are what? Wrong?"

Sam shrugged and leaned his back on the earthy wall.

"We chose to go and find you because we have faith that you are more than just some random child. You chose to come back because, even though you don't want to admit it, you believe that they are right. Sam, you must learn to have faith in yourself. Perhaps *that* is the most important journey you will take."

Sam was considering everything Orga said. He knew that he wanted to fight for Imagia, regardless of his power to imagine. It was the most important thing to him.

Orga clasped his spindly fingers over Sam's shoulder. "You will imagine again, Sam. And *if* you don't, I have faith that you will do what is right for this world. Never forget: It is all about the choices we make."

With that, Sam gave the old Guardian a hug. "Thanks. Be safe, Orga." Then he went back to join the others.

As he slowly walked towards his own group, he looked around. In the corner of his eye, he spotted Garrett and Maggie under a tree together.

Maggie had her head down. She looked upset. Her and Garrett had their hands clasped together as he spoke to her. She shook her head slowly. Garrett appeared as though he was trying to reassure her of something.

Sam watched them. Even though he couldn't hear what they were saying he felt a bit intrusive. He just couldn't bring himself to look away.

Something shiny glinted in the sun as it fell off of Maggie's cheek. She was crying. Garrett put his hand to her chin and softy lifted her face to his. Whatever words he said next caused Maggie to take one hand and put it on his chest over his heart. They exchanged a very powerful look and Garrett flashed her his signature smile. She threw her arms around him and he embraced her. When they pulled away from the hug, Garrett leaned down to her face and began to kiss her softly.

With that, Sam turned away and felt himself blush. As he turned he nearly jumped out of his skin when he saw Taren standing next to him.

"Maggie's worried about him," Taren answered Sam's unspoken question. "She doesn't think he's healed enough to leave yet. And…well…we all know how Garrett is."

Sam looked at Taren questioningly.

He laughed quietly. "He's always been sure of himself and way more optimistic than most. I think we can agree on that."

Sam laughed too. That was the exact first impression of Garrett that he'd had. He risked another peek at them and was thankful that they were no longer kissing.

Taren pat Sam on the back. He motioned with his head for Sam to follow him. Sam was glad to go. He had his own goodbyes to think about.

By this time in his life, Sam was tired of saying goodbye. Most of the time, he didn't even actually get to say the words. So, when Titus (who knew him the longest) trotted over to him, they both simply stood there in silence.

Titus sat down on his haunches, neither facing the other, but rather staring out into the forest. It was very reminiscent of their many evenings back home. Titus was the one who willingly broke the silence.

"I suppose you're thinking about pizza right about now."

Sam burst out laughing. It was the exact perfect thing that his friend could have said at that moment. When their laughter simmered down, Sam sighed as they both gazed out into the morning shadows of the forest.

"Well," Sam started, "I'm not saying it."

Titus mirrored Sam's sigh. "Yeah. I'm not either."

It was mutual. Saying goodbye wasn't needed. Not this time.

"Okay then." Sam turned to Titus. "Watch out for Garrett. I think maybe Maggie might be right about him rushing into this."

"You have my word." He grinned.

"And…ya know…be careful out there."

Titus nodded. "You too. Though, you do have quite the entourage. I have a feeling you'll manage just fine. I'm glad Roz is going with you. I don't know why, but that makes me feel better about not being there."

"You and me both. He gets me. Know what I mean?"

"Yes. I believe so."

Taren called for Sam. It was time to set out. Exile wasn't far, but they weren't taking the shortest route. The trip would take a few days this time because they tried not to use the same path more than once for safety reasons.

"I'd better go," Sam said, a small lump forming in the back of his throat.

"Same here. Garrett is waiting. If all goes to plan we should see each other back here soon enough."

"See you then."

Titus nodded once and trotted away towards Garrett. Sam watched him leave. The lump in his throat wanted to form the word '*wait*' so that he could give his dog a hug. But he caught Garrett's eye. Garrett waved with more enthusiasm than Sam could muster but he returned the gesture. Their waves translated as a goodbye and see you later. Then Sam turned to join his own group.

Their group was ready, each carrying a rucksack and an array of weapons. Taren led them out of the clearing. The familiar sight of Orga's home was gone too soon.

Taren took the lead with Hawke. Sam stayed in the middle of the group, walking with Yetews and Roz at his sides. Foo, Arthur, and Pax were fanned out behind them all, each one looking alert. Iggy and Arty talked Yetews into being their ride. They'd convinced only themselves that it was so they were at a higher vantage point to see any potential threats.

The day dragged on as they traveled. It had been a long while since the last time Sam had ventured into the wild of Imagia. In a way, it was refreshing. But there was also a very strong ominous feeling about it. He shook it off for the time being, hopeful that he was wrong.

By the time they stopped to eat, it was midday. Sam opened his own backpack that he'd brought from home. He'd packed most of the stuff he'd brought with him before coming to Imagia and changed into clothes more fitting to this world. Taren had made sure to give him more of the clothes he'd used at Sam's age. It worked out perfectly.

The forest was quieter than usual. The chattering of birds didn't fill the canopy. Sam couldn't help but notice. Roz was sitting next to him enjoying some of the bread Orga had sent. He was mid-bite when Sam asked him, "Am I the only one who thinks it's too quiet? For a forest, I mean."

Swallowing his bread, Roz looked around and listened. "Huh." He hadn't noticed until now. "Strange. You know," he said, "I think you're right. Where's Taren?"

They both looked around. Taren was nowhere in sight. Iggy and Arty were napping on the ground, both using the same exposed root of a tree as a pillow. Sam poked Arty.

Arty opened one eye casually and when he noticed it was Sam who nudged him, he closed it again. He muttered, "What is it?"

"Do you know where Taren is? I can't see him anywhere."

Arty settled himself further into the ground. "He had to check something up ahead. He'll be back shortly."

"Oh." The quiet was unsettling. He decided to question Arty a bit further. "Roz and I were just saying how quiet the forest seems. Does that worry you guys?"

Arty didn't answer, a little snore coming out instead. Sam looked up at Yetews who rolled his eyes. He snorted and then grabbed Arty and Iggy by their feet, tugging them enough that their heads fell off of the root with a soft thud waking them instantly. Sam and Roz both laughed while Yetews feigned innocence.

"Hey!" They both shouted out at the same time. Yetews pointed at Sam.

Iggy got up, dusted himself off, and growled, "What's the big idea? Can't a guy nap in peace?"

"Yeah! What he said!" Arty jabbed a clawed thumb towards his counterpart.

Just then, Foo came sidling up to them looking quite put out. "What's going on here?"

Roz, trying to look like the responsible one, mentioned to Foo their concerns about Taren and the quiet of the forest but he didn't seem concerned in the slightest. He grumbled something about them being worried about the wrong things and then said, "Taren is perfectly fine. He has duties that are not our concern at the moment and you lot would do well to stop chattering like a bunch of overactive children."

Foo turned to leave and was instantly stopped in his tracks by Iggy's next words.

"Ahh, don't worry about old Foo. He's always been grumpy. But I'd be grumpy too if I had his name." Iggy and Arty were chuckling now.

Seeing the dark look that appeared on Foo's face made it evident that he didn't want this conversation to be happening. And Sam, not in the habit of keeping his curiosity to himself, let the question slip past his lips too late. "What's wrong with his name? I think 'Foo' is pretty cool name, actually."

The look on the two ferrets' faces was devious. Iggy nudged his friend in the rib lightly. "Did ya hear that, Arty? Sam thinks it's cool."

"Ha! Well," Arty replied, "if Foo was his name, then we could see your point. But that's not your *real* name, now is it Foo?"

Foo looked absolutely murderous, but he refrained from answering their snide remark.

"Go on now. I always say that if you don't know a friend's name, you can't really call him a friend. Besides, he's bound to find out one way or the other." Iggy was enjoying this way too much.

"Yeah. He's a smart one. Our children name us, and it's nothin' to be ashamed of!" Arty's voice was mocking at best as the two continued to poke at Foo.

Sam was intrigued more than he wanted to admit. He couldn't resist. "What's your real name?"

Sam and Foo's gaze met and his eyes softened slightly. One of his hands went to the mysterious pouch hanging around his neck and clung tightly to it. Foo stood a little straighter and growled, "Fine. My name is…" He trailed off and the words got lost behind his gritted teeth.

"I didn't hear you. What?" Sam asked.

Foo rolled his eyes. He didn't manage to repeat himself because Iggy did it for him.

"What he said was that his name is actually Mr. Foofykins."

There was nothing for it. Iggy and Arty lost all composure and their laughs, rude and obnoxious as they were, became infectious.

Roz tried not to laugh, so he covered his mouth casually with one hand and asked. "Seriously? Foofykins?"

Sam kept his composure, but he was the only one. "Well, I don't think it's that bad. Really."

Though his look could have killed the others, he looked at Sam differently. With every bit of sincerity, he said, "Thank you." He turned on his heel with all intents on storming away. Before doing so, his ears laid back against his head. He looked as though he was about to add something, but shook his head softly and thought better of it. With that, he left, disappearing into the branches of a tree as far away from the others as possible.

At that moment, Taren appeared and noticed the commotion going on in Sam's little group. He appeared to be asking Foo something and it was easy enough to see what they're conversation entailed. He looked annoyed and was shaking his head in disapproval. When he reached the cackling group, they quieted halfway down.

Iggy, apparently having already been in this same situation before, tried to stop Taren before he could preach to them about their obvious wrongdoing. “Ah, come on, Taren. We were just havin’ a bit of fun. Foo can take it. He’s just grumpy, that’s all.”

“That’s irrelevant. You two just need to stop being such…such…” Taren was getting irritated with them and any civil words failed him.

Arty tried to finish his sentence. “Being such what? Meanies?”

He frowned down at them. “No. Complete jerks!”

Iggy and Arty both ‘oohed’ at Taren and then got up to walk away. As they walked off, they passed under the tree Foo was perched in, still joking with one another. Sam watched Foo. He could only see his back, but as the two passed by him, Sam was sure that Foo’s posture changed. His shoulders fell slightly. He looked hurt.

Sam, though part of him wanted to laugh at their antics, knew that Arty and Iggy crossed a line. It wasn’t uncommon for them and had been more of a defense mechanism for the duo than anything else. But that didn’t excuse it.

Roz, seeing the look on Taren’s face, suddenly had the need to leave. “Excuse me,” he said. “I’ll uh…be over there if you need me.”

Glancing at Foo again, Taren said to Sam, “Don’t let those guys get to you. The three of them haven’t gotten along from the beginning. They had an argument about you.”

“Me?” Sam was taken aback.

“Foo was against bringing you back initially.”

“Why?”

“He’s a Guardian. We were hard pressed to find any that weren’t against it. Messing with the gateways is unnatural at best. Despite what you could do to help us, most Guardians weren’t very supportive. Iggy and Arty, they meant well. But they got into it with Foo. Ever since then it’s been rocky.”

Sam felt bad. He didn’t want to come between anyone and cause problems. Foo seemed like a nice enough Guardian to him, even if he was a bit rough around the edges. “Sorry.”

“Not your fault,” Taren assured him. “Just don’t be too hard on Foo. He’s been through a lot.”

“What happened?”

Taren didn't answer. He was considering what to say. Finally, he said, "It's not my story to tell. If you want to know his story, you'll have to ask him yourself."

Sam nodded. He understood. But today was not going to be that day.

"Now," Taren changed the subject, "we need to get moving. We need to backtrack and go east for a bit. After that, we'll stop for the night."

There was still no answer as to why things seemed off balance in the forest, but the fact that Taren didn't seem wary of anything was a relief. He'd been protecting these lands far longer than any of them. If Sam couldn't trust in that, then where would he be?

Yetews nudged Sam playfully. He grumbled something with a smile.

Smiling back, he answered his friend. "Yeah. I remember. Too bad I grew so much or I'd be riding on your shoulders again. I'd just end up kicking you in the head now. Maybe on our next break we can sneak off by ourselves for a few minutes. And by 'sneak off' I mean that the entire group will know exactly where we are going and when we'll be back."

They both laughed. Yetews rumbled another question, this time more seriously.

"No. I'm not going to bother Foo today. He'd probably…I don't know…shoot daggers out of his eyes or something if I tried talking to him. Some other time."

Those last few words struck a cord he didn't expect. Essentially, they were at war. What if another time never came? He didn't linger on that thought and pushed the anxious feelings down deep where he didn't have to worry about them.

Taren called out for them to get moving. Sam couldn't help but to feel it was going to be a long trip if half their party was upset with the others. He liked Iggy and Arty. But sometimes, he wondered what went through their heads. He let the thought trail off as they began the next leg of their journey through the wild of Imagia. His feet already hurt just thinking about it.

* * * * * * * * * * *

It seemed like ages since the last time Sam was able to truly enjoy the vast forests of Imagia. The tree that he and Yetews were resting under had a familiarity to it that Sam was struggling to place. Across the sun kissed grass of the small glade, was a group of bushes donning wide, fragrant flowers. Even in the shade of the tree, Yetews felt warm as he leaned on his friend. His mind was empty of all but one thought. "*What does this place remind me of?*"

Sam stared at the flowers across the way, still trying to place it. He felt Yetews' body behind him rising and falling with every breath. It was very peaceful, yet something didn't seem to make sense. All the troubles of this world had melted away. He thought, "*What troubles? Was I worried about something?*" He couldn't remember what even made him think that and he shrugged and sighed happily as he listened to the strange calls of birds in the canopy.

"*But that bush looks so familiar,*" thought Sam again. He screwed his face up in concentration, trying to connect a memory to this perfect place. He began to retrace his steps back from where him and Yetews had been that day. But no matter how hard he tried, he couldn't do it. His head started to ache a little, but he couldn't remember why. He rubbed the back of his head, his fingers getting lost in his messy hair. He tried to remember how he'd gotten here, but no amount of effort helped.

Sam didn't feel relaxed anymore. His chest felt tight, anxiety creeping in. "Yetews?" Sam began. "Do you remember how we got here?"

Yetews didn't respond.

Something wasn't right. Sam wanted to turn and look at Yetews, but he couldn't. The only thing he could do was stare at those flowers. Something sneezed in the bushes, flowers flying through the air. Two eyes, green and familiar, shined in the shadows. Yetews was in the bushes, staring at him.

It was at this precise moment that Sam's memory began to work again. This was the same exact place that he'd first been united with Yetews four years ago after coming through his gateway. The tightening in his chest worsened, almost as though a weight was crushing down on him. His eyes connected with Yetews'. But the look he gave Sam was one of fear in its deepest form. The bush was shivering around Yetews, leaves and petals falling to the ground.

The harsh reality hit him like a rock.

Yetews wasn't the one breathing behind him.

Sam's head was no longer aching. It was pounding. Fear gripped his every sense and he winced as the tightness in his chest began to burn as though he was being cut a hundred times. He looked down and saw that there were root like tentacles, black as night, wrapped around his entire body. They were squeezing him, digging into his skin. He could barely breathe. He looked at Yetews, eyes pleading, as he wheezed, "Help…"

But Yetews couldn't help. In place of the beautiful bush that was once there was nothing but dead, spiny brambles, and Yetews was twisted awkwardly in them, the thorns growing into his arms and legs. The ground below him cracked and swelled, slowly swallowing the Guardian.

Sam tried to yell, but he couldn't get air. Yetews was helplessly sinking into the ground. Out of the corner of his eye, Sam saw something shining and could hear someone calling. A gateway was there and the shadowy figure of a small boy was calling out, lost. "Hello?" the boy called from outside the gateway. "Are you there?"

Sam wanted to yell to the boy and tell him to run away. He wanted to call for his friends. He couldn't understand how he'd gotten into this hopeless situation. One last thought went through his mind as he watched his Guardian disappear. "*How did this happen? I can't even remember waking up this morning…* "

It was that single thought that shook his core. He couldn't remember waking up that morning because he never had.

He was still asleep.

Sam tried to scream out. He had to let someone know that he was having a nightmare. But the harder he tried to scream, the tighter the creature behind him squeezed; the deeper the tentacles dug into his flesh. Every breath stung as he tried to focus on pulling air into his lungs.

The boy outside the gateway kept calling out to the Guardian that would never come. Sam finally realized what he was seeing. That boy was himself. And the Guardian that would never come was Yetews. His Guardian was unable to escape the evil of this world. As the gateway shimmered and closed, a new image took its place. It didn't come out of the shadows because it *was* the shadow, creeping eerily from the darkness. Hovering off of the ground, wisps of smoky blackness billowing around him, was Nadaroth. His red eyes pierced Sam's soul. There was no mouth speaking the words that penetrated the forest. In a whisper sharp as a knife, Nadaroth's voice consumed every part of Sam's mind. Slowly, almost painfully, he said, "I...will...*break*...you..."

Those words made Sam use the last air he could find. Through gritted teeth, he whispered loudly so that Nadaroth could hear, his voice shaking and fierce. "Never!" It didn't matter how hard Sam convinced himself that this was only a nightmare. He was afraid.

Nadaroth didn't move for a long moment, hovering silently in the darkness. Sam watched him as he fought the pain in his body that he knew wasn't real. But his head pounded so hard that he struggled to form clear thoughts.

Suddenly, the thorn-laden thicket that had been pulling Yetews into the ground shook violently. Yetews was obviously struggling against his bonds. Sam's chest began to hurt worse, a deep pain he'd never felt before. Then, with one last great effort, Yetews yelled out and was instantly silenced as the thorns tightened severely. Yetews' once struggling hand went limp. Blood dripped from the punctures and trailed to the forest floor.

Sweat was dripping off of his clammy face and he tried desperately to convince himself none of it was real. Nadaroth's raspy laugh echoed all around for only a few seconds. Then, the shadowy figure sped towards Sam with ghostly speed. His eyes blazed and Sam forced his own eyes closed, willing himself not to meet his adversary's gaze. Nadaroth whispered in Sam's ear, "*Death...*"

With that, Sam's head was surely splitting in half. His chest tightened so badly that he could no longer breathe. With a final, weak thud in his chest, he felt his heart stop. He tried to open his mouth to scream and wake up from this nightmare. But there was no air left in his lungs; no fight left in his body. He could no longer feel the thick tentacles holding him. He felt nothing but a choking darkness.

Then, as the darkness was just about to fully consume him, he felt a new pain. His chest ached, but different than in his nightmare. Something was hitting him over and over again. Whatever it was, he wanted it to stop.

Sound returned to his ears. The voice of his enemy was replaced with the many worried callings of his name. He wanted to tell whoever was hitting him to stop when he realized that the thing he desperately needed was air. Sam gasped loudly, as if surfacing from a near drowning. His eyes fluttered opened as he heard someone yell, "Stop! He's breathing!"

Sam recognized Taren's voice. As his eyes focused, he realized he was on the ground below the tree he'd fallen asleep under. There were several concerned faces staring down at him, the closest one being Roz's.

"Sam? Can you hear us?" Roz's voice was shaking as he panted from something that had required a lot of effort.

Sam started to sit up and felt a pain in his chest that stopped him. He wheezed, "Yeah," and relaxed back into the soft earth around him. His skin was clammy and he felt shaky all over.

There were several sighs and sounds of relief all around. Roz looked relieved and said, "Oh, thank goodness. I didn't even know if I was doing it right."

"What happened?" Sam wheezed again. "And why…do I feel…like my ribs are broken?" He felt weak. Waking up from a nightmare had never been so physically draining before.

"Because they probably are," Roz answered reluctantly.

"What?"

Taren's face came into Sam's field of vision. "We couldn't wake you up. You looked like you were struggling for air. Then...you stopped breathing."

Sam was suddenly very afraid. He asked, "*What*?"

"Your heart stopped." Taren looked as frightened as Sam felt.

Sam's palms went cold. He had a sinking feeling that he should be very grateful that he was alive.

Taren looked at Roz who was still shaky. "Luckily," he stated, "Roz knew what to do."

Sam was still feeling horrible, but he looked at his friend. "H-how?"

Roz shook his head, not sure he believed it himself. "Honestly, I'm surprised it worked. I had to go to this strange meeting with all of the other teachers in your school. They taught something called CPR.

I was hesitant at first, but they assured us that it was life saving. Apparently," he laughed shakily, "they were right."

The pounding on his chest. The gasping for air. It all made sense. In his dream, he'd felt his heart stop. Even though it was part of his nightmare, it had been real.

"Are you alright?" Iggy's voice sounded extra concerned. "You gave us a right terrible scare, my friend."

"I'm fine." Sam lied. His words were soft and not without effort. "It was just a nightmare." He lied again. His nightmares had been few and far between since returning to Imagia. But the ones that he had had were beyond a simple dream. Nadaroth had found a way to create a true danger that went far beyond simple fear.

He'd attacked right where it counted: The heart.

Chapter Twenty-three: The Hard Road to Exile

Sam's ribs ached and his chest felt sore with each breath he took. There was also a noticeable slump to his shoulders as he walked. But he knew that he should just be thankful that he was breathing at all at this point. On top of everything, each time he winced in pain, (which he was careful to refrain from) Roz would look at him guiltily. By day's end, Sam finally convinced Roz to stop apologizing for saving his life.

Taren, on the other hand, was looking at Roz completely differently. The morning after Sam's brush with Nadaroth, Taren approached Roz. Sam was recalling this moment yet again.

"Can I have a word, Roz?" Taren looked nervous.

Roz glanced towards Sam as he drew his attention away from the fire he'd just extinguished. "Sure," he said.

He looked like a man who was trying very hard to say sorry, but was still reluctant to do so. No apology came. What he said was much more significant. "I want to thank you for what you did yesterday. If you hadn't been there…I don't know what would have happened. Had you not known – what was it you called that technique? PCR?"

Roz chuckled. "C-P-R." He said the letters a little slower than necessary.

"That's right." Taren chuckled too. "Anyways, I just hope that you'll be sticking around in case anyone else needs saving."

Not sure how to take this sudden change in attitude, he simply said, "Of course."

"Good." He stuck his hand out towards Roz. "Thank you." His eyes spoke as loud as his words.

They grasped hands and shook. As Taren walked away, Roz turned to Sam and gave him two very enthusiastic thumbs up.

The memory faded and Sam found himself smiling. Yetews was watching him. He grunted low, a question in his eyes.

Considering Yetews' words, he shrugged. "Not really. It's not that I have a lot on my mind. Just thinking about how so much has changed. Shoot! I don't even know for certain just how long I've been back in Imagia."

Yetews purred low with a sideways look at Sam.

Reaching up to scratch behind Yetews' ears, he said, "Yeah. I'm glad I'm back too." As he scratched he made a mental note about how much easier it was to reach this time."

The Guardian stopped and Sam followed suit. He looked at his boy affectionately and then placed a flattened palm sideways against his chest. His eyes went back and forth from his chest to Sam's head and then he took the other palm and held them both in front of him, noting the difference in height. He cocked his brow and didn't say a word. He didn't have to.

Sam had to remind himself that Yetews was still rushing to catch up from how much Sam had changed in the three years they'd spent apart. "Yeah, I know. I'm not so little anymore."

Right at that moment, Foo marched past them. "Come on you two. No dawdling. If we're to make it to Exile before the end of the year, we've got to keep going."

Yetews rolled his eyes and they both followed behind Foo.

Whether it was the pain or the heat, Sam didn't know. But the day was dragging on quite slowly. All of the back stepping was starting to be felt. Just like his ten-year-old self, Sam did his best to not complain. Somehow, being older forced him to want to be stronger.

Eventually, after a long day of traveling through some of the thickest forest undergrowth possible, Taren called it quits. It had been enough traveling for the day. Hawke and Pax were busy getting stuff gathered to start a fire while most of the others were stationed around the camp on lookout. Taren disappeared into the forest after briefly talking with Arthur. Sam wondered where he could be going yet again. He tried not to dwell on it too much as it tended to agitate him.

The traveling for the day had left everyone exhausted, but Sam was sure that he was the only one whose feet ached so badly. He'd been away from such strenuous traveling for too many years while the others were used to it. It also didn't help that his ribs and chest were so bruised. Taren, having been taught some healing arts by Orga over the years, had decided that the ribs were likely not broken, but rather bruised. Roz hadn't had to do chest compressions too long.

The tree trunk that Sam finally leaned up against was more comfortable than it should have been. For a moment, he thought about his bed back home. That would have been lovely right about now. But in just a couple more days, he'd be at Taren's home. Providing Taren hadn't gotten rid of the beds, he'd have something softer to sleep on soon enough.

After his last nightmare, Sam struggled with the idea of sleep. He talked it over with Yetews and Roz for a bit and eventually, they decided that sleep was worth the risk. Someone would be assigned to check on him frequently while he slept. That wasn't nearly as comforting to Sam as everyone thought it should be. He may not have enjoyed nightmares, but he wasn't sure that he could sleep knowing someone was always watching him.

Yetews tousled Sam's hair, a familiar gesture that was welcome and nostalgic at the same time. The only difference was that afterwards, Sam ran his fingers through his hair and straightened it up as best as possible. Then Yetews grumbled something reassuringly.

"Thanks buddy," Sam said. "I appreciate you being the first watch. Not as awkward…I think."

The forest was still quieter than usual, but the sounds of the dusky evening couldn't be completely silenced. Cricket-like songs echoed through the trees and fireflies danced lazily in the shadows. The fire had finally taken hold and the crackle of the flames was equally enjoyable. The faint smell of smoke filled his nose and he sighed as he massaged his ribcage. As usual, there was only a light breeze. It wasn't too strong, but just enough to cool off after a sweaty day of traveling.

Sam closed his eyes and was more aware of the headache that he'd had most of the day. Sleep would be easy enough, he thought. And it was. He felt himself drifting off and before he knew it, was standing at the edge of sleep, right in the midst of his in-between. He was faintly aware of the light chatter going on around the campsite as well as the dream that would come should he choose to dive into that peaceful abyss.

In his in-between, he saw the vague images of his family back home. He saw flashes of his future baby brother and of school days with Lizzy. He started to think of his mom calling him back inside as he sat on the hill behind the fence in his backyard. When she called his name, it sounded more frantic than usual. Each time she called him, it seemed to get louder. Now it was somehow right beside him, and sounded like Roz. It gave him a jolt.

Sam's eyes exploded open when he heard it again.

"Sam!"

Their entire party was standing in a circular formation around the campsite, weapons drawn. The fire had been doused. Sam joined them, jumping to his feet instantly. "What is it?" Sam asked anyone who was listening.

Clutching onto Yetews' curled horn, Iggy was the one to answer. "Don't know yet. Taren came rushing in and told us to be on our guard. He has a scout in the forest that warned him."

A terrible roar sent chills down Sam's spine. It sounded familiar somehow. He rushed to place it. Whatever it was roared again. This time, Sam knew. He'd heard that sound before and was equally apprehensive about it. This time it sounded much angrier.

"A dragon." Sam hadn't said it to anyone in particular, but his observation didn't go unnoticed by those around him.

Arty, standing on Yetews' other horn, cursed quietly. "I knew I recognized that roar."

Roz backed up and stood next to Sam. His bow was drawn and aimed towards the trees. "Are you sure?" he asked.

"Yeah. Only the last time I heard a sound like that, it wasn't this angry."

He didn't respond to Sam, but rather called to Taren. "We aren't equipped to handle a dragon."

"No. But we don't have a choice. Our only chance is that it's too big to land in this thick of forest."

Roz's shoulders fell. He looked around the trees and muttered, "Well *that's* encouraging." Looking back towards Sam, he asked, "Any chance that imagination of yours is getting stronger?"

"I can try."

Another roar came from above them. The dragon was circling and getting closer.

"Now's as good a time as any." He pointed an arrow to the sky. It was still dusky out so they all saw the silhouette of the beast as it closed in.

Several arrows were loosed, but if any actually hit their target, it didn't show. Another round of arrows flew into the canopy as a great crashing sound sent everyone running away from the timber and leaves that were falling to the ground.

The dragon was large, but not nearly as large as the roar it emitted. Hawke was struggling to get to his feet again after taking a fall while avoiding a branch. He called out as the monster untangled itself from the wild trees. "It's a small one! Take out the eyes and then go for the wings! Cripple it and then we can take it down!"

Taren was on it. He shot an arrow, straight and true, towards the eyes. It would have been a direct hit had it not turned its head suddenly. Instead, the tip of the arrow chinked off of a bony spot in between its yellow eyes.

Now that it was close, Sam could see that it had deep, bluish-black scales and a gray, fleshy underbelly. Its head was covered in sharp, ivory horns, one especially long one on the tip of its nose. It was finally free, and about the size of two elephants. It crouched low. Its long tail was covered in an array of deadly spikes and it thrashed the tail around behind it, taking massive notches out of the tree trunks around it.

It began to charge at Hawke so Pax jumped in front of him, deftly swinging her large sword. The sound of metal connecting with flesh was sickening to hear and the dragon threw back its head to roar in agony. When it dropped its head back down, it clawed frantically at the place where an eye should have been. Pax had a triumphant smirk on her face and she whooped loudly.

Sam was concentrating on the scene and tried to imagine roots, thick and strong, growing all around the feet and tail of the beast so as to hold it down. As he did, his head began to ache. For a brief moment, it seemed to be working, but aching turned to pounding and it broke his concentration. The vines, intertwining around the dragon's legs, faded away leaving nothing changed.

Taren was out of arrows by now, as were Hawke and Arthur. Roz was trying to get a clean shot to the face and had saved several of his for that purpose. It was down to brute force and they were at a disadvantage. The only advantage they had was that the size of the dragon made it difficult for it to move around the thickly treed area.

The dragon's massive head was low to the ground, its damaged eye now closed. It hissed, massive teeth lining the black jaw. Like a snake poised to attack, it swayed its head to and fro picking the target. It zeroed in on Arthur. It snarled, baring its awful teeth. Quick as lightning, it struck out and just missed him, catching his bow and biting it in half with a loud crack. Arthur dove and went into an agile front roll across the ground.

When he jumped back to his feet, he yelled out to the dragon, "You missed, you worthless snake!" He pulled a dagger from a sheath in his boot. He didn't notice how close he was to the dragon's equally deadly tail.

"Arthur, look out!!" Taren yelled out the warning a moment too late.

A terrible thud was followed by the sound of Arthur screaming as he flew threw the air and landed hard against a tree. Something cracked, but as Sam watched the events taking place, he didn't know if it was the sound of the tree breaking or Arthur.

Sam felt helpless. His imagination was useless and he had no weapons to fight. He decided to run to Arthur and see if he was okay. In his panic to get there, he failed to notice the dragon turning towards him. Taren did not.

"Sam, stay where you are! Yetews, get him out of there!"

Even though Pax and Hawke had been trying to attack its weak underbelly, the dragon's attention went directly to Taren when he called out to Sam. Taren didn't notice that it was poising to strike again, only this time at him.

Sam watched on in horror as Yetews grabbed him from behind and pulled him towards the trees. "TAREN!!" Sam tried to imagine a wall between the beast's head and Taren, but only a faint shadow flickered and disappeared.

Taren spun just in time to see open jaws coming at him. But instead of the sensation of teeth clamping down onto him, someone hit him from the side, both bodies flying quickly away from the powerful jaws that barely missed them. Roz had dived at Taren and both of them now rolled across the ground. Taren had the wind knocked out of him and Roz was grabbing his shoulder and wincing.

And then, out of shadows of the trees, a streak of tawny fur blurred into the middle of the battle, deftly landing on the dragon's head. It took their foe completely by surprise and it raised its head high, thrashing wildly to remove the claws that were hooked into its fleshy nostrils. Two saber-teeth clamped down on the softest spot it could find and the dragon roared in pain.

From the safety of the tree, Yetews held Sam against his will. But Sam had stopped struggling the moment that he saw three crystal-blue eyes, terrible and gentle at the same time, fighting on their side. He whispered in disbelief, "It's not possible." He squinted his eyes to look harder. "Keesa?"

From one of the highest branches above, a small furred shape dropped down. The metal of a curved dagger glinted as it fell. Sam saw the striped fur and knew it was Foo. He landed directly above the eye and his dagger thrust downwards, completely blinding the beast.

Foo clung to the horns on its head for only a moment more. It began to thrash about in pain, its head breaking branches high above. Foo took his chance and leapt off, falling to the ground more agile than any human could. The kupa cat leapt off as well, roared loudly, and disappeared into the forest. Sam was sure he was seeing things at this point.

Blind and bleeding, the dragon knew it was beat. It struggled to escape the twisted ceiling of the forest, but managed to get into the air again. It flew off, screeching in agony.

On the forest floor, everyone struggled to their feet, breathing hard after the fight. Taren, having gotten knocked hard by Roz, finally managed to clear his head and called out, "Is everyone okay?" Each one called back to reassure they were fine – all but one.

Pax looked around frantically and said, "Wait. Where's Arthur?"

Taren's eyes went wide as he remembered seeing him take a hit from the dragon's tail. He spun around towards the direction where he'd last seen him and spotted him under a tree several feet away. He took off, holding his ribs with one hand as he ran.

When he reached the fallen Protector, he called to the others, "Over here!" He was lying face down on the ground not moving. Taren rolled him over carefully and felt for a pulse.

Standing over them with the rest of their group, Sam looked down and saw Arthur's eyes, open but unseeing. His heart began to pound almost painfully and the world felt unsteady around him. He watched hesitantly as Taren pulled open Arthur's shirt to reveal a wound so deep that nothing could heal him.

Putting his hands over Arthur's eyes, Taren verified what everyone already knew. "He's gone."

Everyone bowed their heads. Foo, Iggy and Arty each knelt on one knee at the same time. Taren quietly blessed Arthur's journey to the beyond. "You fought well, Arthur. Rest in peace, friend."

With that, Sam felt the world around him go quiet. He had to get away from this moment. He didn't want to see anymore. This wasn't what he wanted. He didn't know Arthur very well, but he most certainly didn't deserve this ending. The only word that he could get out was, "*No…*" and then he turned and quickly headed for the tree furthest from the scene of sadness and death.

In the back of his mind, Sam could hear Taren sigh sadly and then quietly say, "Roz…go help him."

When Sam reached the tree he grabbed it for support. His chest was rising and falling too fast and he couldn't understand why he felt so dizzy. His blue eyes were wide, taking in the world around him. Something heavy was sitting in his stomach and he was sure it was his dinner. From behind him, a quiet voice asked, "Are you ok?"

He wanted to answer yes, but only managed to nod once before his dinner decided it no longer wanted to be in his stomach. He was doubled over, retching, as Roz held onto one of his shoulders. When he was done, Sam stood back up. His eyes were tightly closed and sweat was dripping down his gray, clammy face. His hands shook slightly. "Sorry," he muttered feebly.

Roz glanced over at the mess and ushered Sam away to a different tree. "Here. Sit down for a minute and get your bearings."

Grateful for the advice, he slumped back against the rough bark of the tree and slid down. He all of a sudden felt weaker than normal. "I don't know what happened. I just…I don't know."

Roz placed his bow on the ground and joined Sam. "It's okay, you know? Death isn't an easy thing to see."

"I know. But I've seen it before. I don't know what happened," he repeated.

Nodding, Roz said. "But it's been years since then. Don't beat yourself up. You're not invincible. No one is."

That's when it dawned on Sam. It wasn't just that he wasn't invincible. He was helpless. A dragon attacked his friends and he was useless to them. Everyone around him could have been saved if his imagination was still powerful. He'd brought down beasts bigger and more terrifying than that dragon during the battle with Nadaroth. He'd healed friends, found ways across impossible grounds, invaded the dreams of his enemy, armed his comrades when they needed it most, and protected his friends from harm. Now he was nothing more than a simple boy in a world he couldn't help.

Sam took a hard look around, taking in every detail he could. Hawke and Taren were digging a hole with their hands and swords under the tree where Arthur fell. Taren's shirt was torn on the sleeve and stained a deep shade of red where a nasty gash was hiding. Hawke had a black eye forming and sported a fat lip, a trail of blood seeping out the side of his mouth.

Pax was nursing her own wounds, her cheek looked like she was dragged along pavement. Yetews had taken a hit from the dragon's tail as it slashed around violently and he had a bloody nose as a result. Iggy and Arty, with all of their experience collecting marked beasts had been in on the action as well, and neither looked their best.

As Sam's eyes came full circle, his eyes went to Roz's hands. Each was bloodstained and Roz noticed Sam eyeing them with a worried expression on his face.

He lifted up his shirt, wincing lightly as he did. "I'm alright. Just took a hit on something on the ground when I knocked Taren out of the way." Lifting his shirt revealed a gnarly wound that traced beneath his rib cage on one side. He slid his shirt back down when he noticed Sam go a shade whiter. He cleared his throat uncomfortably. "It's a bit ridiculous though. Fight a dragon, get beat up by a stick on the ground." He smiled, hoping to get Sam to do the same. It failed.

Sam looked away quickly. The blood didn't bother him. But how the blood happened did. There had been so many injuries from one fight with one creature. In fact, there wasn't a soul there who came away unscathed from the attack – except Sam.

"I never should have come back."

Roz didn't understand why Sam would say that suddenly. "What are you talking about?"

"Look at them. Everyone is hurt. And that was just one stupid dragon. One!" He shook his head and then looked down angrily at his feet. "I'm here to help with my power and I can't even imagine a blasted shovel to help bury someone who died because I couldn't help save him." Sam was getting madder the more he thought about it.

Though there was a sense of hesitancy, Roz stated, "There was nothing you could have done to save Arthur. That wasn't your fault."

Shaking his head, he said, "I could have blocked the hit. I could have stopped the dragon before it even got that far. And now he's dead because I'm helpless. It *is* my fault."

Now irritation replaced the hesitancy. "This is war. He isn't the first one to die and I can damn well guarantee he isn't going to be the last."

It was hard not to notice Roz's agitation, but Sam didn't care. He was angry too. "I know what war means. I'm not stupid. But what did I do? Nothing! I stood there and was dragged away by Yetews so I wouldn't get hurt. Everyone else at least has weapons. My only weapon is my mind and now I don't even have that. I can't even protect *myself* let alone my friends." He turned his face away from Roz, not wanting to look at anyone.

For a moment, it seemed like Roz wouldn't say anything else. Then he shook his head slowly. "Hmph." He started to walk away, but not without some final words. "You know," he started, "for the first time since we met, I'm disappointed in you."

Sam refused to look up at him, still too upset with the situation. But those words stung. He frowned and muttered, "You just don't get it."

"Oh no. I get it. You feel sorry for yourself." He watched Sam turn his head away even more. "I was under the impression that you were the kind of person that would never give up, no matter the circumstances."

Sam didn't respond, but frostily ignored his friend's remarks.

Roz no longer held back his annoyance. "You want to blame someone for what happened? Fine. But no matter who you blame – whether it's someone else or yourself – that won't change what's happened today or tomorrow or any day after that." He turned to leave, the sound of leaves crunching beneath his boots. But he paused for a moment then turned back around. Anger fueled his next words. "You want to change this problem?" He pulled his quiver and bow from over his shoulder. He threw them both down on the ground by Sam's feet. He watched as Sam's eyes flashed to them. "Then do something about it."

With that, Roz turned and left, leaving Sam alone.

Sam chanced a quick look in Roz's direction. He'd joined the others in digging a grave for Arthur. His eyes fell back to the bow and arrows lying by his feet. He wanted to be angry at Roz for not understanding how he felt, but after thinking about it for a moment, he realized that his friend was right. He *was* feeling sorry for himself.

After everything Sam had experienced in his short years, never had he felt so guilty for his own emotions. Orga had told him that everyone has to live with the choices they make and Sam was no exception. He'd chosen to come back to Imagia and unfortunately the unexpected actions of someone else changed how things worked.

The longer he sat there stewing in his own thoughts, Sam began to think about all those who fought by his side so many times. Not a one of them had a special power to defeat their enemy, but time and time again, they did so. If they could do it, then so could he.

Sam was a strong child from day one who had never let any of his failures define him. He wasn't about to let them define him now. He closed his eyes and tried to focus. As his mind cleared, he formed an image and held his hands out, hopeful for the weight of the object to form in his palms. His fingers wrapped around a wooden handle on one end and cool steel on the other. He opened his eyes and grinned victoriously.

Standing up, Sam brushed himself off, picked up Roz's bow and quiver, and walked quietly over to the others. When he reached them, he cleared his throat. Everyone stopped digging and looked at him, their gazes falling to the object in his hands.

Not saying a word, Sam held out a perfectly solid shovel towards Taren who took it hesitantly. He turned it over in his hands.

"Thanks, kid." Taren looked at him with concern. "You alright?"

"Yeah." Sam glanced at Roz who still looked upset. "But I'm done standing around. My imagination isn't strong right now. Maybe it never will be. I can't protect myself." He watched Roz's eye look intently at him, curious what might be said next. "The thing is, I need to be able to. Because I can't expect everyone to do it for me." He looked at the bow in his hand and held it awkwardly, not sure where to put his hands.

Taren furrowed his brow. "What are you saying?"

Sam let his stare fall on Arthur's broken body for an uncomfortable moment. He shook his head, not wanting to replay the events in his head again. Then, without a sliver of doubt in his voice, he stated, "Imagination or not, I'm not going to be helpless anymore. So somebody better teach me how to use this thing so I don't put out an eye." He was holding the bow up so they knew what he was referring to. With as much bravery as he could muster, he said, "I don't want to be just Sam Little anymore. I'm going to be a Protector and I plan on learning from the best."

Roz had a smile so big that his eye patch went slightly askew on his face. He reached up to adjust it and then proudly said, "Awesome. Now that's more like it!" He held out a fist, no longer angry, and Sam gladly reached his own out to bump it.

He wasn't the only one who looked pleased. Taren may not have said anything, but he stood a little taller and the pride he had couldn't be hidden.

Arty nudged Iggy in the side and said, "Sam Little – Protector! Has a nice ring to it, if you ask me. Eh Ignatius?"

"Indeed it does, Artemus. Indeed it does!"

Sam joined in on the digging. The dirt scraped his palms and his fingers were getting sore, but Arthur deserved a proper burial. He ignored the pain and dug harder.

The next morning, he'd wake up a Protector in training. If ever he had to bury a comrade again, it would be too soon. And it most certainly wouldn't be for not doing everything in his power to stop it from happening.

Chapter Twenty-four: Hope Restored

Everyone in their group paid their respects to Arthur, but Pax was most upset by his loss. She'd known him the longest having done their training together. Sam didn't know what to say except to express how sorry he was that he couldn't have helped him more.

The night was restless for everyone. Though everyone took turns at sleeping, most were hard pressed to actually stay asleep for long at all. Sam was exhausted and managed to sleep the most, but not without constant tossing and turning.

When the morning arrived, Taren and the others had come to an agreement that they'd move forward quicker and get to Exile as soon as possible. No one wanted to risk another attack like they had the day before. In the end, it only took them the rest of the day to reach the outskirts of Exile.

When they breeched the forest wall, Sam and Yetews had a rush of memories from the first time they'd both stepped foot in the village. This time, there was not nearly the same amount of caution as before. Those in the village were now accustomed to frequent and sometimes strange visitors. In fact, some of the inhabitants saw their party standing in the shadows of the forest and came to greet them.

Taren told everyone to go ahead and assured them that he'd be joining them shortly. But as Sam watched him turn back into the forest, he stopped him fast.

"Taren, wait!" When he turned back to see what he wanted, Sam asked, "I know I'm being kept in the dark about certain things. But I needed to ask you something important."

He looked over his shoulder at something that Sam couldn't see and impatiently said, "What is it?"

"During the fight with the dragon, I was so sure I saw a kupa cat attack. But it happened so fast that I…I guess I don't know if I saw what I think I saw."

"What's your question?"

"I guess I just…well…I want to know if I'm crazy."

Taren was grinning, but the gesture didn't touch his eyes. "No. You're not crazy. I'll explain more later, but I have to meet with our lookout rather quickly. I'll explain soon." When Taren saw doubt cross Sam's face, he added, "I promise." And then he disappeared into the forest without another word.

Sam caught up quickly to Yetews who was standing just a few yards away in respect for privacy. Which, of course, didn't matter. Sam would tell him everything later anyways. "Do you think I'm crazy?" Sam asked Yetews.

He replied with a shrug and then rocked one hand side to side, grunting shortly.

Elbowing his Guardian playfully, Sam said, "Har, har, har. If I'm going crazy, then I'm taking you with me."

They followed the others through the town and made their way to a very familiar sight. Taren's home, still rugged, stood before them. It looked different from Sam's memories. What used to be a cold and unwelcoming building was now filled with a friendly glow in the evening dusk around them. There was chatter drifting out through the open windows and when the door opened, delicious smells wafted out to greet their noses.

Sam sniffed and could smell some kind of meat cooking inside. His stomach growled loudly in response. The food Orga had packed for the trip was good, but had gotten stale over the last day. He didn't care what kind of food it was. He'd eat just about anything at the moment.

Sam and Yetews were the last two through the door and the room erupted into cheers.

Sam went red in the face. That was definitely unexpected.

There were some recognizable faces, but most of them that welcomed him in were unfamiliar. He wondered idly if any of them knew his ability to imagine was, for all intents and purposes, broken. Perhaps if they'd known, he wouldn't have gotten such an enthusiastic welcoming.

The events of the evening were short and fairly uneventful. Taren joined them shortly after and within an hour, most of the crowd dispersed. Everyone headed back to the places they were staying while in Exile. After a warm and much appreciated meal, their group found places to sleep.

Exile, for the time being, had rarely experienced much in the ways of attacks. Too many Protectors were there to defend it. The few times they'd had to protect the village, it was rarely a significant battle with any losses. No one could explain it, but they'd gotten quite accustomed to the safety of the village.

Nevertheless, Taren had posted extra guard rotations as a precaution now that Sam was with them. He was heading out the door, Sam patiently waiting to talk to him, when he turned and said, "I'll be back soon. I have plenty of Protectors close by in case anything happens. I have some things I need to attend to. Try to get some sleep." He turned to Yetews. "If Sam seems like he's having a nightmare, wake him up fast."

Taren didn't return that night. It wasn't until morning, when Sam woke up from an unnaturally peaceful sleep, that he noticed he'd never returned. The only answer he got from anyone when he asked about it was: "He had things to do."

Sam sat down heavily at the table in one of the aged wooden chairs. He leaned his head on his palm and yawned. The chair next to him scraped loudly across the wooden floor.

"Sleep good?" Roz sat down grabbed the ceramic pitcher in the center of the table and poured some water for himself.

Sam let his hand fall and sighed. "I guess so. Still feel tired though. Any idea what the plan is today?"

"Are you kidding?" he said. "Take whatever they tell you, cut it in half, and that's about how much information they give me." He took a long drink of water.

Sam nodded. "Doesn't that drive you nuts?"

"Nah." He noticed Sam didn't look convinced. "The way I see it, I'm just lucky to be back in Imagia. I'm not exactly part of their inner circle of trust. I'm a Defender. I get it. I wouldn't be any less cautious if the tables were turned. Trust is something earned, not freely given. Did you trust me when we first met?"

"No. I guess not."

"See?"

"But I trust you now. You'd think that would count for something."

"It does."

Sam shook his head and frowned. "Then why all the secrecy?"

Roz thought for a moment, rubbing the stubble on his chin. "You can never be too careful during times of conflict. Be patient. Have faith in your friends. They're doing what they believe is best. And," he grinned and pat Sam on the back heartily, "consider that lesson one in protecting yourself."

"And here I was thinking I was going to get to shoot a bow." He leaned back in his chair.

Roz smirked. "What do you think lesson two is?" He grabbed a roll out of a large bowl on the table and tore it apart, shoving large portions into his mouth.

Sam joined him and managed to eat three rolls before the door swung open and Taren finally returned. What Sam didn't expect was the tawny mass of fur that followed him through the door. He dropped his roll on the table, his mouth still full.

There was no mistaking the crystalline trio of eyes that peered around Taren. Sam stood up slowly, disbelieving of what he was seeing. Without thinking about it, he stammered, "Kee…Keesa?" He took off across the room and didn't stop until he reached the kupa cat. He threw his arms around her neck and said, "I don't believe it!"

The kupa cat was caught off guard, but remained mostly calm, only stiffening a little at the sudden and quite unexpected contact. Startled at such a gesture from Sam, she let out a little surprised, "Oh!"

Taren said to her, "I'm sorry. I meant to talk to him first, but I didn't get back in time."

Sam pulled away from her, slightly confused at the look of awkwardness on Taren's face. When he turned to look at the kupa cat again, he noticed that she didn't look quite the same. Suddenly, he felt silly about his actions. He chewed on his bottom lip. "You're not Keesa." He wasn't asking, but rather stating a fact. "I'm sorry," he finally said. "There for a second I thought you were…"

The kupa cat cleared her throat and sat down on her haunches. "Keesa. Yes. I know."

Taren apologized as well. "I'm sorry, Sam. I was going to tell you but I got so busy last night. I didn't have a chance to get back here. This is Alaria. She's Keesa's daughter." There was a genuine smile that took over his face. It was obvious that he'd wanted to tell Sam about her for a while. He knew that it would be important to him.

"You're…Keesa's *daughter*?"

"Yes." She bowed her head slightly, the motion reminding Sam even more so of her mother.

The last time Sam had seen Keesa's cubs, they were in the heat of battle. He remembered them, but only small details. They weren't grown yet and her daughter didn't look quite so much like her mother back then. Now the similarities between Alaria and Keesa were so uncanny that it was easy to see how he could make such a mistake. The differences were subtle, but once he realized who she was, it was simple enough to see them.

Sam felt rather uncomfortable for the moment and found himself apologizing again. "I really am sorry. I don't know why I would think that she…that you…that I would see Keesa again."

"Oh, it's quite alright. I understand. Just make sure not to make the same mistake with my brothers. They might not remain nearly as calm as me in the same situation." Her saber teeth would ordinarily frighten someone who'd seen her feline smile.

But not Sam. His eyes went wide. "Brothers? Are they here too? I haven't seen any of you since right after our battle with Nadaroth."

"No," she answered. "They have other jobs right now.

"Oh."

Taren explained. "Alaria is who I've been speaking with in the forest. She's been going ahead of us and making sure our way is clear.

She was out hunting when we were attacked. Keesa's children have been helping scout for us. Her son, Zaru, was there the day that we found you."

Sam remembered hearing his name before. Everything made sense now.

With introductions out of the way, Taren excused himself, saying he had to prepare for a gathering that afternoon. Alaria followed after him, pardoning herself with the same politeness that her mother always used to show. Sam was left alone with his own thoughts until Yetews joined him. He'd seen the entire interaction earlier and had felt sympathy for Sam. As Sam tried to deal with the new information, he tousled his boy's hair playfully.

Sam cocked an eyebrow at him as he tried to straighten it back out. "You know…I might be getting a bit old for that."

Yetews grunted and snorted. He rolled his eyes and they both smiled. Maybe it was true, but there would always be a part of Sam that enjoyed it, teenager or not.

* * * * * * * * * *

Taren's home was packed as full as it could be. The number gathered there now had never been greater. Protectors from southern Imagia joined with Defenders of the north that had arrived early in the day. The hustle and bustle was just coming to a head when Taren, who had gone out into the village to gather the remainder of Protectors for the meeting, came through the door. He made his way through the crowd while having a very serious conversation with Zane who was also looking severe.

When he made his way to the front, he motioned for Sam to join him.

"What's up, Taren?" Sam noticed that he looked troubled.

"I need you to understand something." He was speaking in a hushed voice, not wanting anyone around him to hear.

"Sure."

"What's happened to you has been kept fairly quiet. Most of those here will be hearing things for the first time today. Just the ones that came to Orga's know. And even some of them weren't given the whole story."

"Why?"

"We've been trying to keep it quiet from Nadaroth. If he finds out that you're imagination has been compromised, well…we're not sure what would happen."

Sam understood.

"Just stay close to me for now. Alright?"

"Got it." Would they turn on him when they found out his power was damaged? Why else would he need to stay close unless this was a genuine fear of Taren's? He backed up against the wall and sat on a dusty, wooden crate.

The noisy room quickly went quiet when Taren held up his hand. The crowd focused all their attention on him.

"As you all know by now, our mission to retrieve Sam was a success." A round of applause that forced Sam to go red erupted quickly and lingered for longer than he liked. Taren brought order to the room again. "Yes. Good news indeed!" He fingers began to fidget. "However, not all of you are aware of everything that has happened since Sam's return.

"An unlikely scenario had him fall into Gabriel's hands first. Whether it was planned or simply good fortune for our enemy, Sam returned through the wrong gateway and Gabriel's group caught him before we could get there. Luckily, we'd been tracking them and got to Sam before they could take him to Nadaroth. Short-lived as that moment was, it has caused a problem. In order to keep Sam from imagining, one of Gabriel's cronies knocked him out completely. Once again, we don't know if this was their intent, but the severe blow to his head affected Sam badly. His imagination has been temporarily…affected."

Whispers started to spread until it seemed the entire room was a dull roar. Finally, someone from the back of the room voiced loudly what the others were thinking. "So he can't imagine anymore? His power is *gone*?"

Before Taren could even attempt to answer, another person, someone who Sam recognized from Orga's, quickly said, "Yes. That's true. His mind was damaged."

The crowd became restless, many voices loudly expressing their concern for the situation while Taren tried to regain order. Unfortunately he was unsuccessful.

Roz surprised everyone when he jumped up onto the table. Those around him jumped back. "That's enough!" he bellowed. "Everyone quiet! Taren has more to say so show some respect!" His voice was impressively loud.

Taren looked every bit as shocked as the rest of the room, but grateful as well. "Thank you, Roz." The room was quiet now, eagerly listening for more information.

Taren sent a sideways glance at Sam who knew this wasn't easy for him. He explained to everyone as best as he could. "We don't know how Gabriel knew to be at that particular gateway and have no way of knowing how, even if it were possible, he could have predicted that Sam would come through it. Honestly, we have no answers – only speculations. None of which holds up. But when Gabriel caught Sam, I think he knew exactly what he was doing knocking Sam out. With Sam unconscious, he would be no danger to them and easy to take back to Nadaroth.

"I don't believe that they knew it would affect his power so seriously, otherwise we'd have heard about it by now. That's why we've kept the information from spreading. We need to keep it that way. Understood?"

A collective agreement spread through the room.

"Now," he continued, "Sam's ability was initially gone, but it's proving to only be a temporary effect. He *still* has his power. But it's been slow healing."

A woman in the back corner asked, "Have you ever considered that leaving Imagia and coming back is what took his power away?" She wasn't trying to hide her skepticism.

Just as Taren was about to answer her, a voice Sam had come to know quite well spoke up. Everyone turned to look at Foo. He was perched in the open window, idly spinning his curved dagger into the wooden frame. "I can guarantee you that this is not the case."

"How?" the woman asked.

"Garrett and I were the two who went to retrieve Sam from the other world. While there, we watched him use his imagination."

Gasps whispered across the crowd. The words "in the *other* world" kept echoing through the room. The lady Protector voiced it the loudest, with disbelief thick in her words. "You're saying he kept his power *after* leaving Imagia? That's not possible." She shook her head, eyes guarded.

The way that Foo stared back at her was most dangerous. But he didn't respond again.

Taren did though. "Foo is a Guardian of Imagia. He wouldn't lie." The woman nodded apologetically and he continued. "Foo is speaking the truth. They were attacked outside of Imagia from something that escaped into that world. Not only Foo witnessed his power. Garrett did as well. And Roz," he motioned for Roz to join him, "he was there as well. Through a series of very unfortunate events, he had been trapped outside of Imagia and sought Sam out. He's a Defender from the North. He can tell you as well."

Roz looked around the room briefly. "He's right. I didn't know Sam before meeting him in the other world. I will tell you that the power I witnessed was more impressive than any of the stories I'd heard. But I think Sam can tell you better than me." He grabbed Sam's arm, pulling him to the front with him. "Go on Sam."

Sam never enjoyed being the center of attention. He swallowed hard. It wasn't the first time he'd stood in this room having to prove his powers. It was uncomfortably silent. He knew he was the only person who could prove anything and ease their worried minds. "I don't know what to say. In the time I was gone, my imagination got even more powerful. The longer I was away, the more I could do. I don't know why, so don't ask." He could tell there were those with questions.

Someone he couldn't see asked, "What about now?"

"I…can still imagine. But it's weakened. I'm getting better every day though. I don't get headaches as often and my nose rarely bleeds."

Taren went rigid. Sam saw this from the corner of his eye and realized he'd said too much. But it was too late.

Taren spoke through the worried mutters. "It's a setback. That's all!" He was trying to be heard above the commotion. It didn't work, his voice now lost in the noise. The frustrated comments and questions came too quick for Sam to see who said them.

"Everything we did to bring him back was all in vain!"

"We endangered Imagia for *this*?"

"How is this going to affect the plans?"

"You mean he's just some normal kid?"

"We risked our lives to bring him back here!"

That last and loudest comment caused Taren to grow furious. It was something that Sam rarely saw from him, but Taren slammed his fists down on the table next to him. The room went quiet immediately as he bellowed, "We've *all* risked our lives! We were risking them well before Sam ever came to Imagia and will continue to do so no matter what the future holds! As Protectors and Defenders of this world, not a one of you should expect any less!" He took a deep breath, controlling his anger. Somehow, he looked defeated as he stared down at his fists, still balled up on the table.

Calmer, but with the same warning tone, he looked around and said, "If any of you no longer feel that your life is not as important as the safety of Imagia and the Guardians we protect, then you do not deserve to be in this room."

Sam suddenly felt an overwhelming desire to support Taren in any way he could. In all the time he'd known him, Taren had never failed to show his faith in him – even at Sam's worst moment. Roz's words to him rang loud in his mind: "*Have faith in your friends. They will not fail you if you do.*"

Digging deep for the bravery that he hoped was there, Sam stood taller. He walked up to Taren, putting his hand on his arm. "Let me try," he said, his voice quivering slightly.

With a sideways grin and a glimmer of hope twinkling in his worried brown eyes, Taren stepped aside.

For a moment, Sam wondered why he was standing there. He had no idea what to say. He looked around the room of Protectors and Defenders – a few familiar faces in a sea of strangers. Their curious and desperate faces, all quiet now, watched him warily. Each looked as though they were fighting a hopeless battle.

It was then that Sam knew the toll Nadaroth's war on Imagia was taking on them. Taren had been so good at spreading hope. But even he looked worn from the woes of a life in this broken world.

Sam opened his mouth, hopeful that whatever words came out were enough. His mouth felt dry, like he'd had cotton on his tongue. But he struggled past the feeling. "I know that this isn't what you hoped for. Believe me. You can't be more mad about it than me. But…" He hesitated, not sure of the promise he wanted to make. "A wise person told me to have faith in my friends." He could see Roz smile out of the corner of his eye. It gave him a little more confidence to continue. "I think that maybe, I've lost faith in myself. But I can't let that happen. It's what Nadaroth wants. I came back here…to Imagia…to help. I promise that I will not fail to do all I can. I'm healing more every day. If we don't have hope, we can't win. Just…don't lose faith in each other…or me."

The crowd didn't move, waiting with bated breath. Sam knew what they wanted. More than a want, it was a need. His stomach rolled. He only had one shot at this moment. He looked down at the dusty floor, closing his mind to where he was and what was at stake. He disappeared into his thoughts, remembering what it was like before he'd been hurt.

There was an aching feeling lingering in the back of his head, but he ignored it. He told himself it wasn't that bad and it was working. He'd forgotten he was standing in a room full of eager onlookers. Memories began rushing past him. Images began to flicker in front of his mind's eye. Though he couldn't hear them, gasps of shock and whispers replaced the quiet anxiety of the room he was standing in.

At last, one memory stood out brighter than the rest. It wasn't a good memory, but it was a powerful one. He remembered that one moment in the boy's bathroom when he'd lost control at school before truly knowing Roz. It wasn't what he wanted to happen that day, but on *this* day, it was everything that he needed.

Sam looked up, seeing the awed faces staring back at him, images, ghostly and amazing, were fading now. They were all fleeting imaginings of the past. The pain in his mind was poking at him a little harder, but he shrugged it off, pushing back harder this time. Concentrating hard on the dingy room around him, he imagined. Trees broke through the floor, their bark winding and twisting into form. Vines hung from the ceiling that was now covered in foliage. The hard wooden floor became a thick carpet of grass and weeds. The room took shape around the shocked crowd, now a mirror image of the forest outside.

The nagging pain could no longer be ignored. Sam's hands began to shake and sweat beaded across his forehead.

Taren's cool hand was shocking against the warmth of Sam's arm when he reached out to stop him. It pulled him out of his stupor with a bit of a start. As Sam jumped, his head erupted with pain, but instead of screaming out, he closed his eyes tightly and tried to push through, desperate not to let the others see.

Taren knew he was in pain. And all of those who knew Sam the best could see he was holding back for the benefit of everyone else there. Iggy and Arty did what they did best and provided a distraction as Sam struggled in silence.

Both ferrets scrambled up onto a table and Yetews stepped in front of Sam nonchalantly, hiding him from view, giving the appearance of simply helping Iggy and Arty get a higher vantage point. When both ferrets climbed high up on Yetews horns, they held on tight and Iggy hollered out as loud as his voice could carry, “Do you doubt him now? Look around you!”

Arty joined him. “Sam is getting stronger by the moment and he stood before you proving himself! So we ask again: Do you doubt him now?”

The crowd, still in awe of the forest around them shouted out in near unison, “NO!”

With a sideways glance at one another Iggy and Arty both chanted, “Three cheers for Sam Little!”

As the crowd cheered back with Iggy and Arty’s every prompt, Taren took advantage of the distraction and made sure Sam was okay. He turned Sam around now that Yetews was cleverly blocking him from view and noticed the blood trickling from his nose. Foo walked past Taren slowly as if merely crossing the room. But he managed to secretly hand him a piece of cloth. Taren nodded his thanks to Foo as he moved on and then he pushed the cloth into Sam’s hand. He whispered, “Your nose.”

As Sam heard Taren, he opened his watering eyes. The pain in his head was subsiding gradually. He felt he could hold his composure together better now and reached up to wipe his nose. It wasn’t bleeding badly, but he knew that he’d pushed himself too far.

Looking around the room, even Sam was impressed. He wasn’t sure he could still do stuff like this. As he glanced over Taren’s shoulder, he saw some of the leaves begin to disappear and his eyes grew concerned. Quietly, he alerted Taren, “It’s beginning to fade.”

Taren looked around the eager room. The crowd would be too excited to notice a few leaves fading at a time, but knew that if it disappeared too quickly, doubt might spread even quicker than before. He moved around Yetews, back into view of the crowd.

"There are many reasons we have for meeting today!" The room quieted as he spoke. "I know that this was impressive, but it comes with a price. Sam needs to rest his mind if he is to heal and become stronger. He has given us plenty of reasons to have hope. We must have faith in each other to keep us strong. And we *must* have trust. Even when things don't go as planned." Even as Taren spoke, he witnessed a vine in the distance disappear.

Keeping very cool about it, Taren continued. "We lost another comrade. Arthur will not be forgotten. He was a good friend and a great Protector. So tonight we will eat, drink, and rest. We'll remember the lives of those we've lost and celebrate those who have gained our trust." Taren focused most of his attention on Roz now. Those who knew him could see how surprised he was. "Roz…Sam…tonight you're getting tattooed."

The room exploded with excitement. Suddenly, everyone in the room was cheering. Getting the flower tattoo signified a very big moment for them. It was reserved for those Protectors and Defenders that the utmost trust was given. It was indeed a very big moment. Sam, though familiar with the code of the flower, hadn't realized just how big of a deal it was. He also didn't think that they would ever agree to let him get one. Not only was he much younger than any of them, but he also wasn't a Protector. Not yet, at least.

Taren walked up to Roz with his hand extended in a congratulatory way and a toothy grin. Roz took his hand, a shocked look still on his face. It was a tough moment for Taren in many ways, but a welcome one at that.

Taren told him, "I'd be dead if it weren't for you. You've earned it."

"Thank you," Roz replied.

When Taren looked at Sam, he was still grinning. "I can tell you're surprised. But if anyone here deserves it, it's you, kid." Sam's face brightened even more. "If you want it, that is." He knew he didn't have to ask, but was happy to see Sam grow even more ecstatic despite the pain he was in from imagining too hard.

More of the foliage in the room was disappearing and if everyone stayed much longer, it wouldn't be easy to miss. Taren called to the roused group, "Go! Sam needs to clean up this mess he's made." Laughter broke out. "Make preparations and we'll celebrate at dusk."

The room cleared quickly and it couldn't have happened at a better time. Sam sunk into a chair, clutching his head and breathing heavier than normal. He felt like he'd just ran a race. If it weren't for the thought of getting his tattoo later, he would have been happy to just lie down and sleep.

Yetews, Roz and Foo were the only ones left in the room. Sam whispered thanks to Foo and received a welcoming nod in return before he walked over to the window and leapt out. Roz joined Sam, slumping down into the chair next to him.

"Well," Roz started, "I sure didn't see that one coming."

Sam shook his head. "Neither did I."

"Still," he seemed to be considering something, "it is kind of cool. You, uh…gonna be able to handle it? It's probably going to sting a bit."

"Ha!" Sam rubbed the bloodied piece of cloth under his still oozing nose. "I can't imagine what pain feels like." He knew Roz was joking for that very reason.

They sat in silence for a few moments. It wasn't uncomfortable. It never seemed to be with Roz. They both looked drained from the events of the meeting. Yetews pat Sam on the back and grumbled something to him.

Sam nodded and Yetews left as well.

Roz looked at Sam questioningly.

"Crowds are rough on him. He's still trying to heal too."

They sat awhile longer, both thinking about the evening that was approaching. Roz yawned loudly. "So…"

Sam inhaled slowly. "So."

Holding a fist out for Sam to bump, Roz said, "Let's do this."

Sam bumped fists and Roz left as well, leaving Sam to his own thoughts. He knew that what was going to happen that evening was going to shift many things in his life. Even though it was just a small tattoo, he knew what it all really meant. He'd be the youngest one in Imagia to go through this. But as the room finally faded back to its original state, he pushed through the pain once more. While no one was looking, he imagined the very flower that would be tattooed on him in just a few short hours. It grew up from the cracks of the floor and bloomed, its brilliant yellow petals spreading wide. Then, just as quickly, it faded away.

It hurt. The pain would have sent him to his knees had he been standing. Sam dabbed at his nose again, fresh blood staining the cloth.

Alone in the room, he sighed heavily and quietly hoped that he was ready.

Chapter Twenty-five: The Biggest Night

Somewhere in the pit of Sam's stomach were several feelings stirring that made him both uncomfortable and excited at the same time. Yetews was the only one who noticed that something was off and he caught Sam pacing alone in Taren's bedroom.

When Sam turned around he startled a bit when he saw Yetews sitting on his haunches in the doorway with his massive arms crossed.

"What?"

Yetews cocked an eye and grumbled back.

Sam sighed. They may have been separated for years, but Yetews still knew him the best. "Fine. Something's bothering me."

Yetews growled another question.

"I'm not afraid!" He hadn't meant to snap at his friend. "Sorry about that. But it's not fear. Actually," he looked a bit ashamed, "I'm kind of excited. I *want* to get the tattoo. I think I'll finally feel like one of them when I get it. You know?"

Yetews nodded. He looked on as Sam stopped his pacing and settled down onto the bed.

"It's just so weird is all. I'm *fourteen.* I know this probably doesn't make sense to you, but back home, fourteen year olds don't get tattoos. So…I'm excited…but something else. There's this part of me that thinks about mom and dad. Would they be disappointed in me? Mad? What would they say?"

Sam's question hung on the air. Other than what he'd been told about them, Yetews didn't know Sam's parents. He didn't know what to say and gave a feeble shrug.

Sam ran his fingers through his hair. He laid back on the bed and growled out, frustrated. "I know it was my choice to leave! And coming here meant I had to learn to take care of myself and make my own choices. If I want to get a tattoo, it's my choice now. I mean," he began to argue with himself, "it's not like I'm doing it to rebel against them. It has a purpose."

As he lay there, Yetews still not knowing what to say or how to comfort him, he reflected on his family. With every passing thought, his heart seemed to ache a little more. It was the exact reason he tried not to think about them. His throat seemed to close as he quietly said, "I chose to be alone. I guess I just…" He closed his eyes, forcing himself to continue. "I miss them." Before this moment, he had tried his best to not say those words out loud.

Yetews' heart ached as well, but not for Sam's parents. He hurt for Sam. He knew that it was, and always would be, a struggle for him. But to hear Sam actually utter the words was tough. He crossed the room and sat down next to him beside the bed. He didn't have to say anything. His presence was plenty. But he did. He purred his words sympathetically.

Sam processed Yetews' words. *You'll never be alone.* He was right and it helped.

Outside, the forest was turning a dull gray as evening set in. The clouds in the west were ominous. It would rain before nightfall. The air was thicker, moisture building before the storm.

Yetews grumbled a question, breaking the silence just as thunder rolled in the distance.

"Yeah. We should go."

As if reading their minds, Taren appeared in the doorway. "You ready, kid?" He had a large grin across his face.

"Yeah."

"I have a feeling we might get soaked if we don't leave now." He looked out the window towards the gray sky. When he looked at Sam, he noticed there was something going on. He speculated and decided to reassure him. "You don't have to do this. I just thought you'd want to. You said – "

"I do!" Sam interrupted him. "I want to. Really."

The look on Taren's face said he wasn't entirely convinced, but he nodded anyways. "You know, the tattoo comes with a bonus.

Something I think you'll like even more." He knew he'd piqued Sam's interest. "The secrets of Imagia."

When Sam looked like he would positively explode with questions, Taren held up his hand to stop him. "Tattoo first. Questions later." Another round of thunder struck, this time much closer. They left and headed for a large building that stood in the village's center.

Sam, in all the time he'd spent here, had never been to this place. A well-weathered wooden sign hung above the entrance that read: The Lost Tavern. The words were neatly carved into the wood. Rain was dripping off of the sign as it cascaded off of the roof.

When Taren, Yetews, and Sam walked through the door, they were welcomed by loud cheering. The room was full of people, all from their morning gathering. There were sturdy tables and chairs placed all over the room, nearly all of them occupied by now.

A delicious aroma filled the room and Sam looked around for the source. It was darker, but warmly lit by the many candles on the tables and lanterns that hung about the room and from the ceiling. In the corner was a large, roaring fire that had some sort of beast roasting over it. The smell was a mixture of meat, breads, and something sweet that Sam couldn't quite place.

In one corner of the room, Roz sat around the largest table with Foo, Iggy, Arty, Hawke, Pax, and Zane. Even Keesa's daughter, Alaria, was quietly sitting in the shadows cast by the firelight.

Sam joined Roz, his stomach now totally filled with butterflies.

Roz gave him a hearty pat on the back. "Thought you might have drowned or something on the way here."

Sam laughed nervously. "No kidding."

"It's quite a party. Are you ready for this?"

Though there was an obvious jitteriness to his words, he said, "Totally."

For the second time that day, Taren called attention to the crowd. "Alright, alright! Settle down for a minute, will you?" Unlike that morning, Taren now had an excited glow about him as he spoke. He paused somewhat dramatically, looking directly at Sam. "Sam forever changed our world and has given us hope!" Between each sentence, the crowd would let out a loud guttural cheer.

Hurrah!

"It was a great day indeed when he came to Imagia!"

Hurrah!

"And an even better one when he came back!"

Hurrah!

"He has sacrificed more than most of us and is fighting with us to bring peace back to Imagia."

Hurrah!

"Roz, you've shown time and again to be worthy of this moment as well. You've saved not just my life, but Sam's. Thank you."

Hurrah!

"Lift your cups!" Everyone did so and Taren directed his words to just Sam and Roz. "You've earned this night. To Sam and Roz!"

There was one last loud *Hurrah!* Then everyone in the room took a drink. Roz picked up the cup in front of him and pushed the other one beside it towards Sam. They clinked their cups together and Roz downed his quickly. Sam, on the other hand, was more apprehensive. The sweet smell he'd noted earlier was coming from the glass. He sniffed it and shrugged. He took a good-sized gulp and recognized the flavor instantly. It was the same drink that he'd had on his birthday. Only this time, it tasted much sweeter.

A man walked over to Taren and handed him a wooden tool that had a sharp metal tip set into the end. When he sat down next to Sam, he held the metal tip in the flame. Most of the room had gone back to enjoying their food and drink, but some gathered around the table to watch.

Taren noticed that Sam's eyes were wide while watching the metal grow red hot. "It's to sterilize it so you don't get infected."

Sam merely nodded. He was beyond thankful when Roz opted to go first. At the very least, Roz could tell him how badly it hurt. The good thing was that Sam had never had a fear of needles.

"All I need now is a location and color, Roz," Taren said.

Roz began to pull his shirt up. He exposed his back and said, "Left shoulder blade, to the right of my scar. Red." A four inch silvery diagonal scar was just to the side of his shoulder blade that looked as though he'd been run through with a sword. The scarred skin was thick and raised. His back was muscular and there were several smaller scars all over, some of which looked like they would have been very painful to get.

Taren checked the metal tip to make sure it wasn't hot anymore and pulled a small jar of thick, black liquid towards him. Someone set a smaller jar next to him that had a rich scarlet liquid in it. He asked Roz, "You ready?"

"Always." Roz winked at Sam, which was still incredibly impressive with just the one eye. He leaned against the table and Taren poured a clear liquid that smelled very harsh over the area he was going to get tattooed.

Sam watched Taren intently. He was fascinated by the way he moved his hands as he poked and cut the skin, each time dipping the point in the black dye. Sam said, "You're really good at this."

Taren glanced quickly as he concentrated on Roz's shoulder blade. "Well, I've done so many now, that it's quite easy. I think I might be the only one with any artistic talent among us. So I got the job."

It took some time to etch out the outline of the flower, but once he began the red, Roz was wincing as the metal pierced his skin. It made Sam wonder if he'd be able to handle it so calmly. Now that he was nearly finished, and the crowd had grown around them, the butterflies disappeared only to be replaced with a slight queasy feeling.

Finally, Taren set down the tool and wiped the mixture of blood and dye from Roz's back, finishing with another round of the clear liquid from earlier. When the liquid hit his skin, he drew in a sharp breath and said, "Well that wasn't very pleasant."

Taren admired his work for a moment, Sam peering closely by his side. "Finished," he stated. "Red, left shoulder blade. You ready, Sam?"

With more hesitancy than he was hoping for, Sam nodded. He'd had so many injuries in the past, some of them very painful. He knew he shouldn't be nervous about this, but he was. More than the pain, he was nervous about the actual act of getting the tattoo. In a way, it was a right of passage for him. And he needed to go through with it.

Taren began to clean the tool and then placed it back into the flame to sterilize it. As he did, Sam joined Roz who was craning his neck, trying to admire his own tattoo. When he'd gotten a good enough look, he slipped his shirt back down and smiled at Sam.

Before Sam could even ask, Roz spoke very quietly. The crowd was loud enough that they wouldn't be overheard. "It didn't hurt that bad."

"Really? Because it looked pretty terrible to me." His voice was a pitch higher than usual.

"I've had a lot of wounds in my time, and the one place that didn't seem to hurt as badly as the other places, was the shoulder. That's probably your best bet if you want to keep it as painless as possible. Just don't tell them I said that."

Once again, Sam was grateful for Roz. Taren was cooling the metal now, so Sam took a deep breath and headed to the table. An even larger crowd had gathered around, so eager to be a part of this major event.

Taren asked him, a crooked grin on his face. "Where do you want it and what's your color?" He looked around and then whispered, "The shoulder doesn't hurt so bad."

Sam smiled wide, his nerves suddenly much calmer. He looked around the room. So many excited eyes were watching him, waiting for his choice. A rush of excitement hit him and he caught Roz's eye. He took his shirt off. He had the build of a typical teenage boy, awkward, but gaining muscle. He was briefly aware of how much younger he was than the many men and women in the room and felt small. But he said loudly, for those around him to hear. "Left shoulder blade. Sapphire."

The whole room seemed to be cheering him on now as he sat down. Yetews sat next to him. Even though no one but Sam would understand what he said, he lowered his voice and asked Sam a question.

With an anxious look, he tried to smile and said, "No thanks, big guy. I've got it." As much as he would have loved to have a hand to hold, he wanted to look as tough as possible.

Yetews nodded. He wouldn't leave Sam's side during the process.

"You ready?" Taren asked.

"Yeah. Let's do this."

The room erupted into cheers and some of them began a chant of "Sam, Sam, Sam!" over and over again that caught on and lasted until the metal pierced his skin for the first time.

The moment the metal touched his skin, the muscles in his back tightened and his eyes went wide. A wave of nausea swept over him. It wasn't the worst pain he'd had, but enough that he had to try very hard to hold his tongue. Taren, of course, noticed immediately. But he was kind enough not to say anything as the room exploded excitedly.

With each new puncture of the skin, Sam felt pain. But it seemed to lessen with each fresh poke. Whether he was simply getting accustomed to it or the skin was becoming numb, he pressed on. A fine sheen of sweat developed over his face as his stomach continued to churn uncomfortably.

Taren worked quickly. His hands felt cool on Sam's skin, a welcome sensation to the white-hot pain on his raw shoulder. The sharp pain stopped as Taren wiped the tool clean. He had to speak loudly to be heard above to rowdy crowd. "Almost done. Just the color now." A bit quieter so that only Sam could hear, he added, "Hang on, kid."

Sam blew out his breath slowly, gearing up for the next round. He wiped his head with the back of his shaky arm, wishing he had his shirt on to soak up the sweat.

Taren was trying hard not to show his concern for Sam, but he was finding it difficult to do so. He knew that this was a hard moment for him on several levels. Roz was doing his best to not show worry as well and tried to distract him, albeit unsuccessfully, with conversation.

As the blade, now soaked in the brilliant sapphire dye, pierced his skin again, Sam pinched his eyes closed tightly and tried not to yell out in pain. In order to do so, he tried to escape to the confines of his mind. He tried to picture something – anything – to distract himself from the pain. After his morning incident with imagining, he knew his mind wasn't nearly healed enough to push further. But the pain was bad enough that he had to do something. Closing his eyes, he began to filter though images in his mind, only concentrating on each one long enough to have fleeting images appear. With each half creation, Sam could hear the ooh's and ahh's around him.

The distraction worked well enough. He could still feel the metal cutting him, but it wasn't overwhelming anymore. Suddenly, the pain stopped and he opened his eyes. He'd forgotten about the clear liquid, but was quickly reminded when it hit his freshly cut skin. It burned like white-hot fire. Without a thought, he jumped up and yelped out in pain. "Oh man! Not cool!"

"You're all done." Taren placed the bottle of clear liquid down, trying hard not to laugh. The rest of the room was not so kind.

Sam was wriggling around uncomfortably so Taren used a piece of cloth to wipe the remnants of everything off of his shoulder. He slapped another cloth that he doused in water on the finished tattoo and Sam instantly felt better. The coolness soothed the burning. Carefully, he put his shirt back on, keeping the wet cloth in place as he did so.

The rest of the evening, Protectors, Defenders, and even Foo had come up to congratulate Sam. The tattoo had proved to be one of their best security measures since they'd started using it and Sam hadn't realized just how big of a deal it was until tonight. Using the flower code had saved them too many times from danger or spies. It just made good sense to keep using it.

Having the tattoo not only proved they were trusted, but also gave reason to celebrate when someone was deemed worthy to receive one. Sam, though in considerable pain at the moment, felt like he was truly a part of something big.

The celebrations went well into the night. Yetews noticed Sam tiredly staring unseeing at a candle for longer than usual, so he nudged Roz. He pointed at Sam and Roz nodded, took another swig of his drink, and told Taren that they should probably get back.

"That's probably for the best," Taren agreed. "Why don't you go back with him and I'll be right behind you. We need to talk."

Walking back into the quiet of Taren's home, now very much deserted, was refreshing. Sam felt drained. His feet were heavy. As he moved, he felt as if weights were tied to them. His head throbbed dully and his shoulder was burning. He welcomed the idea of crawling into a bed and sleeping his aches away.

Taren came in almost as soon as they'd closed the door, followed by Iggy and Arty who were being exceptionally loud, laughing about something they'd been discussing. Taren called everyone over to the table. There was a notable slump to Sam's shoulders as he moved that way. Any other time, Sam welcomed new information, but it had been a long and emotional day.

Sitting down and pulling over a large pitcher of water, Taren poured three cups full; one for him and two for Sam and Roz. "We need to discuss what our task is for the journey we are setting out on in a few days." Though it was masked well, there was a definite look of reservation on Taren's face. He was struggling speaking about whatever he was about to reveal.

Iggy and Arty scrambled up onto the table to join the others. "How's the shoulder?" Arty asked Sam.

Sam answered with a shrug and regretted it immediately. He winced. "Sore. How come you two don't have tattoos?"

Arty stood a little straighter, somehow looking offended. "We're Guardians, mate. Remember?"

Iggy added, "If you can't trust a Guardian, then who can you trust?"

"Oh. I didn't think about that. Sorry."

Iggy waved it off. "No offense taken." Though he did look slightly taken aback.

Taren drank his water completely down. "As you know by now, there have been many measures taken to keep certain information from Nadaroth and his ilk. There are several tasks that must be done. Each is essential in its own right, but ours may be of the most importance. Which is why details have been slim up until now. You also know that several groups have been forming. Each are being sent out in different directions with their own goals. What you haven't been told up until now is the most highly guarded information.

"Now Sam, I know you've felt a bit shut out from things." He saw Sam about to protest and stopped him. "Yes. You have. And I understand how frustrated that must make you feel." Taren stopped for a moment and glanced at Roz who was just as interested as Sam in this new information. "But," he continued, "What you *need* to understand is –"

There was a knock at the door. Taren sighed, balled his fists up in frustration and said, "I'll be right back." Taren opened the door and Zane was waiting for him, asking him for a moment. He joined him, closing the door on the way out.

"Well," Iggy said, "that was anticlimactic."

Roz went to start a fire. "No sense in being cold while we wait." The rain was a dull mist by this time, but had chilled everyone on the walk back. The fire was roaring in no time and the room warmed up quickly.

Several minutes had already passed since Taren left and the only disruption to the quiet of the room was the consistent yawning that seemed to spread like wildfire.

Sam's eyes were heavy and the fire wasn't helping keep him awake. His head was getting harder to hold up by the minute. "I wonder what's going on," he said lazily, and then laid his head down on his crossed arms upon the table. The room was now comfortably warm and Sam blinked hard, trying to keep his eyes open. Without even realizing it, his eyes closed and he began to drift into the in-between.

He was staring off into the abyss of his mind when he spotted a bird too black to be real. Its eyes were even blacker than its feathers. Without thinking, Sam set chase, hoping to catch it. As he ran, he slowed to look around and noticed that he was in Exile. The bird had landed on the roof just ahead of him. Something about that bird was intriguing and he climbed up onto the roof hopeful to touch it.

By the time he reached the peak, the bird had disappeared. There was no sign whatsoever that it even existed. So he sat perched atop the roof and stared up at the starry sky. By this time, Sam knew he was dreaming. Once it dawned on him, he looked around, all the time wondering if this was a dream or a nightmare. He peered through the night for the glimpse of Nadaroth or some other fear that might take hold of him, but was only met with the sound of two familiar voices talking just below him.

The first and more familiar voice said, "You're being ridiculous. I can't change it, even if I wanted to."

"Yes you can," said the second voice. "You've just grown soft about it. You've let that boy warp you into trusting too easily."

"You're out of line, Zane. Not only has he saved my life, but Sam's as well. That boy has been a better judge of who to trust than any of us. I trust him, so I trust Roz." By now Sam recognized the voice as Taren's. Why was he dreaming about Taren? He leaned forward to try and see better.

Zane said, "I don't think that proves anything. You can trust him all you want. I have nothing against Sam. But willingly divulging information like this is dangerous. I'm not even certain that Sam should know. He's so vulnerable – especially with his nightmares. Even you can't be so blind as to dismiss that."

Taren sighed. "Nadaroth hasn't been invading his dreams. But even if he did, he's shown great control of his mind when he sleeps."

"All of the time?"

He hesitated. "I don't know."

"See?" Sam wondered why Zane was so against him in this dream. He'd always been so friendly before.

"Now look. We have risked too much to change the course of our plans now. You have your task, and in three days we leave for ours."

This dream was feeling more real than it should have been. Something was familiar about this whole thing, but he was having trouble pegging it. He searched his mind as he listened on.

Zane turned around as if he was about to leave and then faced Taren again. He pointed a finger accusingly at him. "You'd better be right about this. You know how much is at stake. If the Guardian Tree is compromised, then – "

"Shhh!!" Taren looked around cautiously, eyes wide and furious with Zane. "Are you mad?! I haven't even told them about that yet for fear of spies!" he whispered harshly.

It was at that moment that it dawned on Sam. *Spies*. Sam looked around suddenly. He only had one thought before waking up with a jolt: The bird.

Sam jumped up so unexpectedly that no one in the room had time to react. He shot out the door in a flash, not saying a word, afraid of being heard too soon. He ran to the place he had been in his dream and saw it instantly. Sitting quietly atop the roof was a black bird, darker than the night. He knew that if he yelled out to Taren too quickly, that the creature would take flight.

Sneaking quietly behind the house, he could hear Taren and Zane talking quietly and his heart began pounding in his ears. He slipped around the corner, careful to stay beneath the overhang of the roof and out of sight of the bird. He knew he couldn't yell out and tried to think of what he could do. He saw a rock on the ground and bent to pick it up. Just as he raised his hand to toss it, a voice came from the dark behind him. "Sam?" It was Roz. He'd naturally gone to see what caused him to run out so suddenly.

Sam closed his eyes and cursed quietly.

Taren turned, confused, and saw Sam at the corner of the house. "Sam? What are you – "

There was no time. Sam jumped out and yelled two words while pointing. "Roof! Spy!"

There wasn't an ounce of hesitation. Taren drew his bow so quickly that it seemed inhuman and he pointed it towards the roof. He spotted it quickly, but the bird took flight.

Taren squinted and pulled back on the bowstring. He loosed the arrow and with a dull thud, it hit its mark. The bird fell, landing in a puddle with quiet splash. It flapped its wings feebly as everyone approached it. One of its black eyes was glowing red but fading quickly. It gave one last weak twitch and then the red eye turned a milky black, as if it were blinded.

Sam stared at it, fearful of meeting Taren's gaze. He was unsure how to explain what had happened. He knew now that the dream that he had when first arriving in Imagia was the same situation. They would have questions for him. Unfortunately, he didn't have the answers.

Roz joined the group. "What happened?"

Taren shook his head. "I'm not sure I know. But I think it might be best if we move inside." He gave a reproachful look to Zane. He was frowning back at him and then turned to leave. "Roz, can you go meet Alaria in the forest? She can dispose of this thing." He kicked the bird so that its face was covered in the murky water.

Roz left at once, leaving Sam alone with Taren. When they returned home, Taren asked Iggy and Arty to go alert some of the Protectors at the Tavern and have them sweep the area for any other threats. He shut the door after them and stood with his back turned to Sam. "How did you know there was a spy?" His voice was guarded.

When Sam didn't answer immediately, Taren turned, his eyes just as guarded as his words. He was scared. Sam was wrestling with how to explain. Taren's voice was raised enough that it startled Sam when he repeated himself. "How did you know?"

Yetews growled threateningly and Sam jumped, having forgotten he was behind him. Taren placed both hands up in a sort of surrender. "I'm sorry. But Yetews, Sam knew there was a spy on the roof – a bird that was listening sent by Nadaroth. Did you see anything?"

Yetews' eyes flicked to Sam who kept opening his mouth over and over as if he couldn't form the words properly. The Guardian shook his shaggy head, pointed at Sam, and then made hand movements that indicated that Sam had been sleeping.

"He fell asleep?"

Sam finally found his tongue. "Yeah. I did. And in my in-between, I saw a big black bird. When I chased it, it led me through Exile. I followed it up onto the roof and when I reached it…it disappeared. And I don't know how to explain this, but I knew this time that it wasn't just a dream. So I woke up and ran to where I saw the bird and – "

Taren huffed. "Wait a minute. This has happened *before*?"

Sam's shoulders slumped. He now regretted keeping the first dream a secret too. "Yes."

The sound that came out of Taren was far more than a simple sigh. He was disappointed. "How did you know it was a spy?"

"You'd mentioned that there were spies before. I don't know how to explain it. I just…knew."

"Alright. I don't know what to make of this situation. I have a hard time believing Nadaroth would have wanted you to know about this so I'm a little lost for words right now. You said it happened before. When?"

"My first nightmare back in Imagia. The one in the forest when you killed the bird in the tree."

There was an awkward period of silence. Neither of them knew what to say. The conversation seemed to have fizzled out and Sam tried to change the subject. "What were you saying before Zane came earlier?"

He was hesitant, his voice still highly guarded. He was thinking very hard about something. "Not tonight. It's late." His spirits seemed to lower even further as he continued. "You've had a draining day and this little incident didn't help. I need to inform the others about what happened. We've never had a spy in Exile…that we know of."

Sam knew deep down that he shouldn't press the matter. He'd been eager for sleep earlier, but things had changed and he wanted to hear what Taren had to say. Whatever he was going to be told tonight was important. Tired or not, he needed to know. His thoughts went directly to the moment in the dream that piqued his interest most.

As Taren started back towards the door, Sam spoke before he could stop himself. “What’s the Guardian Tree?”

Taren stopped dead in his tracks, his boots scuffing the floor as he did. Without turning around, his eyes went wide and in barely more than a whisper he asked, “What did you say?”

Sam knew that he shouldn’t have known this. He swallowed hard. “The G-Guardian Tree.”

Taren spun on his heel, his eyes severe and disbelieving. He looked at Sam as though trying desperately to see something inside him. And it didn’t take him long to start piecing things together. “How do you know those words?” He could see that Sam was afraid, but only because his own look was mirrored back at him. When he failed to answer, Taren’s words were accusing. “Sam…what are you not telling me?”

Sam stared back at him. This was going to be hard to explain.

Chapter Twenty-six: No More Secrets

Roz returned with Iggy and Arty in tow. They walked in and the tension in the room couldn't be thicker.

"Well, *this* should be interesting," Arty muttered.

Iggy looked up at Roz. "Do you have any idea what's just happened?"

"No. But I have a feeling we're about to find out."

Sam wanted to run from the room. Taren was looking at him as though he was the enemy. But he had no control of these things in his dreams. He didn't even know exactly what it was or how it happened. But if there was one thing he did know, it was that he'd hardly be showing much in the way of trust if he didn't reveal everything now. And after his speech about trusting each other, that wouldn't look very good on his part.

He swallowed the knot in his throat. "In my dream, when I chased the bird up onto the roof," he began. "I sort of…became the bird. At least I think that's what happened. The first time it happened, I thought it was all just a coincidence. But this time, I recognized what was happening. I heard you and Zane talking. I heard him say 'Guardian Tree'." All the Guardians in the room stiffened noticeably. "The moment you said the word 'spies', I knew I had to wake up and get to you before it was too late." Taren was unreadable by this time. Sam couldn't take it. "Taren, I swear that I had no control of this. I don't even know how it happens! It feels kind of like invading Nadaroth's dreams like I did the last time I was here. But it's…I dunno…different. I didn't *mean* to do it. It just happened."

It was obvious to everyone that Sam felt as though he was being attacked. Taren knew this wasn't the case, but he couldn't hide his concern. Regaining his composure, he met eyes with Yetews who looked nearly as anxious as he did. "I'm not angry with you. But I don't think I'm leaving you unguarded for the moment. I believe we have a lot to talk about."

Before anyone divulged too much more, Taren thought it best to keep their entire group informed. Foo joined them later. Pax and Hawke, though having traveled with them on the way here, had been assigned to another group. Taren explained that they might be joined by another somewhere on their journey, but wasn't specific about who it was. Alaria would be keeping watch from a distance, constantly checking ahead of them to make sure the way was safe.

When Sam asked why there would be so few in their group compared to the larger numbers in the other ones, Taren explained that a smaller group would go more unnoticed than the larger groups. In fact, two rather large groups were being sent out in different directions as distractions from Sam's group.

Taren watched Sam yawn. "Perhaps you should sleep."

"No!" He didn't even try to hide his eagerness. Whatever the Guardian Tree meant, he didn't want to wait any longer to find out.

Roz shifted in his chair to get more comfortable. "Well, I'm definitely intrigued."

"Who wouldn't be?" Iggy agreed.

After Sam recounted what happened from the moment he'd fallen asleep to the moment that Taren killed the bird spy, everyone was caught up to the current moment. So Taren took over.

"Zane, as you all now know," he still looked concerned about how Sam found out, "would have me not telling you this. But as I've said before, I have all trust in you." With a very meaningful look at Roz, he added, "Both of you."

Roz gave a nod of thanks, Taren acknowledging him silently.

Taren had been sitting at the table thus far, but got up to slowly pace the floor while speaking. "This information *must* be kept secret. You can't speak of these things unless we have secured the area. As you saw, we have good reason for this. Is that understood?"

Sam agreed, but not without a question. "But what about tonight? If Zane knew not to – "

"Zane was a damn fool!" Foo barked out. It was unexpected coming from Foo as he rarely seemed to want to talk at all.

Taren held up a hand to him. "Enough, Foo." Foo took offense to this but merely scowled and said nothing else. "Yes. Zane was foolish tonight. He will not make that mistake again," he said severely.

Sam was taken aback by his tone. It was obvious that Taren was angry with Zane. He wasn't about to push him further and as if perfectly timed, there was a scratching sound at the door.

Taren looked at Foo and jerked his head towards the door. Foo didn't bother to open the door, but rather jumped out the window, disappearing into the night. He returned shortly after. "Alaria has checked the perimeter. She's going to patrol the house until we are finished. It's safe to speak." He jumped back up onto the windowsill. His back was turned to everyone as he peered out into the darkness.

"Alright. This will require that we start at the very beginning."

"The beginning of what?" Sam asked.

"The beginning of Imagia. Now, Roz, you won't know about this. But Sam, do you remember when you first met Orga?"

"Yeah. How could I forget? You told me he was the first Guardian of Imagia."

"Yes. But he wasn't the only one. There were twelve First Guardians of Imagia. They were all created together and reside well hidden throughout the world."

Sam didn't speak. He simply sat there, mouth slightly ajar, and listened intently.

Taren went on, his face becoming more and more serious as he spoke. "When you overheard about the Guardian Tree, you stumbled upon the deepest secret of this world. In the wrong hands, this information can be very dangerous. It could be the downfall of Imagia."

Roz was nervously looking towards the door and the others couldn't help but notice. Even though Sam was trying to compute this new information, he asked his friend, "Are you ok?"

Taren watched him and asked, "Is something wrong?"

Roz, trying to grin but failing terribly, appeared very worried. "I'm fine. But…maybe I'd better go out and help Alaria keep watch."

Taren shook his head. "You need to hear this as well. Everyone in our group needs to know. Alaria is very thorough."

"I suppose you're right," Roz agreed. "I just don't want the wrong ears to hear."

It seemed a bit strange to Sam that Roz was so nervous, but he didn't dwell on it as Taren started to speak again.

"When the twelve First Guardians were born, they became tied to Imagia through the Guardian Tree. It is basically the life force of this world. It has twelve branches – one for each of the First Guardians. Each branch is made up of countless lights. When a new Guardian is born, a new light joins the tree on one of the twelve branches. When that Guardian fades, the light remains, growing even brighter than before."

"What are the lights?" asked Sam.

Taren smiled, "The souls of the Guardians."

"Wow," Sam whispered as goose bumps prickled all over. "Have you ever seen it?"

With hesitancy, Taren said, "Yes. But other than the twelve, I am only one of a few who have. It's impossible to get in to see it without a First Guardian. This is where we come in.

"When Nadaroth took power and began destroying Guardians, the First Guardians went into hiding, leaving Orga as the keeper of the Tree. Up until now, Orga could enter to see the Tree at will. There was one handprint engraved, as it appears, in the stone. Orga had but only place his hand in the spot that matched his own hand, and he could enter. Shortly before we left to retrieve you from the other world, the entrance became closed to him – three handprints replacing the one, each unique. Orga immediately realized that there must be a reason for Imagia to require three instead of one to enter the cavern."

Roz had been quiet up until now. "Three? Does anyone, perhaps Orga, know why?"

"No." Taren sighed. "Orga, as always, has theories. Strangely enough, his theories are generally right. So we had to start coming up with a plan. If Imagia has required three to enter, then there is a reason. Orga is confident that if we gather three First Guardians to open the way, then there will be something inside to help us fight Nadaroth."

With his eyebrow lifted high, he doubtfully asked, "I don't suppose he has a theory for what that might be, does he?"

"Unfortunately, no. But never in the history of Imagia has it required more than one First Guardian to enter the cavern. And Sam, as strange as it may seem, the prints didn't appear until we decided to bring *you* back."

"Me?" Sam asked, flabbergasted. "What could I have to do with that? I'm not a Guardian!"

"Obviously," Taren stated. "But one thing's for certain: You're more important to this world than you realize."

Pressure.

It always came down to the pressure with his abilities. Sam didn't want to feel frustrated. But he was. He'd been trying his best and his imagination was getting better. It was slow, but steady. But still, it wasn't anywhere near as powerful as it used to be. Now he knew that not only the people of this world were counting on him to do something about Nadaroth (again), but also the world itself felt need of him. He started to grind his teeth unintentionally as he listened.

The night wore on as Taren explained everything he felt necessary. They were to leave in three days, heading north in search of another First Guardian. The other groups, each much bigger than their own, were assigned their own tasks. Two of the groups were diversions, looking to lead any enemy away as they consistently spread word that they have found something needed in the war against Nadaroth. Four other groups were each going separate ways, one each going north, south, east, and west. Their tasks were all the same.

Orga had given Taren his best guesses as to where the other First Guardians might have been hiding. Unfortunately, he only knew of three and their general locations.

This is where Taren had been when he disappeared from his home since their return to Exile. He'd been sharing the locations with the leaders of the groups as they were formed. Now that Sam finally understood what all the secrecy was about, he started to put things together. When all was disclosed to Sam and Roz, Taren looked at Sam, his expression one of someone who was patiently waiting.

True to form, Sam had questions. There was a small part of him that was upset that no one ever thought to trust him with this amazing part of Imagia. Especially after all he'd done and sacrificed for the good of this world. But, he looked past his selfish angst to see the bigger picture. "You said another group is going north. So why are we going that way too?"

"We'll be headed towards the Impossible Way."

"*The Impossible Way*?" Sam's shoulders slumped and he covered his eyes with both hands in frustration. His head started to throb as he considered how much they would need his imagination to even attempt to go that way. "Oh, man. I don't think I'm ready for that kind of challenge, Taren."

"Now calm down, kid. I said *towards*. We won't actually be going there. There is a place that is hidden near there that we will stay. Actually, there are three hidden places. We'll be traveling from one to the next as we wait until we are needed."

"Oh." Sam breathed a sigh of relief but then considered what they were doing. Or rather, not doing. "Our task is to just hide? That doesn't sound very important."

Jabbing a thumb in Taren's direction, Roz said, "I think I'm going to have to agree with him on this one. I think that you could use the time to heal and train."

Taren agreed. "Precisely. That, and we have to keep you safe. It's not a very good idea to put your injured mind in the thick of the action, however little there might be for now. We will keep watch while we wait."

"Wait for what?" asked Sam.

"News. When we get word from the others that a First Guardian is found, it will be us that goes to get him…or her."

"I don't understand." Roz's face was screwed up as he considered this. "If they find a First Guardian, then why can't they bring them back? Their groups are significantly more equipped for the task."

Sam was nodding in agreement before Roz even finished speaking. It wasn't that he enjoyed sitting idly by as others did the work. He was simply remembering the many months of traveling the first time he was in Imagia. It was long, tiring, and uncomfortable at best. "Yeah. What he said," He pointed at Roz. "What's the point of making the trip if they're already there?"

Arty crossed the table, his face more serious than Sam was used to. As he approached, Sam felt as though he was looking into his soul rather than his eyes. "Don't you get it, Sam? It's you. You're the reason we have to go."

"Huh?"

Arty pinched the bridge of his snout just between his eyes. "The First Guardians have been hiding for years. They know how dangerous it is for them. They won't leave their sanctuary lightly. Orga has already warned us that they won't leave unless they see you – and your power."

Sam wasn't sure he bought that. "Seriously? How can you know that?"

"Because," Iggy answered this time, "you seem to keep forgetting that *we're* Guardians. Remember? And it's what I would do if I were in their position. And…uh…"

"Iggy!" Arty hissed. "No!" Iggy frowned, sighed and looked to Taren, unspoken conversation between them both.

To Arty's dismay, Taren gave a curt nod. He shook his head slowly. "Fine. I guess we'll just divulge everything then." He crossed his paws in front of him and waited.

With a little conviction, Iggy finished his earlier comment. "Well…the thing is…we already found a First Guardian." Yetews, Roz and Sam all sat a little straighter, each one surprised for their own reasons. "Here's the thing: He refused to come with us. He said that unless there was proof that the boy who imagines is back in Imagia, he wouldn't come. None of them would. When we got you back, we returned to his home. He was gone. And we have no idea where he went."

Taren looked defeated. "This is why we can't risk something happening to you. Without you, the First Guardians refuse to return to the Guardian Tree."

Sam couldn't believe what he was hearing. How did they even know about him if they'd all been in hiding for so long? How did such secrets stay hidden for so long and how could they have never shared this with him if he was so important? He wanted to complain and ask these questions, but all he got out was, "Great. No pressure." Roz overhead and pat him heartily on the back. As he did so, he nicked Sam's newly engraved tattoo and it caused him to jump and wince. Roz apologized and pocketed his hands with a small wince.

For the most part, there was nothing left to reveal. Short of a few questions here and there, it seemed that there was no reason to continue. Sam was exhausted. He could feel it all over his body. Even his mind was tired from all the information that he'd taken in tonight.

He knew he would have more questions as he considered everything, but he could no longer form coherent thoughts.

At this point, there was a lull so long in the conversation that a loud yawn managed to escape Sam's mouth. Both Taren and Roz agreed that they all needed rest. Yetews looked sympathetic when he noticed the dark circles under Sam's eyes and was more than eager to see him get some sleep.

After another tap on his shoulder courtesy of his Guardian, Sam yawned again and muttered, "Alright, alright. I'm going to bed." Though he tried to look as though he was annoyed, Sam was actually very grateful. He'd been tired since he'd woken up this morning. He barely made it into a comfortable position on the bed when his eyes gave in. He was asleep before he knew what hit him.

* * * * * * * * * * *

Sam didn't dream that night. But in Imagia, a dreamless sleep was a welcome occurrence. When he awoke the next day, the hustle and bustle that was all over Exile was almost overwhelming. Over the next two days, Taren was gone so much that Sam hardly saw him. Luckily, Roz was there to keep him company, teaching him about the bow. Roz had told him that he'd only allow him to shoot it after he could manage the proper form and care.

Sam had a good chuckle when Roz stated his reason. "As much as I'd love to let you loose a few arrows, I'm rather attached to my only eye. I'd like to keep it, if it's all the same to you."

Between his bow training sessions with Roz, Sam spent as much time as possible preparing for his own journey. Each of the four groups that were to go in the four directions had all set out by now. The two groups meant as distractions had left as well. Several Protectors remained permanently in Exile so as to keep those that lived there safe. There were, however, two smaller groups, each consisting of three, that were on a completely different mission. They were to seek out Garrett and Titus' location. There had been no word from them, but Taren wasn't too concerned about it. It had been Garrett's way to find his brother quietly. The main reason for seeking them out was to update everyone about what was happening. There had also been word from the north that Gabriel's group had been spotted moving east as if with a great purpose.

Sam was genuinely concerned for Titus. He hadn't been separated from him for this long before and it was really sinking in as to how much he appreciated having him around. He tried not to worry, but it was hard. He missed his furry comrade.

At last, it was time for Taren's group to leave. It had been a strange thing this time, leaving Exile. There was an ominous feeling in Sam's gut that made him think that perhaps he might not return this time. It was mostly nerves, but it was still mildly unsettling. Without relying on his imagination as much, this journey may prove to be the most difficult one yet.

Even though they were going to a safe haven and would mostly be hidden away until they were needed, it certainly seemed as though they were taking a very big risk while doing so. Taren was extra cautious as they set out, hardly finding time to even look at Sam let alone speak to him. He would systematically disappear into the trees to check in with Alaria, whom they only seemed to catch a rare glimpse of. Sam kept remembering Keesa and how she was always within sight of him when they traveled. Alaria may have been her daughter, but she wasn't Keesa.

Iggy and Arty were the same as always. They stayed entertained by constantly finding ways to drag Foo into some form of argument, usually about his overly cautious nature.

On the other hand, Yetews seemed to be back in his element. Aside from the fact that Sam would see him frequently wrestling with something internally, he was very happy that he was there and protecting Sam once again. Sam knew that he was still struggling with the madness and the forest seemed to bring it about much more easily. Sam tried to ignore it.

Roz was doing his best to continue training Sam even as they moved. He drilled him on proper form and stance when it came to holding and firing a bow. But he also managed to get Sam to attempt to use his imagination from time to time. Pending they were in a safe area and not in a place where it would cause them danger should something go sour, it seemed to help keep Sam's sanity in check.

It'd already been several days since they'd left Exile and so far nothing extraordinary had slowed them down. It would be at least a five-day journey under the best of conditions. The forest around them was familiar, bringing back floods of memories from years before. Several times, Sam had to fight back the memories that would pop to mind of Keesa stealthily making her way through the thick foliage above. Regardless of losing her many years before, it was still a hard thing to think about.

Yetews lumbered on next to Sam as they came to a very unfamiliar area. There was a small creek that trickled idly across the path ahead and it's calming, bubbly sound was relaxing. They stopped and Taren removed his pack. It was time for a break.

As Sam peered around, he tried to remember crossing this way before but was unsuccessful. "Where are we?"

Taren answered, "About two days from our destination. We'll follow this creek until we reach one of the darkest parts of the forest. That's where we'll be staying for a time."

Thunder rolled in the distance and everyone turned their eyes to the sky. The trees were thick. From what they could see, the sky was blue. But there was a hint of gray that began to creep in.

Sam grumbled, "Is it just me, or has it been raining more than usual?"

Iggy responded first. "It has been a bit damper than it normally is. I don't think my fur has dried out since the last one." He lifted his arm and took a long sniff. "Gah! Nope. Not dry."

Arty took a note from Iggy and sniffed his own armpit only to wrinkle his nose. "Ugh! Maybe a bath is in order." He made his way towards the creek and began to follow it upstream.

Iggy followed close behind. "If you smell something foul and unnatural, it's not me. It's him," he said pointing towards his counterpart.

"I heard that!" Arty called back.

Roz started to remove his gear. "You know something? I think I could stand to get clean myself."

Each one in turn realized how good of an idea this was and began to head towards the creek. Sam was the last to join them. He removed his mucky boots first. They were the only part of his attire that was not of this world. Shortly after arriving, he'd had a strangely large growth spurt, so the clothes he'd come here in were almost worthless.

His boots, the kind you'd hike in, had been larger than he'd needed so fortunately they still fit. But just barely.

Sam dipped his toes in the water and shivered involuntarily. He turned to Yetews. "I know this makes no sense to you, but I sure do miss warm showers."

He grumbled something, a smirk on his face.

"Har, har, har," Sam chided. "Hilarious. If there *is* a deceptor hanging around, I'll be sure to let you check it out first." He pulled his shirt off and waded into the shin deep water. The thunder cracked again, this time closer. Sam sighed. He casually wondered what the point of bathing was if they were just going to get soaked again. As the too-chilly water hit his skin, he promised himself that he'd try to make them shelter from the storm, even if it meant a headache for the rest of the day.

* * * * * * * * * * *

It had been raining for hours and Sam was nearly convinced that the gray, heavy clouds were following them on their journey. As the rain fell in sheets around them, Sam called out to Taren. "Maybe we should stop! I can't see anything!"

The water cascaded off of the Protector's face, but he didn't stop. Instead, he pointed down-stream, shaking his head. "We're nearly there!" he shouted over the sound of the rain.

The creek was swelling, chest deep at the center now and at least thirty feet wide. When they reached a bend in the creak, Taren stopped and waited for the others to get closer. "We have to cross here. The water's moving fast, but the ground at the bottom is sound." He hiked his gear up over his head, his bow in one hand, his pack in the other, and began to traverse the water.

Yetews was gracious enough to put Iggy and Arty on either of his horns and grumbled to Foo. He pointed up at his shoulders and waited for Foo to get on.

Foo looked up at Yetews' shoulders hesitantly and then over at the creek. As short as he was, there would be no way he could cross without swimming it. As he wasn't the best swimmer, he trudged reluctantly to Yetews and climbed up. He clung on to the soggy mop of fur and gave a very reproachful look to Iggy and Arty. They looked as though they were holding in a burst of laughter. Foo growled, "Not. A. Word."

Yetews growled regretfully to Sam who was no longer small enough to ride atop his shoulders.

"It's alright, buddy. Just stay on my right so I don't get swept down the stream."

Yetews gave a confident thumbs-up and then Roz joined them. He held his gear high as well and said, "I've got your back too." He grinned wide and they all followed Taren across. There was no sign of Alaria, but it was highly likely she'd found a much drier path through the trees.

Stepping into the water was a shock. Sam half expected it to be cold, but when it began soaking through his clothes, he started to shiver. The rain poured down, causing their vision to be skewed. And then, for a reason that he couldn't explain, Sam felt a familiar sense. His goose bumps were no longer because of the cold water.

They were being watched.

Sam stopped suddenly, his eyes wide and frantically searching through the downpour. Roz and Yetews hadn't noticed him stop yet, but Sam didn't think to raise an alarm. Something swam past him; it brushed up against his leg and made his knees buckle slightly. He jumped, his heart pounding as he fought against the current of the water.

Yetews heard Sam gasp and was immediately aware that Sam was no longer next to him. He spun his head back, nearly sending Foo tumbling off his shoulders and causing Iggy and Arty to cling tighter to his horns. Roz saw Yetews spin and turned to see Sam in a state of panic.

Roz yelled out to Taren who was closing in on the other side of the bank. By the time Taren turned, he could hear Roz hollering to Sam. "What is it, Sam?"

Roz's voice carried to him, but was dulled by the sound of the rain on the water. He yelled back, eyes still hysterically searching for what swam past him. "Something's in the water with us!"

Only a few seconds after his warning, Sam saw a dark shape coming towards him in the water. It was some kind of reptile, with a long snout surrounded in white, eager teeth, searching for a meal. It looked like a crocodile, save for the triple line of bony spikes that lined its spine and the tree bark-like skin. It could have been mistaken for a floating log had the head not been sticking out of the water, jaws opening in a menacing hiss.

Backing through the water was impossible. The current was going too fast. Sam desperately tried to get to the bank. He'd always been a fair swimmer and dove forward. As he did, he saw another of the creatures sliding into the water from the bank, this time headed towards Roz.

In a flash, Roz threw his pack around his shoulder and reached below the water. When his hand surfaced, he was gripping his dagger. As the creature swam towards him while hissing horribly, Roz jumped. The creatures were the size of a full-grown man, but they were heavier and faster in the water. Roz leapt onto its back as Sam tried to escape.

A strong hand grabbed Sam from the back and jerked him out of the way of what turned out to be a third creature. But as Yetews pulled him, the first creature rammed into his side, causing him to unintentionally drag Sam under the water. He let go, leaving Sam to rise to the surface, gasping for air. He wiped the water out of his eyes. Beneath Yetews' soaked fur, Sam could see his muscles were working hard to pull a large log out of the water.

Raising the log above his head, Yetews brought it down hard on the head of the creature as it double backed to ram him again. Sam gasped, trying to make sense of the scene through the torrential rain.

Roz had managed to embed his dagger deep into the back of the creature he'd been fighting, and Taren was trying to get there to help. But the dagger only angered the creature and it growled, poising to strike a now unarmed Roz. Sam was about to yell out to his friend when a shadow from above leapt stealthily into the water right on top of the creature. Her saber teeth sank deep into the barky skin. There was a struggle from the creature as Alaria clamped down onto its throat and backed out of the water, dragging the dying body with her into the forest.

Taren was helping Roz up out of the water. He was holding his forearm now, blood mixing with the water as Taren helped him get his bearings. Yetews grabbed the head of the creature that was feebly trying to move away and pulled its jaws open. He was furious. His teeth were bared as he pulled hard and yanked the creature's jaws apart with a sickening crack. He tossed it aside and the body floated down stream and out of sight.

After a quick mental count, Sam realized that one of the three creatures was unaccounted for. Before he even had a chance to look for it, he felt himself being dragged back as the third beast snapped down on his backpack, pulling him under. Beneath the water, Sam struggled as he tried to break free of his pack. He wriggled out of it just in time. He broke through the surface and saw the creature coming at him, its tail smoothly trailing behind it like a snake on the water. It opened its mouth, eyes on Sam.

Faintly, Sam heard the shouts of his friends behind him. He heard the water splashing as they came to his aid. But he knew they'd never make it in time. He didn't close his eyes, but rather squinted as he imagined with all the power he could muster. Just as the creature opened wider to snap down on Sam, another set of teeth emerged from the water behind it. The jaws were wider, had more teeth, and it gave no warning as it chomped down on Sam's attacker.

He heard its back break and watched as the mouth fell open, lifeless. The beast that Sam imagined waded through the murky water. Its prey dangled from its giant jaws. It was easily the size of a hippo and everyone moved out of its way as it passed. It made light of the flowing water as it moved down the stream and out of sight.

Something warm grabbed Sam's arm. Sam yelled out suddenly and then stopped when he realized that it was Taren.

"Come on, kid. Let's get out of here."

Everyone pulled themselves onto the muddy bank, panting from the ordeal. As Sam sat in the muck, trying to recoup, Roz dangled something in front of him. It was Sam's backpack, soaked to the core and torn, but still quite functional.

"Thought you might want this back," Roz said as he set it down next to him.

It may not have been the most important thing in the world, but it was all he had left from home. He was grateful and said very earnestly, "Thanks."

Roz cleared his throat and excused himself to tend to the puncture wounds in his arm.

Before anyone could have much time to rest, Taren called out, "Come on everyone. The shelter is just ahead."

If anyone could have spotted the underground cave, it would have proved to be an impressive feat. The moss and vines covering it were the perfect camouflage. It may have been formed from a rocky outcropping, but it was well hidden.

Soaked to the bone and shivering, their entire group entered the cave one after the other. It was a small entrance, barely wide enough to fit Yetews. He had to duck down quite a bit to get through. Taren went in first and found what he was looking for. He walked back to the little light that the rainy day offered just at the cave's entrance and was holding a lamp. He made himself busy trying to light it.

Even though Sam had just used his imagination, Roz asked him if he had it in him to make a fire. If not fire, then perhaps some dry wood, as they would be hard pressed to find any during the storm. Just as Sam was about to give it a go, Taren stopped him and shined the now lit lamp towards the back wall of the cave. There was enough wood stacked against it to keep a fire going for a week and next to it were several crates and sacks filled with food and provisions. Taren saw the look on everyone's faces and innocently shrugged. "What? We've had some time to prepare."

Once the fire was roaring, everyone sat around it, doing their best to dry and warm up their exhausted bodies. Sam kept trying to hold back his shivers and welcomed the warmth that the fire's glow provided. He could've stayed by the fire all night, but saw Taren standing at the cave entrance, staring out. The rain seemed to slack off a bit. With a little regret for leaving the warmth, he went over and stood by him. "So," he started, "that was crazy."

Taren snorted. "Yes. I don't think they were Nadaroth's though. I've seen those creatures before. They usually hang out in deeper waters. The rain must have swollen the creek a lot."

"Huh. And here I was thinking this was supposed to be a *safe* place."

Taren smiled weakly, still not making eye contact with Sam. "You're not hurt, are you?"

"I don't think so. Couple of scratches and I feel like I swallowed half the creek. I've definitely had worse."

"Good."

They stood there in silence, the rain and the crackle of the fire the only sounds around them. Another shiver ran through Sam. “So…now what?” he asked as he wiped the mud from his face.

Taren looked off into the distance, the weight of the world in his eyes. “Now…we wait.”

Six Months later…

Chapter Twenty-seven: Uncharted Territory

Sam's heart was pounding in his ears and his lungs were on fire as he ran through the forest at top speed. He ducked beneath branches and jumped over tree roots as he sped on. Behind him, he could hear Roz running close by.

"Did you lose it?" Roz yelled.

Through gasping breaths, Sam called back to him. "I don't know!"

"Do you see it anymore?"

Sam growled in anger, stopping quickly. "No. Dang it!" He pulled the bow over his shoulder and kicked the rock in front him into the bushes. "I hit it. I *know* I hit it!"

Also gasping to catch his breath, Roz bent over and put his hands on his knees. "I know you did. But – it wasn't – a kill shot."

"Don't you think I know that?!" He instantly felt bad for snapping. "Ugh. Sorry. I know it went this way."

Roz stood straight and as his eye swept across the area, he shirked off Sam's outburst and explained, "The problem is that if you can't hit a moving target then you might as well not use the bow at all. All targets that count are going to be moving in some way or another. The enemy doesn't just stand there willingly while you kill them." He held out his hands, palms down. "Steady hands. Now show me yours."

Holding out his hands for Roz to see, Sam knew instantly what he'd say. His hands were shaking. He pulled them back quickly and growled out again. He was just about to say something when Roz zeroed in on something just ahead of them on the ground.

He pointed. "Look. Blood. It's leading that way." Roz pointed to the right and they both set off at a run, following the drops of blood. They slowed down and tried to not make any noise as they came to a thick patch of high grass.

Lying in the middle was the beast, no longer moving. It was an ugly creature, with sparse wiry gray hair and four savage, yellow eyes. It was somewhat rotund and each leg ended in a sharp two-toed hoof. The arrow Sam had hit it with was jutting out from just near where the heart would be. The wood of the arrow was splintered from where it broke off as the beast ran through the brush.

"Well, would you look at that? I guess it *was* a kill shot," Roz stated. "Kind of."

Sam grinned proudly. It was his first official hunt. Up until now, he'd never actually hit his target. They'd run out of meat a few days ago. Roz convinced Taren and Yetews to let him take Sam out hunting. They were strongly against it at first, but Alaria promised to go with them and make sure the way was safe.

They tied some rope around the beast's feet and found a long, sturdy branch to hang it from. Together, they carried it back to camp. The beast, known as a yumix, was one of the best meat sources in Imagia. They were plentiful and somewhat easy to hunt. As long as they weren't backed into a corner, there also wasn't much danger in hunting them. Which, of course, made it the perfect thing to hunt for a beginner like Sam.

At the first glimpse of Sam returning, Yetews breathed a sigh of relief. The grass where he had been standing looked as though he'd been pacing. When Sam approached, he took notice of the well-trodden ground.

"I'm okay, buddy. Really." He scratched behind Yetews' ears as he passed to enter the cave.

In all their waiting for news, they'd already been to each of the three designated safe havens. Since leaving Exile, they'd also managed to find and safely retrieve one First Guardian. The whole journey had gone without a stitch. It wasn't very far from Orga's home, only a two-week journey there.

This First Guardian's name was Zarcanis. He was much taller than Orga, by a foot at least when he wasn't hunching. The greens of his skin matched the leaves of the trees he'd made his home in. Which is why he lived high up in the canopy of the forest. He was wiry, but muscular, owing to how easily he navigated the high branches. His eyes were just as friendly and warm as Orga's despite the fact that they were black as night. In fact, there was a moment when Sam was staring into Zarcanis' eyes and he was sure he'd seen stars gleaming in them.

Now, they had come full circle. They were back at the cave they'd first come to and had been there now for nearly a month already with no word from anyone – until today.

As Roz and Sam entered the cave, they were greeted by the sound of Taren speaking with Brock, another Protector Sam had met years ago.

"Hello Sam!" Brock beamed enthusiastically.

"Hey!" Sam set down his end of the stick, settling the yumix onto the ground. He was quite happy to see someone new, hopeful that there was something in the way of news. "We haven't had anyone here in weeks!"

"That's because there has been nothing to report in as long," Brock stated.

Taren asked Roz to go and get Foo, Iggy, & Arty and to attempt to locate Alaria if he could manage it. When he returned, everyone was with him. Alaria had been close by, resting in a tree. When she entered the room, she chose to stay close to the entrance, her ears constantly swiveling around, listening for danger. Alaria may have looked like her mother, but Sam remembered Keesa being much softer around the edges.

Brock, a husky man with an impressive dirty-blonde beard, got to work updating them with new, very welcome information. They all sat around a rustic table that Sam had imagined for them to eat at.

For all intents and purposes, the third First Guardian had been found. She had disappeared sometime ago and it had been extremely difficult to find any information on her until a Guardian from the North had come to Brock's group when they were getting ready to go west in an attempt to start over.

This Guardian, that chose not to be exposed for helping out, had been trying to escape some collectors that were trying to capture him. In his desperation to hide, a very old Guardian had stumbled upon him and took pity. She helped him, taking him to a very secluded place somewhere deep within the swamplands in the east. When asked to describe his rescuer, the Guardian told them what she looked like, but mostly spoke of her kindness. He'd failed to get too much information out of the old one, save for two things: She had been hiding since Nadaroth had taken over and she knew Orga.

As soon as Brock had discovered this, they'd returned at once to see if Orga knew who she might be. Upon hearing her description, he identified her as one of the First Guardians. Her name was Sentreece and she would be very easily picked out of a crowd should anyone be searching for her. It had made perfect sense for her to go to the gloomiest and least traversed place in Imagia.

By this point, Taren was pinching the bridge of his nose, eyes closed tight. "The swamplands." He shook his head slowly, thinking for a moment. "Of all the places we would find one, why did it have to be the swamplands?"

At first, Sam tried to wrap his mind around the idea of a boggy, unpleasant place even existing in Imagia. Swamplands, if they were the same as what he was used to reading about back home, were wet and hard to travel through. Even so, he was curious why Taren was so bothered by it, as they had traveled through much worse places before. "I didn't even know there were swamps in Imagia. Why is it so bad?"

Taren and Brock exchanged a look. Taren put his elbows on the table and explained. "There are many places in Imagia that are, for the most part, uncharted and not well traveled. There is a place in the east that we simply refer to as the swamplands. Very few have ever been there, so it is mostly all hear-say as to what is there. The Guardian that explained this, gave a very detailed account of where he found her so we will be able to find it fairly easily."

"So what's the big deal then?" Sam asked.

"The swamplands are on the northern shores of Imagia. Which means –"

Sam interrupted him and answered mostly to himself. "We have to cross the Impossible Way."

Beside Sam, Yetews growled his disapproval.

Roz was almost giddy. "I haven't been back to the north since I fell through the gateway."

Sam had almost forgotten that he had come from northern Imagia. That statement had caught him a bit off guard.

As their conversations drew on well into the evening, many things were revealed. There were fears that something was stirring in Nadaroth's lands. Not only had the shadows that covered the land grown, but more movement from creatures and people were being seen coming and going from there. It had put several of the Protectors on high alert and they were gearing up to defend themselves should an attack happen.

At this point, no one knew what kind of control Nadaroth had gained or just how many he had at his command. His absence from Sam's nightmares had actually been unsettling for everyone, including Sam. The unknown was making everyone nervous.

This all had led them to get to Taren and his group as fast as possible in hopes that they could retrieve the next First Guardian quickly. Orga, though still calm by nature, had suspicions that Gabriel's disappearance might be dangerous for her future. He requested that Taren be told that they leave as soon as possible as a precaution. Reinforcements would hopefully be arriving at the Impossible Way if they could be reached in time.

Taren agreed that leaving at first light the next day was imperative so everyone was given things to gather to prepare for the trek. Brock bid everyone farewell so he could return to his group. They were waiting not far off in the forest. They were eager to get back to Exile in fear that the village would be attacked.

As he was leaving, Taren called to him, "Just a moment, Brock." He turned to Sam who was busy packing his scattered belongings into his tattered backpack. "I'll be right back."

Something in the urgency of Taren's voice tickled Sam's curiosity. He was the only one left in the cave now. Yetews had even left to go gather some fruit from a nearby tree. He quietly crossed the cave floor towards the entrance trying to look as though he was retrieving something important. He picked up a rock and wondered how he would explain its importance should someone walk in on him eavesdropping. He hoped if he was quiet enough that he would catch part of Taren and Brock's conversation.

He was within earshot and caught Taren's question. "Has there been any word about Garrett and Titus?"

Brock sighed heavily and hesitated. "Nothing. Perhaps it's time to admit that –"

"Shh! Not here." Sam could hear Taren shift his weight and was sure that he was looking towards the cave. He quickly moved away. He knew that the others were hesitant to mention Garrett and Titus around him. Sam had simply stopped asking, fearful for what news might actually come. Brock's words were not meant for his ears. Now he regretted eavesdropping. Since Garrett and Titus had left, there had not been one word about their whereabouts. And even though Sam was choosing not to lose hope that they were fine, he couldn't ignore the whispers when others spoke about it.

Taren returned to the cave, Sam having been long since packed. There was weariness in his face, but he looked determined. He walked over to Sam asking with a bit too much joy, "All packed then?"

Sam was staring blankly into the dying embers of the fire while he sat on one of the logs placed in the center of the cave. "Yeah." He tossed a pebble into the ash releasing a stray flame.

"Good." He cleared his throat. "There's something I need to talk to you about." The false joy was gone. But he didn't get a chance to say anything else.

There was no point in hiding that he'd heard their earlier conversation now. "I know. I heard you and Brock talking."

Taren's eyes went wide, but there was a hint of a smile at the corner of his mouth. "Of course you did." He was trying to make light of the situation. "Curious forever and always, eh?" When Sam didn't respond he sat down next to him on the log. "I haven't lost hope. And neither should you. Understand?"

"Sure."

Nudging Sam in the ribs lightly, he said. "You have *met* Garrett right? Because honestly, I'm not sure anything could hurt him. He's way too proud to let that happen." He smiled and Sam did too.

It worked. Sam felt better. Without another word, they went back to preparing. It wasn't far to the Impossible Way, but once they got there, it was going to get tricky. After a good meal, courtesy of Sam's earlier hunt, they all went to bed, restless for their journey. Sam went to bed with thoughts of Titus, Turtles, and time…hopeful that he would see more of all of them.

* * * * * * * * * *

Coming out of the forest into the grasslands that preceded the water was nostalgic and bizarre. They'd come through further east than the last time Sam was here, but the grasslands were the same. Only, this time it was Sam who had changed. He was much shorter the last time and remembered fighting his way through the tall blades of grass. Now, it was easier and he could actually see what was in front of him.

In his flood of memories, Yetews walked beside him and watched as his boy remembered. A lopsided grin formed at the corner of his mouth as he recalled that day. Reaching out, he snagged a few blades of grass and nudged Sam. He held them out to him, grumbling a question.

Sam smiled so widely that nearly every tooth in his mouth was showing; something he'd not done in awhile. He chuckled and answered, "No thanks. I already had breakfast." He took the blades of grass from Yetews anyways and basked in the memory that came to mind. At just ten years old, he had actually tried to eat that grass because it looked so delicious when Yetews crunched on it. At nearly fifteen, he knew better. It was a good memory. He slowed down, letting Yetews move ahead of him and out of sight. When he was certain no one was looking, he took the wide blades of grass and placed them in his backpack.

From the corner of his eye, Yetews didn't miss this moment. But he moved on, not saying a word, his heart warmed from the moment of innocence.

Iggy and Arty ran ahead with Alaria, quite stealthily for their size. They weaved expertly through the grass, seemingly at home with the terrain. At the rise of the hill, they all stopped, keeping low to the ground. They called back to assure them it was clear. They cautiously approached the shore.

It wasn't long before the deceivingly calm water began to tremble, a familiar smooth, mottled skin surfacing just after. Roz, having never seen this before, gasped and stepped back in surprise. Alaria began to pace uncomfortably, never taking her eyes from the water. The others in their party were unfazed. The giant catfish opened his mouth dully, ready to give his warning to the potential passers of the Way, only to stop mid prose with a start.

In a gasping gurgle, he turned one eye closer to the party and took notice of Taren. "Taren! Good to see you, friend!" he boomed.

"Always good to see you Dolimus. We've brought a friend this time." He motioned to Sam who was already alight with excitement.

It took a moment before realization hit him. With more excitement than any normal fish should be able to express, Dolimus gasped and belted out, "Sam Little?! Is that really you?"

"Hi Dolimus!"

"Well, aren't you a sight for old eyes? You've grown up!" He disappeared briefly beneath the water to take a breath. When he surfaced, he was a little closer to shore. "So it worked then. You've returned to Imagia. How amazing! Welcome back, my boy!"

"It's great to see you again too."

Taren was looking to the skies, his eyes searching. With some sense of haste, Taren brought his eyes back to the old catfish and disrupted their reunion. "I'm sorry Dolimus, but we have a favor to ask. We are in need of passage."

If ever a fish could look confused, it was now. "Well, you have Sam. Surely he can be of more service than I."

Sam's face flushed. Every time he had to explain the problems with his imagination, he felt like a failure. Even though it had been well past half of a year since his return, he still struggled with his power. But he wouldn't hide from it. Before Taren had a chance to say anything, He decided to explain it. "Actually, there's a problem." He watched as Dolimus listened with curiosity, his snake-like whiskers calmly floating on the water's surface. "I got hit hard in the head right after coming back. It has made imagining really difficult. I'm getting better, but it's…well…taking a long time. I can imagine fine, but the more complex it is, the less reliable it seems to be."

A quick breath again beneath the water and Dolimus asked. "How long have you been healing?"

He didn't want to say, but did. "Since my return – eight months ago."

Dolimus didn't react. He merely considered it in silence.

Breaking through the awkwardness, Taren asked, "Do you think that the turtles can be found?"

With one eye still turned to Sam, he answered. "I will do my best to try." He spoke not another word and disappeared, his whale-sized tail the last to vanish.

They waited. During the time, the others tried to convince Sam to practice and try to imagine like he had the last time. Even though the only one's in their party that had witnessed it were Taren and Yetews, the stories were well known. But nothing they could say would convince Sam to try. He had been so hesitant to use his imagination lately. He could see their concern in their eyes, but he didn't know how to tell them that he just didn't think it was going to ever be the same again. He avoided the stares. And when Yetews tried to coddle him, Sam shrugged him off, frowning. "Just drop it, Yetews."

Yetews was taken aback. Sam could see that. He sighed and considered apologizing, but his pride got in the way.

Over half the day passed before the water quaked and Dolimus surfaced in front of them. A ways behind him, the water was moving, dull wakes where something swam just beneath the surface. Dolimus said, "I'm sorry for the wait. They are very good at hiding."

Three heads, each the size of boulders, broke the surface. By the time they reached the edge of the Way, three giant turtles waited peacefully. Upon seeing Sam, they're heads dipped in a respectful bow. Sam didn't feel worthy of such a gesture.

Dolimus reminded them of the dangers of the water, but also of a much more important detail. "They must not touch the land and you must not touch the water. Just as last time, you must find a way onto their shells."

All eyes were on Sam now and once again knots seemed to form in his throat. That feeling was getting more common now. Each time they expected something of him regarding his imagination, he felt as though he would let them down if he weren't successful. Swallowing the knots, he put all his focus on creating a set of steps reminiscent of those he had created last time. They jutted just slightly out over the water – enough to get on the turtles, but not so much as to tip it over.

"Well done, Sam." Roz beamed. "With the steps *and* the turtles. Fascinating what your mind is capable of."

Sam snorted under this breath and quietly said, "*Was* capable of."

"And still are. You're just – "

"Healing. Yeah. I know." He couldn't mask the sarcasm in his voice.

Roz shook his head and made his way to the stairs. "You know what your problem is?"

Sam Frowned. He didn't need more opinions on what was wrong with his mind.

Turning just before the steps, he stated, "Confidence." He boarded the first turtle with Alaria hesitantly leaping on after him, her claws out and ready. She had the same distaste for water that apparently all kupa cats had.

Taren boarded the second turtle with Foo. Even though the stairs were steady enough, Foo was more nervous than any of them. His poor water skills made him jittery and he clung to the wood as he climbed, careful not to look into the water below. Despite Taren's reassurance that he wouldn't let him fall, Foo's eyes were wary as he made the wide step across to the shell. Taren grabbed his arm to help and, for once, Foo didn't complain. He sat right in the middle of the shell, still looking anxious.

Iggy and Arty went over to Yetews. In passing Sam they agreed with Roz, agitating Sam further. "He might be on to somethin', you know?" said Arty.

"Yeah. We agree with Mr. One-eye there." Iggy jabbed his clawed thumb in Roz's direction who was doing his best to look innocent.

Yetews held up a finger, his mouth open, but upon seeing the look on Sam's face, thought better not to say anything at all. He scooped the ferrets up and helped them onto his shoulders. He waited until the next turtle reached the platform and climbed carefully onto the slippery shell.

Sam leapt lightly from the end of the stairs when it was his turn and slipped as he landed. Yetews deftly caught him and pulled him to a steady position. They both exchanged a look that said all was forgiven.

Once everyone was safely on their mounts, Dolimus said, "I will accompany you across the Way."

"Actually," Taren started, "We aren't crossing. Not directly at least."

"What?" Dolimus was shocked.

"If they are willing," he motioned towards the turtles, "we have need to travel east…to the swamplands on the northern shore."

Dolimus grew angry, which was something Sam hadn't expected. "The eastern waters are very rarely traveled. The water tastes different there and is harder to breathe in. You are asking them to risk their lives."

He understood. "Which is why we will ask them. If they do not agree, we will cross here and make our way slowly there. If it weren't imperative that we reach this place quickly, we would never ask. Sam?"

It was discussed on their journey here so Sam knew that he was to speak with his creations and ask them for help should the need arise. He nodded and bent closer to the turtle he was riding atop of, the largest of the three. "Will you help us? We need to get there fast. I…don't want any of you to get hurt." He began to stroke the shell of the turtle. He didn't know anything about where they were going, but he didn't like the idea of risking the lives of creatures as peaceful as them. It wasn't right.

The turtle sensed his touch and his sincerity. She turned her head slightly to look at him. "We will help you."

Part of Sam hoped she would say no. He had a terrible feeling about this. But without any hesitation, the three turtles swam to deeper water and headed due east. The sun was setting and the air was chilly as it passed over the water. Even though the situation wasn't ideal, riding the turtles that he'd created over four years ago was refreshing compared to the doldrums that they'd been experiencing tethered to the safety of the cave.

Dolimus surfaced next to Sam. He swam in silence for a long moment. His gaze was piercing and Sam tried to ignore him. "Your friend is right," he finally said.

"About what?"

"I can see it in your eyes. You're afraid of something."

Sam rolled his eyes. "I'm not afraid," he said defensively.

"I've been a sentry to these waters for a long time. I've seen what fear looks like too many times. It's in their eyes, like a cloud forming in a clear sky. When I first met you, you didn't have that look."

Sam tsked, "I was terrified the first time we crossed, so I think you might have missed something."

"Just like every emotion, there are several types of fear. The one I see in you is self-made." He dipped below for a quick breath and then continued. "What is it that Sam Little is so afraid of? Hmm?"

He looked around at all of his friends. Ever since he'd made the choice to return, he had had the same concern. And when his head was hit and it changed everything so much, it just justified what he had been afraid of since the beginning. He didn't want to answer, but something in him forced the word out, shocking not only Dolimus, but Yetews as well. He stared straight ahead, not meeting anyone's eyes, as he said, "Failure."

"An entire world believes in you. Perhaps, you simply need to believe in yourself again." With that, the old catfish left. Every once in awhile he would surface just long enough to speak with Taren. Sam didn't talk for a while. He rode in total in silence for a very long time.

The trip east went far quicker than anyone expected. The turtles were fast in the water. It was just past dawn and they'd been on the water for over two days by this time. Everyone was ready to be on dry land again. So when the trees on the northern shore began to shift into a dark mess of willowy trees and thick vegetation, everyone was grateful.

The turtles came to a sudden stop, Dolimus surfacing for them all to see. "This is as far as I go. It is beginning to hurt to breathe this water."

Taren nodded. "Thank you for helping us. I know it comes with risks for you."

He took in a great gurgling breath. "I don't know what you are here for and I do not wish to know. But my hope goes with you." He turned his wizened eye to Sam. "You are here for a reason, boy. Never forget that."

Something in the way that Dolimus looked at him caused emotions to stir deep within. He knew he shouldn't have been so sharp with the old sentry and he regretted it. Sitting up straight, he assured him. "I won't." Dolimus gave a fishy grin and turned to leave. "Dolimus, wait!"

He turned back around, curiosity twinkling in his old eyes.

"I'm sorry…for earlier." Sam fought to find the right words. "You *are* right about me. I just don't know how to find my confidence. But…I won't stop trying. I promise."

Dolimus laughed, a strange baritone sound. "I believe you. Goodbye Sam."

"Bye."

With one last splash of his tail, Dolimus was gone and the turtles began to swim towards the shore. They were barely a stone's throw away when Alaria stood up, her claws digging deep into the shell, and growled fiercely. Sam spun to see the hackles on her back raised and her ears and eyes darting about frantically.

She hissed, "Do you feel it? The water…something is moving." The moment she said this, the turtles stopped and began to look below them.

The lead turtle whispered, fear taking over her voice, "They are coming."

Taren and Roz looked at one another from their separate mounts and Taren asked, "What is it?"

The turtle simply said, "Evil."

The water around them began to ripple more violently. Shadows of creatures swimming below began to threaten the surface. Sam yelled out, "What do we do?"

The shore was close, but Sam's turtle was the furthest away. Taren barked out orders. "Get us as close as you can. Sam, create a platform. When we reach it, we'll have to jump. Quickly!"

Sam concentrated on the shoreline just in front of where Taren's turtle was. A wooden platform came into existence just in the nick of time. Creatures from the deep were now surfacing – a mixture of things with sickly gray skin or thick, black scales and teeth. There were so many teeth.

Whatever was stirring beneath the water began circling the turtles. Menacing jaws were snapping at their shells. The turtles began to panic, but fought against the threats to get their riders to the dock. They had no defense, but they did have sheer size on their side.

The turtle carrying Foo and Taren were the first to reach the dock and each one of them jumped to safety. Foo yelled out to the turtle, "Get to safer waters!" As a Guardian, he was concerned for the creatures that so selflessly risked their lives to get them here. The turtle nodded his head, fear in his eyes for his companions.

As he was trying to escape, a set of razor sharp jaws swam towards him and he began to double back. In his panic, he accidentally ran right into the turtle carrying Roz and Alaria. As the two collided, their turtle was also rammed from behind by one of the creatures. It sent Roz flying forward and caused Alaria to slip. She began to slide towards the water but grasped the shell with her powerful claws. She yelled out to Roz, "This one is being attacked! Get to the other turtle! Now!"

Roz pushed up hard, jumping back up onto his feet. He turned to help Alaria first.

She growled fiercely, "Don't worry about me! I'm fine! Go!"

They were rammed again and something from below began to pull the turtle backwards. Roz didn't hesitate. He ran and jumped to the back of the other turtle, barely making it. "Come on!" he yelled to Alaria.

Her muscles rippled beneath her slick fur. She grunted and pulled herself to the top of the shell. The turtle was now several feet away from the one Roz was on, but Alaria dug her back claws into the shell, leaping hard. She landed next to Roz. The turtle they had left was under full attack. It was nearly impossible to see how many creatures were now tearing at him. He bellowed out in pain, the whites of his eyes fully visible and taken over by dread.

Sam watched as the turtle fought to get away and yelled out. But they began to pull him under, blood tainting the water. "NO!" He squinted hard in concentration. He knew he had to concentrate harder than normal, as anything that he imagined would be destroyed by the evil within if it didn't come from below. The turtle he was on was shifting and moving constantly, trying to get away from the beasts attacking her. He tried to ignore the chaos as Yetews held him tight. Then, five gray fins, easily belonging to something that matched the size of the turtles, broke the surface.

As soon as Sam saw them, he willed them to the turtle being attacked and yelled, "Help him!" He was nearly under the water now, fighting a losing battle. But now five larger than life sharks tore through his attackers, ripping as they went. It was just enough of a distraction for him to escape. Diving below, he was gone and headed to the safety of the deeper waters.

Sam was just about to breathe sigh of relief when his own turtle was rammed as well, knocking them to their knees. Iggy was clinging to Yetews' horn as he belted out, "We gotta get to the dock!"

Their turtle spun in the water, sending waves rippling behind her as she swam quickly towards the dock. Her frantic attempt to get there made it even more difficult to avoid touching the water. By now, Roz and Alaria had made it safely to shore and there were arrows being blindly shot into the water. They were just hoping to distract whatever was attacking. But the water was moving too violently now to tell what was wave and what was beast. The turtle that had taken them to safety was nowhere in sight, having dived below to escape the moment his riders were free. Sam hoped that she made it to the safer waters.

Though she was fighting back hard, desperately trying to get Sam to safety, the last turtle was struggling with bleeding wounds all over. She'd nearly made it to the dock when her eyes went wide. Something was pulling her backwards. "You must jump now!" she ordered Sam.

Sam knew that he couldn't make the jump. He may not be as small as he used to be, but they were just too far away for him to make it. "I can't! Yetews, you have to jump first and when I jump, you'll have to catch my arms."

Yetews shook his head and protested loudly.

"I'm too heavy for you to throw me! It's the only way! I can't make it and your arms are long enough to reach the rest of the way."

The turtle had managed to kick off what was holding her, but it returned and caught her by the tail, pulling harder this time. She was giving it everything she had but fading quickly. "*Please! Go!*"

Yetews growled and tensed his muscles. Iggy and Arty tightened their grip on his horns. He leapt the distance, barely catching his back feet on the edge as he landed. The others were there to stop him from slipping. Iggy and Arty leapt off, falling into clumsy somersaults as they landed. When Yetews turned, he reached his hands out, stretching them as far as they could go.

Sam felt as though time slowed down. He could see all of his friends calling to him – urging him to jump – but the only sound he could hear was his own heartbeat. He ran to the back of the shell but she was being pulled so hard that there wasn't much left above the water. He took a deep breath, and ran. He focused on Yetews' outstretched arms and when he ran as far as he could, he jumped.

As his foot pushed off, his turtle was suddenly pulled further under water, throwing him completely off balance. He felt his feet leave the shell, but knew as soon as he was airborne that he wasn't going to make it. He reached desperately for Yetews and could hear someone yelling his name. He closed his eyes, waiting for the pressure of the water to take him.

He wondered what it would feel like when he died. Would it hurt for long? Would the white thread-like tentacles take him slowly like the ship he'd imagined years ago, or would the frenzy of beasts devour him like a worm on a hook?

The splash never came. Out of nowhere, two huge, scaled claws clasped him tightly around the waist and the sensation of falling was gone. Now he could feel himself climbing high into the sky and away from the frenzy in the water below. He opened his eyes and saw brilliant green scales all around him as two wings beat against the wind. The dragon turned smoothly back to the shore and set Sam down before landing next to him. When he folded his wings to his body, he shrank almost instantly to the size of a goat.

Sam couldn't believe it. "Enoch!"

His brilliant white teeth flashed. "Hello Sam. I guess I got here just in time."

Iggy and Arty were clutching their chests in mock heart attacks. They were both panting as though they'd run a mile and Arty chided, "What do you mean 'just in time?' More like almost too late!"

"Blasted dragons! You just can't trust them to keep a schedule!" Iggy added. Though they were trying to sound upset, their relief was transparent.

On the other hand, Yetews looked as though he was about to pass out. He rushed Sam and threw his shaggy arms around him, pulling him into an inescapable hug. He growled almost angrily, but also grateful.

His voice was muffled through all the fur, but Sam hugged him back saying, "I know, big guy. I know. But I'm okay now." When he looked up into his Guardians green eyes, he saw tears that were threatening to spill. Sam didn't want to admit how truly terrified he'd been and made a promise to himself to never mention it for fear of pushing Yetews back into the madness he'd been fighting so hard to keep at bay.

"Enoch, your timing is impeccable," Taren assured the dragon with a grateful grin. "What took you so long?"

He flared his nostrils, "It's complicated. Perhaps a tale for another time." The voice seemed too deep to belong to such a small creature. It fit his more impressive stature. It was just part of the mystery of shrinking dragons. When his wings were expanded he became a full-sized dragon but shrank down to barely the size of a large dog when he folded them to his sides.

Wasting no more time, Sam walked straight up the dragon, knelt down, and wrapped his arms around his cool, scaly neck. "It's so great to see you."

The dragon wrapped an arm around Sam. "And you as well. You've grown!"

"That seems to be the popular opinion." Sam heard someone approach him from behind and saw that it was Roz. He looked very taken aback by Enoch's presence. "I know you told me you were friends with a dragon, but I guess I never really thought too much past that."

Enoch stepped back, squinting at Roz. "Who is this?" he asked. He voice was suspicious.

"Enoch," Sam introduced, "this is Roz. He's a Defender from the North. Roz, this is my friend Enoch."

Taren noticed Enoch's hesitance. "He's a friend of Sam's…and to all of us."

It seemed that was all the dragon needed. He bowed his head briefly and said, "If Sam calls you friend, then I shall too."

Roz whispered a quiet, "*Wow. Amazing,*" as he walked away.

Alaria walked past Sam, her tail brushing against his leg as she passed. "I'm glad you are safe, Sam." She smiled and then went to sit quietly near the morning shadows of the trees. Sam was surprised how truly grateful she looked.

The water was calm now, no signs of any creature – good or bad. Sam's heart was heavy as they all tried to recoup from the incident. "Do you think they made it back to safe waters?" he asked anyone who would listen.

Roz was the only one to answer. Everyone else seemed wary as to what they should say. "I think they had a good chance. They are very big."

Sam heard the doubt in his voice, but hoped he was right.

They rested briefly but didn't want to linger. The shores of the Impossible Way couldn't guarantee safety. But, as they looked into the cypress trees that led to the heart of the swamplands, there was undeniable uncertainty. The shore was muddy and the water that spread beyond the trees was murky and ominous.

For a moment, Sam wondered what life would've been like if he'd just stayed home. He didn't let the thought fester. It wouldn't help him now. "So…"

Taren nodded. "So."

"She's in there somewhere?"

"Yep."

"Huh. And you know where we're going?"

"If our source is accurate, then yes."

Brushing the muck from his filthy hands, Sam looked around at all the apprehensive faces. "Well…let's go get her."

They each had their weapons at the ready. One by one, they entered the swamplands, hopeful and unsure what lie ahead.

Chapter Twenty-eight: Swamplands

Enoch had been in contact with the group that remained at the north shores. He was meant to meet with Taren's group well before they left the southern shores, but had run into some problems. There were other creatures making a straight line to the swamplands and Enoch and his clan of dragons had been stopping them for fear they had discovered the First Guardian.

There were too many whispers that Nadaroth had discovered her and possibly others of her kind. Though it had taken some effort, it seemed that they were successful but Enoch had thought it best to help them secure the First Guardian's location. Once Brock and his group returned to Orga's, Enoch was given the responsibility to show Taren where Sentreece was hiding.

This made locating her hideaway simple. The biggest problem they were running into was the terrain. It was murky at its best. They had spent hours wading through waist deep water. When they weren't in water, they were shin deep in mud. Much to the distaste of Alaria, the trees were knotty, wild, and difficult to travel through. Though she tried her best to stay dry, there were too many times she had to make her way through the mire along side of her companions. She was becoming more vocal by the day about her distaste for it. They had just managed to find some dryer ground to make camp on for the night and Alaria sat beneath a particularly twisted tree cleaning her fur. Though it was the driest she'd been in awhile, she muttered for the fourth time that day, "My undercoat will never be dry again."

It was precisely at that moment that a large amphibious creature swam past her and splashed its tail, soaking her again. She frowned furiously as Iggy began to laugh hysterically. Arty chimed, "That was timing if I've ever seen it!"

Much to her dismay, the laughter spread and everyone, even the ever-serious Foo, was laughing. She tried to keep her scowl, but after watching Sam laugh, her expression softened and she chuckled low. "I'm so glad to amuse you all."

After their third night, they reached the place Enoch had been leading them to. They were meant to have reached it on the first day, but a dense fog had set in and caused them to get turned around. Before them was a twisted tree that dwarfed every tree around it. It was actually a series of trees that had grown together to form a sort of super tree. There was moss hanging down from every limb that created a curtain around it, keeping any entrance well hidden. Unless one knew what they were looking for, it would easily be bypassed.

Sam stared at the tree and tried to see how anyone could live in it. "I don't get it," he said. "How can she live in that thing? It's a mess."

Enoch pointed very low to the ground near the base of the tree. "Not in it. Under it."

That's when Sam saw it. At the base, there was an opening that looked as though the roots grew apart specifically to make a door. It wasn't a massive opening. Yetews would have to duck just to fit through it. But it was dark. As they moved closer there was no sign of movement.

Roz quietly said, "Well I certainly hope she's friendlier than that entrance looks." Yetews nodded in agreement.

"We've spent too much time getting here. Let's get moving. We'll go in and you can work your magic, Sam." Taren was concerned and Sam could hear it in his voice. "Orga said that she will be very reluctant to leave."

Sam started to move towards the entrance when Enoch and Keesa both hissed, "Wait!" His skin prickled with sudden fear. Taren and Foo both rushed around Sam and without the slightest hesitation entered the opening.

They'd only gotten a few yards inside when Foo came rushing back out, panic on his face. "There's been a cave-in of some kind. We can get through, but we need to move now." He had his dagger out and ready.

He was afraid to ask, but Sam did anyways. "Is there something in there?"

"No." Foo looked over his shoulder into the dark of the cave. "But there was." His voice was grim. "Enoch, keep watch out here."

The dragon nodded and unfurled his wings. He burst into his more impressive size and kept guard.

Beneath the tree was a tunnel that led deeper underground and it was made up of thick dirt that was heavily lined with rock. Deeply cut into the harden ground were claw marks. What used to be a path was now cluttered with earth that nearly blocked them from going further. But with effort, mostly thanks to Yetews' powerful arms, they were able to clear the path enough to get through. It was a slower process than any of them liked, but necessary.

The air was thick with mold and dust that had been knocked loose from the cave-in and everyone was coughing as they struggled to move the debris out of the way. After great effort, they reached a clearing that led to a makeshift doorway created by roots that had grown into an arch. Yetews had to work very hard to squeeze through it. When they came through the other side, there was a wide cavern supported by countless thick roots from the cluster of trees above them. Once they were all inside, they stopped and took in the scene before them.

The only light in the room was from one small candle and the glow of the torches that Sam had created and given to Taren and Roz. When Sam's eyes adjusted to the dim light, his heart fell. He was the first to speak and the whisper of his words hung on the air. "We're too late."

The cavern was destroyed. The belongings of the First Guardian were strewn about. A table was broken and lying on top of a great mound of dirt and rock, a part of the earthen ceiling fallen in. Pieces of the First Guardian's possessions were littered amongst the rubble that used to serve as her home. There was no sign of life. There was only destruction.

When Taren directed the torchlight towards the ceiling, there were more claw marks that matched those in the tunnel. And as he brought the light down, smears of blood stained the rocks by his feet. The fury that came to his eyes was frightening. His fists balled up, knuckles turning white. He yelled out in anger. The echoes quieted quickly as the roots absorbed the sound.

Foo fell to his knees and cupped his hands over his eyes. "No…"

Yetews bowed his head and his ears hung low. Arty and Iggy walked slowly over to Foo and each placed a paw on his shoulders. They bowed their heads as well. Roz was simply stunned and had no words.

The torch fell from Taren's grip as he dropped to his knees. Sam watched everyone, lost as to what to do or say. He walked over to the pile of rubble to pick up Taren's torch and a sense of desperation to search for the First Guardian took over him. He couldn't stand there and do nothing. As he reached down to grab the torch, the glow of fire touched something in the rubble. A white hand, smaller than his own, was sticking out – and it twitched.

He didn't pause to think or speak. Sam dug into the ruins and began to throw giant clods of heavy dirt and stone out of the way. Roz rushed to his side and started to dig as well. He could see the hand too and didn't hesitate.

"She's alive!" Roz shouted.

Within seconds, everyone was pulling together and digging Sentreece free. The hope in the air was guiding them and pushing them to move quickly. When her head appeared, Sam gasped. Even through the dirt and blood that matted her smooth face, she was beautiful. Her skin was as white as snow. She had long silver hair and pointed ears that stuck out slightly. Her face wasn't human, but very close to it. Her eyes were too big and her mouth too small. She had two dainty antlers that stuck out from her hair. One was broken at the tip. As they freed her completely, Sam spotted two wings sticking out from behind the ancient cloak she wore. They looked like the wings of a gray-brown moth, but were tattered from the cave-in.

Taren picked her up and cradled her gently in his arms. "Clear a space," he directed the others. He moved towards the clearest spot in the cavern. As soon as the ground was free of debris, he laid her down gently.

Sam rushed to her side, terrified for the worst. "Is she going to be okay?"

Taren was working to clean her wounds and doing his best to see how far the damage went. "I don't know. I'm no healer, but I can tell she's badly hurt."

"What can I do to help?"

"Here." Taren handed him a rag he'd soaked in water from his pouch. "Try to clean the wounds on her head while I get some more water."

Sam knelt close to her, his hands shaking. He had no idea who did this to her, but he was angry. Sentreece wasn't very big. In fact, she probably wouldn't even be Sam's height if she were standing. Orga was right about one thing: She would be easy to spot if someone was looking. The idea that anyone could hurt something so pure rattled him. He did what Taren asked and shakily wiped the blood away from her wounds.

Sentreece began to stir. She whimpered, startling Sam even more. As he pulled his hand away and was just about to call for Taren, she opened her eyes. The shade of blue was too bright and Sam found he couldn't look away. With a feeble arm, she reached up and touched Sam's cheek. Sam stiffened and closed his eyes, beginning to shake all over.

Images began to flood his mind. Faces he couldn't place were laughing and something large was ripping through the cave as Sentreece tried to hide amongst the roots of her cavern. Sam could feel her dread as she watched the room around her being turned upside down. In a singsong voice, someone called, "Come out, come out, wherever you are!" When she didn't respond, the same voice spoke again in a very bored tone. "Oh well. Tear it down." As the ceiling fell down around her, she saw one last face. He looked familiar but Sam couldn't quite place it. The images went black.

Sam opened his eyes, almost certain of what just happened. He'd experienced something similar before with Nadaroth when he entered his mind through sleep. Only this time, he didn't remember falling asleep for those few moments.

A hand went to Sam's shoulder. Yetews looked concerned and grumbled at him. Sam was sure his own face must mirror that of his

Guardian. "I…I don't know for sure what happened. I think…I think she showed me who did this."

Foo furrowed his brow. "What do you mean she showed you? How?"

He was shaking his head, no idea how to answer him. "There was something big that destroyed the walls and then…a man."

"What did he look like?" asked Foo.

"I don't know. I think I might have seen him before, but I can't place it."

Taren had been listening. He didn't try to push Sam for more questions, but his voice was serious. "We need to get her to Orga's. Now."

The sense of urgency was high. Thanks to Enoch, they were able to get to the edge of the swamplands that led back out to the shores of the Impossible Way in a quarter of the time it took them to reach Sentreece's cavern. The biggest problem was the murky water and keeping her body dry, so Yetews was the one to carry her. The thick vines and knotty trees weaved a net out of the canopy and made it impossible to fly. Otherwise Enoch would have taken them out quicker.

They reached the shores and as they were emerging from the trees, still sloshing through ankle deep water, Taren said to Enoch, "We'll need to get her to Orga's as quick as possible. Do you think that – " He didn't have a chance to finish his question.

A voice in the muddy shadows of the shore had interrupted him. "I see she survived. How fascinating!" Once again, the familiarity of that voice struck a chord somewhere with Sam. It was polite, yet dangerous. And when the man stepped out of the shadows, Sam knew instantly it was Sentreece's attacker. It was the face he saw through her eyes.

Taren drew his bow and had an arrow pointed directly at the man dressed in black. "Gabriel!" he thundered. Everyone fell in behind Taren, drawing their own weapons as Enoch spread his wings and grew. But they didn't get a chance to act because they were threatened.

"Ah, ah, ah! Weapons down, or your friends will die." Gabriel was grinning and almost singing the words.

From behind Gabriel, a ragtag group appeared. Some were human. Others were not. But they were all intelligent and one looked very troll-like, towering above the others with a great, ugly grin on his face. His hands ended in heavy claws that matched the grooves in Sentreece's cavern. He held ropes in his hands that were tied to something behind him.

When Taren saw this, the tension on his bowstring slackened. "What friends?" he asked warily.

With a snap of Gabriel's fingers, the beastly thug holding the ropes jerked hard, pulling their captors forward into view. They were both tied tightly with the rope and were very bruised and battered. The moment they came into view, a collective gasp filled the air, all weapons were withdrawn, and Sam jumped forward. Taren and Roz both grabbed his arms, holding him back, as he yelled, "Titus! Garrett!" He fought against the hands that were holding him and spit out in anger, "Let them go!"

Gabriel stepped closer, his lips spread wide in a devilish grin. He spoke as if he was simply greeting an old friend. "Ah…Sam! Almost didn't see you there." He leaned a little closer, cocking his head slightly. "How's the head?"

Sam relaxed, no longer fighting to get away. He shrugged off Taren and Roz's grip and scowled at Gabriel. In a most deadly voice through gritted teeth, he answered, "It's fine."

"Well, don't go trying anything funny or Garrett will not live to see the night fall."

Sam looked him in the eyes and then turned away quickly. He didn't want to risk his friends' lives.

Gabriel chuckled, a merry sound that was out of place. "That's better. See? Now all you have to do is just hand over that pretty little Guardian. These," he gestured half-heartedly towards Garrett and Titus, "for her. Fair trade. Though, I do believe you're getting the short end of the deal."

Garrett was staring at the ground, one eye swollen closed, dried blood on his face from old wounds. His lip, however, was still bleeding from a fresh cut. His hands were tied in front of him. Judging from the raw skin around his wrists, the ropes were very tight. Sam had never seen him look so broken – body and mind.

Titus was tied by the neck and had bloody matted fur in several places. One of his ears was jaggedly split in the middle. His innocent, brown eyes stared back desperately at Sam. He was afraid and in pain. Sam's heart felt sick and it beat desperately inside his chest as he tried to figure out what to do.

"Garrett." Taren addressed his friend and fellow Protector. When Garrett raised his head, they looked hard into each other's eyes. Garrett's nostrils flared, and his lip quivered. They both had determination in their eyes. Taren's knuckles were turning white and they both nodded to one another so slightly that Sam wasn't even sure it really happened. He snarled at Gabriel. "No deal."

His eyes wide with surprise, Gabriel paced slowly in front of his group, occasionally looking at his brother. After a tense moment, he came to stand next to Garrett and smiled. "Well," he started, "I suppose we are at an impasse then." In one fluid movement, he reached into his belt and pulled a long dagger out from its sheath and then held it directly under Garrett's throat.

Garrett closed his eyes tight, waiting for the inevitable. His lip continued to tremble. But Gabriel stopped suddenly when Sam yelled out.

"NO! YOU CAN'T!" Roz and Taren were holding him back again.

Gabriel smiled wickedly and clucked his tongue. "Oh dear," his tone was mocking. "Don't tell me that you actually *care* about my brother. Because if that were true, then I would be holding the knife to that Guardian in his place."

Sam looked desperately at Gabriel. He couldn't understand how this was happening. It was very possible that he was a big brother himself now. Even if he would never see his baby brother, he would never do anything to harm him. Gabriel waited patiently for Sam to respond. "You *can't* kill him." His voice was small.

"Actually," he chuckled darkly, pulling the blade closer to Garrett's throat, "I can." There was no remorse or regret in his face. In fact, he looked perfectly at ease with the situation.

"But," Sam shook his head in disbelief, "he's your *brother*."

Gabriel considered what Sam said for a moment. "For the powers that be, you're right!" He promptly removed the dagger from

Garrett's throat. "It would be a shame to rid the world of my *entire* family. After all, he has been quite useful."

Garrett's face fell and he looked apologetically at Sam who stared back baffled. Garrett would have died before betraying them. Of this, Sam was certain.

It prompted Gabriel to say more. "Oh, don't you worry now. He didn't give us any information. Well…not willingly." Garrett was cautious as he watched his brother raise a hand in the air as if beckoning something to him. A small legion of winged leviathans landed behind them on the shore, each one matching Enoch's full size. Most of Gabriel's group began to climb onto their backs. The only ones that remained on the ground were the biggest one that was still holding the prisoners' ropes, Gabriel, and another man that had a murderous stare. Gabriel smiled again. He really did look like Garrett. "Well, my dear brother," he swiped the dagger between Garrett's hands, cutting through the rope with ease, "you're free to go."

When Garrett didn't move, Gabriel shoved him from behind. He stumbled and then walked hesitantly away, looking down at Titus as he walked past. Titus whined quietly and then looked to Sam.

Stuttering slightly, Sam asked, "W-what about Titus?" Garrett was halfway to Taren by now.

"Ah yes," he said. "I nearly forgot." Gabriel looked at the thug holding the rope and nodded once. Sam watched with relief as the rope dropped out of the thug's hand and Titus began to slowly walk away, limping on his front foot.

Titus made it about halfway to Sam when Gabriel said, "Unfortunately, I couldn't care less about your pet." He pulled his dagger back and then threw it forward. It flew straight and true, hitting Titus right behind his front leg and into his heart.

With an agonizing yelp, Titus fell forward onto the muddy ground. Sam screamed out. "NOOO!!" No one tried to hold him back because everyone was in shock. He ran to his friend, and fell at his side. "Titus?"

Titus was gasping for breath, a trickle of blood trailing out of his nose. "I'm…sorry Sam."

"No! No, no, no, no, no! You…you can't die!" Sam was trying to imagine of a way to heal him like he did for Keesa, but he couldn't think straight.

Titus whimpered. In a ragged breath, he said, "I…really…lived."

Sam nodded, trying to smile and be strong, but the tears were blurring his vision now. "Yeah," he sniffed. "You did."

His words were hard to understand, and Sam leaned closer. "I'm…not…saying it."

Sam didn't want to say goodbye either and remembered those last good moments with Titus before they left Orga's when they had this same exchange. He sobbed hard, "I'm not saying it either."

He pulled Titus closer to him, hugging him as best as he could and Titus weakly pulled his paw up and laid it on Sam's arm. The moment lasted only a few small seconds. His body went limp, his paw slipped from Sam's arm, and his heart beat its last. Sam sobbed hard again and whispered in his fallen friend's ear, "Goodbye."

In the background he heard commotion. Taren and Roz were loosing arrows at Gabriel, but it was too late. He was already on the back of his heavily scaled leviathan, the arrows pinging off its hide like gnats on an elephant as it took flight.

Gabriel called down to Sam, a smirk on his face, "So sorry, Sam. But I *am* the bad guy after all."

Something inside of Sam boiled. As he held onto Titus, he didn't look up and give Gabriel the satisfaction of seeing his pain. His blood felt hot, as if he would surely explode. He began to shake as he gritted his teeth together in fury. It was a rage he'd never known. The pain was great, but his anger was greater.

It consumed him.

The sky darkened, heavy gray clouds forming at an unnatural speed. Thunder rolled and lightning flashed across the sky. Sam got off the ground and stared up at Gabriel as his leviathan beat its wings higher into the encroaching storm. Sam's eyes were ablaze. Wind began to blow and the water of the Impossible Way became turbulent. White tips formed on the water's surface as the sky grew even darker. Somewhere in the background Enoch roared, calling to his clan.

Sam was deep in concentration, his eyes on the man that slaughtered his friend. "I'LL KILL YOU!" he screamed. As he concentrated on Gabriel, a bolt of lightning struck inches away from his beast of burden. It faltered, nearly throwing Gabriel from its back. Just as this happened, lightning struck twice more, each bolt hitting their mark and causing two of Gabriel's men to fall into the

Impossible Way. Thousands of eerie, white, string-like tentacles met them in the air before they hit. They screamed out in pain, but the sound drowned out quickly.

The look on Gabriel's face was pure shock as he stared back at Sam. He was disbelieving of what he was witnessing. He looked around the sky and then to Sam, realization settling in. The storm was Sam's creation and it was more powerful than he obviously thought possible. He pulled hard on the reigns of his beast.

For a split second, Sam was sure he could see Gabriel smile again. Just when it looked as though he was fleeing, he double backed and charged them head on. He urged his beast to swoop low to the ground forcing everyone to jump out of the way as his leviathan's tail hit the ground. Then he pulled back on the reigns and climbed high. He followed the others north towards Nadaroth's lands. But they were no longer alone in the sky.

With another mighty bellow, Enoch took flight. The hair on Sam's head flew wildly as he burst into the sky to join his clan of dragons. They had heeded their leader's call and attacked the fleeing enemy. They disappeared into the dark clouds, the echo of their roars barely heard over the storm.

Sam watched them disappear into the storm as his power surged. His chest heaved as he fought back the pain he was feeling. He stopped concentrating on the retreating enemy and closed his eyes tight. Memories flooded his mind of Titus and everything they'd been through. He remembered the moment that he'd first met Titus when he was just a puppy. Every good memory he had flickered into existence around him, ghostly images that faded as the next memory surfaced.

His fists were balled up so tightly that his fingernails dug into his palms and though it hurt, he didn't care. The ground was shaking beneath him, as if it were mirroring the breaking of his heart. He was remembering the time he sat on the outskirts of the forest – just him and Titus. The night was peaceful and they were laughing. With that last memory, Sam felt a hesitant hand on his shoulder shake him lightly. Taren's voice quietly said, "It's okay, Sam."

He didn't turn to look at Taren when he opened his eyes. The earth around them was shaking as the last ghostly image of him and Titus faded. When it was gone, he dropped to his knees and covered his face in agony. Titus' body still lie where he'd taken his last breath. Everyone took a knee in his honor, surrounding his body in a circle with heads bowed.

Sam felt no shame as he cried hard because he knew they were sharing this pain. Garrett was devastated and apologized quietly to Titus. "I'm so sorry, my friend. I'm so sorry."

Not much time passed when Enoch landed heavily next to them. He folded his wings and joined the others, completing the circle.

The storm slowly dissipated, the sky returning to normal and the water finally calm. Yetews, still cradling Sentreece, did his best to sooth Sam's pain, but it was too deep and raw for words to heal. When Sam finally stood up, the determination in his eyes replaced the agony as he looked to the injured First Guardian. "Nadaroth has destroyed too much. We have to stop him. I *will* destroy him." Everyone listened and watched as he walked defiantly towards the edge of the water. "We need to start crossing the water now so we can get her back to Orga's."

Before Sam could imagine anything, Enoch stopped him when he tilted his head to the skies and roared. Several dragons returned the call. "You're journey is a long one, Sam." Four dragons descended, landing behind Enoch. Each one dipped their heads and Enoch acknowledged them with a returned bow. He raised his emerald green wings and returned to his more impressive size then said, "But as the dragon flies, it will be a much shorter one."

Sam shook his head. "We can't fly across. There are these tentacles…I've seen what happens."

"You can if you fly high enough."

Foo intervened to explain. "It's true. We discovered this some time ago. But it still has its dangers." He looked darkly at the dragons and then asked Enoch, "Are they actually willing?"

"They will heed my call."

"But are they safe?" Foo's tone was accusatory.

Sam asked, "What do you mean?"

Enoch sighed. "My brothers and sisters have no love for Nadaroth and his ilk. But we are an intelligent kind. Many do not wish to trade one form of slavery for another by becoming simple ferries to the water."

"So I ask again," Foo demanded, "are they safe?"

Taren stopped Foo before he could cause damage. “Enoch, we know how they feel. But it’s imperative that we reach the southern shores as fast as possible. If they could simply carry us across then – ”

“Stop,” Sam ordered. .Everyone turned to look at him, some angry and others curious. He walked over to Enoch and spoke loud enough for all to hear. “They’re right. They aren’t slaves.” He smiled weakly at the dragons, impressed by their noble stature and sheer size. He addressed them this time. “Thank you for your help… from before. You should never feel forced to do anything. No one should. We’ll find a way to across. I’m sorry.”

The dragons exchanged looks as Sam walked away amidst very upset looks from his companions. Taren stopped him. Cautiously, he said, “Sam, I understand how you feel, but we need all the help we can get.”

“No, Taren. When I came back to Imagia to help, it was a choice. *My* choice. They deserve to make that choice as well. If we don’t give them that, we aren’t any better than Nadaroth.”

Taren’s hand dropped to his side. He knew that Sam was right.

The next voice that spoke was deep and unfamiliar. It was the biggest dragon, black and silver with more horns on his head than teeth. “Enoch was right about you, boy.” He moved to the front, his shadow covering everything before him.

Sam turned back to look at him. “What do you mean?”

“You have a pure heart.”

Squinting, Sam asked, “What’s your name?”

Though it was a bit frightening, the mighty dragon smiled and dipped his head within inches from Sam to examine him closer. “You’re the first human to ask.” It was obvious that this impressed him. “My name is Bakka. And we will take you to Orga’s home.”

“Why?”

“Because you gave us a choice.”

It was an unforeseen gesture and the one most impressed was actually Enoch. The lot of them split up onto the dragons, keeping their loads as light as possible. Yetews and Sam were the last to go. Yetews was still cradling the First Guardian. Enoch wanted to carry them. Iggy and Arty had opted to ride on Enoch’s head, as per their usual place. As he helped Sam up onto his back, sitting just before his wings, he said, “That was a noble thing you did. Bakka is my second in command. His mind is not easily changed.”

“Oh. Well…no biggie.”

Enoch chuckled low. “It really is good to be with you again. You are a breath of fresh air in these dark times.”

Sam didn’t know what to say to that, but didn’t have to worry about it. The last remaining dragon, who had no riders, approached. Her scales were a rich shade of purple. She directed her words to only Sam. “I am sorry for the loss of your friend. I will safely return him home to you. You have my word.”

A sharp pain struck Sam’s heart and he swallowed the lump in his throat. Tears formed in his eyes again as he choked out his words. “Thank you.” He looked back one last time. He had imagined a blanket for him just like the one Titus slept on back home. The soft blue cloth covered his broken body as it rest on the murky ground. Then they were in the air, the wind cool on his face.

As they climbed, Enoch gave Sam a warning. “Hold on tight. We have to go very high. It will be very cold and the air will be thin for you. Breathe slowly. This is going to be a fast trip.”

The four dragons climbed so high that the stars could be seen and Sam felt his chest tighten as the air entered his lungs. He looked at Yetews who was clinging tightly to Sentreece. His Guardian grumbled sadly.

Sam looked into the sky ahead as they reached the height they needed and began to travel straight ahead. “Yeah,” he said quietly. “I’ll miss him too.” The air was bitterly cold and bit their skin as they flew. Sam was grateful for it. It was just the distraction he needed as they flew on their path to Orga’s home and on to the cavern of the Guardian Tree.

Chapter Twenty-nine: The Guardian Tree

The flight to Orga's wasn't necessarily short, but had they walked it, it would have taken weeks after crossing the Impossible Way. Time was something they didn't have. Sam wasn't shy about showing his gratitude towards the dragons. As dragons are a proud species, they were more than accepting of this.

Dragons are strong and the cold of the sky doesn't bother them, but everyone else became chilled very quickly. They only stopped to rest for the sake of their riders. Regardless of the breaks, they reached their destination just days later.

They stopped a half a day's walk from Orga's so as not to draw too much attention to the location. It was a glade just in the forest where, one at a time, each dragon landed and let their riders off. The final dragon to land was Enoch. There wasn't much room in the clearing. Not all the dragons could fit. But Bakka remained with Enoch who shrunk back down again to give them more room. Roz and Taren had thanked the dragons and waited for Sam with the others. Alaria, on the other hand, despised the flight the most and upon reaching the ground, gratefully leapt into the trees while saying, "Cats were most certainly not meant to fly."

The sense of urgency was hard to miss. But Sam wasn't about to let Bakka go without thanking him properly. He went to Bakka who appeared to be waiting with something of his own to say. He let Sam go first. "Thank you, Bakka. When I was younger, I always wanted to meet a dragon. After meeting Enoch, I knew how amazing you all were. And…well…it's an honor to meet another one."

Bakka's head tilted to one side as he considered Sam's words. "The honor is mine as well. You are a rare thing in this world. I see now why Imagia needed you to return. Now," he continued, "I must go back to my clan. I will help my sister bring your friend's body back to you. I truly am sorry for your loss."

Just as Bakka spread his wings and began to turn to leave, Sam called to him. "Bakka!"

The curious dragon turned his golden eyes on Sam once more.

"Thank you – for everything. I promise you, we'll never ask for you to do something like this again."

Bakka bent his head low in a bow and grinned. "You'll never have to ask." He gave an approving nod to his leader and then was gone. Enoch told everyone that he would be close by if they needed him. Until then, he also needed to return to his clan for the time being. He bade them farewell and followed after Bakka.

Alaria was already leading them in the direction they needed to go, weaving through the trees as if she was a part of them. There wasn't much in the way of conversation. By the time they'd landed in the forest, Sentreece was in much worse shape. The trip had been difficult for her ailing body. Yetews had done his best to keep her protected and Sam had imagined her heavy clothes that appeared right on her as they flew across the chilly sky. At least the forest was warm, the sun shining down brightly through the canopy.

Yetews was having more difficulty than expected carrying her through the dense underbrush. So Sam took it upon himself to create a sling of sorts that she was cradled in. It gave him back the use of both arms, which sped things up significantly.

Roz watched him imagine again, as easily as if he'd never had damage to his mind before. He caught up to Sam. "So," he started, "it looks like you've gotten your confidence back." He smiled wide, trying to lighten the mood of uncertainty that hung over them.

With an answering crooked smile, Sam said, "I guess so."

"What happened?" Roz was rubbing the back of his head and winced a bit.

When Sam saw him cringe, he half-heartedly answered. "Dunno. It just…happened. I lost control. It's happened before. Remember?"

"How could I forget? Ouch." He grimaced.

"Are you okay?"

"Oh sure. Took a tail to the head when Gabriel double-backed. Didn't get out of the way fast enough. Knocked me out for a minute. Now I've got a headache. Don't suppose you have any secrets to getting rid of them?"

"Don't I wish! I still get them."

Roz began to laugh but then stopped in his tracks, grabbing his head with his mouth open in a nearly silent scream.

"Roz?" Sam began to panic. He shook Roz on the shoulder lightly and called for the others to stop.

Taren came running back to them. By the time he got there, Roz was back to normal. "What's wrong?"

Sam's eyes were wide. He looked into Roz's eye. "I…er…I don't know. Roz said he got hit in the head and he just suddenly stopped and looked like he was in horrible pain. Are you okay?"

There was a light sheen of sweat across his brow. He rubbed lightly at his temples and shook his head. "I don't know what happened. I'm okay now though." He looked at Yetews and then at Sentreece. "Don't worry about me. I'll be fine. It's her that needs the help." He pointed at the First Guardian.

Sam was looking at him with concern, but Roz pat him on the back and said, "Really. I'm okay. At least I didn't get a nose bleed."

That seemed to satisfy Sam for the moment and they pressed onward. With Garrett being injured, Roz having his strange episode, and Yetews carrying the extra weight, they weren't making great time. The longer the day wore on, the more pressure they felt. Time didn't seem to be on their side.

* * * * * * * * * * *

Coming out of the dense forest and back into the welcome sight of Orga's home would have been refreshing had they not been so rushed to get Sentreece inside. There were two Protectors near the entrance, each pointing an arrow at them. One of them ordered loudly, "Not another step!"

Taren was holding Garrett up as he was struggling to make the last leg of the journey. But he removed his arm with a grimace so that Taren could address them. "I'm no imposter, William. None of us are." He had his hands out in front of him in surrender.

The Protector called William lowered his bow and let Taren step out of the shadows. As soon as he recognized his face, he aimed the arrow at him again. "Proof."

"Sapphire, right shoulder."

Garrett weakly said, "Purple, center back."

When the two Protectors failed to lower their weapons, their eyes went to the other humans in the group. Taren turned and looked at Sam and Roz. They'd never had to answer with proof of their allegiance. He whispered to them, "They need to know you're not imposters," and raised his eyebrows meaningfully.

"Oh!" Sam said too loud. "Um, sapphire…left shoulder blade." He felt odd saying it out loud for the first time, but strangely proud as well.

Roz stepped forward. "Red. Left shoulder blade."

The two guards lowered their weapons and William said, "Good to see you, Taren. Where did you find Garrett and what the blazes happened to him?"

Taren led the way, their entire group following quickly. He dismissed William's concern. "I'm sorry. No time to explain. We found the third First Guardian but she needs Orga's help. She's badly wounded."

They all rushed down the slope and inside. Orga spun around when they opened the door and his large jowl briefly widened into a grin until he saw Yetews. "What happened?" The grin disappeared. He rushed to the table where Yetews was gently placing Sentreece. He began to check her then rushed about the room gathering as many items as he could carry to work on her.

"Gabriel," Taren growled. "He ambushed her right before we got there. She didn't stand a chance. It may have been a trap." He then explained everything as Orga nursed Sentreece's many wounds. He intentionally left out the part about Titus.

Orga listened intently and was especially interested in the exchange that Sam had with Sentreece in the cavern. But he didn't miss a very important detail. He eyed Garrett and then asked, “Where is Titus?”

Sam instantly looked to his feet. He didn't want to relive this memory again.

Taren answered, "He didn't make it."

Orga's face fell, and he began to offer his sympathy to Sam who he knew had suffered the greatest loss of them all. "Oh Sam, I'm so - "

But he was interrupted when Garrett unexpectedly fell to his knees, weakened from all of his injuries. He gasped and his face paled. Taren rushed to help him. Roz went to his other side and both of them half carried him down the corridor as Orga said to them. "Get him in a bed." He then called to Alaria. "Quickly. Get Maggie. She is keeping watch nearby in the forest. "

Alaria nodded and left with haste. Foo looked as though he wanted to kill something. "I'll go help her." With that, he stormed through the door, slamming it as he left.

Iggy and Arty had been uncharacteristically quiet. Seeing the First Guardian in her waning state had taken a toll on all of the Guardians. Iggy spoke up finally, addressing Orga. "It's been a rough trip. Things haven't gone nearly the way we'd planned." Sam didn't think he'd ever heard Iggy sound so disappointed. If this wasn’t a sign that things were bad, then nothing was.

With heavy concern in his voice, Arty asked the question they were all thinking. "Will she live?"

Orga was just finishing cleaning the last wounds on her pale hands. He wiped his own hands on his shirt. "I've done all I can do. We need to get her to the Tree. There’s a chance it will help her heal."

Sam looked around the room. They'd just reached Orga's and now they would have to leave again. He was tired. Sleep was nearly impossible when flying on the back of a dragon. And on top of everything he felt emotionally drained. The little sleep he'd gotten was filled with self-made nightmares of Titus' death and collapsing caverns. But he knew, above all else, they had no choice but to push through it. There would be a time to mourn, but it wasn't today. Sam tried to stand a little straighter. He was already thinking of ways he could imagine something to help them get there quicker. "How far away is the Tree?"

The room went quiet. Taren had come back to join them, leaving Roz to stay with Garrett until Maggie could come. Each set of eyes looked to Orga as if waiting for some unspoken sign. It was an awkward feeling. Sam knew that they were hiding something.

He got angry. "I'm not stupid, you know. I know you're keeping something from me. What don't I know this time?"

With Orga's approving nod, Taren said, "We know you're not stupid, kid. So don't go acting like we did this to spite you. We had full intentions on revealing this to you once the third First Guardian was found. We didn't want to have the information too fresh in your mind in case Nadaroth got in your dreams."

"Fine. So what is it?" He didn't sound entirely convinced, but he did soften his tone considerably.

"Remember when I told you that Orga became the keeper of the Guardian Tree?"

"Yeah."

"Well…I'm surprised you didn't figure it out already. The reason we don't want anyone stumbling upon Orga is because the Guardian Tree is here."

"What?" He looked around the room as if he was going to see a tree appear out of thin air that he'd missed all this time.

"Haven't you ever wondered where the west corridor leads to?"

"It's…just an empty room. I've walked past it tons of times before, but thought that's where it ended. There was nothing there." Sam was trying to picture it. The one time he'd gone in that room, he ended up leaving right away. It was empty, dark and boring. He'd never gone back.

"Yes. But there's a door."

"A door? I don't remember a door."

Orga said, "It's very well hidden. For good reason, as you might agree."

He wanted to run from the room and go see for himself. Sam couldn't believe he'd missed this. In all his adventurous desires as a child here, the possibility that he'd missed something so captivating boggled his mind. But he stayed his ground and tried to be patient – a task he never excelled at.

The door to Orga's home burst open and Maggie came rushing in. "Where is he?" She was distraught.

Taren took her to Garrett and Sam followed with Yetews in tow. Maggie rushed into the room and knelt by Garrett's side. Sam peered in from the doorway. Garrett's eyes fluttered open at her touch. Despite his injuries, she threw her arms around him. She began to look over him and assess the extent of his injuries. Taren and Roz both left the room and Roz grabbed Sam's arm as they left.

"Best leave them to it," Roz said. "I imagine she's got it under control. He's in good hands."

Watching them did feel intrusive in a way and Sam glanced once more over his shoulder before leaving. It warmed his heart to see them together. Love was something that Imagia needed to cling to. It was a bright light during a dark time.

But the warmth he felt dissapated quickly when he returned to the main room. Seeing Sentreece on the table, a beautiful creature like she was, lying there broken from evil acts was a harsh reminder of the past few days.

"What can we do, Orga? She's unconscious. The doorway won't open unless there are three." Taren was concerned. He lowered his voice. "She might not even survive."

The room was filled with all the familiar faces Sam had spent so much time with. Even Alaria had come back in to join them. After much debate, the most vocal amongst them being the rag-tag group of Guardians, it was decided that they were to try and open the entrance with Sentreece regardless of her state. The very least they could do was try.

Yetews gently lifted Sentreece up and held her carefully against his chest. He grumbled his worry to Sam who did his best to reassure him that she would be okay.

Orga looked around the room at the group that was there while Taren went to retrieve Zarcanis. He'd been staying in the room that Yetews had been locked in. He strode across the room and placed his hands on Sentreece. "She is weak. This may not work."

"We have to try," Orga said. "There has not been a gathering of First Guardians in a very long time. Perhaps it is all we need." His eyes fell on Sam last, lingering too long. "Let's get her to the Tree."

Roz waited for Sam who followed behind Yetews. "Did you know it was here?" he asked quietly.

Sam shook his head. "Did you?" He was quite certain he already knew the answer to that question.

"No." Roz reached up and rubbed the temple of his head beside his eye patch.

"Are you sure you're okay?" Sam whispered now so that no one could hear.

"Of course." He said it deadpan and Sam was sure he was lying.

They went into the west room that led off the corridor. There was a cleverly concealed door that, when opened, looked as though it was merely an empty space much like a closet. As they passed through, the darkness expanded and the lanterns they carried illuminated another wide corridor that was even capable of comfortably fitting Yetews. It led downwards underground.

After several minutes of steady walking, they reached a dead end – or so it looked. Taren quietly motioned for Yetews to come forward with Sentreece who was still unconscious. "We're here," he said.

The door to the Guardian Tree wasn't so much a door as it was a blank, stone wall that had tree-roots growing around it in an arch. There were three very subtle handprints set in the stone. Two of them matched perfectly for Orga and Zarcanis. But the third print was much too big to be for Sentreece.

Orga started to reach for his own handprint, but stopped. He looked around at the large group that now stood outside the place he was meant to keep watch over.

Taren placed a hand on Orga's shoulder. He was concerned for the old Guardian. "Are you sure you want to do this?"

He hesitated. "Yes. It's just that this is the largest group to enter and see the Tree. I'm not sure what will happen." When Taren didn't respond with more than a sideways reassuring grin, Orga's gaze fell on Sentreece. Determination coursed through him. "Come now. We'd best hurry."

As soon as Orga's spindly fingers touched the wall, his print began to glow an iridescent blue. He removed his hand and the print continued to shine. Zarcanis approached next and gave a very meaningful look to Orga. "I hope that we do the right thing." His words were slightly broken and heavily accented. He reached his hand up and touched his own print. It also began to glow with the same light as the first.

As Sam watched, he couldn't find any words. He was in complete awe. And he was not alone. Every eye reflected the blue light. Taren asked Yetews to bring Sentreece forward and to lift her up so that her hand would reach. The moment Taren lifted her hand towards the wall, her eyes burst open and she gasped loudly.

The penetrating blue of her eyes sparkled in the otherworldly glow from the stony door. With all the strength she could muster, she pulled her hand away and whispered, "No." Her eyes traveled across each face there until her gaze stopped on Sam. She motioned for him with one finger to approach.

With a nudge from Roz, Sam went to her. Her lips were barely moving as she struggled to get the words out. Sam leaned in closer to hear what she was muttering over and over again. After Sam finally understood, he nodded to her and stepped back.

"What did she say?" Iggy asked.

"She said, 'prove your worth'." Sam didn't wait to explain it because he knew what she meant. He'd have to imagine for her. He gently took her hand in his. It felt too small and fragile to belong to a being so important to this world. He smiled at her and concentrated on what he wanted to create. He wanted it to be perfect for her. The dimly lit room that they all stood in was now gaining a new brightness. From wall to wall and ceiling to floor, tiny firefly-like creatures filled the room. They drifted about, each one a different shade of green. Pretty soon, the room looked as though they'd been lifted into a starry sky.

"Sam," Foo said a bit unexpectedly, "you truly are amazing."

"Yeah," Arty and Iggy both agreed. Arty said. "Took the words right outta my mouth. Which is pretty difficult to do as I'm pretty good with words."

Yetews looked on at his boy with pride while Taren said, "It's beautiful."

Sentreece gazed at the living starlight as it reflected in her eyes. She reached a hand up and one of the lights landed on her pale skin. She turned to Sam and nodded once before closing her eyes again. Taren lifted her hand up and placed it on the large handprint. It shifted and shrank down to match her hand and then began to glow.

The stone wall shuddered, dust drifting down and mixing with the living starlight. The roots that were around the entrance came alive and revealed a hidden crack in the middle of the doorway that they began to twist and curl through. The very roots of the trees above were pulling the stone apart and opening the door. As it opened, a soft light illuminated everyone's faces. They all squinted as their eyes adjusted from the darkness.

Orga stood in the front and turned with a smile. Without a word, he walked through the opening and gestured for everyone to follow. Zarcanis followed him and they both stood on either side of the entrance and waited for everyone to enter. The cavern was huge and filled with all sorts of plants. Nearby there was the gentle sound of water babbling through a brook that traveled through the cavern.

But most impressive of all was the mammoth tree that towered in the middle of everything. The branches were twisted and old and the leaves were wider than dinner plates. Shining out from within the canopy were millions of brilliantly glowing lights – the souls of Guardians.

Sam had barely gotten inside the door when he stopped and stared in awe. He had never seen anything more beautiful in his life. But he wasn't the only one. Aside from the First Guardians and Taren, everyone was standing in the presence of the Tree for the first time. A peace washed over Sam and he knew it was because he was standing in the actual heart of Imagia. The ancient roots curled and dug deep into the ground. No other tree was its equal in size or beauty.

Orga's voice traveled over the group as he said, "Welcome to the cavern of the Guardian Tree."

Zarcanis clapped his fellow First Guardian on the shoulder and approached Yetews. "Come," he purred.

Orga chose to remain at the entrance to keep watch from a distance. He appeared to be quite at peace about the situation. The others quickly moved towards the base of the Tree. But Sam lingered when he noticed that Roz stopped moving. He was holding his head tightly between his hands while his mouth was ajar in a silent cry of pain.

Sam approached him, worried now for the injury that he must have taken and was keeping so quiet about. As he reached a hand out to tap him on the shoulder, Roz went rigid. Sam asked, "Are you sure you're okay? Cuz you don't look okay."

Roz opened his eye and looked at Sam. He pulled his hands down from his face, no longer appearing in pain. "I'm quite alright."

Sam's forehead wrinkled in confusion. Something about the way Roz said those words didn't sound right. Roz saw that Sam was confused. He began to smile in reassurance but then his mouth opened in another silent scream and he slapped a hand over his eye patch, his other eye closed tight.

"R…Roz?" Sam knew what pain felt like and he recognized it immediately. His friend was in agony. "What's the – "

"No!" Roz interrupted him and his voice was panicked. It came out in a harsh whisper as if he was struggling to say the words. "You have to…dangerous…I can't…" His face was contorted painfully as if he was fighting to scream out in torment. But it suddenly stopped when he wretched forward, doubling over briefly.

Sam's eyes went wide. He had no idea what kind of pain his friend was in or what he was trying to say. He glanced towards Orga who was watching them intently. Just as Orga took a step towards them, Roz straightened up slowly. He smiled crookedly at Sam. "Apologies. I'm much better now."

Sam was lost. He shook his head slightly and asked, "What just happened?"

Roz, still donning the same crooked smile, bent closer to Sam. Ignoring his question, he simply said, "Thank you."

Now even more baffled, Sam asked, "For what?"

Roz cocked his good eyebrow and whispered, "Your unwavering trust." He didn't wait for Sam to respond. He simply turned towards the entrance to the cavern and calmly walked away.

Sam looked back at the others and saw they were circled around Sentreece's body that was now being cradled in the giant roots of the Tree. She was surrounded by an iridescent blue glow. He didn't know what just happened with Roz, but when he turned back to ask him what he was talking about he watched as his friend calmly approach Orga.

Sam made to follow him but stopped in his tracks when he saw Roz reach behind his back towards his dagger. With the same manner of calmness he had when walking away, he pulled the dagger from its sheath. Orga looked confused for a split second but then made eye contact with Sam. His jowl turned up in a sad, knowing smile.

Roz pulled Orga close, as if merely hugging him, and then stabbed the dagger through the Guardian's chest. Sam stood frozen to the ground. He couldn't scream out. It was as if the entire thing wasn't happening. His mind raced to make sense of what he was seeing. Surely, he thought, he was having a nightmare.

Roz's body seemed to shiver for a moment and Sam watched him look down at his hand with some form of strange horror going across his face. He looked as shocked as Sam felt. He pulled the dagger from Orga's chest, his hands shaking uncontrollably, and dropped the knife as if it was burning hot. He lowered the Guardian gently to the ground. Orga's lips moved as he whispered something to Roz.

Sam's mind began to scream at him to move…to run to Orga. His feet jerked a little, but he didn't budge, still unbelieving of what he was seeing. Roz stood up, turning to Sam. His shirt was covered in Orga's blood and the shock Sam felt began to turn to anger. Roz was looking down at his shirt in alarm as if he also didn't believe it. His bottom lip quivered as realization struck him. The calm look that Roz had had only a moment ago was now replaced with a pained expression. For a split second, their eyes connected. Then Roz turned to the cavern entrance and ran.

No words of warning or screams of panic escaped Sam's lips. His once frozen legs now ran full tilt to Orga. He landed next to the dying Guardian in a slide and put pressure on the gaping wound in his chest.

With every effort in Orga's dying breath, he reached up and placed his hand over Sam's heart. A strange wave of warmth traveled through Sam's body. It filled him completely with a familiar peace. Then just as quickly, the sensation was gone. Orga weakly said, "F-forgiveness...is…a ch-choice. Tr-trust…in yourself…" His chest fell and Orga's hand dropped lifeless to the ground. The room around him seemed to grow slightly darker. Sam turned to the tree and watched as the lights on one of the main twelve branches began to fade out followed by several shocked gasps.

Sam didn't hesitate another second longer. He leapt to his feet, leaving Orga behind, and ran. He could feel his heart slam against his ribs and with every beat he felt his rage grow stronger. He sped through the dark of the corridors that were still dimly lit by the dispersed glowing lights he'd created for Sentreece.

He burst through the doorway into the empty room and saw a shadow running down the hall. He pushed himself to run faster. One thing Sam had going for him was his speed. He had outrun Roz more than once while out hunting. The thought of this once good memory stung sharply. He rushed past the room Garrett was in and vaguely heard him holler, "Sam, what's going on?" but ignored his calls.

The door to Orga's home was wide open and Roz's shadow was more visible this time as he fled. Sam followed him through the door and climbed the slope at an alarming speed. He flew past the two Protectors guarding the entrance, leaving them behind, stunned and confused. He didn't call for their help. He wanted to deal with Roz alone.

Sam could see Roz ahead of him. He had already entered the forest but Sam was gaining quickly. He shouted, "TRAITOR!!" Roz turned his head to see how close Sam was to him. His eye was wide with panic.

"Come back and FIGHT!" When Roz didn't' stop, Sam knew he had to do something. With barely any effort, he imagined the trees in front of Roz growing together. Vines creaked and roots groaned as they created a wall between him and freedom.

Roz desperately looked around and started to turn away from the barrier. Just as he turned, an arrow flew past him, grazing his shoulder as it hit the tree in front of him. He reached up in pain to grab the wound, spinning on his heal to face Sam.

Sam stood back from him. A bow that he'd imagined was drawn and another arrow aimed. He was breathing heavy, a murderous look in his eyes.

Roz watched on as Sam hesitated. He could see the boy's fingers shaking; hear his breath trembling.

And Sam could see the same look mirrored on Roz's face. He pulled the bowstring back harder and took a few steps closer to get a better aim. He yelled out again, "Traitor!!"

The look of fear in Roz's one good eye disappeared. He was out of breath, but the dread turned to something else – sadness. He let go of his shoulder and the blood seeped out, staining his clothes. "Go on, Sam," he said quietly. "Kill me." His voice wasn't mocking, but rather pleading.

Sam's grip on the bow loosened. He hadn't expected him to say that. And now he wondered if he could really do it. The fact that Roz put him in this position made him even angrier and he growled out, "Fight back!"

The way Roz looked back at him was as if he'd given up. He shook his head. "Never."

"What?"

"I won't fight you. Aim for my heart…just like I taught you." He stepped forward to give Sam a closer target.

Roz's actions just confused Sam further. But the image of Roz digging his knife into Orga's chest flashed in his mind. He pulled back on the string again, aiming the tip of his arrow. He watched as Roz closed his eye in anticipation. But Sam couldn't do it.

He dropped his hands to his side, the arrow falling dully on the ground. And then he growled out, yelling in frustration. He felt the unwanted moisture building in his eyes, stinging as he tried not to let it overtake him. "I *trusted* you!"

Roz's head hung low now as he tried not to look at Sam in the face. Had it not been for the quiet of the forest, his words might have gotten lost in the air. "I know."

Whether or not he believed it was possible, there was true regret in Roz's words and Sam desperately tried to control the overwhelming emotions that were taking over him. "Then *why*?!"

"I didn't…I can't…" Roz was struggling with his words. "It wasn't…*me*."

"LIAR!!" Sam thundered. He pulled his bow back up and an arrow appeared out of nowhere, aimed once more at Roz.

Behind them, the sounds of footsteps broke the silence and Taren's voice rang through the trees. "Sam!"

Sam turned and saw Taren rushing through the forest and was followed closely by several others. But he noticed that there was one face missing just as Taren yelled out in a panic, "Sam, it took Yetews!"

His heart nearly stopped and he turned to throw an accusing look at Roz. But the look Roz gave in return was equally as disbelieving as the one Sam had.

The trees above weren't terribly thick, so the shadow that suddenly overtook the ground was shocking. A huge winged beast that matched that of the one Gabriel had ridden crashed down through the canopy and landed deftly in front of Roz.

There was a brief moment of hesitation before Roz climbed up on the beast's back and clung to it tightly. He gave Sam one last look of pained regret and then the beast beat its wings wildly, climbing into the sky.

Taren reached Sam first and aimed his bow at the creature, but stopped when another of the winged beasts joined it in the sky. Taren's reason for wavering was seen immediately. Clasped in the heavily clawed feet was Yetews.

Sam screamed out in horror as he watched the creature climb higher with his Guardian in tow. "NO! YETEWS!" Everything was happening so fast and the world felt like it was crumbling down around him. He could feel the confusion in his own mind and the ache in his heart was overpowering his thoughts, muddling them.

He picked out the clearest image in his mind and only half focused on it, imagining a winged creature of his own. Sam rushed at it, leaping onto his creation's back. It took flight. But it only climbed a dozen feet off of the ground before it faded, which left Sam plummeting backwards towards the hard ground. He hit the grass heavily, knocking the wind out of his lungs.

Taren ran to help him up. Sam brushed his attempt at help away and leapt up the moment his lungs filled with air again. "NO!" Another creation appeared in front of him again and he ran to jump on it, but was shocked when he felt himself being held back.

"No!" Taren pulled him backwards. "It's too dangerous!" He held Sam tight as this newly imagined creation also faded.

Sam was panicked, but Taren wouldn't let him go. Every eye in the forest was watching silently as Yetews disappeared from view with Roz and the two dark beasts of burden.

Sam bellowed out as loud as he could, Taren still grasping tight to his arms, "TRAITOR!!" His next words were mixed with a broken sob, but equally as angry. "BRING HIM BACK!!" He knew there was no hope in Roz hearing him now and he stopped struggling against Taren's grip. He tried to yell again. This time his effort waned as the realization of what was happening set in. "Bring him back!" He knew what a nightmare felt like and this wasn't one. This time it was real.

Taren let him go as he felt Sam's body become almost limp. Sam slumped to the ground repeating his pleas to bring Yetews back in a feeble voice. The Protector didn't say anything and whoever was in the forest with them chose to remain in silence.

Sam felt himself settle into the thick grass. It was an oddly comforting sensation. The events that had transpired washed over him. Titus…Orga…the Guardian Tree…Yetews. And then one more thought: Roz…his *friend*. He wanted nothing more than to close his eyes and forget everything. He pulled his knees to his chest, clasping his arms tightly around them, and then rested his forehead on his legs. He didn't care anymore who was watching him. He didn't care about anything right now. In a great crashing wave of emotion that he could no longer control, Sam let go. And finally, the immense grief overtook everything that he was.

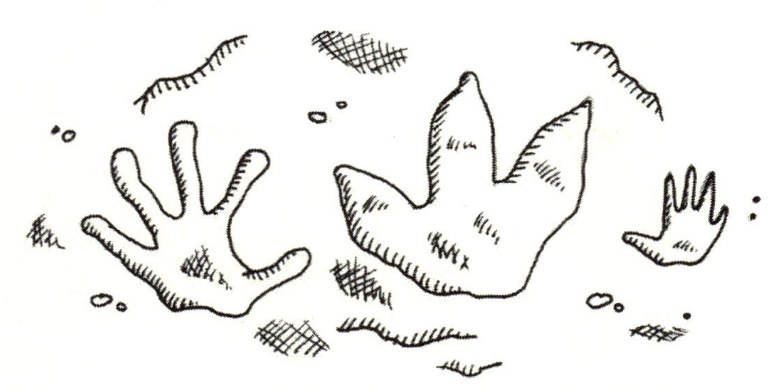

Chapter Thirty: Choices

All was quiet in Orga's home. Evening had come to the forest and it seemed darker now that Orga's friendly face was no longer a part of it. Barely any words had been spoken since the unfortunate events of the day. There really wasn't much anyone could say as each of them had lost a dear friend. Even the forest itself seemed to be mourning for his loss. The once peaceful tunes of the birds and creatures in the woods sounded sadder somehow.

But no one was in as much pain as Sam. He lost not one, but four friends. If a broken heart could bleed, his was surely doing so now. He sat alone in what was once his room. No one could comfort him. Taren had offered what he could before he left Sam alone, saying, "I know you're hurting, kid. We all are. I can't fix this. But we won't give up on Yetews. If you need me…I'll be here." As he left the room, Sam didn't even acknowledge him. But he turned back once again to add one more thought. "I know you. I know you're blaming yourself. But don't. None of this was your fault. Orga wouldn't want you to give up. Remember that." And with that, he left and didn't bother Sam again.

He had overheard Taren telling the others that he was to be left alone. "When he's ready, he'll come to us." There was a faint sound of agreement that followed. Then the door opened and closed leaving nothing but silence behind. Sam was truly alone.

After Roz's betrayal, several things happened and everyone was rushing to make sense of it. The moment that every individual stepped out of the cavern door to the Guardian Tree, it sealed itself. Orga was left inside and they couldn't return to retrieve his body. Once the door was closed, there were no longer three handprints carved into the stone, but twelve. Each one was unique. The problem was that there were no longer twelve living First Guardians. So it seemed that the reopening of the cavern would be practically impossible.

The Guardian Tree had healed Sentreece, but she was still weak. The sadness that both she and Zarcanis felt for the loss of their fellow Guardian was causing them to struggle. It was thought best to hide them both, so multiple Protectors were sent out in separate directions to get them to safe havens until they could find a way to gather the remaining Firsts. Though it seemed an impossible task, it was the best course they had at the time. Too much had happened to discuss it further for the time being.

Night came. The sounds of the others returning to the safety of the indoors was nothing but a bunch of muddled noises to Sam. He vaguely heard the sounds of footsteps as the others passed his room. He didn't turn to look at them. He didn't care to see or speak to anyone. He was silently grateful to Taren for keeping everyone away. Mostly, he felt numb. The pain that he had succumbed to became nothing more than a dull sense of emptiness.

Sleep evaded Sam even as everything became silent. The sounds of gentle snoring came from random places throughout the home. Iggy or Arty (Sam couldn't tell which one) was talking in his sleep, accusing dragons of cheating. Only a dim glow from one last lamp was burning feebly from somewhere in the main room, its oil nearly gone. In the quiet of his own room, he lay staring up at the ceiling trying not to think of anything painful.

There was no way to know what time it was, but Sam knew that it must be past midnight by now. His eyes felt heavy, but he still couldn't sleep. Only nightmares waited for him on the other side. He rubbed his eyes.

He sat up on the bed, swinging his feet over the edge. He sat there in silence for only a short while when something caught his ear. He strained hard to listen again, certain that it had only been in his mind. An ethereal voice whispered to him.

Sam...

This time he heard it clearer. A shiver travel through him. The last time he'd heard a voice call to him, it hadn't ended well. But upon hearing the voice yet again, it felt different this time.

Sam...

The voice, he was almost certain, could only be heard by him. It sounded as though it was actually coming from inside his mind. At first, he wanted to ignore it, but then a spark of curiosity flared. He didn't know why, but he got up off of the bed and walked to the door of his room. He stopped. Looking both ways, curious if anyone else was hearing this voice, he listened carefully for movement from anyone. But all was quiet. Until…

Sam...

He had no idea where the voice was coming from, but he began to walk through the dark. Through the corridor, he passed the other rooms and could see faint outlines of his friends sleeping peacefully. Why couldn't they hear it?

Sam stopped again, having no idea where he was going. Then just ahead of him, at the end of the corridor, he saw a light glowing. Had he not been looking, he would have easily missed it. It pulsated slowly, as if the light itself was a heartbeat. He should have been frightened, but the feeling that he had was familiar and not one he was at all concerned about. The voice, feminine in nature, whispered again.

Sam...

The light was pulling him now, and with every step he took, his heart seemed to beat harder. The voice kept calling to him and each time it whispered louder and louder, the sound filling his mind. The further he walked, the brighter the light became and the faster his feet fell against the ground. He could now hear himself breathing heavily. He was running. He was sure that no matter where he was going, he could just as easily get there with his eyes closed. He was flying through the dark and heard one last call, the loudest of all despite it being a whisper.

Sam...

The voice trailed off and by instinct, Sam stopped suddenly. He realized instantly where he was – the stone door to the Guardian Tree. He stepped back, trying to remember how he'd gotten here. Then the twelve handprints glowed blue. Sam stepped back suddenly, looking around for the Guardians that should have been there. The door opened. The light from the Guardian Tree, though dimmer than before, was bright in the darkness. Sam blinked as his eyes adjusted.

He took a deep breath and stepped through the door. It closed instantly, trapping him inside the cavern. He looked around and realized that even though it was night in Imagia, it shined almost like a late summer's evening inside. Sam's eyes traveled around and unwillingly stopped where Orga should have been lying. But there was nothing there. He was gone.

Sam wasn't afraid. He was confused. And just as he was about to call out into the abandoned cavern, a beautiful, bodiless voice spoke.

Who are you?

Sam hesitated, startled. He looked around carefully but didn't see anyone there. He answered the disembodied voice. "I'm Sam. Sam Little."

Who is Sam Little?

Confused now, he answered again. "Um…I am. I'm Sam Little."

A bright light shimmered just beneath the canopy of the Tree, temporarily blinding Sam. He shielded his eyes with his arm and when he looked again, the light had taken shape. A beautiful woman stood at the base of the tree, clothed in natural earth tones. Her dress seemed to grow into the ground at her feet. She was tall and lean and had a kind and welcoming face. And she was staring intently at Sam. She responded to his answer. "Yes. I knew your name from the very first moment you came here."

"Then," Sam furrowed his brow, "why are you asking me my name?"

She smiled gently. It gave Sam a warm, familiar feeling. "Your name is not who you are. *Who* is Sam Little?"

The question struck a nerve inside of him. He thought about it. After everything he'd gone through and everything he'd lost, his power changed nothing. Whoever he thought he was seemed worthless now. It had been eating at him and he had a feeling that this strange being knew exactly what he was feeling. He was angry that she asked him. "I don't think I even know anymore."

There was no response from her. She simply waited.

He took two hesitant steps towards the Tree to look her over more carefully. "Who are *you*?"

She smiled again and sweetly replied. "A friend."

The closer he got, the more certain he was about where he had felt like this before. It was the same peace he had when riding on the great beasts across the Land of the Behemoths and when he rode atop the turtles on the Impossible Way. He remembered a moment, however painful it stung, when Roz referred to Imagia as a 'she'. He stopped walking towards her and stated, "You're Imagia. Aren't you?"

"I am a Voice of the Whole."

Whatever she called herself, Sam was sure that if he wasn't speaking to the world itself, that it was the closest he would ever come to doing so. "It was you who called me here. That's why no one else heard it." She nodded once. "Why?"

"Curiosity. You still have not answered the question. *Who* is Sam Little?"

Sam sighed. He shook his head and shrugged. "I dunno. I guess I'm just some kid who made a wish."

"Ah. Yes." She showed a flicker of excitement. "But do you remember what you wished for?"

"Yeah. For my imagination to be real." It seemed silly to think about the wish that had brought him here all those years ago.

"No. Do you remember your exact wish?"

He thought back to that day nearly five years ago. He remembered the birthday cake and the exact words he wished in secret. "I wished…that I could make my imagination real."

This time, she smiled wide. "Precisely."

"I don't understand. Isn't that the same?"

The Voice of the Whole stepped down from beneath the tree and walked towards Sam. Her movements were surreal as she glided around him, observing him as she circled. "Nearly every child that is welcomed here wishes the exact same thing." As she spoke again, whispering voices echoed throughout the massive cavern, each repeating the same words.

I wish my imagination was real.

The voices were each unique, belonging to countless children that had wished for the same thing.

She stopped right behind Sam, his back turned to her. "*Almost* every child."

Sam shivered, goose bumps forming on his skin as he heard one more voice, loudest of them all. It was his own ten-year old voice that now filled the air, standing out amongst the rest.

I wish I can make my imagination real.

He remembered saying those exact words in his mind before blowing out the candles on his birthday cake. He'd never spoken them out loud, but it was definitely his voice. And as he heard the words, he knew. What the Voice of the Whole was trying to make him understand was perfectly clear.

As the realization began to show on Sam's face, she smiled boldly. "You understand."

He nodded, eyes wide. "So…*this* is why I can imagine things…why I have this power?"

"Yes. In a way."

"But I can't be the only one in all of the history of Imagia to wish that."

"No." She suddenly looked sadder.

It didn't take Sam long to come to his conclusion, but the moment he did, his heart fell. "Nadaroth. He wished this. Didn't he?"

She nodded, watching him carefully for his reaction.

He stared down at the ground. His voice was meek as he said, "So we *are* the same."

She began to circle him slowly again. "No." She paused, still watching Sam. "And yes."

He was confused, and it showed on his face. "What do you mean?"

"This is not the first time you were certain you and Nadaroth were the same. Wise words from a wise soul were given to you."

He knew exactly what she meant, but thinking about it made his heart ache. He closed his eyes. "Orga," he whispered. "He told me that it was about the choices we make."

The Voice of the Whole stopped circling Sam and had settled in a place just a few feet in front of him. She appeared to be pleased with his answer but didn't say anything.

Remembering Orga opened the floodgates that he had been trying to keep closed. At first, his voice was quiet. "I *chose* to trust Roz. And look what happened." His voice began rising in anger, his eyes flashing as he spoke. "He pretended to be my friend. And he killed Orga!" He was yelling now. "He betrayed me! And now he's taken Yetews away from me! Again!" He saw a small rock on the ground by his toe and directed his anger at it, kicking it as hard as he could. It flew into the Guardian Tree, rustling the leaves as it went.

The Voice of the Whole didn't flinch, but continued to observe him carefully.

As Sam watched the rock fly, his eyes traveled across the canopy of the Tree. The gentle lights reflected in his eyes as they finally came to rest on the darkened branch that was once Orga's lifeline to Imagia. His anger ebbed away, only sadness remaining. "This is all my fault." He hung his head and let the pain wash over him again.

Finally, the Voice of the Whole spoke again. "The Orga that you knew has died. This is the truth. Mourn him, for this is part of life. But know that he is not truly gone. He is here now. He remains a part of Imagia. His soul is very much alive."

Sam's head jerked up. "You mean he's here?" He gestured all around him.

"Yes. And no."

With a crooked grin on his weary face, he asked her, "Do you *ever* give a straight answer?"

She grinned back. "It depends upon the question being asked." She saw the disheartened look on Sam's face and chose to expand her answer. "The lights of the Guardian Tree can only be extinguished if all the branches are destroyed. Orga's branch is still very much alive. But it is weak…vulnerable. Easily removed."

The look she now gave Sam was intense. She meant for him to see beyond her words. He wasn't sure how, but he understood. His eyes drifted over the darkened branch that was once alight with the souls of Guardians. If every branch went dark and was broken off, it would be the end of the Guardian Tree…and all Guardians in Imagia would perish.

But amongst the darkness on the branch, there was one small green leaf budding out. And inside of the leaf, he could see a faint glow. For one fleeting moment, Sam felt hope inside of him. But the moment passed quickly. He turned away from the Tree and faced the Voice of the Whole. He shook his head. "It doesn't matter. It's my fault this happened because I *chose* to trust. It was the wrong choice."

"I don't believe that is entirely true. And neither did Orga."

His eyebrow's pulled together in frustration. He muttered low and heatedly, "What do you know anyways?" He spoke so low that he was certain she wouldn't hear him.

But then the air filled with the sound of Orga's voice. Several times he had told Sam about choices he made and each one of those times now echoed throughout the cavern. It ended with Orga's dying words: "*Forgiveness is a choice. Trust in yourself.*"

Hearing the old Guardian's voice was a welcome sound, but also stung like salt in an open wound.

Circling Sam slowly again, scrutinizing his every action, she explained. "I know that you have put your trust in many that others would easily have destroyed. Your heart, Sam Little, sees in others what no one else can see. Perhaps even what they cannot see in themselves."

Something churned inside of Sam as she spoke. Hearing the hope and the good that everyone was so certain he was made of sparked a darkness inside him. He had buried these feelings so deep that he'd never really let it out. He knew that she was watching him – waiting for him to show her what he truly was.

"What if…" Sam paused, unsure if he should speak his thoughts for her to hear. But then he continued, curious how she would feel afterwards. "I chose to come here on my own. No one forced me. But things are so…" He faded off. He didn't need to say how much pain he was in. He knew she already saw that.

A darkness flashed in Sam's eyes when he looked at her. "I could do it, you know. Just find the next gateway and leave. I could do that…just go home and leave this world to fight its own battles. I'd never have to look back."

As she watched him, she didn't bat an eye or react to his threat. She simply listened in silence. And Sam knew that she could see far beyond the words he was speaking. It wasn't the first time he'd felt like this, but it was the first time he'd ever let it show. He wouldn't dare let his friends see this part of him. But with her it was different. He knew that somehow she could see the darkness in him even before he entered the cavern.

He was being tested.

With a graceful wave of her hand, she motioned for Sam to look behind him. A tinkling sound, like that of wind chimes, filled the air as he watched a gateway open.

He walked slowly up to the gateway and looked out into the world he'd left behind. Just beyond the trees, he could see his home and in the backyard –

It was his mom! She was gently pushing a small swing that hung from his old swing set.

Sam got as close to the gateway as he could without crossing its borders and watched with a heavy heart as he realized that the small swing was cradling his baby brother.

Home.

He could just walk through and leave it all behind. And he knew that the Voice of the Whole was watching his every move. He could feel her gaze upon him. He didn't look at her when he said, "All I have to do is walk through. Then it would be over."

"Yes."

Sam thought of his friends, but then his thoughts quickly shifted to the pain of the ones he'd lost. As he watched his mom swinging his brother, a warm smile on her face, he knew that everything that made him who he was came to this single moment.

"And I can't say goodbye."

"No." She could sense his hesitation.

"I want to go, but…" He looked back to the cavern entrance, his thoughts on those that would wake to find him gone. Abandoned and betrayed.

There was harshness in her voice this time. "Just as you alone chose to come back, you must also choose this path on your own. But know this: Once you step out of that gateway, you can never again return to Imagia. It will be lost to you…forever."

Sam looked back out to his mom and his home. He growled out in frustration, balling his fists up in anger. "I'm just so tired of the pain! There's always pain…suffering…loss. I don't want this! I want an ordinary life!" He sighed. "But…I'm not ordinary. Am I?"

"No," she answered. "I believe you are extraordinary."

He didn't know if he thought the same of himself. Shaking his head, staring longingly at his mom, he said, "My friends. I'll never see them again."

"I'm afraid not."

Sam faced his judge, confused. "I don't understand this world. Can you just open a gateway whenever you want?"

"Yes. But if used, it comes at a great cost." Her voice was grave.

"What will happen?"

She simply raised an eyebrow in response.

He knew she wouldn't answer even before he'd asked. "I don't want to hurt anyone."

"You must make this decision on your own and live with the consequences – good and bad."

Sam's heart was beating in his ears again, like it seemed to do so often these days. It was almost painful. As he watched his mom, a flash of a future life danced through his mind. It was filled with joy and love. He was playing in the backyard with his brother…Seeing Lizzy's smiling face in class…His mom hugging him at graduation…His dad playing baseball with him and laughing…Thanksgiving…Christmas…His family whole and happy.

He slowly reached his hand through the gateway. The cool air touched his hand and it felt different to him than the warmth of Imagia. Somehow, though he knew it was all in his mind, the air was lighter and free of burden. He could feel the weight of the world leaving him. Then he quietly asked, "Are the rules the same here? A gateway only closes when a human goes through."

Her pale lips turned up in a curious grin. "Yes."

Sam brought his hand back inside. He imagined a thick piece of paper and it appeared in his hand. He considered it carefully for a moment. Words began to form on the paper as he imagined them. He hid them from sight so that only his eyes could see what it said. He imagined a simple bird, like the ones that his mom enjoyed feeding, and it landed on his arm. He whispered something to it and then handed it the piece of paper rolled up with a string. "Thank you," he whispered to the little feathered messenger.

With a small nod, the bird flew through the gateway and Sam watched eagerly as it landed on his mom's arm. It startled her, but then she saw the paper it was holding and took it. He watched her read it. She grabbed at her heart in surprise. Even though he couldn't hear her, he knew she had called out for his dad.

He came bursting through the backdoor and she thrust the letter at him. After reading it, they both embraced. They turned to the forest and were talking hurriedly. Sam knew that they couldn't see him through the shadows of the forest, but he pretended they could.

He took another step towards the gateway, now dangerously close to leaving its boundaries. He closed his eyes tight, and reached through the gateway, his heart surely about to stop. When he opened them again, he could see his parents running to the back of his yard. He pretended that his mom and dad could hear him. With a lump in his throat, he quietly said, "Goodbye," and then pulled his hand back in.

Sam turned to face the Voice of the Whole. "I will not let the Guardian Tree die."

The Voice of the Whole smiled defiantly and the gateway closed with a small gust of unnatural wind rustling Sam's hair from behind. The weight of the world returned to his shoulders.

Sam knew his time in the cavern was at an end. It was time to return to his friends. He walked past the Voice of the Whole and stopped suddenly. He turned to address her. "I saw the twelve handprints in the stone. I shouldn't be in here." The look she gave him in return let him know he should be cautious with his words. "Did you get the answer you were looking for?"

She smiled again, sweetly this time. "Sam Little – you choose to see the light in the dark. *That* is who you are."

His eyes narrowed as he chose his words. "Everything I've seen tonight…it's dangerous to know. I know it is. Why did you show me?"

She leaned towards him and simply said with a smirk, "Curiosity."

Sam laughed a little, a sound that he didn't think he could make after everything. He turned to leave and stopped once more before the entrance to the corridor that was once again open. "Thank you for trusting me…" he turned his head so he could see her beautiful face once more and called her by her name. "…Imagia."

She bowed her head once and then Sam felt her light disappear. He stepped out into the dark and the stone wall sealed behind him. As he walked back to his room, he knew that he couldn't give up on his friends. Pain or not, it was the right choice. And it felt good.

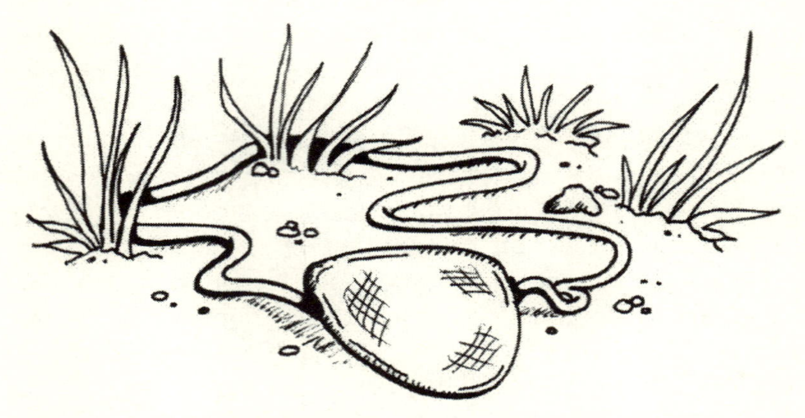

Chapter Thirty-one: Redemption

Smelling breakfast in the air was almost cruel when Sam opened his eyes. For a moment, it seemed as if the events of the day before were nothing but a nightmare. But the feeling was short-lived. Every moment – good and bad – came crashing back down and he wondered if he could really make himself push onward.

The others in the house must have wondered the same thing about Sam, because when he appeared out of the hall and joined them at the table it was difficult to miss the surprise on their faces. Out of respect, not a word was spoken about it. Even Iggy and Arty managed to hold their tongues, which was a surprise in and of itself.

Sam didn't speak a word of his encounter with the Guardian Tree. Not because he didn't trust anyone, but simply because he knew it wasn't meant to be a shared experience. If the time ever came to share that story, he would know when it was right.

In all, the room stayed fairly quiet. Alaria had chosen to help the other Protectors take Zarcanis and Sentreece into hiding. So the only ones remaining behind were Taren, Garrett with Maggie, Iggy, Arty, Foo, and two Protectors that remained at the entrance to Orga's home. If there was anyone else, they were out of sight at the moment, keeping watch in the forest.

Even though he had left his room and tried to not be angry, Sam still didn't know how to move forward. Yetews being gone had left him feeling more lost than ever and his unsure fate was frightening. Other than Yetews, Roz had become Sam's best friend. He'd taught him how to live again and how to enjoy his power – even when it was broken. The constant thought of his betrayal was almost more painful than anything. He wanted to hate Roz, but found it hard to do. And that made him angry at himself.

It was obvious that everyone was being careful what to say or how to act around Sam. It was maddening. So after a long round of awkward silence in the room, he stood up and walked towards the door to leave.

Taren got up as well, concern on his tired face. "Where are you going, kid?"

With his hand on the door handle, he answered. "I just need to go for a walk…clear my head."

Taren gathered up his bow and quiver of arrows. "Then I'm coming with you."

Sam faced his friend. "No. I need to be alone. I'll be fine. I won't go far."

Taren was obviously nervous, and from the stiff looks of everyone else in the room, it wasn't just him who felt this way. "Look, I know that you're…dealing with things." He was choosing his words carefully. "But it's not a time you should be wandering around alone and unprotected."

Sam raised an eyebrow. Without a word, he walked back to his room and reappeared a minute later carrying his own bow and arrows. "Better?" he asked.

With a cautious shake of his head and against his better judgment, Taren chewed on his bottom lip for a moment and then agreed cautiously. "Alright. But at least let me show you which direction to go. And if you're not back after an agreed amount of time, we're coming after you. Deal?"

Sam sighed. "Fine. Deal."

After yet another lengthy explanation of where he should go, Taren finally left Sam to himself. He was instructed to go north on a straight path until he came to a clearing and then turn back. He'd never really gone out on his own before. Roz had let him take the lead several times during hunts and he'd gotten pretty far ahead, but this was a first.

Sam wasn't afraid. More than anything, he was lonely. The forest was serene. It was a beautiful day, the sun beginning its trek into the sky. Sam traveled in the exact direction he was told to go. A small part of him wanted to defy everyone and stray from the path, but he didn't.

It was a dull walk and he reached the small glade quicker than expected. Seeing as how he had plenty of time left, he set his bow and quiver of arrows down beneath a tree and sat in the shade. He leaned his head back and reveled in the peace of the woods for a long while.

There were a pair of birds chirping and dancing about playfully across the way and he let himself focus on them. He hadn't watched them for more than a minute when all of a sudden they flew off, squawking angrily. Sam instantly heard why. Appearing out of the shadows of the tree was a man. He didn't quite come into the light, but Sam snatched up his bow and leapt to his feet.

The man stepped into the light, his arms raised in a gesture of submission. "I'm not armed."

Sam couldn't believe it. "Roz?" He hesitated to draw his bow, but only for a moment. He aimed an arrow at the traitor's chest. "What are you doing here?" He didn't even know why he was asking. Or why he was stalling, for that matter.

"I came to return something to you."

Sam, though furious, stopped. He couldn't tell if what Roz said was a threat or something else entirely. "What?" he asked hesitantly, his eyes darted around looking for a potential threat.

The bushes behind Roz moved and Sam began to back up in fear of what was coming. But when he saw a familiar peachy snout emerge out of the shadows, his heart leapt into this throat. Yetews walked through the bushes, carefully looking to the sky for a moment before crossing quickly to Sam. He didn't look at Roz as he went, but showed no fear in passing him.

"Yetews!" Sam ran to him, throwing his bow to the ground and wrapping his arms around his Guardian's shaggy neck. Yetews pulled him tightly to his chest and hugged him back. He grumbled something low, his eyes wide and unbelieving.

Sam couldn't wrap his mind around what Yetews was saying. He went to stand behind Sam.

Taking a cautious step forward, Sam shook his head in disbelief. "He said you saved him. And then brought him back here. Is that true?"

“Yes.” Roz stated.

Sam was struggling. He was worried that this was some form of a trap. But he couldn’t help himself from asking. “Why?”

“Because it was the right thing to do.”

“The right thing?” Sam sounded dangerous all of a sudden. “The right thing?! Was killing Orga the right thing as well?!”

Roz flinched at those words, which caught Sam off guard. He closed his eye and sighed. “I didn’t want this. I never wanted to hurt you.” His voice was shaken and quiet. “And I certainly didn’t want to hurt Orga.”

“LIAR!” Sam thundered. Roz looked as though he’d been punched in the stomach. Sam couldn’t fathom how he could be pained by his own actions. It didn’t make sense. He tried hard to soften his tone. “How did you even find me?”

“I’ve been waiting since yesterday. I hoped you would come out alone. I knew you’d need time to…to be by yourself. So I waited. If the others saw me first, I didn’t stand a chance to explain.”

From behind Sam there was a sudden sound of harried footsteps flying through the forest. He looked up into the sky at the sun and realized too late that he’d been gone too long. Within seconds, both Taren and Garrett came flying out of the trees into the clearing.

Each one of them were shocked and quickly trying to grasp what they were seeing. Taren yelled out, “Sam!” He saw Roz first, drew his bow and paused as he realized that there was another standing in the clearing. “*Yetews*!?”

Sam watched as Garrett and Taren pointed their weapons at Roz, ready to kill. He didn’t know what came over him, but he spun on them and made a split decision that he hoped he wouldn’t regret. In the blink of an eye, stone walls appeared and completely encircled the Protectors. The walls were steep and smooth, impossible to climb, and surrounded them everywhere but on the top. So Sam could hear them perfectly as Taren shouted in panic. “No, Sam! What are you doing? He’s going to kill you!”

Garrett, who in all rights wasn’t even strong enough to be out here, called out as well. “It’s a trap, Sam!”

Sam turned back to Roz, glancing at a very nervous Yetews before doing so. Part of him was filled with rage and distrust, but yet…there was something else.

"Thank you," Roz said.

Sam shook his head with a warning look. "Don't. Just…don't. I won't hold them long. Explain."

"Don't listen to him! You can't trust him!" Taren was frantically trying to get Sam's attention.

In a way, Sam had just committed a betrayal of his own. He interrupted the constant pleas from his friends. "I know what I'm doing Taren! Just…trust me!" He only half believed his own words, but Taren went suddenly quiet. Turning his attention back to Roz, he said, "Go ahead."

Roz kept nervously glancing at the sky. "I don't have much time. The beast that took Yetews away will come back soon."

"How do you know?"

"Because I told it to."

Stepping back, Sam's voice was small. "You're going to kill me."

"No. I'm not."

Sam couldn't remove the anger from his voice as he asked, "How can I believe that?"

"Because," Roz stated, "you should already be dead."

Those words made Sam incredibly uncomfortable.

Roz could see that Sam was about to ask a question but stopped him fast. "I don't have time to explain everything and by all rights, I can't ask for your trust." His voice was thick with regret. "I don't deserve that much."

Sam listened carefully, watching every move Roz made, readying himself for an attack.

"You've never asked about it before, but years ago, Nadaroth gave me this." Roz pointed to his missing eye. "You've seen the red eyes of the spies?"

Sam nodded.

"He took my eye and replaced it with his own creation. A spy with a conscience – it would be his most dangerous weapon. But it didn't work the way he planned. I fought it…he couldn't control it all the time. I escaped and removed it myself." He shuddered almost too lightly to see. "The day I went through the gateway to the other world…the creature that attacked wasn't after the Guardian. It was after me."

Though he was sure that Roz's words were meant to help his case, they were simply making Sam angrier. "Why would it be after you?"

"Of all those he tried to do this too, I was the only one who survived." He jumped as if someone had poked him with something sharp. His eyes went to the sky as a shadow passed over the clearing quickly. "We're running out of time."

Sam didn't care about time. He wanted more answers. "How does this change anything? You're still a traitor and a *murderer*!"

Looking at the ground now, his head hanging low, he raised his face only a small bit to connect with Sam's eyes. "I thought I was free of him. When I was knocked out back at the Way, Nadaroth reconnected. I didn't realize…" his voice broke, "…I didn't realize it until…I tried to warn you when I felt it again, but…it was too late. When I took back over and saw what I'd…" Roz trailed off. He didn't try to finish after that and his hands were trembling when he looked down at his open palms. "Orga was my friend too." The words came out in barely above a whisper.

Sam didn't speak. It was in that moment that he saw something in Roz that couldn't easily be faked: Regret. He was trying to put everything together in his mind, but his anger kept blinding him. He desperately wanted to believe Roz. He wanted to know that this tragedy wasn't what it seemed. His heart ached for this to be true, but he was just so furious. He'd been quiet too long and Roz tried to say more.

"Sam, I – "

"I *trusted* you!!" As he yelled, Roz flinched and stepped back. But Sam didn't stop there. "You were my friend!" Sam drew in a ragged breath. He was very close to losing control of his emotions. "You killed Orga!" He pulled back on his bowstring, another arrow appearing. His anger was taking over, but the arrow began to quiver as his hands shook.

Roz didn't try to run or protect himself. He simply stood there, as if already defeated. Sam's eyes began to blur from the tears building in them. He blinked and they spilled over, his lip quivering. He couldn't do it. No matter how angry he was at Roz, he couldn't kill him. The arrow dropped to the ground and Sam yelled out in frustration.

The silence between them was deafening. But after a moment, Sam's anger was replaced with his own sense of regret. "Why didn't you tell me? I would have understood."

Roz answered him. "It was my greatest mistake. I should have trusted you…like you trusted me."

"Is he controlling you now?" Even after Sam asked, he wondered how he would ever know if Roz was lying or speaking the truth.

"No. If he was, you'd be dead. I ran because I had to get away from you, Sam. He was going to use me to kill you next. I have control. I am me." Another shadow darkened the forest floor and Roz looked up nervously. "He can only control one at a time." When he looked back at Sam his voice was foreboding. "Which is why you need to let Taren and Garrett go."

He was confused. "They'll kill you."

"That's a chance I have to take. You're going to need them."

"No." Sam squared his shoulders, unafraid of Roz's warning. "I'm not afraid of you. Orga told me something. His last words to me were to trust myself. And I can't explain how I know this, but you won't hurt me."

With a cautious grin on his lips, he whispered, "I'm not the one he's controlling right now."

With those words, the shadow crossed the ground below them once again, this time moving slower. Now Sam's eyes went to the sky. He understood. Roz's words weren't a threat. They were a warning. He called out to the friends he had trapped. "Garrett and Taren, I'm taking the walls down. But you can't kill Roz. Promise me."

There was a short silence followed by Taren's voice. "Agreed," he said.

Garrett grumbled, "For now."

The walls around the Protectors crumbled into sand, disappearing into the grass and weeds around them. Garrett's look alone could have killed, but Taren looked very calm, his bow held at his side. Sam looked back, wanting to apologize, but unable to follow through.

The way Roz was looking at the ground told them that he knew something that they didn't. His eye was wide. "It's coming," he warned in a hiss. "Listen," his words were hurried as he spoke, "The only way I could get Yetews back to you was by telling the beast it was a trap to get you. It *must* look this way."

Roz began to walk towards Sam but only got a few steps before Garrett's bow was aimed deftly at Roz's face. "If you lay a hand on him you will find out what the tip of an arrow tastes like."

A strange impulse took over and Sam jumped in between the arrow and Roz. "Garrett," he pleaded carefully, "please. I don't know how to explain this…and maybe I'm wrong…but I *have* to trust my instinct."

Taren reached over, pushing Garrett's arrow towards the ground. Garrett was obviously upset, but complied. And it couldn't have been better timing. At that exact moment, the circling beast was now visible and would land soon.

Trying to hide his concern, Roz reached back to grab for his dagger. But it wasn't there. He had come unarmed. "Sam," he whispered loudly, "I need a dagger."

Without hesitation, though he realized that he should have shown some, he imagined a dagger that appeared on the forest floor by Roz's feet. As soon as he picked it up, he whispered quickly, "Remember the forest and your not-actually-sprained ankle?"

Sam nodded once. How could he forget? He'd fooled his parents that night with a clever bit of acting. He wanted to grin, but refrained.

The winged serpent-like beast, black as night, crashed through the clearing in the canopy and landed. The ground shook as it settled. Glowing like a hot ember was one of its eyes and it was looking right at Sam.

Roz reached out and grabbed for Sam, pulling him in front of him while facing Taren and Garrett. He pulled the silver dagger up to Sam's throat and barked out a threat, "Weapons down!"

Garrett and Taren could not have looked more worried. Whether they were acting or the fear was genuine, it was convincing. They slowly lowered their weapons to the ground. Taren had his arms out in front of him. He looked like he was trying to reach for Sam. "Let him go, Roz," Taren pleaded. "You've done enough damage. Please…let him go."

The knife pulled closer to Sam's throat and Sam winced. He wasn't acting. It felt uncomfortable to have the sharp blade dig into his skin. A thought flickered in the back of his mind. What if he was wrong? He squashed the thought quickly.

Roz stepped backwards, bringing Sam with him. “This beast will follow my command. One step towards your weapons and it will kill you both.”

Sam’s brow furrowed. He felt the anger for everything he’d been through rise to the surface and it fueled his words. “You’re a traitor,” he growled. The knife moved over his throat as he spoke. He flinched and Roz loosened the blade slightly.

Roz grabbed Sam’s arm and spun him so that he was now facing the beast, its lips curling over deadly, eager teeth. “My master wants the blood of his greatest enemy to spill on the grounds of Imagia.” Roz now held tightly to Sam’s arm and lifted the knife to his heart. He called out for the beast, Garrett and Taren to hear. “It ends today!”

Sam watched as the eye of the beast focused eagerly on the scene. He saw the look on Roz’s face. Suddenly, he wasn’t certain of anything. Fear crept in and one word stood out in his mind.

Choices.

Sam closed his eyes. There was nothing he could do. He could imagine, but what? He could fight, but how would it end? The questions began to form in his mind, but he was interrupted by Roz’s voice.

He barely moved his lips, but the words were clear. “You ready for this?”

The words weren’t threatening in the slightest and it forced Sam’s eyes open. He saw the look on his friend’s face. And it was all the reassurance he needed. The crooked grin pushed up Roz’s eye patch slightly. Whether or not it was all in his head, Sam thought he could see a faint glow of red beneath. But the grin Roz had held his true allegiance. Sam knew and he returned a crooked grin of his own. His eyes flickered to the beast and then back at Roz. He answered in only a voice Roz could hear. “Always.”

Roz, his back still to the beast, pulled his free hand from Sam and curled it into a tight fist. “One last time?”

He tried to hide his sudden surge of excitement as he reached over and bumped fists with Roz.

Subtly, Roz made eye contact with the two very confused Protectors very pointedly looking back at the beast. Each one of them somehow knew what he was thinking and Taren gave one slight nod to acknowledge him. They both became very tightly wound springs ready to bounce.

In one fluid motion, Roz grabbed Sam and pulled him in tight to his chest as he spun around, both now facing the beast. His dagger swung up and he held it there for a tense moment before bringing his other hand up to his covered eye, releasing Sam from his grip. He ripped the patch off of his eye, throwing it to the forest floor.

Though he wasn't facing Roz, Sam could see the glow of his red eye. The beast's eye went dark and it became confused, shaking its head as if coming out of a deep sleep. Roz shuddered.

Through the piercing pain of revealing his eye, Roz yelled out for Nadaroth and all those around him to hear, "I am no longer your puppet! Long live Sam Little and the Guardians of Imagia!!" The dagger flew up, but not to Sam. In a most shocking scene, Sam turned to watch as Roz used the knife on himself. He dug at the glowing eye and stabbed it out, blood now the only red left to be seen.

As soon as the glow of Roz's eye was gone, the beast was back under Nadaroth's control. He'd seen it all and the creature roared out in rage as Roz dropped to his knees in agony.

Taren and Garrett flew past Sam in a blur as the beast thrashed its head in fury, snapping its powerful jaws. There wasn't much room in the clearing for it to move, so braches cracked and shattered as it moved. Sam wanted to go to Roz, but he knew he needed more time.

The trees around the beast began to weave around it like snakes and pulled it away from them, holding it fast as it fought against the thick wood. Sam imagined more and more trees that each found a path around the beast's hide. It was fighting hard, but was struggling to get free. It gave Sam the time he needed and he knelt down to Roz. "Are you okay?"

Though it was obvious he was in considerable pain, Roz held a hand over the empty eye socket and barked, "I'm fine! Help *them*!" He gestured to Taren and Garrett who both were loosing arrow after arrow into the maze of wood, desperate to kill the enemy.

He didn't want to leave Roz bleeding and in pain. But he knew he had no choice. This creature couldn't survive. He reached the others just in time to see an arrow pierce the wrong eye. The branches and roots tightened as Sam imagined them crushing the still fighting beast.

But a sudden burst of strength caused the beast to free its neck. Wood splintered in every direction as it whipped its neck around and hit both of the Protectors, each flying backwards and landing on their backs. The wind got knocked out of them and they struggled to catch their breath.

Sam had to concentrate harder this time as he created more woody vines entangling the beast again. His head was beginning to ache again. But he pushed past it. The powerful roots and vines tightened and the creature's head became trapped once again as the roots started to constrict it like a great snake capturing its prey.

Now that he had the opportunity, Sam rushed to the fallen Protectors to help them. Garrett was nowhere near full strength and it was actually foolish that he was even out here. He was lying on his back and holding his chest in obvious pain. Taren was still trying to get his bearings. He kept shaking his head and appeared disoriented. Sam looked at Yetews as they both ran towards their friends. "Go help Garrett!" he called.

Sam reached Taren fast, sliding beside him on his knees. He tried to help him but didn't know what to do. "Taren, are you okay?"

He didn't answer.

Sam was getting nervous about how much cracking of wood he could hear behind him, but his first priority was to get his friends to safety. They were much too vulnerable lying on the ground like this. "Come on," he said as he tugged on Taren's arm. "We gotta get you out of here! Garrett's hurt and we need to move."

He shook his head hard trying to snap out of it, but his eyes were out of focus. He'd hit more than just his back when he landed. Sam had gotten him into a sitting position, but no matter how hard he pulled, Taren just wouldn't stand up.

In all the panic Sam was in, he'd stopped paying attention to the creature behind him. He failed to hear the silence. But Taren was finally coming around enough to speak. "Sam…I'm sorry. I should've…I should've trusted you quicker."

"I'm not worried about that right now. Come on!"

Sam tugged harder on Taren's arm and this time Taren nodded and started to get up. But before he got his feet under him, his eyes went wide and his face paled. Sam noticed the look in the Protector's eyes and instantly felt his skin prickle on his neck. The light of the sun disappeared and a shadow fell across them.

It happened quickly. Sam turned, two thoughts rushing through his mind. First, the vines had faded because his mind had gotten tired too quickly. And second – the beast was about to kill him.

A lot went through Sam's mind as he watched the inevitable moment unfold and terror filled him fully. He quickly tried to accept this ending to his story as faces of those he'd loved and lost sped through his thoughts. He closed his eyes and wondered briefly how badly it would hurt.

As if it came from out of nowhere, a warm body jumped between him and the deadly strike. Sam opened his eyes quickly and saw Roz.

At that exact moment, the beast snapped down and was met with the harsh feeling of cold steel being rammed up through the roof of its mouth.

Roz's muscles strained against the weight of the beast's head as he thrust it further into the skull. His arm was bleeding where razor sharp teeth had torn through his flesh. The angry, dying beast pulled back hard, one last feeble attempt to flee. It's neck arched back in an unnatural bend. It was going to fall right on top of them.

There was no time to move. Sam threw his arms up as he screamed out. An almost invisible barrier shimmered above them, protecting all three of them from the crushing weight of the dead beast as it crashed to the ground. It slumped off of the shield and lay motionless on the forest floor.

Roz was on his knees, bleeding and exhausted. Yetews lumbered up to them, an arm supporting Garrett. His ears were alert and his eyes were worried. Taren had his wits more about him and Yetews was able to coax him to his feet and lead him away from the beast. Dead or not, its red eye was still glowing brightly.

Sam saw this and it made him even more wary. His eyes flicked nervously back to it as he got to his feet and began tugging at Roz. He put his arms under Roz's and lifted him with all his strength. "Come on," he grunted as he pulled. "Let's get out of here."

Though Roz was badly wounded, he still managed to catch a glimpse of the glowing eye as well. He struggled to get to his feet, but did so nonetheless. Once everyone was several yards away, they took time to catch their breath.

Even though Yetews hadn't been injured, he was extremely frazzled. He was just on the verge of losing control and Sam could see it. Too much had happened and his mind was rushing to stay focused. That left Sam as the only one there who was able to make decisions. He had to take control of the situation.

He looked at Roz's arm and eye – or lack of eye, as it were. His arm looked bad, but he was sitting up on his own, so he decided to go check Garrett. When he stood up to go, Roz grabbed at his arm, pulling him hard. Sam shot him a confused look.

Roz's face was panicked. "The eye," he whispered harshly. He looked back at the beast pointedly and then back at Sam. "He can *see.*"

A sick feeling made Sam's stomach churn as he realized who 'he' was. If Nadaroth could still see them then they weren't safe. Sam and Taren exchanged concerned glances. Yetews grumbled something quite panicky.

Sam shook his head at his agitated Guardian. "I don't know. But if he *does* know where we are at, then we need to get out of here fast."

Roz was getting up and Sam jumped in front of him. "Where are you going?" He held a hand to Roz's chest to stop him.

Roz grabbed Sam's hand and started to push him away. "The eye. It has to be destroyed."

As Roz went around him, Sam knew he had no choice. "No!" He spun and grabbed Roz's wrist. "I'll do it."

For a moment, Roz looked unsure. He knew the dangers that the red eye held from a first hand experience. But he also knew Sam. With reluctance, he agreed and moved out of Sam's way. He was in pain and joined Taren at his side, lowering himself heavily to the ground.

Sam could hear their concern as he built himself up to approach the fallen beast.

Taren spoke low. "I'll go with him."

"No," Roz stopped him. "Let him do this."

There was a hesitant pause from Taren, but then he asked, "Is there a danger here?"

"I don't think so. But it should be him."

"Can we trust you?"

There was an even longer pause. "I hope so."

Yetews went with Sam and no one tried to hold him back. As they approached the beast together, they stopped before the eye's line of sight. Yetews grumbled quietly, lines of worry beneath his tired eyes.

Sam looked up at his Guardian and half-smiled. "I think so. But I *want* him to see me."

Yetews growled his disapproval.

Sam knew his friend had been through a lot. But so had he. He had a message for his enemy. "He's taken too much," Sam answered Yetews quietly. "I'm tired of losing everything – everyone." His blood began to boil as the events of the last few days flooded his thoughts. He gritted his teeth. "It's his turn to lose." Without another word to debate the situation, he stormed towards the gaping mouth of the beast. With a good deal of effort, he heaved Taren's sword that Roz had used from the skull of the creature. The sound it made coming out was nauseating, but Sam ignored it.

He stepped directly into the view of the still-glowing eye and stared into it angrily. Certain that he was speaking directly to his enemy, he growled, "You lose again." He lifted the sword high above his head and hissed out, "Roz is no longer yours."

Sam aimed and started to thrust the sword down, but something stopped him. He connected with the eye. Everything around him changed as he was pulled into the place where dreams form. The sword was gone from his hands and the forest around him was empty of everyone. He spun around and tried to figure out how he was here.

He knew this sensation. Sam was in someone else's mind and the faint red hue to the forest was familiar. Realizing what mind he had been connected with, he started to turn wildly around, looking for him.

Nadaroth didn't disappoint.

Laughter, deep and sinister, echoed around him with no source. This time, his enemy didn't appear as a disembodied, smoky nightmare with his fiery eyes. He stayed hidden in the shadows, laughing madly.

With effort, Sam calmed himself. Words wouldn't come, but he did his best to show no fear as the ghostly shape of a man walked from behind a tree and into the light. It was Roz, just as he was. His face was covered in blood from his lost eye and his wounded arm hung loosely at his side. He looked afraid.

Helplessly, Sam watched as the image of Nadaroth's vision continued to take shape. Another creature appeared out of the sky. It snatched up Roz and pulled him into the air.

Sam's coolness slipped as he watched another friend being ripped from his grasp and Nadaroth took advantage of his weakness. The laughter stopped and a cracked whisper spoke directly into his ear. Shivers violently tore through him both mentally and physically as Sam heard his own words repeated back to him.

"*You* lose again."

Sam's eyes flew open. He was no longer holding the sword. Instead, Roz was standing next to him having taken the sword into his own hands. He'd pierced the eye and broken the connection that Sam had with Nadaroth.

The beast was motionless on the ground. Its eye was burning out in a wisp of black smoke. Sam was breathing hard, his heart beating terribly fast as the sweat beaded across his forehead. There was an obvious change in the air around them. Nadaroth's presence was no longer there and everyone could sense it.

Roz was leaning on the hilt, trying to keep his balance. "I'm sorry, Sam. I didn't know he could connect with you. Are you okay?" His voice sounded weak, but genuinely anxious.

But Sam's responding look only worried him more. He looked back at Roz, his eyes wide with terror. His heart was racing as he searched the sky. But nothing was there.

"What did he show you?"

Sam breathed a sigh of relief. "Nothing. It was nothing," he lied. "Let's get out of here."

Roz groaned as he pushed off the sword that was deeply embedded in the now dead eye. "Good idea. Cuz I've got a killer headache."

Sam saw Roz's crooked grin and couldn't help himself. He grinned back. "You know," he said as they walked back to Taren and Garret, Yetews following close by Sam's side. "I think I might be able to fix your eye."

Roz was keeping what was left of his eyelid closed in an attempt to hide the gruesomeness of his wound, but it was difficult to look at. "How's that?"

Sam stopped and Roz did as well. "I did it once before…with a friend. I healed her. It wasn't perfect, but…I could try. I mean…if you want me to."

It was difficult to hide his leeriness, but Roz ultimately agreed. "What have I got to lose?"

Sam took a deep breath. He was tired but also determined. "Just hold still."

Before Sam could do anything, Roz stated, "Just in case you were wondering, this eye is fine." He smiled and pointed to his good eye.

Sam shook his head and rolled his eyes half-heartedly. He looked deep into the damaged eye socket and began to imagine. He thought about eyes and how they were built, going back to his science class at school. He pictured the nerves and the veins, all of it growing around the pupil. The skin around Roz's eye began to knit together. Roz winced and grabbed at his temples as the eye socket filled with a brilliant white globe that began to take shape. The eye formed as Roz struggled to hold still. But as it filled the healing socket, Sam knew something was wrong. It wasn't working. The eye was forming, but it wasn't right. Roz was screaming out.

The same problem had happened with Keesa when he'd attempted to heal her. He had to know exactly what he was imagining and he didn't know enough about eyes to make it perfect. But he did what he could and finally stopped trying so that Roz could stop hurting. "I'm so sorry! I shouldn't have tried. Are you okay?" Sam felt terrible.

Finally, Roz stopped wincing. In a twist of surprise, he opened his eyes and reached his hand up to the healed one, gingerly feeling it. He looked at Sam with sheer gratitude. "I can…see you." He didn't believe his own words.

Neither did Sam. "What? You're kidding."

"No. I can actually *see*!" But then he slapped his hand over the new eye and closed it with a shout of pain.

Sam panicked. "What's happening?"

"Too bright! It's too bright!" he held the eye shut. It was hurting him.

Sam didn't know what to do. "I'm sorry! I'm sorry! I can try to change it back." He felt horrible.

"No!" Roz hissed. "It's okay." He regained his composure. He tried a couple more times to look out of it, but the brightness was overpowering and painful.

"Here." Sam had imagined one more time and a new eye patch appeared in his hand. Handing it to Roz, he apologized again.

"Well, it's better than the alternative." He slipped the eye patch over his new eye. "We can work on your eye building skills later. Let's get out of this place."

There wasn't any more hesitation. With Yetews' help, Garrett got to his feet, clinging weakly onto the Guardian's arm. He didn't say anything, but he was white as a ghost and having a hard time breathing deep. Taren was slow to get up, but managed to push through everything to walk ahead of them and lead them back in the right direction.

As Sam and Roz passed the body of the beast, Roz stopped. "Hold on a minute. I'm gonna get Taren's sword. Be right back."

He waited for Roz, watching the others slowly make their way into the trees. He idly thought about the scene Nadaroth had showed him but shook off the nightmare and told himself not to dwell on it.

It was quiet, as it generally seems to be after a fight. But something about this time felt wrong to Sam.

His feeling came too late. There was no warning. A shadow briefly covered the ground, but it was so quick that Sam only had a moment to turn around and see what it belonged to. Come to life right out of Nadaroth's vision, was the winged beast.

Sam watched in vain. Time slowed down just enough to burn the image of Roz's expression of horror into his mind. His friend made a desperate leap away in an attempt to dodge the open claws of the monster. But it caught him in mid jump.

As Sam screamed out, it alerted the others, "ROZ!!" he yelled. Taren was at his side almost as quickly as Yetews, but it was all for not.

As the beast pulled Roz into the sky, Taren's sword fell from his hands and landed on the ground. Other than the sword, the scene was nearly identical to that of the one Sam pretended was just a nightmare.

There was no time to imagine and no time to fight. The moment the monster reached above the trees, it shivered against the blue of the sky and disappeared.

Roz was gone.

Somehow, Sam heard Nadaroth's mocking laughter. Whether it was in his mind or in the trees, he was sure that it was meant for his ears alone. He felt the tender, cautious touch of Yetews' large hand on his shoulder. Sam looked up at him. Their eyes reflected each other's pain.

Sam wanted to scream out in the anguish he felt at that moment so that the whole world could hear him. More than that, he wanted to give up. This only meant that Nadaroth was winning. So above all else, Sam knew this couldn't happen. He was alive. And if anything could be taken away from this day, it was that Roz hadn't betrayed them.

As Sam's mind reeled with thoughts he couldn't control, one particular thing stood out in his mind: Nadaroth was going to pay for what he'd done today – and every day before this. His reign over this world was coming to an end. And Sam was going to be there to make sure it happened.

Chapter Thirty-two: Small Victories

Orga's home was dark. Sam had spent enough time in there to know that it had never felt so dreary. There was always a light in the air around Orga and now that he was gone, his home was difficult to be in. But because the Guardian Tree was hidden below, there was no hope in abandoning it to waste. It needed protection more now than ever.

Sitting on the edge of his bed, Sam tried not to let his mind wander through the grief that was still so raw. It was difficult. The others were grieving as well, but they all focused so much on Sam's reaction. After Titus and Orga's deaths, he'd shut down almost completely and everyone looked at him as though he was just moments away from doing the same thing again. So he decided to disappear into his room to avoid any further stares.

Yetews had stayed with him, despite Sam's constant reassurance that he was fine. In reality, Sam was equally worried about Yetews. The events of the day had worn on him greatly. He was struggling with becoming captured again. It was short-lived, but the potential for enduring more torture was weighing heavily on him. And then there was Sam's near brush with death. It was far more than he wanted to bear. Finally, after some pushing, Sam convinced Yetews to take some time.

Yetews had seen the concern in Sam's eyes and heard the worry in his voice. He also knew that if he didn't control his own emotions, that he'd be no good to Sam. He nodded and pulled him into a tight hug. The warmth of Yetews' fur was welcome and Sam held on longer than he expected to. Yetews tousled Sam's hair and left.

It wasn't long after he left that another face appeared at the entrance to the room. "Want some company, kid?"

Sam had been so lost in his own thoughts that he hadn't noticed Taren until he spoke. He simply shrugged one shoulder and said, "Sure."

Taren joined him on the bed and they both sat in silence for some time. Finally, Taren said, "So…"

After a deep breath, Sam repeated him, "So."

He nudged Sam with his elbow lightly, his arms still crossed. "You doin' okay?"

His response was too quick, but he tried to sound convincing. "Sure."

"Yeah," Taren looked at him knowingly. "Me neither."

Those words were a relief to hear for Sam. It was the realest conversation he could have asked for.

They sat in silence again. But Sam knew what Taren was thinking before he could even say it. So Sam said, "I know everyone thinks I'm gonna shut down or something weird like that."

"Nah. Mostly we just don't know what to say." He furrowed his brow. "Is Yetews okay?"

"Yeah." Sam was glad someone was thinking of Yetews too. "He just…ya know…needs some time. He still struggles."

"Good." Taren thought for a moment. "I'm probably supposed to tell you something along the lines of 'it's not your fault' or 'you'll be ok', but I think you know that by now."

Sam nodded. He didn't need reassurance from anyone about his actions. But there was one thing that had been bothering him that he did need to know. He sat there awkwardly as he remembered every moment after Roz's return. Finally, as he stared down at the dusty floor, he said, "You hesitated."

Taren looked at Sam confused. "What?"

"In the forest, when you first saw Roz, I saw you. You were going to kill him. But…you hesitated." He looked into Taren's eyes, searching for the reason.

"Ah," Taren understood. "That."

"Why?"

"Would you accept my answer if I just said it was complicated?"

Sam raised an eyebrow and waited curiously.

"No. I didn't think so." Taren grinned quickly. "The truth is, that when I found you standing there with Roz and Yetews…" He trailed off, not sure how to finish the sentence.

Sam watched him struggle for the words and then he understood completely. He looked at his friend, a mighty Protector of Imagia, and knew he was afraid to say what he felt. Sam said it for him. "You thought *I* betrayed you."

Taren flinched lightly at the word 'betrayed'. But he moved past it quickly now that it was spoken. He looked at Sam apologetically. "Yeah. Yeah I did."

"Still," Sam said, "You could have killed him. You *should* have killed him."

"True. But something Orga said stopped me."

"What?"

Taren sighed heavily. "After you returned…all of you…I don't think it's a secret that I had my reservations about Roz."

Sam snorted out a little laugh.

Taren continued, "Orga and I had many arguments. You know that." He waited for Sam to nod and continued. "One night, we were fighting about trusting him…again. I was *so* angry with him for trusting him so quickly. But he kept saying, 'If Sam trusts him, then so do I. End of argument.' I disagreed."

"What did you say?"

Taren was shaking his head. He looked like he was ashamed of what he was about to say. "I called him a damn fool."

Sam was shocked. "You said that to a First Guardian of Imagia? Wow."

"Yeah. Not my proudest moment."

"Was he mad?"

Taren was sad at the thought. "You know how Orga was. I'm not sure he knew true anger. He just looked disappointed and I started to storm out of the room. He stopped me before I left and told me something that I thought he was crazy for." He was unsure about sharing his next words, looking away from Sam as he considered it.

"What did he say?" Sam urged him.

He was slowly shaking his head, but ultimately turned to face Sam when he spoke. "He told me that a day would come when I wouldn't trust you. And that I should trust you anyways…even if I was sure it was the wrong thing to do."

Right away, Sam remembered Orga's last words to him and all of the things Imagia had revealed to him. He felt sympathy towards Taren.

It seemed to be hard to say it, but Taren apologized again to him. "I'm sorry I didn't trust you. Even if it was for only a moment."

"That's okay." Sam felt comfortable with his next confession. "Honestly? I kind of felt like I *was* betraying you. But I just had this…feeling."

"I know. Orga was…" Taren's voice broke. He cleared his throat and Sam tried not to look at him out of respect. He tried again. "Orga was my best friend. It took everything I had not to release that arrow. But…I'm glad I didn't. Because then I would have killed *your* best friend."

Sam immediately thought of Yetews and looked nervously at the door. He'd always considered Yetews his best friend. But Roz had pushed him and understood him in ways that his Guardian couldn't. Regardless of what Roz had done – or had been forced to do – he really had become Sam's best friend in a time that he needed it most.

The silence between them wasn't uncomfortable, but Sam knew he needed to say something to Taren. "I'm not gonna leave Roz to die." He didn't expect Taren's response.

"Neither will I."

Sam smiled at his friend. He knew that must not have been the easiest thing for Taren. And he had a lot of respect for him for saying it.

The moment between them was brought to an abrupt halt when one of the Protectors that had been stationed in the forest came rushing into the room. "Taren," he was out of breath and looked frazzled. "It's Roz."

"What?" Sam jumped off the bed, not believing what had been said. "Where?"

The Protector, who Sam only partially recognized, threw a worried look at Taren. "He approached us just outside of the main perimeter. He's asking for Sam."

There wasn't an ounce of hesitation as Sam ran past the Protector. But Taren followed quickly after him and exchanged an uncertain look with the one who alerted them. "Wait, Sam!"

Garrett was sitting at the table as Maggie was trying to tend to his tender ribs, but he jumped up against her wishes and followed them.

When Sam pulled the door open, Taren continued to call out to him and he only stopped when he heard, "It might not be him!"

Sam stopped, remembering the many times things weren't what they seemed in this world. He considered Taren's warning. He shook his head. "I have to know!" He shot off up the slope, leaving Taren rushing to catch up. Just outside of the perimeter in the forest, Sam saw him.

Three other Protectors were holding Roz at bay, all of which had weapons drawn and aimed. The moment he saw Sam, he smiled. Sam tried to rush to him, but Taren had caught up and grabbed his arm.

"Wait, Sam!" He stepped in between him and Roz and whispered. "How can you know it's *him*?"

It was a good question. There was only way to find out though. He knew Taren was being careful and with good reason. He stepped around Taren and cautiously approached Roz. The other Protectors wouldn't let him get too close so he asked his question from there. "How did you get away?"

"Not without difficulty." He lifted up his shirt, exposing four deep gashes across his ribs. He winced as he covered the wounds back up. "I know I'm not trusted, but I'm also not armed." He looked pointedly at the three Protectors still keeping him from approaching.

He wasn't sure if it was the right thing, but Sam ordered them to back down. They did so, but only after a leery nod from Taren. Sam approached Roz closer, but as he did, something inside of him felt off. He stopped a few feet away.

Roz noticed Sam falter. "Sam…it's me. I swear it."

"How do I know you're…ya know…you?"

Roz lifted his eye patch up and the eye that Sam had imagined was there. He covered it back up quickly.

Even though he knew this should have been proof, it wasn't good enough. The uneasy feeling was growing. He thought about what Taren had said. It looked like Roz, but if there was any part of him still being controlled by Nadaroth, then he would be a danger to everyone. He could ask him a hundred questions, but no good ones came to mind. He wanted to believe it was Roz and that finally something good was going to happen. But there had to be proof.

Surprising everyone around him, Sam started towards Roz.

Taren hissed, "No! It's not – "

Sam turned, eyes wide in warning. "I know what I'm doing."

Though he looked ready to spring, Taren didn't argue further.

Sam's heart felt heavy, but he had to be sure. He knew that the tattoo should be the best way to find out if it was Roz. But if Nadaroth had control of him, there was no telling if that was reliable. So he had another plan. Calmly, he walked up to Roz with a smile on his face. "You got away from that beast all by yourself? That is awesome!" He held up his fist and waited patiently.

A curious expression crossed Roz's face, his smile wavering. He looked down at Sam's fist and then around at the others. Sam's smile disappeared as he lowered his fist and began to back away slowly. He was shaking his head as he quietly said, "It's not him."

Instantly, every weapon was directed at Roz, and his hands went up confused. "I don't understand!" he fretted. "Sam, it's me!"

Sam turned away and saw Yetews appearing. He was growling low as soon as he saw Roz and Sam whipped back around when he heard Roz yell out at him. "Turn around and face me Sam Little!"

Taren and Garrett were both holding Roz, his arms behind his back. As he began to fight against them, his face contorted in anger. When he continued to struggle, Taren kicked behind his knees and they buckled. He was kneeling on the ground now and surprised everyone as he began to laugh quietly.

Sam's anger began to rise. He looked up at the others. Taren watched him. He would not shed Roz's blood in front of Sam. Garrett on the other hand, looked ready to kill. A decision had to be made on what to do. "You're not Roz."

Still laughing, he looked up at Sam mockingly. "Oh but I am."

"Why are you here?" Sam was devastated.

When Roz didn't answer, Garrett punched him in the face. "Answer him!"

Sam closed his eyes. He didn't like seeing Roz get hurt, even if it wasn't really him. Taren shot Garrett a look and said, "Garrett. Enough."

Roz's lip was bleeding and Sam looked into his good eye. Even when Nadaroth had been in control before, Sam could still feel the good in Roz. But now there was nothing. His eye looked empty. He was almost sure that this wasn't even Roz's body. So he repeated his question, this time between gritted teeth. "Why are you here?"

He spit blood out onto the grass but still didn't answer.

"Last chance."

"Or what?" Roz mocked him further. "You'll kill me? You can't."

Sam knew he was right. If this was Roz's body, then it meant that Roz was somewhere inside. Which meant he could still be saved. They had to find out if it was his body. "We need proof." It was what they all asked for when needing the location of the tattoo.

One of the other Protectors said, "We asked him before. He couldn't identify himself." Everyone there knew what this meant.

As Sam searched Roz's face, he simply stared back with a sort of madness in his eyes that didn't add up. Nothing made sense to Sam right now. He had to know for certain. Nadaroth hadn't been in control of Roz when he'd received his tattoo. There was still a chance it could help.

Sam looked at Taren, his eyes hopeful. "Check his shoulder."

Taren was hesitant for a split second, but quickly jerked back Roz's shirt, exposing his shoulder blade. Roz looked baffled. When Taren's eyes met Sam's again, a triumphant grin spread across his face. "Nothing."

His heart skipped a beat as it filled with hope. It wasn't Roz. "I'd tell you to give your master a message, but you're not leaving this clearing alive."

The imposter knew he'd been revealed for what he was and his face twisted in anger. In a voice that was too harsh to be Roz's, he said, "I have a message for you."

Sam wasn't sure he wanted to hear it, but curiosity held him. "What?"

His mouth turned up in a wicked grin that most certainly did not belong to the Roz that Sam knew. "You will lose everything." Blood began trickling out of his mouth. Garrett must have broken more than just his lip with that punch.

The way the imposter said those words made Sam uncomfortable. He tried not to show his fear, but must have slipped. The imposter began to laugh again as a faint red glow began to show beneath the eye patch. Sam backed into Yetews when he saw it appear. "Taren…his eye."

Both Garrett and Taren saw it and got noticeably more nervous. They were too close to Orga's home. They turned him around to face the forest in another direction.

The imposter cackled, his voice now barely recognizable and twisted. "You'll never win this fight. Rozalam is mine."

Those words sparked a kind of courage in Sam that he hadn't felt in a long time. Slowly, he walked around the imposter and came face to face with him. "His name," Sam stated with confidence, "is Roz. And I'm coming for him."

The imposter grinned, his bloody teeth tight and his voice shrill. "You want him? Come and claim him – or what's left of him."

"Where is he?" Sam's fury was rising. He knew the imposter wouldn't tell him even as he asked the question. His hand was shaking as he reached for the eye patch, ready to uncover it and speak to the master behind the puppet.

Taren held tighter to the prisoner and said, "Are you sure you can do this?"

He didn't care if Nadaroth could see him or how dangerous it was. He had his own message. He reached his shaky hand to the patch and lifted it up. Instantly, the once normal eye burned red. The imposter stiffened in pain when it was exposed and began to struggle, his breath coming in harsh gasps.

Everything in Sam wanted to look away but he pushed past it and looked right into the eye. Everyone around him seemed to disappear as he spoke to his enemy. "Roz made his choice. He's not yours anymore." He got even closer to the eye, his face reflecting the eerie red glow. In his most threatening voice, he warned, "Be ready. I'm coming. Your rule is over. The time has come for the rise of the Guardians."

With those words, the imposter began to scream out in agony and Garrett pushed the patch back down to block Nadaroth's sight. The imposter was panting. "What are you going to do now, Sam Little?" he mocked. "You can't destroy me. I look like *him*. You're too *weak* to kill me." He started to laugh when he saw Sam shudder at the word 'kill'.

Shaking his head, Sam looked at the imposter one last time. "You're right. *I* can't." He looked at Taren and Garrett and nodded once. They nodded back and waited while Sam began to walk away.

When Sam turned, he looked at Yetews. They both began to walk away and Sam could hear the imposter yelling out in desperate pleas as he realized what was about to happen to him.

The sky went dark, gray clouds forming across the brilliant blue. Thunderclouds gathered as he tightened his eyes in concentration. Thunder rolled loudly. He knew that his imagined storm couldn't drown out the fight that was coming. But for the moment, the rain began to fall and it drowned out every sound around him that he didn't want to hear. Sam walked into the storm with Yetews by his side. As the rain soaked them, he looked up into the emerald eyes of his Guardian and they both smiled proudly.

Sam knew that even with so many losses and so much turmoil, this moment was a win. As the rain dripped off of his face, he felt as if it was washing away the pain, even if it was for only the moment. And he felt stronger than he'd ever felt. Yetews nudged him with his shoulder and Sam knew that somehow, they would win. Today, no matter how small it seemed, was a victory. He said quietly to himself as he left his fears behind him, "Hold on Roz. I'm coming."

Jessica Williams

Author's Note

Thanks for reading *The Gateway to Imagia: The Gathering.* I know that the wait was long for this sequel. But rest assured that I am currently working so that the wait won't be as long next time. I appreciate your time and interest!

Sam *will* return in the final book of the Imagia Trilogy:

"*The Gateway to Imagia: The Rise of the Guardians*"

If you enjoyed the newest installment of Sam's journey, please like and share my page on Facebook.

www.facebook.com/TheGatewayToImagia

Leave me a comment or a review. I'd love to hear what you thought of it.

Thanks for reading!

And remember – keep on imagining!

67529512R00246

Made in the USA
Charleston, SC
14 February 2017